PAGE TURNER

David Lowe lives in North London. Working life in the corporate salt mines of information technology has influenced this, his first novel, as have musical interests. Other literary ventures, besides crossword setting, include short stories (available on www.davidclowe.co.uk) and a second novel in progress.

David Lowe

2

PAGE TURNER

Published 2013 by completelynovel.com

ISBN 978-1-84914-331-8

To Celia, for her support and patience

Thanks to Ruth, Rob and Beryl for their reading and editing efforts, to Gavin who helped spark the initial idea, to Tally Ho Writers Group for their ongoing help and suggestions and to friends and family for their encouragement

Book cover by Jessica Holloway (www.studio5258.com)

CHARACTERS IN 'PAGE TURNER'

Carl Trenchard	Professor of Paginatorics, Arts University of Peckham ("AUP")
Paul Körnthofer	Distinguished Paginist visiting AUP, from Dresden
Pete	Pianist
Henry	Pianist
Ben Cordell	Senior Lecturer in Paginatorics, AUP
Alan Westwood	Head of Manucussionists Department, AUP
Crabtree	Resources Officer to Faculty of Ancillary Music, AUP
Stephen Pendleton	newly appointed Reader in Phoniotics, AUP
Viola Trent	Lecturer in Paginatorics, AUP
Alison Somers	Internal Auditor, AUP
Mike Esther	Lecturer in Chordology, AUP
Rupert Llewellyn	Lecturer in Faculty of Ancillary Music, AUP
Graham Fender	Faculty Chairman, Faculty of Ancillary Music, AUP
Rt Hon Ranulph Fraserman	Vice Chancellor, AUP
Janet	Student Paginist
Atinuke	Nigerian girlfriend of Ben Cordell
Tad	Postgraduate Media Designer. AUP
Eva Koniecka	Research Assistant, AUP

Jane Fredricksson	Friend of Viola's, a philologist
Paul Fairley	Second-year student Paginist
Tony MacLeish	Composer; graduate of AUP and former student of Carl Trenchard
Karen Swindells	PA to Ranulph Fraserman
John Librarian	Librarian avatar
David Wetherill	Senior member of AFFREM
Joe	Military historian; friend of Viola
Carly	Alison's younger sister
Sergeant Brown	Police Negotiator based at Denmark Hill Community Security Condominium
Inspector Fox	Senior policeman at Community Security Condominium
Mohammed Khan & Farooz Karmal	Waiters from Memories of Helmand
Superintendent Mike Osler	Chief of Denmark Hill Community Security Condominium
Sylvia Smith ("Sylv")	Member of the "Cowingdon"
Sadie Conant	One of Karen's predecessors as PA to Ranulph Fraserman
Inspector "John Doe"	Member of the Office of Security and Co-operation
Sue	Member of Corporate Planning, friend of Eva
Leke	Albanian security expert used by Stephen Pendleton
Harold Morrison	Head of Department of Visual and

	Plastic Arts, AUP
Grand Temple (Herb Summerson)	Pendleton's superior in AFFREM
Daoud Amin	Afghani Official Community Representative
Jack Kavkazian	Leader of Outvesta bid team
Purveen Aqsa	Senior civil servant with ASBA
Clare Bowman	Accountant; member of the Cowingdon
Tom Warrendell	Local MP
Bernard Saintsbury	Secretary of Real Fellowship of Franchised Reamers.
Stavros	Security supervisor for AFFREM
Tala Amin	Daoud Amin's wife
Valerie	Receptionist at AFFREM offices
Neil	Jane Fredricksson's second cousin
Director	Giles: Purveen's Director in the Government Service
Kevin	Crabtree's successor as Resources Officer

CONTENTS

I

MASTER CLASS

An audience lulled by the glasshouse effect of the sun, mesmerised by the particles of dust dancing in its rays – the student paginists jittery, unable to catch the rhythm of the piece securely, distracted by the sunbeams lancing at arbitrary angles through the seminar room skylight and, in Janet's case, by a wasp – there had been better workshops.

Körthofer, struggling against the prevailing nervous lassitude, was increasingly excitable, even manic. "Passion! You need passion. The smooth page turn, the turn like silk, that is great, that is very okay, but it needs it communicate. Turn page like you making love!" His gaze moved from Paul, who maintained an unconvincing insouciance, to Janet, gazing at him with a slightly hysterical concentration. "As if make love," he repeated. He turned to Paul again. "This is Ravel Valse – it need passion, movement."

"From top. Again!" The two pianists, exchanging sideways glances, embarked once more on the cumulative cascades of notes over which they had laboured for the past two hours. The lead students, Paul and Janet, resumed their choreographed, figure-of-eight dance around the pianos, timing their arrival at the shoulders of the pianists just before they played to the end of the page.

All went well for several minutes, but the original scores on the piano stands had not been printed with paginatorics in mind. The page timings were uneven, causing difficult tempo changes. A poorly balanced rise and snatched execution by Janet led to a loss of a few notes and a noticeable intake of breath from the maestro. The ripple died down, but was succeeded shortly after by a repeat dither from Paul and a screamed "no, no, no, you make like you never done this before. Concentrate, think: you make love. Give it passion!" The performance paused. He looked at Janet. "Why she crying?" The tears increased. He turned abruptly to Paul. "No cry, just perform." He turned back to Janet. "The music. Is becoming chaos, yes. But not here. Now is sophisticate. Later is chaos. Now, you give it passion. You give it ..." He paused, looking upward to the lecture room ceiling, struggling with his exhortation and the slippery intransigence of the English language. "You give it ..." His face lightened with successful recall. "You give it fuck!"

The audience, half-asleep, showed no reaction. Janet collected herself. The piece teetered on from where it had left off. Then, several page turns later, catastrophe. The yellowed, brittle paper of the antique score to the second piano part, seized at the edge and pulled gently (but a little too passionately), ripped straight across the page, the unexpected diversion of force yanking the music off the stand, and much of the paper around the edges of the score disintegrating in the fall.

The first pianist played on for a couple of bars and segued briefly into a quiet up-tempo rendering of the Blue Danube, halting abruptly as he caught Körthofer's eye.

A ghastly silence preceded the storm. Körthofer stood still for several seconds contemplating the wreckage, before wailing, on a rising note of panic, "what you done? Gott in Himmel!"

Janet started to cry again.

Körthofer, apparently unable to move, continued to look down at the debris. He shook his head, willing it away.

"Is history. Look what you do. History!"

"Was history", Carl thought. He knew it to be Körthofer's own score, a present from the daughter of one of Ravel's pupils, autographed by the master himself.

Janet's crying gathered in force. Haplessly, students assisting the class attempted to collect the paper pieces scattered over the floor, but these disintegrated further as they were touched. Ravel's signature, unseen, reduced itself spontaneously to powder.

"No, no, no! No touch. You make destroy. Cretins!"

The students retreated, bowed down by the developing screams of fury. The two pianists sat in the middle of the maelstrom, wearing, with difficulty, expressions of studied neutrality. The remains of the score became a no-go area, upside-down on the floor and, in appearance, the beneficiary of a particularly brutal haircut.

"A disaster waiting to happen, bringing his own heirloom," Carl reflected. French scores were trouble: outsize, the paper's ingredients auto-guaranteeing their destruction.

It was not to be reflected upon out loud; Körthofer was gaining his second wind of outrage, and only subservient contrition would be wise. Carl had never thought his friend's paginatoric artistry top of the tree (though it was much better than his English), but he was a big name and as vindictive as a wounded bear when crossed. This would need much unction if the department's name were not to suffer.

Speaking to Körthofer at this stage was unlikely to be useful. And he had other urgent things to do. The mise-en-scène was his senior lecturer Ben's immediate responsibility to sort out. He slipped inconspicuously through the lecture theatre's unlit rear exit, just as Ben walked to the front with the demeanour of a dispensable Christian stepping into an amphitheatre.

It struck Carl, as he reached the safety of the outside landing, that it was a lesson in choosing one's metaphors carefully. One could say that the students had done to the piano score – if not necessarily in the way intended – exactly what the maestro had urged.

SPRING 2063

THE IDES OF MAY

II

COMMITTEE

The Faculty Resources Committee would consume the next few hours. The usual, plus an anticipated budget coup by Westwood to be fended off. It shouldn't be difficult. Framing his put-down, Carl manoeuvred past a gaggle of students and into the Symposium Room.

Five minutes to the meeting, there was little sign of interest. A bored technician cast an eye over the integrated media suite, which would no doubt malfunction on cue. Crabtree, the resources officer, sorted a formidable stack of paper into neat piles calculated to lower the spirits and discourage enquiry. A newcomer, unused to faculty meeting timekeeping, vegetated in a corner. Carl helped himself to the vending machine's least repulsive offering and walked over.

"Carl Trenchard:" he introduced himself. "You're new here, I think?" He added a brief smile. It was not returned.

"Stephen Pendleton": with an ever so slightly dismissive nod. A slight touch of American in the accent – Boston?

"It's often slow starting; won't be long". Carl's gaze quickly toured the room. Another nod; the new man looked unimpressed. "My area's Paginatorics. Relative to this faculty, one of the more long-established subjects. How about you?"

No crack in the expression; after a protracted pause: "Long-established, I would certainly say so." Another pause, before he continued: "Phoniotics!" "My subject."

That rang a bell with Carl: the enigmatic Readership funded none knew how and apparently personally sponsored by the Vice

14

Chancellor. He knew a little of Phoniotics, his professional status made it unavoidable. But its books challenged wakefulness and, weightily American, tended to cut off circulation at the knee; he did not much care for it.

"You deconstruct scores for a living?"

"I would state that more precisely as a professional commitment to deconstruction, rejection of value judgements and a focus on the musical score, considered as an objective entity. Too great an emphasis on the actual score as published, the 'partition concrète', obscures the underlying themes of the composer's, or, more correctly stated, 'auteur's' moral and societal objectives and can prevent analysis of the score in the light of sociological concerns, such as feminism or racism."

God above! Research needed to move on, but to this? Carl's subject operated at the smallest remove from actual performance. Struggling to find common ground, he became aware of the newcomer's focused gaze and the droop to the facial expression – very much like the puritan stiff with the pitchfork standing by his wife in that American painting – who was it by? The gaze intensified slightly; the reverie had better stop. He composed his features into a look of earnest enquiry and remarked, "some interesting concepts there."

The newcomer's mouth twitched slightly but the face remained in general terms unreadable. A pause and then: "It is a system of thought, far more than a simple assembly of concepts, that can facilitate a properly rigorous framework for thinking and acting. An effort by the faculty to define its objectives and policies along these lines could be much to its benefit, imagewise."

What was he on about? More to the point, what was he on? The face remained straight, severe and expressionless.

Several departmental colleagues came into the room together and the meeting preliminaries gained momentum. Carl moved away to chat to his junior lecturer, Viola, and Pitchfork – he must remember to call him Stephen – turned to convey austere disapprobation elsewhere. He could be masking uncontrollable lechery, for one or other or both sexes – or, indeed, the faculty cat. But it seemed unlikely.

The chairman, Graham, with his usual air of unfocused worry, called them to order. "Is Rupert on his way? Quarter of an hour? Right, let's make a start." They settled without enthusiasm around a rectangular table, long and wide enough to require good voice projection, its blankness broken only by random coffee stains and a large plate of assorted biscuits placed in the geographical centre. "The 15th May meeting of the Resources Committee of the Faculty of Ancillary Music is now in session. Can we approve the Minutes of the previous meeting?"

The meeting adopted its familiar drone. Carl settled into semi-comatose awareness, just distanced from actual sleep, running a mental sweepstake on who would first take the fateful step of choosing a biscuit from one of the plates in the centre of the table and whether the manner of so doing would put them at the top or bottom of the pecking order. Though biscuits were badly needed as a means of taking away the taste of the coffee, it was important to get it right. Nothing could be expected to combat afternoon drowsiness before the needle match: agenda item 6 – budget allocations for next year.

But it was item 3 that started the war. The agenda item in question was innocuous to the point of self-parody: Internal Audit Report Summary on Health and Safety Procedures Applicable to Ancillary Music Teaching Practice.

The auditor, Alison - much prettier than her irreparably drab calling might suggest, dark hair, short but abundant, with a tendency to curl, framing a lively face, tapering to a delicate but probably determined chin - Carl concentrated on describing it to himself - had meandered uneventfully through the first eight or ten Holopoint images projected in the air before them. Technology of the utmost sophistication displayed endless lists of recommendations in text. It had all been discussed well beforehand; there were no surprises.

A recommendation - "to improve effectiveness of the internal control processes relating to expenditure on teaching aids for enhanced awareness of health and safety issues arising from advanced solo paginatoric technique for piano duet performances." - provoked a comment from a Chordologist, Mike Esther. Nothing unusual: asking questions in presentations could be the only practicable way of staying awake.

"Internal control of a Paginist: that sounds expensive." He got a ripple of laughter.

Pitchfork picked it up. "Nevertheless, a necessary mandate and not exclusively in monetary terms."

Asking what he meant could provoke a debate of significant tedium. Carl let it go as a graceless attempt at establishing committee soundness.

But the Chordologist asked it instead, taken aback that his aside should have hit such a seam of seriousness.

"Threesomes" (Carl registered the word: he knows the slang too) "can facilitate problems, in Paginatorics just as well as in other areas of activity. What does our colleague think?"

Shit, thought Carl, he knows about it. The Körthofer debacle. How? He did an elaborate rising-to-full-consciousness routine, stifling a small yawn, smiling wearily in the general direction of Crabtree (who did not reciprocate) and, after a little further thought, commenting: "That's an interesting symbolic connection between old and new professions for one of your students to research, Stephen, but Alison's point is about money for wobble boards to improve performers' balance. Just under £200 last year, to set Mike's mind at rest."

Mike grinned and nodded slightly, but Pitchfork was not giving up yet: "The point is about rigour" (mortis? thought Carl: it seemed to be one of Pitchfork's words) "and professionalism, which should be unexceptionable demands for any area of the faculty". He looked round at the meeting, which, daunted, nodded earnestly, almost in unison and murmured a general sense of assent.

"Quite so." answered Carl with a profoundly serious timbre. "Alison, have you anything to add?" Alison hadn't, and the next Holopoint slab of text burst thankfully into the air. Carl noticed a smirk flit across Crabtree's features, like a whimper of radiation from a black hole. A put-up job? he thought, then no, don't be paranoid; he's just a pillock.

The meeting resumed its slumber, the biscuits still untouched. Faculty Resource Committees, Carl reflected thankfully, happened only once a quarter: you couldn't afford to miss them, but at some point in the proceedings you lost the will to live; the frequency of meetings could probably have been calibrated to a desired rate of cull of academic staff if there hadn't been more straightforward methods available.

He surfaced again, with an uneasy sense that something had been said. Viola was looking at him and so was Crabtree, though the meeting as a whole was looking at the Holopoint display. Item 5: "Short-term Options for Overspill Accommodation for the Manucussionist Department". An unexciting topic; the Manucs were regarded as overspill by most serious artists anyway, unimaginative middlemen for drummers in need of a stick, marimbists looking for a hammer etc. Put them in the container conversions where they belonged. His mind rewound on the sounds recorded in recent seconds…something about "flexible working and adaptation to circumstances that could be expected to arise". Crabtree. What the hell did he mean by that? They weren't going to try handing drumsticks over from home, for God's sake! The postal service didn't do sub-day response, let alone sub-second. Asking for clarification would be a give-away, so he let it pass, but made a conscious effort to listen more closely.

The accommodation item ground on. The container park, acquired several years ago by the performance artists as part of a degree project, was indeed one of the options. There was no decision. Crabtree was asked to produce a position paper with fully developed business cases for three of the options. As if! Carl thought. The Manucs were going to have to continue boxing and coxing day and evening for the foreseeable future.

"I would be happy to lend assistance in constructing the business cases." Accepted. Pitchfork – Stephen! Stephen! What was he hoping to get out of the bullshit and faked arithmetic that would at best ensue, for a department nobody else cared about? Carl found it obscurely threatening.

The chairman announced item 6, the budget bids, provoking a studied lack of reaction from all present and an almost tangible atmosphere of heightened attention. Crabtree studied his fingernails, waiting for the summons. Pitchfork metaphorically held his implement to attention. Though a newcomer, he was showing unmistakeable signs of interest: less well concealed than for any other person present; perhaps he had early hopes of a new department.

Crabtree distributed copious papers and summarised the state of the budgets for this year (slightly overspent), the state of the funding for next year (uncertain) and the total of the departmental bids (wildly optimistic). The chairman asked departmental heads to give brief presentations.

Mike Esther expatiated on teaching aids for string-tensioning skills and emergency gut-plaiting techniques in an amusing but expansive style that was cut short of the funding denouement by the chairman. Looking wounded, he gave way to Westwood, who went for the importance of Manucussionism as a founding discipline of Ancillary Music. There was much reference to the department's commitment to professionalism and ongoing research ('Hermeneutics and Relativism: Cross-Cultural Contexts in Drumstick Handling' and like papers, Carl thought, with an inward sneer) and its commitment to temperance - an odd addition in the context of an appeal for more funding; it was normally the cue for quiet derision.

Carl kept his short, concentrating on objectives. Not yet sensing the degree of change in the wind, he left the reputation of Paginatorics, the original and still the most glamorous of the Ancillary Music subjects, to speak for itself. The approach had been effective in two decades of such contests.

Presentations followed from the minor subjects – the Reedsmiths and Presentation Technicians. The chairman asked for questions, and a melee of open discussion erupted: statements of interest - often of startling irrelevance – of rebuttal – often startlingly tangential – of indignation – often startlingly ill-focused – of peace-making – often startlingly irritating. It advanced nothing, but was necessary, allowing easement of accumulated opinions, the equivalent of farting and belching after a meal and with a similar gradation of discretion.

Suddenly, Pitchfork – Stephen! – rose from his chair, reached across to the plate of biscuits with a masterful gesture, swept up the chocolate orange cream and, unwrapping it, used the slight pause caused by drawing attention to comment: "It is clear there are many competing priorities and insufficient funding to meet them all. We shall need a co-ordinated statement of faculty objectives to decide how these stand relative to each other and to allocate the money that is available. Do we have such a statement? For that matter, do we have its genesis: a banner statement?" Crumpling the biscuit foil, he flicked it back towards the biscuit plate, hitting the outstretched arm of Crabtree, who, ever the loser, had reached out too late and was forced to settle for a chocolate digestive.

The chairman, groaning audibly at the mention of the banner statement, announced a 10-minute break.

There was a general move to secure a biscuit, and to seek relief. Carl sought out Rupert Llewellyn, a mere Reedsmith, but always well informed on faculty manoeuvrings. He was curious as to whether the spat over item 3 and Crabtree's lank air of subdued triumph had any significance, but Rupert could relay only Mike Esther's very public liaison with his administrative assistant and Viola's invitation to present to the Bucharest conference, the latter already known to Carl and a source of quiet pleasure. Pitchfork – Stephen – was definitely in with the Vice Chancellor and on first-name terms with his PA, but nobody seemed to know any more: probably just another American purveying a new, shiny subject to satisfy the VC's perceived rampant Yankophilia.

The meeting resumed, with an introduction from the chairman. "Stephen, to whom, incidentally, I owe an apology for not doing a proper introduction at the beginning of the meeting…" everybody smiled in Pitchfork's direction and murmured some species of greeting "…Stephen…Stephen Pendleton, has asked whether we have a faculty banner statement and consolidated statement of objectives covering the various departments. The answer to the best of my knowledge is that the two are taken as subsumed into the faculty's Banner Statement, which originated as the Mission Statement and appears in the Annual Report, where it normally forms most or all of the section on faculty objectives. I'll read it out, and we can then discuss whether this meets the purpose of the present discussion." Deadpan, he read out:

"To passionately and at the highest quality educate learning-seekers in the craft of assistance to primary-delivery musicians and in the principles of artistic performance outreach to sonic stakeholders"

"I think we must overlook the phrasing; we're here for music not literature. But it does seems to cover the essentials."

Pitchfork jumped in. "With respect, Chairman, I cannot see that this states the faculty's objectives at the level at which we can usefully attempt to prioritise departmental demands. And the banner statement itself makes no reference to the primacy of the market-led approach, to professionalism, or to the moral issues involved in ethical standards."

Oh God! Carl thought, we've got a post-neocon. Surely that ground had been poisoned forever twenty years ago after the spectacularly ill-judged attempt to create Pakafiran, a national territory running from the Zagros Mountains to the Karakorams and constituted as a commercial subsidiary of HallTech, an East India Company of our century, but rather less successful; it had lasted just four years. Seemingly not - Pitchfork continued:

"I have been asked by the Vice Chancellor to be instrumental in establishing a working group to scrutinise the faculty's objectives and the effectiveness of its study methods and scope of syllabus in achieving these. Naturally, questions of ongoing allocation of funds, particularly as regards new initiatives, will need to be considered in the context of the working group's findings, and I propose that decisions on the present agenda item be deferred at least until the group makes its initial report. I would like to add my apologies for springing this on you at this meeting in this way. There is to be an announcement in the next couple of days, and I had forewarned your chairman" (the chairman nodded miserably) "but it is clearly necessary now to avoid premature decisions made without full knowledge of the facts."

Shit! was Carl's first thought. 'Facts', as an official construct of reality, looked as though they had mutated. More considered reactions started to crowd in, but his attention was needed for the vote on Pitchfork's proposal.

Its fate was determined by the reputation of Pitchfork's boss and confidant, the Vice Chancellor (known generally as the VC); the resolution went through swiftly and without opposition. It wasn't inarguable, but no-one fancied being seen as a troublemaker by the VC. Not after VAPA's fate. "Personality differences" between the VC and head of faculty had inspired Visual & Plastic Arts' rationalisation on market-led principles. Its Fine Arts department now devoted most of its output to computer-generated designs commissioned by advertising agencies. Just the design: production happened in one of the more southerly and poverty-stricken countries in the Russian Federation. Performance Art had been contracted out to a regular licensed busking spot at Elephant & Castle tube station. Sculpture led a peripatetic existence doing whatever they were paid for and had been last heard of reproofing the Angel of the North. Textiles had possibly fared best and now ran training courses from a base in Tuscany, largely self-funding and further supported by the takings from craft shops in San Gimignano and Siena. Ceramics, or such of its staff as were prepared to emigrate, had relocated to a town in North China to "facilitate enhanced synergy with contemporary production approaches". There had been much resistance and some violence, but all had proved beyond prevention. VAPA had set a standard.

The coup achieved, the meeting disintegrated rapidly. There was a token attempt to discuss the remaining agenda items, but even the ongoing saga of staff kitchen facilities, that had on at least one past occasion led to a senior lecturer throwing a punch at Crabtree (unhappily, though perhaps happily for the senior lecturer's career, it had not connected), roused virtually no interest or discussion. The chairman terminated the meeting just after 4.30pm. Such promptness was unheard of - meetings had been known to straggle on well into the evening - but there was no air of pleased release as people dispersed. Westwood looked quietly smug (had temperance's hour come at last?); Crabtree had an almost-concealed smirk that Carl longed to wipe off his face; Pitchfork continued simply to look like Pitchfork. All others were subdued.

Carl hung back a little, making a show of collecting papers, to avoid getting into conversation with colleagues. First reactions were rarely productive, and the necessary touch of insouciance edged with hard seriousness would need a little time to mature within. Pitchfork and Co. were easy to avoid, having already got together in a huddle near the Holopoint projector. First things first, though: Viola. They had nearly an hour and a half more than they'd planned. After Viola he'd need to talk to Ben. He would call him once he was out of earshot of the others. Assembling the papers in readiness for filing or recycling, he jettisoned the spent coffee cup and made a swift exit, shouting "Au revoir!" to the stragglers and the huddle and "Splendid biscuits, Graham!" to the chairman, now locked into the huddle with an air of martyrdom. Responses of "Bye!" or "Ciao!"; Graham smiled weakly; Pitchfork raised his hand hieratically; Westwood grunted; Crabtree sniggered. No surprises there. Outside, having crossed the road to the gardens in front of the university buildings universally known as The Old Bin and established that no colleagues were in earshot, he rang Ben, turning the videophone off.

Ben answered immediately. "Ben, it's Carl."

"Carl. Where are you? I can't see you."

"Battery's a bit low for video. How is it going?"

"Not well. We've only just about scraped Körthofer off the ceiling; at least one of the students: Janet, the slim one with nice tits, is going to need counselling; God knows what we're going to do about the music, I've not even had time to think about that yet. And Körthofer, when he was flailing about just after it happened swiped one of the pianists on the back of the head: the one who started on the Blue Danube, so there may be an assault charge there, let alone a personal injury claim. There's staff looking after each one of them, and they've got Körthofer back at his hotel now, but it's an uphill bloody battle"

It didn't sound good, but it didn't sound like an ongoing riot either. "Look, Ben, I can't stop now, but we'll need to discuss what to do, and something else has come up that I need to talk to you about urgently. Can we meet this evening?"

"I've a tutorial till seven thirty and an appointment with the lovely Atinuke around eleven, but I'm free between, though I'll need to eat."

"Okay, can we make it eight thirty in the Oast House?"

"Yeah, okay. See you there! You owe me a pint or two."

"Maybe. See you there!"

He rang off. That was good; the Oast House was big and anonymous; its acoustics made conversations inaudible more than two or three feet away at the best of times. And it served decent food.

He set off to the flat and to Viola.

III

DIFFICULTIES WITH GIRL

She avoids me now; we can't even talk.

The Brighton trip started the trouble. A group of us, including Ali, went down for the day. We split up after lunch and went off separately. I went to look at a bookshop in The Lanes: I like books, even though they're old-fashioned, and there are very few proper bookshops about. That's how, after I'd spent a couple of hours working right through the shop, I ran into Ali: she'd gone shopping in The Lanes too, and we met near the Meeting House. She was minus Eva, her constant companion, that day, so I had her to myself for a rare couple of minutes.

The thing is, I think she's wonderful: sexy and funny. Curly dark hair, a face that always seems on the edge of laughter. I met her just over a year ago. But getting near enough to try anything has been problematic. There's Eva, they go around together: everywhere. And when I've suggested, in the odd moments there's just been the two of us that we meet, she'll agree, but it'll be somewhere crowded, like a pub, and at least a couple of weeks away. Well, I've never been the type to say "nah, don't like that. Wednesday round your place," as somebody like Wayne might. I doubt I'd get away with it, anyway, you have to be Wayne, but it's what I'd have preferred. I'm not totally without experience, but it doesn't seem to help; it's back to square one.

When she said "Hi, Tad!" and smiled, a fraction of a second before I saw her, I assumed at first she'd be in company.

I responded, "Hi. Bought anything?"

"Just this." She showed me what she said was a scarf, so small and insubstantial it might have been a fancy handkerchief. "I was thinking about a dress, but I'm not sure. I came out to think about it."

She really was by herself. I grasped the opportunity. "I could give an opinion on it if you want"

She thought about that a bit. "Would you? I don't want to take up your time."

"No problem."

"Well, it'd only be five minutes. If you don't mind. Normally I'd have Eva."

We walked round the corner to the shop where she'd found a dress she liked, reduced in a sale. She went to try it on, reappearing five minutes later from the changing room, to do a twirl in front of me.

"It looks great on you," I said. It did. It was a darkish red, which suited her.

She stopped, looked down at it, held out her foot for comparison with the shoe and looked doubtful. "You say everything I wear looks great."

"No, I mean it. It suits you" And it did, really. She was right in one way; anything would look pretty good to me if it had got Ali inside it, but she dresses smartly anyway.

"Mmn." She walked over to a mirror and did another twirl, for herself. "Do you really mean that?"

"Yeah." I concentrated on looking at her face; the dress hung quite loosely, but it was tantalisingly close-fitting here and there.

My eyes strayed momentarily downwards, and she must have seen that, for she sniffed, raised an eyebrow and said, "I bet you do." Then she went back to the mirror, posed this way and that, looked doubtful again and, after ten or fifteen minutes of to-ing and fro-ing, said "Mmn" again and went back into the changing room, from where she emerged another fifteen minutes later with a decision I would have made half an hour before.

We were walking along from the shop, towards the sea front, when we noticed a doorway, set back a bit from the street, a stand announcing Sea View Ice Cream Parlour.

"I could murder an ice cream," she said.

Suddenly, I found I could too. I said, "Lets have a look" and went in through the doorway, along a narrow hallway and up some stairs. Nothing special from below, the café was quite a large room, clean and cheerful looking, with a walls-length of window looking over the sea and the bank of pebbles that Brighton calls a beach. Round to one side, you could see Palace Pier. It was nearly empty, just an old couple at a table near the stairs. We headed straight for the window and plonked ourselves down at a table with the view, well away from the others.

We ordered drinks, an ice cream each and a portion of chocolate cake that Ali liked the sound of. It came quickly. The old couple paid up and left. "Just me and you, then," she said, with a flicker of a grin and a slight widening of the eyes, after which she returned her attention to the view.

"And the view." Not that I was looking at it particularly: I was enjoying the moment, watching her sit there straight-backed, rapt, her light-brown eyes fixed on something in the distance, the drinks straw dangling inelegantly from her right hand.

After an interval, she remembered where she was. "Sorry," she said and flicked a glance at me. "What's that?" She pointed out towards the horizon. It took me a minute to see it: a rectangle of shining light hanging a little above the sea near the horizon. There was nothing holding it up as far as you could tell.

I put on an air of serious enquiry. "No question about it: it's an alien spacecraft?" I said.

"Yeah, yeah. Little green men, come to abduct us. And?"

I remained straight-faced. "It may just be a reconnaissance flight."

She rolled her eyes briefly. "Have you ever been abducted by aliens yourself?"

"I look little and green?"

She giggled. "It's the ideas you have." She looked out of the window, thinking hard. "It doesn't look like anything, really."

"Just a big shiny rectangle suspended in space."

She dismissed it and spooned a dollop of ice cream into her mouth.

"Do you want any other ideas?"

"Such as?" She attacked her drink, with a slight slurping noise.

"A spiritual vision."

"No. Try again." She spooned up more ice cream and looked at me questioningly.

"A vision of the unattainable."

She frowned a little. "That sounds serious. I think I'll settle for the big shiny meaningless rectangle."

I laughed. She didn't. "Yeah, I suppose so."

We sat in silence for a few minutes, while she finished her ice cream and the majority of the chocolate cake, more daintily now that she was under direct observation. I picked at my ice cream, but mostly just made a mess of it. There's what I think of as the background radiation in the universe of the opposite sex. It's partly excitement, partly – actually, that's mostly in my case - frustration. Ali had the ability to crank the radiation up to a level that might have set off a real-world radiation monitor. Not by doing anything, just by being. So put what followed down to radiation sickness.

"This unattainable thing. The truth is, I'm crazy about you, Ali. Have been since I first met you. I don't know if you realise that."

She went poker-faced and put on a stage-Irish accent. "Is it sex you're after getting, now, then, Taddy?"

But I'd got stuck on the seriousness track.

"No. Well, that as well, but it's what I feel about you that matters."

She didn't answer, just looked down at her drink, then out of the window, then back at me, then back down to her drink. I blundered on.

"Just a feeling. Well, I love you, you see."

I hadn't exactly understood that until I said it. It was true, but I wished it unsaid soon enough. She looked sort of pleased and unpleased at the same time. There was a long silence. I waited.

Finally, she sighed and looked at me directly: another moment to remember; she has lovely eyes. After a short pause she said, "We hardly know each other, not really, Tad, you can't say that." There was another long silence, she looked down and half-heartedly saw off her diet coke, before eventually looking up at me again. I hadn't said anything more; a prime minister who's just gone for the all-out nuclear strike, then realised a couple of rockets over the border fence would have been a smarter move, would know what I felt like. I suppose I must have looked stricken, for she sighed and said, "look, Tad, you're somebody I really like. You're talented, and I respect you. Let's leave it like that for now, find out who we really are. "

"So nothing then?"

"No, you mustn't say that. We'll both be at the party next Wednesday, I'll see you there."

"You don't want to meet, Ali, just the two of us?"

"We're meeting just the two of us now; you'll be asking for my veep next. And I'd rather be called Alison, you know." She laughed. I didn't.

For those of you who don't know, or pretend not to know, a veep is part of our generation's answer to condoms. In technical jargon, it's a digital profile of sexual response. Avatar technology.

I continued, gloomily. "Would that be so terrible, then?"

"Lighten up, will you? I'm not one of those sex-game avatars you work with."

Actually, the virtual games I work on are educational, nothing to do with sex, but there's never been any convincing her of that. "I never said you were. Anyway, avatars don't use veeps or X-Gloves."

"Lucky them."

"So it does horrify you?"

She sighed again and looked at her hands for a moment. "No, it's nothing like that." Then she looked at me. "Sex really isn't that great, you know; let's not spoil things. Let's just enjoy what we've got."

There wasn't really anything to say to that. "We'd better go," she said, standing up. I followed suit, picking up the bill. "Maybe we shouldn't say anything to the others, keep this between ourselves." I nodded and tried to keep a neutral expression; what would you have done? Cry? She patted my arm and turned. A crowd of people started up the stairs, sounding jolly; it was definitely time to go.

I glanced out of the window. There, near the horizon. A container ship with the sun on it, that was all.

The X-Glove, if you're wondering, is what you use with the veep, a machine, which you fit to yourself – it's neat. They're universal since they drove off the competition a few years ago (leaving millions of pissed-off consumers with profiles in unusable formats). You dodge the problems of sex, of doing it, by letting a machine simulate it for you, using the profile. It's been very popular, except with the religious, who call it, among other things, The Beast of Gomorrah.

I never have got her veep, though I did try giving her my penpro (the male equivalent). She didn't turn it down, but nothing came back, though I heard tell her sister had tried it out.

Then things got worse.

A few weeks failing to enjoy hitting a brick wall, and sometimes saying so to Ali (I still think of her as Ali, not Alison). Mostly she was nice to me, I must admit, but sometimes she'd laugh and I suppose once or twice I got a bit bad-tempered about that. The occasion when things took a downturn, I'd said something like: "you just don't give a toss, do you?" and she said "Giving a toss is up to you, isn't it", which shocked me a bit; I hadn't thought she could be crude like that; I'd only meant what I said in the usual sense.

Anyway, she went on with something like "This is getting me really wound up, and it's not as if there's anything to get wound up about, is there?" Then she said she thought "we should cool things off a bit; maybe we'd better not see each other for a while." After one of her pauses, she switched to the ultra-sincere expression, that I'd got to know quite well. "It's for your own good, you should look for someone better. What's wrong is with me. Honestly, you'd be better off with someone else. Someone like Eva. I'm no good for you really, you know."

And that was that; she's avoided me since.

Eva, as I've already said, is Ali's constant companion. She seems in an equally constant sulk, which I don't find too amiable, and I don't get the feeling she thinks much of me either, so Ali's suggestion washed straight off. Hens often seem to think they know who we'll find attractive, and they're usually wrong. Look at it from the wrong angle, I suppose.

Getting banned from the presence has been devastating, and I've been a bit obsessed about it; got to wondering whether there's something wrong with me. But really it's just yearning, if you get what I mean. I yearn for her every moment that I'm not totally taken over by something else. It's like an ache. I tell myself blokes only acquire girlfriends and veeps and so on as status symbols and true, some do, but I can't convince even myself that I'm consoled.

I'd better go and smarten up; I'm meeting some friends – male friends – at The Oast. Blokes are not so picky about how you're dressed, but you never know who else might be there. Like Ali. Actually, I'm looking forward to an evening out; there haven't been many recently. It keeps occurring to me I ought to feel bad about that: what's emotional turmoil mean if you can soothe it so easily? It's shameful really, especially if you consider yourself a romantic.

IV

SOIREE MUSICALE

Waking, he felt the warmth of her body against his and instinctively reached out his arm to hold her, running his hand down the sides of her rib-cage and along the pelvic curve, coming to rest temporarily on the perfection of her buttocks. The move both wakened Viola and stimulated further exploration, but Viola wriggled effectively, leaned back to read the clock and sat up with a lunge. "That's enough of that. It's nearly half past six. We haven't got much time." Carl groaned lightly but obeyed the summons, moving himself by degrees into a sitting position, then out of the bed, reaching for his clothes.

Viola, already dressed, had retrieved a glass from the kitchen and was skittering about, applying it and her ear to various walls around the study and hall as she did so. "There's nobody there. We've got until just before eight." Carl grunted approval and, having retrieved his shirt from halfway down the back of the dressing table, moved into the study and picked out the Franck piano score from the music cupboard, where it lay half-concealed by files on teaching aids.

"Here's the viola part."

"Thanks." Viola had discovered the version of the Franck sonata for her instrument from a mid-90s recording in the "Reserved" section of the university library, was immediately taken with the idea of playing it and had, with some difficulty, succeeded in acquiring the music as research material. That had required no small amount of ingenuity, as her subject of research was paginatoric contexts in late Dutch polyphony, and only the Belgian, Low Countries connection and Franck's use of chorale-like melodies in his organ ("keyboard") music had averted difficult enquiry. "I'd like to give it a run-through, maybe rehearse a bit." Carl nodded, busily dog-earing and flattening out the piano score.

Satisfied they were not overheard, with the possible exception of the old man across the courtyard, who was nearly stone deaf, they tuned quickly and launched into the sonata, settling, after a slightly shaky first few bars into a steady flow, each sensing the direction in which the other would take the piece, as the piano and the viola alternately took the leading role. At times, to Viola, it felt as if the music was being made by a single instrument and instrumentalist, as if the two of them were symbiotic. Mostly, it was not quite that satisfying, but not bad and, after a brief re-run of the opening page, to re-establish a secure starting point, they passed on to the second movement. This was not so well co-ordinated, and they quickly made a new start and then another. On the third run-through the music started to fall properly into place, the sense of unity becoming achievable, though it would need some dedicated rehearsal. Viola played with a steady concentration and gave an impression of slight distance from the technicalities of playing. Carl, glancing across when the score allowed, or musical co-ordination demanded, was struck, as always, by this and by the slight lift of one corner of her mouth, the beginnings of a smile overlaid on the otherwise steely coolness, perhaps the only hint of her feelings that was not expressed in purely musical terms.

Carl glanced at his watch: it was a quarter to eight. There was not much time left, so they skipped the third movement and ran straight through the finale; enough to establish that it was going to need serious work. There was a noise of footsteps in the courtyard outside, and Viola immediately ceased playing and put the viola aside, away from casual viewing.

Viola was a second generation Paginist, qualified only in Paginatorics. Brought up in a detached house with a cellar that could be sound-proofed, she had been taught to play her eponymous instrument. Also the 'cello, but concealing an instrument of this size in a small flat was simply impractical, so it remained for the moment with her parents. Loving S-class passionately was one thing; making a career and a living was another, and it would do her career in Paginatorics no good at all, if she betrayed this passion.

Carl continued to doodle for a couple of minutes: playing page-transition passages to support research was kosher; it just didn't do to sound too connected, or go on too long.

Viola, caught up in the doodlings, said, "have you ever been tempted just to be open about it, play when you feel like it? I'd have thought a professor, especially with your reputation, might get away with it."

The playing trailed off. "Not so. There's the artistic purity of my profession to uphold and all that. Actual playing is something that artisans do; it'd be thought of as peculiar, a sort of fetish. Why do you take the risk?"

She considered. "The music. Just that, really. And you?"

He doodled a little more. "The same. Not that it's the only thing I enjoy about our meetings." It wasn't. Viola had attracted him from the moment he saw her outside the interview room, but getting her into bed (or more precisely, onto a quilted picnic rug one warm and memorable summer night) had been a revelation. The physical attraction was inextricably bound up with affection: she was a strange girl in some ways, but she had an instinctive empathy, sometimes switched on, sometimes off. He had kept his feelings, at least for the time being, to himself; he sensed that it was highly likely that Viola felt, to some degree, differently about him, and she could deploy a quality of coolness that worked to great advantage when playing music, but might be difficult to deal with when it came to emotional concerns.

She was in a cool mood now. She liked Carl and found him attractive, and the sex was okay, but he was not quite her type: she preferred something with a touch of ambiguity, and sex with virtual assistance: Carl had this odd, slightly fetishistic insistence on trad only, which was fine as far as it went, but not the way her generation did things. The first exploratory caresses on the picnic rug had come as a surprise: there'd been no veep or clip request, an area in which she'd become an expert decision-maker, negotiator and occasional short-order counsellor. No, he'd just made a moderately subtle lunge, after a little flirtation. The surprise had acted as a mild aphrodisiac; she had given way without complaint or resistance: Carl's skills as a pianist were famous in certain circles, well beyond the university, and it had been obvious even from before she had been offered the job what her bargaining point might be.

She changed direction. "Why get into Paginatorics? Starting as a pianist?"

"Me? Oh, the usual. Money. It's all taken for granted now, but M-class was new then and popular because of the things S-Class didn't do: all the theatrical stuff. S-Class - just listening to music, classical music - was something not many people did any longer; they still don't; it all looked old-fashioned. And the money went out of it. So I had to learn to do the Mozart C-Minor Concerto, say, as part of a circus act, or a Flamenco scena, or a mime in three acts, or an ice-skating spectacular. It was a producer's world for a time."

"But it still left you as a pianist."

"For a short while, yes. Then page turning suddenly became the big new craze, this mix of ballet and gymnastics. I got asked to do a couple of dates, they went well, the playing opportunities were drying up, I just followed the money." Viola looked at him thoughtfully. "You look shocked. It's common enough. And it was worthwhile."

Viola shook her head and smiled. "No, I'm not shocked at all, just curious. Actually, you must have got out just in time"

"Too true. The work just disappeared. As a pianist, I'd got to the final of one international competition and had had a couple of honourable mentions, but by the time I changed jobs and became a paginist, it wasn't enough; there was so little work, they only took first and second prize winners. Even they don't get much. Our two pianists today probably earn less than apprentice plumbers and always will. There's not much else than playing in workshops, Trad Pubs, 'live' piped music, because it's cheaper than recorded and a once-in-a-blue-moon live recital. Most of that isn't actually S-Class anyway."

"What I meant was what happened to S-Class after that."

"Oh. The neosoc witch hunt and all that?"

"Yes."

"Well, yes, that was a tragedy for some. I was lucky. The pity was, it was so unnecessary. Driving S-Class into a remote corner was happening anyway. It would have become just a harmless lost cause that the likes of us followed as a hobby. I suppose, though, they realised it'd survived that sort of thing before. Half-criminalising it made life difficult for everybody. Some of my friends … it destroyed their lives, sometimes literally."

They both reflected on the outcome. After the neocon debacle and the swing back to a stylised version of left-wing values ("neosoc"), pursuits that were seen as reactionary had assumed a darker colouring. S-class in particular, though it had remained, in the strictest sense, legal, had become highly suspect, with its consciously minority and elitist appeal. Above all, a series of court cases by the local authorities against a number of the more famous music schools had established a precedent that an exclusively S-class musical education could potentially be interpreted as child abuse. Whilst there was no outright ban on teaching children traditional musical skills, it ceased to be respectable in social terms, unbuoyed even by local government's subsequent demise. S-Class had become risky as hobby or profession; increasingly, the musicians who supplied the necessary cannon fodder for Paginatoric performances came from the Russian or Chinese sectors: usefully beyond the pale and relatively cheap.

The conversation had taken a mournful tinge. Viola changed direction again. "What was that little speech in the meeting by that Stephen character - the American with the bald patch - about?"

He thought about for a moment. "Now you mention it, he does sport a bald patch, doesn't he? What he was talking about, the Lord only knows, really. It sounds like a reorganisation, but we've had four or five of those promised in the past three years, and nothing much has happened. Except for poor old VAPA, of course: which is why we have to stay polite and cooperative. What do you think?"

"Holding up the budget sounded serious enough to me. Where does Stephen come from, anyway? It was the first time I've even heard of him, but he just swanned in and took over the meeting. Pretty cool!"

"The budget's often late; two years ago it wasn't final until seven months into the year; that's just Crabtree. I don't know much about Pendleton yet, but apparently he's well in with the chancellor of vice and his crowd, so we'll have to take him seriously. Would you be able to find out anything on that young-things circuit of yours?"

Viola tossed her head. "The old man speaks! If you mean MiMi, I'll see what I can find, but he didn't sound like the type who'd let everyone in on his life. Unless his interests are specialist, of course."

"That could be useful to know. And anything else you hear. I'll have to run now; I'm meeting Ben at the Oast in fifteen minutes."

"Give my regards to the Sex God", Viola said, eyebrows raised coolly. Though her musical affinities joined her at present to Carl, she found Ben strikingly attractive, even if unambiguous, an attraction that was mutual and had expressed itself, unbeknown to Carl, in an exchange of veep and penpro.

"Will do. Who from? The Sex Goddess?"

Viola, without a change of expression, punched him lightly on the chest and walked with him to the door, where they embraced and kissed at some length to establish a scene of respectable normality to the passers by, then watched him to the corner of the walkway before going back inside, placing the viola inside a concealed cupboard next to the dresser in the kitchen and returning the music to the Chorale Development file. The girly outing at the Afghan café wasn't till nine-thirty. She had some time on her hands and no inclination to Dutch polyphony for the time being, so MiMi it was.

She sat at the computer and activated the Holoplayer and Sense system, grinding her teeth as always at its slowness – fifteen seconds just wasn't good enough; Jane had something that got you there in under a second. But then she also had lots of money on tap from her parents, something that Viola's more self-consciously frugal background denied her.

There were several message presentations, mostly importuning her custom; the virtual market one even had a smell of bread – that idea must be at least a century old, she thought. Three personal ones got replies: one just a smile. Then she activated the environmental surround, with its tang of scorched dust and walked forward into the search library, thinking about where to start.

V

IN THE OAST (1)

A brisk 15-minute walk from Quiberon Road brought Carl to the tramway, which he crossed, eschewing the mandatory but generally ignored footbridge and gaining the safety of The Oast House by a side entrance. Inside, Ben was not immediately in view. He did a slow circuit of the pub, acknowledging a student group with a raised hand, and was heading for the bar when the main door opened and Ben breezed in, with his usual air of cheeky energy. From a mere twelve-year age gap, he often made Carl feel old.

They found a private corner and settled there. Neither private nor corner were really the words for a pub so triumphantly open-plan as The Oast, a compendium of late twentieth century pub architecture, but the effect of the usual crowd of customers on its acoustics made it possible to roar confidences at one's neighbour with little risk of being overheard.

"How has it gone with Körthofer?"

Ben grimaced. "It could be worse. We've got him back to his hotel, more or less calmed down. Janet's ministering to him. I told her to order any food and wine – or anything else he wants - within reason. It shouldn't hit the budget too hard."

"That's good as far as it goes. The problem is what happened to the score. It looked pretty well composted when I left."

"It's completely fucked."

Carl nodded; no surprises there. "We'll have to come up with something quickly on the music. One legal point: we did have our own copies of the music on hand, didn't we?"

"We did. They were on a music stand to one side."

"If the worst comes to the worst, then, we could just say it's up to his insurers. But we can't really hope to get away with just that; it'll be bad for the department's reputation. The snag is, the signed copy is probably irreplaceable, and even if it was, any budget we could get together wouldn't be in the same order of magnitude."

"Forgery?" Ben said with a smile. "The signature, I mean."

"You need to be careful about keeping that sort of suggestion off-record, Ben, but yes, off-record, it might have its charms. It's just so traceable – where would we get the music? Most of the pieces in our library are M-Class and recent. Places like Cecil Court are covered by dozens of cameras and their stock is on every database that matters."

Ben looked uncharacteristically introspective, swallowed some beer and decided to get a dig back. "Your generation had it easy. Nobody had records on anything that far back."

"I'm not that old, Ben. You'd have to go back to the Elizabethans for that – my parents and beyond. Even my parents were used to cameras." Carl was distracted momentarily by this slur on his 52-year-old self.

He regrouped. "It's obvious we can't hope for a like-for-like replacement, but we could make some sort of gesture, give him something that he can show off in the future, even if it's not from Ravel."

He paused, took a mouthful of beer, then turned back to the here and now. "Incidentally, why did you leave Janet with him? She was the one who dropped the music, wasn't she? Last time I spoke to you, she was going to need counselling."

"He's a celebrity: in our world. She seemed to like that – once he'd stopped screaming at her."

Carl raised his eyebrows. "And did he take to her?"

"Very much so. I left them deep in social intercourse." Carl looked momentarily startled. "I said social. Mind you, he likes how she looks, no question. I can't blame him. Amazing tits."

Carl let the observation go. "A diversion by the one who caused the damage could be useful, I suppose. Make him reasonable. Am I right that she was the one; it's what I remember?"

"Yes, Janet was the one. She was set up by the other, though. He fumbled the page-turn just before. It placed the music badly; it'd have been precarious even for an expert. I should have intervened, but you know what Körthofer's like with interruptions."

Carl cast his eyes to the ceiling; he knew only too well. At an early stage in his career, he had shared a concert platform, in Dresden, with Körthofer and could remember with considerable clarity the reaction to his stopping the dress rehearsal to discuss with one of the outlying marimba players why they were repositioning their music stand. It had been difficult to know whether the marimbist was more at fault for interfering with choreography, or Carl for destroying the orderly flow of the rehearsal to discuss things with a player, when a sharp command would have sufficed. That the marimbist turned out to be unable to see the music in the choreographed position had been beside the point; it was not the way they did things in Dresden. The concert had led to a wariness in his lifelong friendship with Körthofer, though it had given them a mutual respect for each other's technical abilities. Carl privately thought the other lacked real finesse in his style, but there was no question that his sheer technique went beyond Carl's own.

"Well, that sounds enough to be going on with. I'll contact him myself tomorrow, say how sorry I am and the department is about a most unfortunate incident et cetera et cetera. We'll need a proper post-mortem on the workshop. Procedures; how we avoid something like this again, that sort of thing. One key point, I think, is not allowing celebrities to let loose their own precious scores on students; not unless we're very confident in the student's technique. I should have foreseen that one. Remind me, who was the other student?"

"Paul, a second-year. He made himself scarce pretty quickly – wisely where *il maestro* was concerned, but I don't suppose it'll get him much further with Janet, leaving her in the lurch."

"They're not thinking of becoming a duet act?"

"No, nothing like that. Think personal."

"He likes how she looks?

"Very much, especially her tits"

"You seem to have a decided view on her tits."

Ben smiled and switched the subject back. "Doing something about the music - we could do an autographed score to another piece of music; not try to replace what's gone, but show willing."

Carl had been thinking the same. "Something contemporary – more affordable"

Ben gathered the glasses. "My turn. Another?"

"Thanks! A Three Kells. Another pint." The sine-curve of drinking fashion had, by chance, landed both Carl and Ben, nearly twenty years apart in age, at the same lodge: both were, in a pub setting, beer drinkers. Wine and lager were on display all around and a variety of diabolical potions favoured by the women, but they kept the true faith. Ben moved to the bar.

"Contemporary could be risky," Carl thought. Presenting Körthofer with a piece of dreck destined for almost immediate oblivion would be unimpressive; a sure winner, on the other hand could be expensive."

Then it struck him: MacLeish; already quite a big name, and there had been that premiere two years back.

"What's your view on MacLeish?" as Ben returned with the new pints.

"Talented. When he can be bothered"

"I meant for a score. For Körthofer"

Ben thought about it. "It'd be possible. Why do you think MacLeish particularly?"

"We could call in a favour."

Ben looked momentarily blank, then laughed. "Oh, yeah; he owes us a good one, doesn't he?"

"He certainly does"

Tony MacLeish, an alumnus with a steadily growing reputation, had been commissioned, three years ago, to produce a piece for a student finals concert that would highlight the skills of the new graduate prize-winners. Written for string ensemble, two pianos and percussion, it had had a difficult gestation and the last of the changes that MacLeish had insisted on had been made on the day of the performance and had, through careless proof-reading, put the music out of synch with the choreography, a fact that Carl and Ben became aware of as the piece was about to start, having both, by sheer chance kept the older copy of the score with them as well as the update.

It had been too late to stop things and had led to an unintended appearance by the two of them, improvising moves and pirouettes to undo then redo page turns, gradually calming slightly, as the students guessed the problem, to a seat-of-the-pants double conducting job from the sidelines, cancelling and reinstating moves to fit the new order of things.

They had all been very lucky, not least in having exceptionally able students, for the musicians would have, with underpaid and low-status malice, simply ground through whatever had been put in front of them. In an earlier era, the ensuing chaos and cacophony might have been passed off as intentional; even the composer might not have noticed. But that era was long past. None had been luckier than MacLeish himself; there had been a large and influential audience and it had been an early boost to his career. In the event, it had gone down very well, barring a grudging criticism from New London Media about tutors and professors grandstanding in student events for no obvious artistic benefit. MacLeish's career had taken off. Carl had left him in no doubt of his debt of gratitude.

Ben said, "If you're going down that route, why not use that particular piece? You won't have to twist his arm for something new. We could get it quickly."

Carl gave some thought to that. It was a good idea; no-one else had laid claim to the piece as far as he knew, and it was very presentable. "It would have to be a corrected version, of course."

Ben back-pedalled slightly. "He may not have made one yet. He was always an idle bastard."

Indeed, MacLeish had been one of their most brilliant students, but only when he could be persuaded to get out of bed.

"I'll chase him about it." An autograph copy, with maybe few enhancements to challenge Körthofer's technique to its formidable limits. He'd get Ben to check that the result matched up before it went out. "Try and divert any monetary claim onto Körthofer's insurance and make it clear that we'll be doing something to compensate the sentimental loss. Via Janet if that seems best."

Ben nodded.

"What about the assault on the pianist, before I forget?" Pianists might be generally regarded only as grunts, but they could be sensitive about their welfare.

"Oh that. I don't think he was much hurt. I apologised on the Prima Donna's behalf, rounded both their fees up, paid in cash and promised them the booking for the Bucharest conference: we were going to give them that anyway. They went away saying nothing and the other one was smirking, so God knows what story's being told about us, but they won't sue."

"Good" said Carl, with inward chagrin at his erstwhile profession proving so easily bought. But the problems seemed, gratifyingly, to be on their way to bed. He moved on. "I said I would update you on this afternoon's faculty meeting, and I'd like your view on what was said." Carl gave a summary of what had happened, Ben listening carefully, except at Carl's reference to "Pit... Stephen, Stephen Pendleton"

Ben grinned. "What were you going to call him?"

("I might as well write it on my forehead", Carl thought.) "He reminded me of that character in an American painting, standing by his wife with a pitchfork in his hand and a sour expression on his face. But keep it to yourself, would you."

"Oh, 'American Gothic'"; Ben had an encyclopaedic knowledge of interesting, if essentially useless cultural references. He continued in an unusually thoughtful vein. "What is it you think they'll try attacking us on? I shouldn't have thought there'd be much trouble on study methods or syllabus. And from what you've told me, we're cost neutral with performance fees, near enough. So why do you think the

VC is going for this all of a sudden? He's been quite happy up to now."

"I don't know, Ben. Not yet. We have to find out, though. Something about Pendleton's attitude and the way he sprang it on the meeting implied that somebody's to be made an example of. And it's preferable that it's not us. Have you got any direct contacts in the VC's office?"

"Not as such. But Paul is friendly with one of the girls who works there, I think. When he's not hanging around Janet with his tongue out."

"We mustn't let students get any hint of what's going on. Could you chat with her yourself?"

"I could try, but I don't know Paul well; I only know about the other girl because of Janet wishing he'd keep his attentions that way."

"Well see what you can do. It may sound paranoid, but I'd say this looks a bit more serious than the latest management fashion having a brief parade over Crabtree's dithering. Whatever Pendleton's up to, he's a heavyweight."

"I'll make enquiries, as they say."

"Use your famous charm. The Sex Goddess sends her regards, incidentally"

Ben laughed. "Thanks; send her mine. By the way, if we're going to hit difficult times on budgets, why not get MacLeish to cough up a second copy of the score for ourselves? We've still only got the intelligence test he set us on the day."

It made sense to Carl, who bought another round on the strength of it. The conversation languished, Ben speculating to himself on the favours that might be on offer later. An attractive and shapely

Nigerian, Atinuke had temped briefly in the department as a choreographic transcriber. He finished his beer and left with a view to turning the campaign plan into practical reality; Carl lingered, ordering some food and relaxing into the subdued roar of noise, the almost tangible pub surround that formed more of his impressions of the place than the just-past-smart furnishings. Snippets of other people's conversations came through, but the pub essentially retained its confidences. At eleven, he made tracks for an early bed.

VI

IN THE LIBRARY

The library came slowly into focus (for all the senses) around Viola, the desk in front of her only gradually presenting the tactile pleasure of good-quality polished wood that she had specified when setting up her virtual environment profile, though the resistance to movement beyond its virtual boundaries was there from the outset. The usual clerical and professional avatars drifted into view; she could see them talking, for a minute or so before she could hear what they were saying. Everything got there in the end, even the taste reflex to the smell of stale coffee from the virtual vending machine, but so slowly! She really must think, when she had the money, about upgrading.

Saying hello to the avatars, she sat down and set to immediately, checking the name files first. Stephen Pendleton was there: she discovered a conventional enough career in the higher reaches of American academe – a first degree at Michigan; Masters and doctoral years at Princeton, then an assistant professorship at Cornell. The appointment here at AUP wasn't mentioned. New, of course, but it was sloppy record-keeping all the same. The MiMi personal profiles offered a bland write-up of an individual with a high opinion of himself and a modest record of achievement; the holoview confirmed this: so far, so boring. She dispatched the avatar, John Librarian, to search for anything that looked relevant in the archives; he had been hanging around for several minutes and needed diversion to a task. While he was away in the stacks, she looked in Careerall, a compendium of all recorded paid work: the usual teenage labouring jobs, burger-flipping, some temporary clerical work to start. The first serious job was as an academic research assistant in Phoniotics, and everything subsequently was mainstream academic. He really didn't seem to have anything out of the ordinary in his background. She printed a summary.

John Librarian returned with an armful of volumes and a pleased look on his handsome, symmetrical face. Also a hopeful look; Viola's heart sank slightly at the memory of a passionate half-hour some months back: one afternoon when she was new here and lonely. Sexual intercourse with a virtual being had been a curious experience. Against the odds – the avatars had no conventional analogue to human reproduction, though they were capable of boredom like any human being and as much in need of diversion – the software developers had left out nothing in terms of body parts or sensory detail. But the electrostatic cloud that generated the tactile element of the virtual environment was only effective externally. That went for the tactile experience also. And a software problem had caused intermittent short-circuits and sparking, Viola's thighs carrying a scattering of small, but painful, first-degree burns for some days afterwards.

More than anything, this had dissuaded her from repeating the experience. John Librarian had suggested it in more or less subtle ways, but she had said no. On the second occasion, he had persisted. "Is it the software problem? There have been upgrades."

"John, it was just a bit of fun. And how do you know the upgrade is any good? What about the filing clerk?" Viola didn't doubt the software upgrade: they were shovelled into the avatars much as she and some of her friends ingested chocolate. The filing clerk avatar had recently been upgraded, only to suffer foot-drop, a disability yet to be remedied.

"I could ask the University support engineers to run a personal test of the software."

"With your history and memories on full view? No thanks." The support team was one of the key centres for local gossip. She had no idea how sex with an avatar might be thought of (weren't they, it occurred to her, supposed to be programmed only to be sexually attracted to other avatars?) but no desire to find out.

There would certainly have been other upgrades since then, but Viola was content to leave things at an impasse. She did smile nicely at him, though, to his evident pleasure.

He handed Viola a small virtual pamphlet; the tag read "Minutes of Ancient Fellowship of Franchised Reamers": she'd never heard of them.

"There is nothing else directly about them. The others here are academic background". He deposited the remaining volumes on the desk simulator. "The archive records show it as an anonymous donation. The Source Librarians must have been uncertain about it, because you will have to use the dirty-reader to look at it. The rest are normal."

The dirty-reader, or Viral Delimiter to give it its proper title, was used to read virtual documents whose provenance was felt to be dubious and liable to infect more obviously respectable volumes. Isolated from the ordinary readers and cleaned thoroughly once a week, or immediately after any incident, it could still on occasion provide a fascinatingly bizarre experience, alternately violent, pornographic, disgusting, fantastic or disintegrating. No dirty-reader had ever been known actually to melt while in action; it wasn't theoretically possible anyway, but several highly convincing simulations of this could be found on the VDUnbound site, a repository of dirty-reader experiences.

The machine this time was fairly clean, so Viola experienced nothing out of the way, apart from a couple of cat avatars that rocketed distractingly across the reader space at intervals. Indeed, the pamphlet was a very sober affair, just a five page account of a society meeting in a fairly standard Minutes format. The contents and the discussion were the oddities, though well concealed under a flat, corporate prose.

The attendance list, 22-strong, included the name Stephen Pendleton: not automatically cross-checked with the rest of the archives, as it was a dirty-reader item, so no certainty that it was the same person. But

the meeting location was Ann Arbor and the date just under 15 years
ago. Actions from the Last Meeting included 're-draft the
Fellowship's Mission Statement'. SP was one of three actioned. An
updated draft was referenced, but not included. That could mean a
long-established group trying to get up-to-date with corporate
fashion, but why wait so long? The mission statement fashion dated
from the previous century. More likely an early meeting in a new
group's existence. Funny about the 'Ancient', though.

The next item recorded the 'Chairperson' (a curiously old-fashioned
term, she thought) as 'reading the Mission Statement with everybody
standing' (it sounded more like a prayer meeting). It was just recorded
as happening, so no wiser on the Statement itself. Then there was a
medley of the usual meeting-type stuff: financial statement (healthy),
rental agreement on meeting premises (OK for six months), provision
of refreshments for meetings (also actioned to SP: no wonder he was
so good at judging biscuit-grabs) and so on. There were reports of a
fraternal visit to a Reamers group in Berkeley and of an email
reporting some unspecified local problem from Cambridge, England.
The Minutes gave very little detail of what that was about, but the
meeting had decided 'to activate the T & D protocol', whatever that
may have been.

There was a discussion of a report: 'Boring then, Reaming now: The
Audacity of Conviction'. As with the Mission Statement, the report
was supposedly appended, but missing; Viola felt simultaneously
annoyed and thankful. The action (for a David Wetherill) was
basically for him to continue the good work, with progress noted.
The title once again evoked a prayer meeting, but the scraps of notes
on the discussion included comments on 'core values' (the meeting
was in favour of them), which sounded more political and on 'cultural
responsibilities' (the meeting was certain they existed), which sounded
more like sociology. Someone had managed to include a mention of
Althusser: an avowed Marxist amid this lot seemed unlikely, so
probably a Structuralist: no wonder boring was such a crucial word.
Somebody (unspecified) had complained that the necessary emphasis
on performance measures in the context of a market economy was

weakly expressed: that sounded like Stephen P. Or perhaps his
Svengali, if he'd had one. She yawned and stretched; like most
research it was potentially interesting in outcome, but often tedious in
detail.

The last item that caught her eye was a discussion of arrangements
for 'a general meeting of the Fellowship in Vishiney'. Dniestria
Rossiya was an odd place for a bunch of American market-oriented
idealists (which seemed to be about it) to meet, even 15 years ago and
even if they did have branches in other countries. It bordered on the
Russian zone and was less than respectable in Western-zone terms:
even Bucharest, where the Paginists conference would be assembling
that summer, was pushing it a bit. There was nothing to say who
would be going from the group, just a note to discuss arrangements
again at the next meeting, which a final note under AOB gave as two
months later.

It was frustrating that so little of the real content of the meeting
could be found, but it was certainly an interesting fragment, if one of
uncertain significance. The Minutes proved impossible to print,
presumably for the same reasons that classified them with the dirty-
reader, though she couldn't imagine how one could seriously corrupt a
printer. Writing a detailed account of the points of interest, she noted
the filing reference.

The remaining papers were indeed standard, mainly academic papers
in Phoniotics, which looked slightly less exciting than Structuralism.
Viola wasn't tempted to learn more. Pushing them into the
Desimulator, she thanked John, still looking hopeful, with a quick kiss
on the cheek (surprising how real that seemed), said "Bye!" and went
into Re-Entry, clutching the prints and notes.

Back in her room the clock showed ten past nine. Time to be getting
ready for Memories of Kandahar – she could never understand why
Joe, her military historian friend tended to wince, or sometimes laugh
when she mentioned it. The heavy green skirt she had picked up
from near the bed was functional enough (and a useful, subtle

dampener for Carl), but it would never do for a girls' night out. Perhaps the silk trousers … fifteen minutes of agonising choice got under way – why so little time? – before, armoured appropriately for her status in the group, she slipped out of the front door of the flat into a mild and honeysuckle-scented evening, observing with pleasure the fresh pale-green of the foliage on the horse-chestnut tree in the park, rising above and illuminated by the buildings on the far side of the courtyard.

VII

IN THE OAST (2)

"He's staring at me again, Eva; it gives me the creeps." Alison looked round. "Swap places with me; he won't see me so easily if I'm where you're sitting." Eva nodded, frowning a little, grabbed her handbag, looked over to the door as if spotting a new arrival and shifted over to Alison's chair. Alison scudded to the toilets for general maintenance and face restoration. The ploy worked; Eva didn't seem to be of the same interest; in fact, she merited no more than a single initial glance. A pity, she thought, he wasn't bad looking. Quite tall, as far as she could tell, a well-proportioned face, short dark hair. He didn't look quite with it, but definitely better value than the others in the group he was sitting in. He and Paul Fairley were the only ones she definitely recognised. Alison 's judgements on men weren't always good, but with looks like hers she had too much choice. Eva often wished the looks and the choice could have been shared out a bit, but you had to be realistic.

She surveyed the rest of the pub. Two of the staff were talking at a table nearby; the older one was a professor, she thought: neatly dressed, quite distinguished; the other was Ben Cordell: now he was good-looking, but didn't he know it? Alison fancied him, probably half the reason she'd changed places: it took her pretty much out of the media designer's sight – what was his name? something like Thad, or Tad – and pretty much into Ben's. Well, good luck to her, but Eva's assessment was that he was conceited.

Alison returned, newly burnished. Yes, she did glance in Ben's direction, but there was no glance in return; he was talking to the professor. "He's quite sweet really, says he loves me, but I know he really just wants a copy of my veep, and I'm not giving him one."

"Ben?" said Eva with disbelief. That was quick work.

"He's called Tad. The one who was looking at me. Do keep up, Eva. He made me take his penpro, but I don't fancy him. I passed it on to Carly; I think she tried it out as well, dirty little cow!" She paused to enjoy a moment's moral uplift, then added. "I'm not risking what happened with Wayne again." God, that had been embarrassing, she thought. She hadn't got round to putting any security on it, and Wayne had passed on copies to all friends likely to be impressed by his coup. "Mind you, his penpro was interesting." The two girls looked at each other and giggled.

Eva, with her Catholic upbringing, was ambivalent about virtual technology, but she did, nevertheless own an XGlove, had had her own veep produced (though as yet undistributed) and had found the copy of Wayne's penpro that Alison had given her impressive, if not exactly subtle. But its best feature, if she was honest, was not having to put up with Wayne himself.

A brief silence fell. Alison stole another look at Ben, but with no better luck than before. "I was in a meeting this afternoon. Presenting a report. There was an American there as well, and he got nasty about one of the recommendations. Not with me, with Carl Trenchard."

"Who?" asked Eva.

"Carl Trenchard! He's sitting over there, with Ben Cordell. You know Ben?" Yeah, wonder boy, thought Eva, who just nodded. "Carl Trenchard is his head of department: that's the Paginists." (So he *was* a professor.) "Anyway, I'd just gone through a list of things; nothing to get excited about, and this American got aggressive about some tiny point that I'd slipped in to make up numbers on the slide."

"An Internal Audit special." She sniffed.

Alison gave Eva a hard glance.

Eva's expression was all inscrutability. "What happened?"

Alison resumed. "Oh, he just made a big thing about the department needing control. That's the American. And there was something about threesomes ... I can't see anyone wanting to do threesomes with him; he's not ugly, but he's a real stiff. Anyway, it wasn't so much what they said - and he got put down about it being trivial - it was the atmosphere; I thought they were going to go for each other."

Eva looked across. "He doesn't look the aggressive type to me."

"Carl Trenchard wasn't being aggressive, not at all; it was the American. He seemed to have something he knew about, but wasn't quite saying." She thought about it. "Like he had a bomb ready under his jacket."

Eva looked across again. "They're looking serious enough about something now. He must have let it off."

"Well, I had to go as soon as I'd done the report. But it still looked tense when I left. I thought I might try asking Ben Cordell - that's the one talking to Carl Trenchard - if he knew what it was about."

"Ha!" Eva stifled a snort. So that was the plan. She didn't think Alison would get much out of him: departments sometimes discussed interesting scandals in other departments with outside staff, particularly when it could harm a rival's standing, but they were usually close about internecine warfare. As a way of getting talking, though, it was a winner. She wished she had the same instinct for that sort of angle. And the looks too, of course.

Eva had a difficult relationship with her features, which she would have liked to be interestingly narrow, dark and Latin, but remained, as the mirror each morning reminded her, obstinately broad, fair and Slavic. Within these annoying parameters, she did the best she could, but there was no doubt that interest from the opposite sex had a tendency to come from those who had lost out in the competition for

Alison. They were, sometimes, better than the ones who had won, but it wasn't exactly consumer choice. Out of the corner of her eye, she saw Tad or Thad, talking to another of his group. He looked preoccupied and rather unhappy; she felt a momentary surge of sympathy.

"Eva, you're not listening to a word I'm saying. Do you like this scarf?"

Eva, caught day-dreaming, focused on the patterned wisp that Alison was holding and went into approval mode. "It's so pretty. Just right with your hair colour." It was, and it did indeed go well with Alison's very English, ever so slightly foxy face and dark hair; it would not have been so good for Eva. "You should wear it when you try to chat up Ben." He'd probably notice, she thought, even though he was a man.

"You really haven't been listening, have you? I asked you if I should wear it to the club later." Eva hadn't heard this, but gave her approval, though privately less enthusiastic. Alison frowned a little and said she thought it was perfect. Eva agreed, and Alison put the scarf down on her handbag, looking pleased. Eva made her way to the bar to refresh the drinks, which arrived quickly, as the nice barman with the humorous penpro advert tattooed on his wrist, who seemed to like her, spotted her almost immediately. Returning, she noticed that the scarf had retreated into the handbag. And Ben had disappeared, so Alison had missed that chance. Professor Trenchard was still there; he looked more relaxed than earlier, so his discussion with the conceited one must have gone well.

"Thanks." Alison sipped at her drink. "What's your day been?"

"Nothing much. I spent a lot of it keeping out of Alan Westwood's way." The life of a research assistant, particularly a Manucussionist's research assistant, didn't tend to be action packed: even the evening visit to the Oast House had to be kept quiet because of the temperance thing, although there was nothing contractual about that for non-tenured staff. "The research isn't going too badly, we're finding there's a mathematical relationship between drummers' heartbeat rate and the hardness and density of drumstick heads. The closer you get to a magic number, the better the performance. The number varies a bit at different dynamic levels and it needs to be graded for the various musical expression marks, but …" Alison's expression was glazing over and she drifted to a stop. The truth was, that day she had nothing more interesting than the research to report.

Eva switched lanes, and the conversation settled to ongoing gossip.

VIII

IN THE OAST (3)

Well, she was there after all, but I didn't see much of her. Ali, that is. Our group was in another corner a little distance away, and then her friend Eva, the broad-faced one under the permanent thundercloud, moved onto her chair when she was away somewhere. Flashed me a not very friendly look, too, so I think she might have made the move deliberately. I don't think much of getting in the way like that: does she think I'll take her friend away or something? Some hope! I didn't let it bother me. Being in love is all very well, but it's not much fun when there's nothing to show for it; I certainly couldn't say anything about it to my friends.

But anyway the conversation was all about technicalities: some new media systems the Chinese are supposed to have produced. Nobody knows anything definite, but it sounds like an accelerated language-learning system for avatars, so they can speak without having to use the standard voice module that makes them so boring to listen to at the moment – if they're speaking English, even the males and females can be hard to tell apart, except by pitch and what they say. We've tried specifying regional accent modifiers, but they're very slow, and the system engineers just love fucking it up: getting a virtual librarian talking to Kansas students in a broad Lancashire accent and that sort of thing: it drives them crazy, particularly in America, where they don't usually see the funny side of it.

It went on some time before it was exhausted, though it was obviously all just speculation: we'll have to wait for a visitor from China, or maybe they'll send a demonstration model once they think there's serious money in it. I sat for a while just thinking, then Paul started talking about this Janet that he's gone on. He sort of implied that he'd got somewhere. It's probably bullshit, but the contrast to my own lack of progress with Ali was depressing.

I stood up and got another round in. That's an expensive cure for depression, but getting the attention of the bar staff at The Oast, if you're male and my age, needs concentration and fast talking, so I was feeling better when I got back. I edged in and sat down on the bench rather clumsily, falling slightly to one side, further into the corner of the small booth area we were in. This was noticed; questions along the lines of "Pissed already" and "You want a stretcher, Tad?" were fired at me. But I also heard, in my right ear, a measured voice saying something about a pitchfork. I sat myself properly on the seat, and the voice faded. Perhaps it was a trick of the acoustics. I leaned gradually backwards again, trying not to let anybody notice as I did so, and the voice came back into focus.

"…somebody's to be made an example of." That didn't sound too good. "…any direct contacts in the VC's office?" Somebody probably replied to that, but I couldn't hear them. Then, "We mustn't let students get any hint of what's going on. Could you chat with her yourself?" Who did that mean, and was it a student they were going to make an example of? Again, there was a gap, then "Well see what you can do: … paranoid, but this looks a bit more serious than … brief parade over Crabtree's … Pendleton's up to, he's a heavyweight." It only made sense in fragments. I couldn't tell where it was coming from; must have been a trick of the acoustics, but, after a comment about some sex goddess sending her regards (why does everybody else but me have these things all worked out?), there were a few scattered comments and a goodbye, then the voice ceased altogether, so I guessed it must have come from the two men sitting twenty feet or so away, one of whom - a lecturer in Ancillary Music, I think - left not long after the sign-off.

"You all right, Tad?" somebody asked, and I dived quickly back into the conversation (about football; somebody prop my eyes open), while having a think. Crabtree everyone would know; he's the dim resources officer, who makes a career out of being difficult about grants and loans; I've had a couple of maddeningly pointless run-ins with him over not following his stupid rules. A parade on top of

Crabtree would be popular with a lot of people. Preferably wearing spiked boots. Pendleton I thought I knew about: a new professor he must be, who I've seen walking in or out of the Vice Chancellor's building. He must be welcome there, which was why they were talking about contacts in the office. But why were they so bothered about him? He looked insignificant to me and a miserable bastard at that. I couldn't work out where the 'heavyweight' bit came from.

I remembered Paul's 'contact' and said quietly to him, "What about that girl you were seeing; works for the Vice Chancellor. Maybe she'd be more willing."

Paul smirked, rather shiftily. "She's keen all right, but I'm keeping it for Janet."

"That's noble, but supposing Janet's keeping it for someone else."

"Who are you talking about?" Paul said suspiciously and with some concern.

"Oh, nobody in particular, but, you know, you might want a fallback if things don't work out."

"Not when it's the real thing. You'll learn that, Tad, when it hits you someday" said Paul, with an attempt at gravity. Somebody sniggered and he looked embarrassed and furious.

I persisted. "What's she like then?"

"Janet?"

"The girl in the Vice Chancellor's office."

"Oh, Karen. She's a nice lass. Neat. Nice bum. Why, do you want introducing?"

"Depends if you're offering. What does she do there?"

"In the office? I think she's a PA. She does a lot of secretarial stuff, anyway. Why do you need to know, all of a sudden? You like shagging secretaries?"

I didn't answer, reflecting gloomily that that was just one of a long list of female categories that I mostly didn't get the chance to shag, even virtually.

One of the others, who'd all started listening, said, "give him a chance, Paul, he's gagging, can't you see?"

I protested: "You've all just got dirty minds".

But Paul was taking his new role of man of affairs and matchmaker seriously. "Meet me at the Bin tomorrow for lunch and we can say hello to her if she's there."

"I can probably interrupt my crowded schedule. Will she be worth it, though?"

"Oh yes"; Paul nodded like the Churchill bulldog, "but it'll be up to you once I've done the 'him Tarzan, you Jane' bit."

We fixed for 12.30.

The conversation drifted back to sport, then back to what the Chinese might do with avatars that had their own voices. Somehow, sex ended up featuring largely.

Just before one o'clock, near to closing time, Paul spotted Janet entering the pub and waved, but she didn't wave back. An old man walked in after her – he had white hair, rather unkempt. She looked pleased with herself, from what I could see at that distance. You'd have almost thought there was something between them, but it couldn't be; not with somebody that age. Paul muttered "Körthofer" and slid away along the seat, bending over his drink. They didn't stay in the pub long, though: just a quick drink, then they left.

Ali and her grumpy friend left soon after; she didn't look in my direction.

After closing, some of my group set off for a club just the other side of Camberwell, but it didn't sound inviting, and I needed to finish this essay sometime, so I said goodnight and set off back to Nunhead.

It was a fine night, mild and clear. You couldn't see much of the stars with all the lights around, but Orion was obvious enough and the North Star, over the City. I thought about tomorrow's – today's – lunch date. It wasn't really my style, butting into other people's problems. A fight with this Pendleton character would definitely be that. The talk about somebody in the faculty being made an example of could just be something I had to worry about. Unlikely, though. But I genuinely was curious. And there was Karen and her neat bum, of course. If Paul's promise to introduce me wasn't just the usual shit.

IX

CORRIDORS OF POWER

The Honourable Ranulph Fraserman was in a sour mood, even relative to normal standards. VAPA (the Faculty of Visual & Plastic Arts) had been kicking up about communications with the Changchun region (they had a satellite 'phone, wasn't that enough for them?) and dragging up Health & Safety issues over the Performance Arts' undeniably dank performing space, as if anybody gave a fart about H & S nowadays, or, indeed, about performance art.

Vice Chancellor of the Arts University of Peckham (generally known as AUP), he was Ranulph or Ran to his family and friends, the VC within the university. A disaffected business consultant colleague had nicknamed him Onran, and this was generally known, though never repeated to his face. He had come to AUP from a senior partnership with Libra Merrick Coutts, an international accountancy conglomerate. Though released by them with astonishing alacrity, his career with LMC had been highly successful, built on contacts and raw aggression. It followed an MBA from Princeton and a 3-year spell in "The Broads", formed with City connections and generally considered in the circles that mattered to be a jolly good regiment, rising to the rank of Lieutenant and developing further the leadership qualities evident in his reign as a prefect at Hertingsbury. Both Hertingsbury and the Army had released him with high commendations and a vague feeling of relief. Princeton kept its own counsel about his qualities, but the MBA had been unquestionably gained with distinction.

Whatever the ambiguities about his colleagues' feelings, there was no ambiguity about the VC's approach to organisational management, which was straightforward slash and burn. VAPA had found that out the hard way. And now they were complaining. Knocking sense into the muddle of artistic administrative arrangements had its rewards, he reflected, not least the salary, but the artists did go on about it; there was no gratitude for the efforts made on their behalf.

And then there was Stephen Pendleton, grinding away in the corner about market principles. The Hon Ran had little more time for ideology than he had for performance art, though ideology could be useful sometimes as a means to an end. He hadn't much liking for Yanks either; particularly the humourless and dedicated type: too large a proportion of the breed in his experience; particularly when he couldn't afford to ignore what they were saying. As now. Groaning subliminally, he forced himself to attend to what Pendleton was bleating about.

"...budgetwise, their case doesn't cut it. You English like tradition, but this is ridiculous. Paginatorics has not been a hot topic for fifteen years. They break even, but they're not going anywhere better than that. Something that's come to a standstill like that, you should be looking at sourcing it as a commodity."

"You mean flogging it to the commercial sector?"

Pendleton winced. "What we are talking about is managed fragmentation; curettage of non-performing sectors no longer in a market-leading position and provision through performance-locked, base-cost third-party agencies, enabling a clear focus on core values and the optimisation of symbiotic opportunities."

"Flogging it off to commerce in bits."

"If you say so. I think we can take a more upbeat and nuanced view of the business benefits. Paginatorics has a lot of brand-optimisation opportunities, and they are not going to be realised in an academe-centric context. It needs the richer air of the open market if it's going to fly."

"Such as?" Pendleton looked momentarily blank. "The brand-optimisation thingies."

"Bring in a competitive edge: broadcast contests; a few dirty tricks, that kind of thing. The broadcast media audience could love that. And reality shows: the daily lives of Paginists, the love interests, the fights. Once there's an audience for the contests, that will be a winner. But I'm not a media geek; you'd need one of those to give you all the possibilities."

"I see. Any place for the music?" Pendleton looked momentarily blank again. "The thing they turn pages for."

"Ran, we're talking an encapsulated product here. Music is there, because it's infrastructure: like the electrics in this building. The product can't do without it, but it's only the S-Class weirdoes who still think it matters any more than that to the public, and it could be the long goodbye if any of us got associated with S-Class."

The Hon Ran mused. He was right, of course; music was just an all-pervasive filler nowadays; better liked than performance art, but no better regarded. Certainly less popular than Health & Safety, thinking back to VAPA. But carving up (or 'managed fragmenting') VAPA had brought difficulties by the truck-load, and not just within AUP. The government advisors who had talked him into the job in the first place had turned out to be deeply committed to and passionate about free market principles for academia, just so long as they stayed as principles. Actually throwing VAPA to the free market wolves had not really been the thing to do at all, particularly when it brought some sneering headlines in the news media and, perhaps worst of all, the barring of one of the more senior advisors from the High Table of his Oxford college as a result. An unguarded flippancy in an interview with the local news media outlet, served up as a reference to 'painter johnnies', had not helped either. Subsequent discussions with the advisors had at times been uncomfortably robust.

"Well, you know what happened with VAPA. Are we going to gain enough from doing the same to Paginatorics and Ancillary Music?

More to the point, what is your lot going to do to help? Last time, they did naff all."

"Our lot, Ran. Our lot. Both of us signed up to the Charter."

The Hon Ran grunted sceptically, but made no attempt at rebuttal.

"No question, what happened with VAPA was not a good scene. You took us by surprise, though; gave us no time to evaluate. The Ethics Committee chairman – you know Bruce? – was going bald trying to report it, Charterwise. The first draft did not look good. The Communications Vice President could only activate an operation after the second draft, and you'd screwed up on that interview by then. Believe me, Ran, there was a lot of work done to save your ass; that's why I'm here. We like your ideas, Ran, truly we do; they just need process. Now I'm on the case, we're wired in. No more snafus. You give us the ideas, Ran, we make sure they have process, Ethics checks them out against the Charter, Communications makes sure everything looks sweet, everyone is a winner."

Except Ancillary Music, of course. Well, stuff them, they had it coming; what they needed was a real job in the world everyone else inhabited. Was there any way of stifling this 'Ran' plague, though? He preferred Ranulph, and Pendleton was certainly not one of the set of old friends who might ignore that preference, even if the fraternity relationship meant he couldn't easily be stopped. Interesting that his language had relaxed a bit, though; the 'naff all' comment must have hit a nerve. Time, he thought, for some circumspection. "I hear what you say, Steve, and there are good ideas there, but they'll need a lot of refining before they have any chance of being accepted here. I have the government on my back, pissing on anything that threatens to make them earn their money. The last thing they want is someone doing what they say."

Pendleton frowned slightly at the 'Steve'. 'Loose cannon', he reflected; that's what the Brits called it. But it wouldn't be the first time he had had to guide one of those into firing at the right time and in the right direction. Time, he thought, for some circumspection. "We're fully aware of the local difficulties you experience here and will work around them. Call me Stephen, incidentally."

"Fine. Ranulph, by the way." They exchanged tight smiles. There was a brief pause.

"So. How do we take this forward?" The Hon Ran settled back in his chair, enjoying its programmed adaptation to his frame and its attention to the health of his back. He stared out of the window behind Pendleton, registering, with a pleasure that few colleagues would have believed, the shading of sunlight through the spring leaves, contrasted with the dappling of the plane tree bark. His office enjoyed a panoramic view of the main campus in an upper floor of the Old Bin. Might have been a painter johnny himself, if Hertingsbury hadn't taken that sort of thing firmly in hand. Damned good thing they did, too, when you thought what he might have become otherwise. Still, the way the light and colours worked had a genuine appeal.

Pendleton was wittering about something; must have missed half of what he said. Come to think of it, he looked like somebody or something the Hon Ran had seen before. But his range of cultural reference was not broad and his ability to correlate faces and names had never been good, so the thought passed on unresolved. Pendleton had now ceased speaking and seemed to be expecting a response. "Interesting, but a few things that need thinking about. Could you just run the key points past me again, and we'll think about them one by one."

Confirmed. He hadn't been listening. Keep it short, or it's dreamtime again. "There are two basic approaches: get the department on-side then take them through a tender process in which they're competing as well, or put out a confidential tender then tell them when they're screwed. The first approach is slow and it always runs the risk that the in-house team puts up a good case and has to be disqualified some other way. And a slow process gives you more collateral shit, particularly political. We recommend the second approach. It's more brutal, but it has fewer problems getting you the answer you started out with, and better for morale: no-one knows anything until the decision is announced."

Still not exactly words of one syllable, the Hon Ran mused, but clear enough: bag them up and throw them in the river. "Makes life easier in the short term, sure enough, but what about the fallout. I don't know if collateral shit is smellier than chicken shit, but there'll be a lot of the latter flying about, mostly from Whitehall. And we don't have the security guards just to march the staff who are axed off the campus with their belongings. One of the more difficult problems with VAPA was dealing with the staff squats. Diaries of occupation, webcams; all that."

Actually, he reflected, it hadn't been so difficult in reality, nothing that MacsForce weren't able to sort out late one night, starting with bolt cutters on the fibre-optic link and a jammer on the wireless comms: just embarrassing. And there had been all sorts of legal idiocy, with the telecoms people and with that lecturer's wife: probably widow, actually, but nobody knew; he'd just not been there after the raid; she had needed considerable persuasion.

"Leave Whitehall to us, Ranulph. We have good connections; they do what we say. Just so long as there are no surprises. And I wanted to talk to you about the security. Your profile is very European, security-wise. Look at this office: three floors up in a building built two hundred years ago; no guards, no armour-plating. You don't do the real creative deals in an office like this; not if you want to stay around to enjoy them."

"There's a small matter of budgets."

"Like I say, Ranulph, leave the budgets to us. AUP can repay in time from the savings this little exercise will make. You're in the front line here, Ranulph, one of our marines. There's to be a big investment in making AUP fighting fit, and we don't intend going into battle unable to defend ourselves."

The military jargon was mounting as fast as the condescension. "You've seen action then, I take it."

"You mean military action? I've been under fire. That's some experience, Ranulph."

"So you'll know the purpose and the value of drill, discipline and esprit de corps."

"Sure do, Ranulph. Gives you something to think about in the long nights without electricity."

Was he trying to pull his wire? He didn't look it: completely straight-faced, and a formula joke he had cracked earlier had been accompanied by loud, if strictly rationed, laughter. "The point is to keep troops working together when they can't think because they're abnormally high on adrenaline or simply scared witless. It turns necessary tasks into reflex actions. Combined with physical fitness, that's what's called fighting fit and there's nothing better for a battlefield. What I can't see is what it has to do with AUP. For a lot of my staff, physical fitness means walking to the pub without getting out of breath. Even for those who do exercise, there's nothing in their working lives that would ever scare them witless – literally too frightened to be able to think. Bored witless, maybe: have you ever read any of the tripe they put into print? Towards a hermeneutics of chickenshit, all that sort of stuff. Scared witless, no; so why should any of us need to be 'fighting fit'? And where have you been under fire, incidentally?"

There was a knock on the door from the secretaries' office and a smartly, not quite provocatively dressed young woman breezed in. "Excuse me Mr Fraserman; I'll just collect the cups. Would you like another?"

With an appreciative glance at the elegant pair of legs on display, the Hon Ran looked at his visitor, who shook his head. "Just the one for me, thanks, Karen," he said. A gin and tonic was what he really wanted, but iconoclasm could only go so far. He was beholden to these Americans up to a point, and alcohol there was close to out of bounds in the evening, let alone midday.

"Right you are, Mr Fraserman." Karen darted around the office picking up the debris of coffee, tea and biscuits from this and two previous meetings, affording a range of angles on her charms. Pendleton appeared resistant to these, maintaining the sullen silence into which he had lapsed as soon as the knock sounded and staring at a copy of The Charter in Brief, which lay, a little too openly for comfort, on The Hon Ran's desk. Karen exited with a tray of dirty dishes and a wiggle of the bum that was appreciated by at least half of the company.

"Pakafiran."

Surprise, surprise! "With the armed forces?"

"With the Management Education Corps. We were facilitating a workshop on Instilling Shared Values with the Iranians when someone outside fired a few rounds through the windows."

"The towelheads?"

Pendleton winced inwardly. "No-one was sure. Intelligence thought it might have been your people, Ranulph."

The Hon Ran grunted. Not in disbelief; if there was one thing a British soldier had hated more than an Iranian (the chief architects of resistance) by the end of the Pakafiran fiasco, it was Management Education. The combined temptation must have been irresistible. He reverted swiftly to the main point. "What has the idea of fighting fit to do with AUP?"

"Fighting fitness is needed by the task force implementing The Charter. Certainly not by everybody in AUP. The Charter demands commitment and discipline; its world-view has many opponents, and the task of implementation can be high-risk. Pakafiran was an early warning of the difficulties and trial that we face in taking its concepts to the untaught. Too strong an injection of concepts can, like a narcotic, produce counter-progressive reactions. We need to be wise to this and ready for action or defence as needed."

Too strong a tendency to reach for their guns, more like. The earlier, test-bed adventures in the region had done nothing for American diplomatic sales technique. But it seemed unlikely that The Charter concepts would have had a smooth ride however they had been introduced. "I came here to shake up AUP and drag it into the real world, not to start hand-to-hand combat. I'll cope with that if it ever happens as I coped with it during my army service, but there's no point provoking fighting for the sake of it."

"The Charter has some very radical concepts, some of them shared only at the highest levels. You Brits take a lot of shit without doing anything; you have for fifty years now, but there has to come a tipping point. We need to be prepared for that."

The Hon Ran doubted that, from what he knew of The Charter and of his fellow countrymen. Extensive immigration had changed the ethnic mix and cultural assumptions over the last century, but had had surprisingly little effect on the national temperament, which tended more to phlegmatic acceptance and cultural absorption than to revolution and cannon-shot. Texans, now, they would be different. An image of drilling Pendleton through with a round of bullets, to the applause and approbation of his fellow citizens, wafted pleasurably through his mind.

A tranche of extra budget would have its uses, though. "So we're to go for the stuffed mushroom approach and put up barricades for when the mob are informed. What are your first steps?"

"Agree in principle which parts of Ancillary Music go first. Paginatorics is a priority, as we've already discussed."

"You didn't convince me. It's the only department we've got, at least on the performance side, that's got real prestige. Why get rid of that?"

"Don't think 'getting rid', Ranulph, "think 'managed growth'. Believe me, there are companies out there, significant names, just poised to run with this, make it big. They just need the word."

"So why not, say, the Manucussionists. They could certainly do with more excitement."

"Not the same potential; nothing like the same outside interest. Then there are internal issues."

"Meaning?"

"Charter restraints. We hold back on action against our own: it's assumed they are changing things as they need on their own patch."

"You don't mean Alan Westwood ..."

"He joined last autumn and has been a valuable catalyst for site action."

The little bumsucker! No wonder he'd looked so smug the last couple of occasions he'd bumped into him. "Why wasn't I told this?"

"AFFREM works on a 'need to know' basis, as I'm sure you know, Ranulph. Truly, the last thing we would have done is failed to inform you if it had been possible to do so, but there are some big issues at stake here."

"What issues? Free market drumstick peddlers! In case it had slipped your mind, I make the decisions here. I need to know about anything that happens, particularly if it's going to end up gang-banging Whitehall."

The secretaries' door sounded again, and Karen returned, searching for a mat and depositing the drink with some care on the desk, before retiring with another - 50% appreciated - wiggle of the bum. The sun sparkled on the surface of the coffee, but the atmosphere in the room remained dark.

"Ranulph, let's ease up a little. This is history already. You know now, and no difficulties have been caused. We need to look forward."

"Depends if AFFREM are going to pull any more rabbits out of the hat. Is there anything else I haven't been told?"

"We are crusaders, not magicians. And there is nothing else to tell you. If you feel you have been misled, I apologise; it was not our intention. We do need to move on this, though."

The Hon Ran looked fixedly at Stephen Pendleton in silence, for an interval that continued well beyond a conventional pause for thought. The atmosphere, in spite of the previous remarks, was unaggressive, but something or someone was being weighed up. Its object remained silent too and focused, returning the gaze at a slight angle. There had been many such moments in the past few years; they were like fevers coming to a crisis. A low-level rumble of traffic, motorised and human, from the outside world grew into the silence, and the slam of a cupboard door permeated from the adjoining office. They would have to improve the sound-proofing, he thought, if the plans they had for AUP were to be discussed with the necessary confidentiality. Or find somewhere more functional. He focused again rapidly; Fraserman was coming to; the crisis might be past.

"You have my authority to get ahead with a service specification for the Paginists. But it's going nowhere if it fails to pinpoint some real, measurable business benefits. I want them written down and signed in blood. And two other essentials. Firstly, Westwood had better come up with proposals for changes 'on his own patch': real changes, with real business benefits, just like the Paginists. I'm not going ahead with the Paginists unless we're going ahead with the Manucs at the same time. Secondly, any information of the smallest relevance and anything at all that even smells like a decision must come to me. If there's more funny business like Westwood's induction that I'm not part of, I'll cut off your balls. Without anaesthetic. Do we understand each other? Stephen."

Kerpow! He'd risen. Time to close and get on to some real work. "We do; the operation will not be necessary. AFFREM's executive cell send their appreciation of your assistance and co-cooperativeness in this."

(He felt sure they did: now for the soft soap). "That's all fine and dandy. Just make sure you don't forget what I said. What about the rest of the Ancillary Music faculty, while we're at it?"

"I make that the Chordologists, Reedsmiths, Case Technicians and Presentation Technicians. And Phoniotics, of course. That so?" The Hon Ran nodded assent. "We intend to sweep them up in a second phase after the Paginists."

"And the Manucs."

"And the Manucussionists, of course; my thanks for the correction, Ranulph. They need more analysis, but our gut feel is that, with the obvious exception of Phoniotics, which represents the future of the Faculty, they are mostly too close to their respective S-Class performers in mission and priorities to form an appropriate cohort subscribing to AM's re-focused core values and objectives."

Ah well, it had been fun bouncing him into something like a real language for a while. Back to normality! "So they're all for the chop in your view?"

"Perhaps a small, strategically-focused core remaining.   The Chordologists seem more capable than the others of sustaining the necessary process of continuous challenge to the hegemony of the S-Class performance matrix. Re-stringing instruments, particularly the more complex and photogenic examples, such as harps or arch-lutes, can if presented in parallel with the S-Class performance, posit a richly visual and formally satisfying alternative to the random posturing of virtuoso playing, while simultaneously questioning implicitly its artificially constructed illusion of perfection. And the Presentation Technicians have always had their limited niche with music stands. Cutting and honing reeds, though, is too detailed for mainstream audience appeal, and the reeds are too small as objects to make presenting them to the players an activity likely to distract much attention from the S-Class performance. Ditto the bag carriers; if S-Class had gone the way of Rock Music and they could be called Roadies, then maybe something could be made of them. As it stands, though, most of the possibilities likely to survive in the global free market seem to be research topics for a strategy unit rather than income-generating actualities.   Condensation and re-positioning, establishment-wise, will be a critical enabler for the greater abstraction of discourse appropriate to a Phoniotics-orientated faculty."

Christ, was there going to be any more of this? The Hon Ran struggled back to full consciousness. "Well, no doubt there'll be a report on it. Any deadline for that?"

"The Paginists are likely to be tricky."

"And the Manucs, of course."

'And the Manucussionists, no question. We're not counting on Phase 2 in under six months, as a result."

"Fine, are we done?"

"I would just like to raise the question of accommodation. My office is next to Alan Westwood's in what look like old industrial units. As a base for the core discipline of a newly re-organised faculty, it lacks many key selling points."

"A permanent solution will necessarily be contingent on release of accommodation through rationalisation of the Manucussionists department, so you should consider giving that first priority." The Hon Ran smiled sweetly at his visitor. "Crabtree can give you a detailed picture of our situation on accommodation at the moment, but you shouldn't expect much to be on offer, I'm afraid; we're very hard pressed for space." Crabtree had had very explicit instructions, so no problem there.

Pendleton, his unhappiness only poorly concealed, promised to speak to Crabtree and thanked his host for "a very positive and forward-thinking meeting, before heading suddenly and quickly towards the door. But Karen made it to the respectability of her desk in time and directed him sweetly past the toilets and down the rear stairs to the fire door that gave out on to the park, where he stood disorientated for a moment or two before striding decisively through a patch of mud. She hadn't heard much, but it had all sounded interestingly unfriendly. How dare he do that to Mr Fraserman, now calling her into his office!

Walking away across the grass and round to the front of the building, Pendleton surveyed its undoubted classical charm and undoubted security problems. Entry from anywhere you felt like, with the minimum of equipment. And that office: he was sure the girl had been listening. No sign as he walked out: that might mean she had useful skills, as well as the sex-bomb bit, but you couldn't risk this sort of program to that physical setup. What about Fraserman? He might be screwing her and telling everything. Probably not: Fraserman was a pro in spite of appearances. But they would have to make a decision on recruiting or firing her. Meanwhile, he should get the Albanians in; a building assessment would be needed in the next 48 hours. He put a call through.

X

MEMORIES OF KANDAHAR

Now well past dusk, just the last scraps of sunset were visible over the station. The air was mild with that pleasant warmth considered, in contradiction of general experience, quintessentially Spring-like. Viola, relaxed, rounded the flat conversion that had served as a Council depot just long enough for Utility to become Heritage, and strolled into the ethnic quarter that was the sole exotic remnant of the huge West African community that had previously dominated Peckham, now long since dispersed by the push-pull forces of upward mobility and gentrification. 'Memories of Kandahar' was in Warwick Park Village, just beyond. Jane was already there, with one or two of the others; she went to sit by her. "Hi!"

"Hello Vile. We're ordering drinks; fancy a Ground-to-Air?"

Not on your life, she thought; they were lethal! Viola ordered a pomegranate juice with a double of vodka (a Lover's Shot according to the menu) and dumped the straw in the recycle chute, before appraising Jane's latest ensemble. Envy, as usual. She did have money, of course, but there was no getting round the taste that made Viola feel her own dress sense to be subtly lacking, a touch commonplace. "Like it?" Jane queried, lifting a sleeve (short, but exquisitely cut) for inspection.

"It's lovely. Makes me feel dowdy."

"Don't be silly Vile; the trousers look very smart, and the top suits you." Actually, Viola had noticed appreciation on her way to the restaurant, but men's opinion on style didn't count. The formalities done, there was a mutual download of the last 24 hours or so of news. It lasted until well after the rest of the group had arrived,

80

placed orders for nut roasts, lamb fusillade and a couple of chicken and chips and received the usual assorted knick-knacks for starters.

Viola got to the question that had been teasing her for the last hour. "Did you ever hear of the Ancient Fellowship of Franchised Reamers?"

"The Ancient what?"

"The Ancient Fellowship of Franchised Reamers."

"Why? Carl want to become vice-chancellor or something?"

"It's just something that came up in my research. It may have a connection of some sort to my Dutch composers, but I can't find anything on what it was, just a reference that said it existed."

"Oh yes, them." Jane conveyed gentle amusement; she had her own theory about Viola's pursuit of Dutch polyphony. "Well, it doesn't mean anything to me, but the word 'reamers' doesn't seem to fit at all; it's the name of a tool in any usage I would know. I'll look it up, but I'm fairly sure there's no ancient usage of it to mean a person or trade, which is the only way it would make sense."

The others had overheard. "Ancient fellowship of free pricks" somebody said to applause.

"It'll be a boy's club."

"It'd be shortened to something like AFFREAM." The speaker laughed. "Never heard of that either."

"Sounds like something that went wrong at the hairdresser's."

The assorted company of philologist (Jane), geographer, writers, artists and ancillary musician (Viola) tore the subject happily to pieces.

Viola let it ride; no-one would forget it now, or fail to let her know if they came across it again.

With lulls for eating, the conversation gradually rose to a high-pitched, super-heated roar, one part intellectual enquiry to four parts gossip, a furnace in which no subject of discussion was safe.

Viola made her excuses and left when she first heard the sound of a dropped plate from the kitchen. There was no telling when Jane's passion for the sound of smashing glass or crockery would bubble to the surface, but surface it would and, though the experience was undeniably cathartic, some of the bills that followed had been sobering. Nowadays, anyway, the group's reputation for plate smashing and food throwing preceded them; the dropped plate could have been intended as a catalyst. The restaurant owners welcomed them, serving up on the cheapest mass-purchase catering units and charging for the family silver. Jane had the money to take that lightly; Viola needed to exercise restraint. Her friend Joe called them The Cowingdon for some reason: typical of his odd take on names. It puzzled Viola, who didn't like it much for its implication that she was a cow, but chose not to get drawn into one of Joe's elliptical Socratic dialogues by asking him to clarify.

Outside, it was still pleasantly warm. A little down the road, she recognised the young woman from that afternoon's meeting - the audit person - and nodded to her, as she passed in the company of a female friend, then shortly afterwards saw the unmistakeable bulk of Körthofer, in conversation with a student, whom she recognised as Janet. Carl had described the "La Valse" debacle when they had met earlier, so she hastily prepared some words of sorrow, in the hope of contributing to a general process of soothing. But he seemed, as they met and greeted each other, quite unbothered. A brief study of Janet's already proprietorial expression made the possible reason for this clear enough, if something of a surprise: hadn't she been the main object of wrath in Carl's account? Whether or not, she certainly wasn't now.

"We have been trying your English pub. Not weinstube, not bierstube, a something of both. And the food, I think, not so fulfilling. But it is good, yes?"

"I'm glad you're enjoying our South London night life" Viola said with a smile "Which pub did you try?"

"The Oast", Janet replied. "Just a quick drink and a bite."

After? thought Viola: no doubt for rehydration…stop it! "That's good, though it's a bit noisy." "Is it your local?" she said to Janet.

"Near enough. A lot of the students go there."

And show off distinguished conquests…stop being a bitch! "Haven't you tried an English pub before?" Viola asked Körthofer.

"No, or not so much. Always the professors they take me to restaurant. Is students, they like more drink beer, I think." He laughed uproariously; the two women laughed with him.

From the middle distance a crash was followed by a bang; something thrown through a window, maybe. Viola winced: that really was going to be expensive. And the police might take an interest. Time to be distant from the scene.

"And now, your English hooligans again. Is a busy night here." He laughed again, and Viola smiled weakly. "Let us walk with you to where is safer."

Viola protested mildly, but the critical thing was to move away soon. They crossed the tramway bridge, to the safe, neutral territory of Nunhead. Conversation proceeded in jerks, but showed no inclination to music or page-turning, though the "hooligans again" might have been a coded reference. In fact, Körthofer remained remarkably relaxed and trouble-free, considering he knew her to be a junior lecturer in the department that had cropped his heirloom with such devastating effectiveness only hours before. Perhaps Janet was just as devastatingly effective in bed; you never could tell with the quiet ones. The issue continued to niggle her, though she avoided making even the most indirect stab at the subject. She asked whether he would be going to the Bucharest conference: he would. Viola sensed a sharpening of interest on Janet's part; she'd be lucky!

Approaching Quiberon Road, she asked them in for a drink, was politely declined by Körthofer, who kissed her hand, a gesture she thought had died out with the romantic novel, and the three parted company, Janet and Körthofer linking arms for the walk back to wherever. It occurred to Viola that she had not found out where Janet lived or Körthofer was staying. It was a rare lapse in her command of social information - probably confusion caused by the window-smashing.

XI

THE SCARF

The exam in progress and the virtual monitors set, Ben could relax. His presence was nugatory, a relic of traditional invigilating, decades old and never tidied up. His thoughts started with Atinuke, but strayed to the young woman who had tugged at his sleeve as he walked into the faculty building earlier that morning. Excusing herself and addressing him as Mr Cordell - an almost unheard-of formality - she had asked him a question about a meeting he had not attended and, when he had pointed this out, laughed in a slightly flustered way and said no, of course, but she had not wanted to bother Professor Trenchard and just wondered if there had been anything going on that she ought to know about.

She was stunningly pretty: a finely drawn, very English face and dark, curly hair, beautifully put together, right up to the wisp of scarf that set off her face to good effect, though it must (it now occurred to him) have been over-warm for the mild, almost sunny May weather. The seeming shyness was intriguingly different from his normal experience. She gave her name as Alison. It was familiar, but he couldn't place her.

Her topic of introduction had been a bit flimsy, very much like a pretext to get into conversation than anything, but who cared? Ben hadn't ever lacked for feminine company and attention in his fifteen or so years on the prowl, but it had largely been 'all my own efforts'. A campaign from the other side was flattering and rather touching. There was no avoiding invigilating, but he had promptly fixed up a lunch date (though only in the refectory). The invitation was accepted coolly, but without temporising.

A light flashed on the monitor; an examinee was downloading a whole sentence or more of text. Ben took no action; the incident was recorded, and the standard warning about plagiarism and the need to reference would come up on the examinee's screen. At the far end of the hall, a student mouthed what looked like abuse at his monitor, though whether in frustration or indignation was unclear.

Ben's thoughts drifted pleasantly back to the mystery woman, before the realisation surfaced that there was an article facing a deadline he had intended to work on. Examiner and examined were in the same situation: the wrong end of the whip.

Alison entered the refectory a precisely calculated seven minutes after the arranged time, immediately spotting Ben in a quiet corner near the window. He saw her as she walked across and waved.

"You've lost the scarf".

"No." Was it his imagination, or had she coloured ever so slightly? "It's too warm now."

"Ah. It looks good on you, though."

Eva had been right. Not that she would tell her so in so many words; Alison enjoyed being number one in that relationship. But she owed her a favour.

Ownership of the table established, they wandered over to the counter and accumulated: steak and gravy lost within a thick casing of suet and accompanied by chips and a small bottle of beer (Ben); a green salad with a slice of feta and a mango and persimmon Frutenlo (Alison). Ben paid for both, averting his gaze: how could girls create such a perfect product inputting rubbish like that? Alison averted her eyes from the suet.

Walking back to the table, he slipped a glance towards her, to find that she had glanced towards him; she looked away.

Ben targeted an early dismissal of faculty politics: "What happened at the meeting, then?"

She dissected a leaf of rocket with some care. "They had a sort of row over one of the things I said in a presentation. Not with me, with each other. What I'd said was a nothing really; I'd only put it in to make up numbers on the slide" (three to five points per slide, no more, no less, Ben thought; they'd all been taught that on the Holopoint course). "But it nearly started a fight. Then they just shut up and tried to pretend nothing had happened."

"Who was there? Apart from Carl, of course"

"Carl: that's Professor Trenchard?" He nodded. "There was Mike Esther: he's a Chordologist, I think. He started things by making a comment about Paginists being expensive, but I think that was just a joke. It was another of the people there, a man with an American accent, who picked it up and tried to make something of it; he got quite aggressive. He was put down by Professor Trenchard on that, but it felt like he was trying to start a fight."

"Pity he didn't, really. Carl's no patsy. What was the presentation about, though?"

"An Internal Audit – that's where I work – report on Health and Safety in Ancillary Music. The point that started the argument was about internal control of expenditure in Paginatorics; something about piano duets, I think. It wasn't at all serious."

Ah, she was *that* Alison! Carl hadn't said anything about this particular spat, just the budget coup d'état later on in the meeting. Funny how the prettiest girls sometimes had the dullest jobs. "The American, that would be Stephen Pendleton. He's new here, won't know the in-jokes. How did he strike you?"

She hesitated, not wanting to make enemies. Still, she thought Ben would be discreet. "Pompous and full of himself. He seemed to have some nice cosy secret waiting to spill. And either he was born tactless, or didn't feel he needed to be on friendly terms with people. Not with Professor Trenchard, at any rate."

"Carl."

"Not with Carl."

Pendleton had certainly been nursing a secret, Ben thought: the budget coup. "Stephen Pendleton's friendly with the VC."

"The VC?"

"Sorry, the Vice Chancellor."

Oh, him. Her boss knew him as Onran, but that name probably wasn't repeatable. "Do you think he's up to something?"

"The VC's 'up to something' all the time. Do you think he was having a go at anyone in particular? Stephen Pendleton, I mean."

"Definitely at Professor Trenchard - Carl. He made several nasty comments in a row. Everyone just sat and said nothing. That creep who looks after resources, Jed Crabtree started smirking." Alison felt on safe ground with her opinion of Crabtree; he was universally detested.

Ben laughed. Poor Crabtree! But he deserved it all. "Crabtree doesn't do any favours for Carl, or anybody else much. Stephen Pendleton is anyone's guess."

"Anyway, what about you?"

The conversation ambled on to more personal topics. Her job as auditor, to be brutally honest, sounded less than exciting, he thought. But discussion of anything else was cut short; he found himself almost belated for the afternoon exams and had to make another speedy exit. "Sorry, got to go." He looked at her. "I'm free Tuesday, if you are. Shall we do lunch again?"

Yes! He'd bitten. "Maybe; I'll have to check with a friend, a girlfriend. Could I ring you?" Ben handed her one of his Information Cards; Alison scribbled a number on the back of her business card, and he left, trying to avoid breaking into a run, the card between his fingers; God knows what the avatars would be getting up to; the examinees were the least of the problem. Outside, he narrowly missed colliding with a stocky man of eastern European appearance, wielding camera and theodolite.

Alison sat over a coffee for five minutes, savouring a feeling of achievement and watching a magpie, magnificent in his lustrous black and white patterning, play King of the Castle in the plane tree outside the window. She must dig out something about this Stephen Pendleton, to keep the conversation rolling. Karen, she thought; Karen must know something. She recalled the Vice Chancellor's copy of the monthly Internal Audit Summary, waiting on her desk. This time she would deliver it by hand.

XII

IN THE REFECTORY

Karen had been close by, though in a far corner well out of Alison's sight. Picking her way without enthusiasm through the refectory's idea of a vegetable bake, she saw Paul Fairley and a male companion snaking along between the tables and headed in her direction. She answered Paul's greeting with little more enthusiasm than she felt for the vegetable bake: he was all right in his way, but a bit of a wanker. The companion, looked more interesting; in fact, quite dishy. "Karen, this is Tad; he does something in Media Studies; no-one can ever tell what. Tad, Karen!" They said hello and distributed themselves round the table, Karen retaining her view of the room. She asked Paul how he was and how things were going with Janet, not without malice: she knew perfectly well from Janet that things weren't going and never would be. Paul's reply, at the usual edge of bravado, she let pass. Conversation trickled on a little further, gradually giving way to the background clamour and the punctuations of bangs of plates and glasses on tables, clatterings of trays and an occasional smash. Paul sprang up, saying "Must catch Mitch: I need to copy his lecture notes from Wednesday morning. See you, Karen! Catch up with you later, Tad!" And withdrew.

Karen threw a glance at his retreating back. "Never can get up in the mornings," she observed, with a minimal spice of affection.

"It can be hard", Tad observed, with a token defence of his friend.

"Tell me more."

Tad, unsure how to respond, lapsed into a discreet appraisal. She had a lively face, topped off by a mop of hair with blonde highlights. Her nose was slightly upturned, creating a subtle air of challenge. She was, without exactly being pretty, extremely attractive. He might have had

90

trouble if he'd had to describe precisely why he found her face so attractive, but there was no difficulty lower down: they were out of this world. He forced his gaze away and became conscious that the silence was prolonging itself; if he didn't speak soon, she was going to notice his survey, and hens could be funny about that.

But she got in first, asking, with a slight toss of the head: "what can I be doing for you, then?"

An honest answer seemed a bad idea. "You don't have any problem with mornings? You're a lark. How did you get to know Paul?"

"A lark?" She laughed, disbelieving, though still friendly. "That's a first. Do you talk rubbish like that all the time in Media Studies?" Before he could reply, she added: "How I got to know Paul, you don't want to know." Karen would have preferred not to know either; it had been a brief, but shaming lapse in taste.

"It's Media Design I'm in, not Media Studies; Paul never seems to get the difference. We spend our days in front of a Holoscreen; talking's not part of the deal"

"Well, I spend most of *my* days in front of a Holoscreen, but the talking never stops. That's others talking at me, mostly."

"What sort of work do you do, then?"

"I'm a PA." Tad looked puzzled. "Personal Assistant. To the VC."

"That sounds grand."

Karen scrutinised him: was he taking the piss? Probably not: just those days in front of the Holoscreen. "It's necessary, if that's what you mean." She leaned forward, chin supported by hand, with an air of inquisition.

"Not too much typing, though?"

Bridling slightly: "Most of that I send out, and Mr Fraserman types more than half his own stuff anyway." She leaned back slightly, to check her well-manicured fingernails. "I get to sit in on a lot of meetings though." A pause for consideration. "They can be dead boring; there's some real half-lifes running departments here. But some get more lively."

"Like serious-intellectual-discussion-lively, or are you talking blood-baths?"

She laughed. "I wouldn't swear they've all of them got any blood. The heads of department, I mean. I have seen a punch-up, though. It was weird. It was a meeting that was all men. Except me, of course. They were talking about critical values, which I hear a lot about, particularly when the Fine Arts people are in. They were starting to shout a bit, but that's nothing unusual, then all of a sudden one of them screamed something and took a swing across the table at one of the others, who dodged, shouted something else and swung back. They both missed, but the first bloke threw himself across the table and got the second by the throat. The others separated them easily enough, but they'd taken out the bottles and glasses on the table, so it was quite a mess. Mr Fraserman was furious."

"Yeah. Personnel's very hot on violence. I got a verbal warning once about kicking a processor."

"Not the violence, that's just Jed Crabtree got hold of somebody else's rulebook. Actually, Mr Fraserman doesn't mind a bit of violence: he was in the Army, you know. But he does mind wasting the best part of a bottle of Gordon's, and one of those went down with the water and the coffee. Ended up all over one of the Manucs, which was quite funny, as they're all temperance. It didn't improve things for Mr Fraserman, though; he kept mumbling about casting pearls over swine for a couple of days afterwards. He hasn't liked them since. I think he held it more against them than he did against the two blokes who were fighting; they just had to pay for the damage."

"It sounds more exciting than Media Design. What were they screaming and shouting about?"

"You tell me. The first one called the second an 'existential opportunist', and the second one called the first a 'structuralist inspissationist'"

Tad was impressed. "Have you studied literature, then?"

She was drinking some water and spluttered most of it back. "Do us a favour." Tad assisted in dabbing with a napkin at wet patches on non-critical bits of her anatomy. She didn't attempt to stop him. "Camberwell Business Skills College, that's me. The meeting was taped: most of them are. I replayed it a few times, trying to work out what they'd become so angry about. It was a waste of time. I still haven't any idea what they were talking about or why it mattered so much. I just remember the words. I sometimes think I could get along okay in one of their meetings", she mused, unusually thoughtful, looking directly at Tad, "if no-one knew who I was. I'm never all that sure they understand each other."

"I'd put money on it. It sounds like you must know everything that's going on around here."

"Most things; some meetings I'm not let in on." She paused, conveying determination. Then she turned and looked at him straight. "What about you, anyway? You spend all your time in front of a Holoscreen. You must get to know something about something."

"I'm not an official hacker, so no, I don't get that much access to information. Media Design means you know every fact about the object you're working on, useful, or useless. Anything else is just chance. I do avatars, particularly information storage ones: I know a lot about the avatars, but not much more than anyone else about the information they store."

"What was it the one you gave a kicking did to annoy you?"

"The verbal warning, you mean?" She nodded. "That wasn't an avatar, it was the one of the processor boxes that generate them. It wasn't working properly."

"Personnel don't do property, do they?"

"That's not it. Kicking the processor made it work properly. The avatar it generated was hacked off at having to put in more hours work than it'd been expecting. It complained to Personnel."

That made her laugh. "And Jed Crabtree took it seriously? This place does your head in sometimes."

"I've been more cautious which boxes I kick since then."

"Do you enjoy what you do, anyway? You've not said."

"Yes, I do, though I could wish for a bit more, you know, human interaction on the job."

"Well, on the job's one thing, but you're getting some human interaction here, aren't you?" She fixed him with a questioning, slightly mocking smile, which he returned slightly nervously. Looking more serious, she said: "I wouldn't do a job for long if I didn't enjoy it."

"It's fine for now; just doesn't feel long-term, if you know what I mean." He blushed inwardly to think what Paul and company would have made of the "on the job" bit, but she didn't seem to have noticed, he thought.

"Which will be?"

"God knows!" She frowned slightly at the exclamation. "I wish I knew. It'll turn up."

"What about – what did you call it? – being an official hacker?"

"No. I wanted to be when I started as a student, but you have to have phenomenal mental fitness to make it to that grade. I'd decided before I got to the test that a hacker's life would drive me round the bend anyway.'

She looked dubious at this, but did not pursue the matter further. She smoothed her skirt, running her hands smoothly down from waist level to hips. "No interesting punch-ups in Media Design?" He shook his head and smiled assent. She continued. "I thought there'd be another punch-up a couple of days ago, actually. It was one of the meetings I wasn't allowed into, so I don't know much of what it was about."

"Sounds like you need bouncers. Who was fighting this time, then?"

"Just Mr Fraserman and this new head of department; I think he's an American. I took coffee in halfway through and they looked like they were ready to bite chunks out of each other. And the rest of the meeting wasn't too friendly either."

"How could you tell?"

Karen looked, for the first time, just slightly uncomfortable. "You can just tell. When he came out: that's the American, not Mr Fraserman, he charged out of the office the wrong way, I had to be quick…" She bit her lip, but Tad showed no sign of noticing anything. "I directed him out the back exit, but he didn't seem to notice he was going in the wrong direction."

"Perhaps they were discussing critical values."

She giggled. "That's not Mr Fraserman's style. The subject in the diary was 'Phoniotic Principles of Organisational Dynamics'. That wouldn't be Mr Fraserman's style either, so I think the American must have put that in." She remembered. "Stephen Pendleton: that's his name."

Tad stretched his arms out, considering. "Seems an odd way to get started with a new boss."

"You won't tell anybody else, will you? Mr Fraserman was being quite crisp when I went in to sort through mail afterwards, and that's not like him. Everyone is afraid of him, but he's a sweetie really."

Sweetie was not the word Tad had heard anybody else use of the VC, but he nodded sympathetically to concur with the request for confidence. "Phoniotic Principles of Organisational Dynamics doesn't sound like a topic to start a fight, but then I suppose neither did … what was it?

"Existential opportunist."

"Yes… In Media Design, we'd probably flag both with a spider's web. Beware the small print."

"Mr Fraserman doesn't do small print."

"Americans, the ones I meet through work, it's always about selling, even if it's just themselves. He'll have small print all right"

"He didn't look as though he'd done a salesman's job on Mr Fraserman."

Tad moved his hand in a rocking motion to signify a (hopefully) sophisticated-looking mixture of uncertainty and scepticism and said "anyway, you haven't said whether this is *your* long-term career."

She moved her hand in an imitative rocking motion and they both laughed. She let the topic move past without saying anything about the Charter thing that she'd seen lying on Mr Fraserman's desk. She hadn't managed to read much of it at all; there was a limit to how much fuss you could make over a single coffee; just something about AFFREM and a solemn commitment to beliefs and something about the free market. It had been out of sight when she went back in and nowhere to be found when Mr Fraserman was out later in the afternoon. It would be confidential for now, at least until she had a more interesting line on it.

A sympathetic silence developed. Tad fetched two more coffees. Karen confirmed her observation as he moved out of and back into sight: he was her idea of dishy; not everyone's taste, but definitely hers. A bit clueless sometimes, but that could be sorted. And he'd given her more than the usual once-over. On an impulse before she went, Karen rummaged in her bag and handed Tad a small plastic card. She didn't believe in wasting time. He looked stunned, but then had the presence of mind to seek out the corresponding plastic card, kept in an inner pocket and hand this over in exchange. Walking out of the refectory exchanging small-talk, he looked around, but no-one seemed to have noticed the exchange: as well to avoid endless comment from Paul and the others. The stunned feeling persisted. Exchanging social data at this stage with somebody you got on with was quite usual. Exchanging veep and penpro just didn't happen this early in getting to know a girl, did it? Not to him, at any rate. Well, it just had. In the confusion, he forgot to mention another meeting, but they parted company with an implicit promise to see one another soon. Paul was right, he noticed as she walked away: she had a neat bum.

XIII

IN THE CONDOMINIUM

Viola struggled awake. Why was she having to face consciousness so summarily? The videophone was ringing in the next room; she had never got round to arranging an extension, and Carl lacked the practical skills. So it was out of bed and scurry into the next room, eyes gummed up and body protesting, though she did summon sufficient wit to turn off the video feature before answering. One automated, but interrupted message and a quantity of clicks and whirrs later, Jane's unmistakeable tones cut through, providing a focus in the just-awakened fuzz.

"Vile, thank God you're home. Carly baby with you?"

"No." Viola tried not to sound stiff, but she was battling a slow starter motor.

"Hope I'm not interrupting any other development." Viola let that go. "Could you be a pal and drop down to the nick and bail us out. Sorry, I know it's not your time of day, but everyone else I know and can trust is in here with me. One of their WPCs got a lamb fusillade in the face and down her uniform, so we've been put in the cells. They've not been at all friendly so far." "Pigs!" she added, though she did not sound very convincingly indignant.

So the police had taken an interest. It must have been quite a session. The action must have been all-engrossing if no-one had managed to make it out of the back door when the plods arrived. It was not as if Memories of Kandahar was likely to be uncooperative: they knew they would be paid; the Cowingdon was probably a vital part of their business plan. "Okay. Give me half an hour to get my head together. Which nick?"

"Denmark Hill; part of the old rail station." She groaned silently; it meant a change of tram to bus, or a lengthy walk, though the latter might be useful in glueing together the façade of competence that would be needed to successfully spring an entire hen party from virtual Siberia.

"I'll see you there, then. But it'll need to be cash on the nail once you're out. I've only got this month's salary in my account."

"No probs Vile; you're an angel. See you later."

She switched the 'phone off, just in time to avoid the nauseatingly (literally at this point of the morning) cheerful and upbeat adverts that would cut in on any lengthy period of silence.

Becoming aware that she had no clothes on and that the music room was overlooked by at least one resident who might take an interest, she retreated to the bedroom and donned undergarments before getting stuck on the Morton's Fork of purpose and colour-matching. She would need to look business-like to be credible to the police as somebody with the means and determination to buy unconditional bail. She would also have to maintain adequate competition to Jane, who would still be wearing last night's ultra-smart outfit. True, she had spent a night in virtualised exclusion and true there would have been a lot of highly spiced and highly coloured food flying through the air last night, but it would have been most unlike Jane for any of it to have been allowed to land on her and most unlike Jane not to be fresh and alert, even at this time in the morning.

Come to that, what was the time? She asked the bedside clock, and it said 08.16 with digitised lack of cadence. Viola reflected, with a twinge of guilt, that that was not most people's idea of early morning. After some agonising, she chose tight-fitting but soberly patterned trousers and a looser silk top. It was warm and didn't seem to threaten rain, so there was no other layer needed. She decided on the walk – Jane and Co. were just going to have to wait - and slipped on a pair of appropriate, though adequately smart shoes. Reflecting that

Carl might come round later, she undertook a minimal tidy-up of the bed and raised the blinds. Then she sought breakfast in the kitchen. Though only a cup of strong coffee and a slice of toast, this involved a series of greetings from fridge, coffee-maker and toaster: they had all been chosen for the greetings to be tolerably downbeat at this stage of the morning. Carl's toaster drove her to distraction with its irrepressible bonhomie; on one occasion she had been provoked into an unwisely ratty reply, after which it had assiduously burnt her toast for several days in a row.

Outside, stripes of sun cut up the courtyard between the two cherry trees that provided shade and, at present, a carpet of blossom in its central area. The little ginger cat that had taken to sunning herself on the balcony presented herself for a stroke and a scratch under the chin. Viola set off purposefully, following much the same route as the previous evening, but with a diversion that kept her away from, but in sight of Memories of Kandahar. The damage certainly was impressive and seemed to have spread to one of the windows of an adjoining house: no wonder the police had been called. The costs should keep the restaurant securely in business for another year or two; she breathed a silent prayer of thanks that she would not have to share in them. The route also avoided the main university campus; she did not want to get involved in conversation with anyone official until a story was generally agreed and firmly in everybody's mind. A left turn up billionaires' row – a long, tall line of preserved early-Victorian houses that were within the means, just, of the Hon Ran, but not anybody else that she knew – brought her to the top of the hill. Just round the corner was her destination: the Denmark Hill Community Security Condominium, as the pedestal-mounted sign outside announced it.

Dealing crisply but politely with the door avatar, she stepped into the environmental surround and was greeted by the reception avatar. He had been programmed to a heritage style of delivery, familiar from the still-popular detective soaps that celebrated the secure world of the previous century. Responding in character meant a quick progression, this time to an actual human police officer, a sergeant, in a bare and functional meeting room. He gestured her to sit in a chair on what was obviously the client side of the meeting table.

She was relieved to see no tell-tale stains on his uniform; hopefully she would be able to discuss things on an entirely neutral basis. The hope was dashed when a WPC came into the room, her uniform jacket substituted by a (quite attractive, Viola thought) cardigan, its neckline pulled out of true by her police identification placard, clearly chosen to avoid disturbing the large bandage on the wearer's neck. The WPC also had two small but painful-looking burns on her forehead. Viola had not taken into account the possibility of somebody getting hurt; civilians were not so foolhardy as to get in the way when the Cowingdon got going; restaurant staff would invariably lock themselves into back rooms, armed only with an inventory and a Holosheet of costings.

The sergeant introduced himself. "Sergeant Brown. You've come about your friends?"

"Yes."

They looked at her in silence for several seconds. "If I could give you some advice, Miss…"

"Ms, please"

"Ms. If I could give you some advice, I would choose your friends carefully. You look a respectable young woman … what's your employment?"

It seemed untimely to object to personal questioning of this sort. "I'm a lecturer at the university."

"The Arts University?"

"Yes. I'm not sure where that's leading us, though."

They looked at her in silence for a few more seconds. "As I said, you look a respectable young woman" (with conviction) "and you have a respectable job" (with slightly less conviction). "Those friends of yours, what they were getting up to last night was anything but respectable. Criminal damage to premises and injuries to police officers. Perhaps you'd like to talk about that to my colleague here."

Viola would have preferred not, but clearly would have no option if she wanted to make any progress.

The WPC, who had been silent up until then said: "See these." She pointed to the burn marks on her forehead. "Those were done by something one of your friends threw at me. They'll leave scars. I could have done without that."

She sat back, hard-faced. Her colleague took over again. "Burns sustained by a police officer in an assault is serious enough. I hope you understand that, Ms …?"

"Trent."

"Ms Trent. It could have been more serious still. That restaurant was bedlam last night. Glass flying everywhere. It was lucky somebody wasn't killed."

Why didn't you just stay out of the way until it was all over, thought Viola. She immediately suppressed the thought. Actually, she was shocked by the WPC's injuries; that sort of thing had never been part of the game. "Whatever happened here, and however they behaved, I can't believe my friends would have intended to hurt anybody." "I'm sorry that you were injured like this" she said to the WPC, who returned eye contact then momentarily looked down. "I'm sure that my friends will be shocked that it has happened too and will want to apologise."

"Apologies will be welcome of course, but they can't take back what is done", her colleague said. "Your friends face some serious charges here, and I'd repeat my advice to think seriously about the sort of company you keep."

Viola stiffened and set her face at this.

He passed on, without pausing. "So what are you here to do?"

She decided on directness; they would know perfectly well what she was here to do and no amount of prevarication would make it possible to get them off guard. "I'd like to go through what's needed to get my friends set free again."

The two registered no reaction. "Bear in mind what I said about the charges your friends face. There is no question of their being given just a caution and let go. We shall be enquiring closely into the background to this disturbance, and your friends will need to be available for questioning at any time as our enquiries proceed."

Enquiries? Into why a pissed-up hen party started throwing food around? They must be short of things to do. "So are you saying you intend to keep them all in custody? That's a bit extreme, even given that someone was injured."

"It is clear to us that there were leaders and followers here. We are in a position to discuss bail."

"What sort of bail and who?"

"Our normal tariff for tagged bail for accessories to this type of offence would be two thousand per person. We could extend that to all but one member of the party."

That didn't sound good for Jane. The tagged price seemed steep, as far as Viola could tell, not having dealt directly with the situation before, though you normally got quite a lot of the money back. There was a deduction for 'expenses', which could be heavy, but the process, nevertheless, was under scrutiny. For all that, it was an unpopular bail option. The tagging apparatus was a non-removable collar, a nuisance and difficult to conceal. Worst of all, it gave the police total access to everything you did, 24 hours of every day on bail. Careless bail subjects were apt to find interesting or salacious moments of their lives appearing on the media, following 'targeted attacks by determined and ruthless professional criminals on the police database'.

"And untagged bail?"

"A difficult one given the gravity of the situation." Gravity? What was he getting at? "If we extended the facility at all, and I would need to consult my Inspector on that, I can't see it coming out at less than five thousand per person. Possibly more; you must realise that objectively it carries a greater risk of absconding."

Absconding? A bunch of lecturers and professionals? Where were they going to abscond to and why? Viola did not like the way this was being built up. And five thousand sounded extortionate, considering you still ended up in court and rarely got much of the money back: untagged bail was discretionary and largely outside scrutiny.

She pressed on; these were only preliminaries to the real bargaining point, as all of them knew. "We may be looking for unconditional."

"It's not an option we have yet explored. It will be a matter for the chief if you want me to pursue it"

Of course it would go to the chief, whatever his title was; he'd take the biggest cut, after all. But the negotiations were now open. "What sort of level are we talking about?"

"As I said, it's an option we've not yet explored. Do you want me to pursue it?"

Unconditional bail meant no tagging and only attending court if you heard again from the police. In practice, you didn't; once paid, it bought off charges. It was expensive, the police's most profitable option. Like hell they hadn't explored it. "Yes. Please do. May I have a word with my friends now? In private."

It wouldn't be private, of course, she knew, it would be recorded, but at least they wouldn't dare use anything they recorded in evidence. Some lucrative prosecutions had, in the past, fallen apart over clumsy attempts to splice private conversations into official interviews.

The party, minus Jane, were brought into the meeting room, and they were allowed to confer briefly. Then the sergeant asked Viola to follow him. At the virtual boundary wall to the cell area, he punched a code into a keypad on a stand, a doorway materialised and they stepped through into a corridor of security doors. He sneezed unguardedly, almost the only verifiably human characteristic that he had so far shown; his features and general demeanour were bland to the point that he merged with the furniture. He ushered her into the second from the end, handing her a virtualphone to use when she needed to leave. She was not to give it to anyone else: usage was monitored closely.

Jane was sitting in the corner of the bed that completed the standard police cell: virtual now, but of a format essentially unaltered in two centuries. It was a cheerless place, less so even than the meeting room, almost featureless once you had accounted for the bed and the small virtual simulation of a window that presented a scene of no obvious interest; no wonder the police did so well out of bail payments. She looked tired and a little the worse for wear, but characteristically unrepentant. "Vile. I'm so glad to see you. I've been cooped up here since the small hours. What time is it?" Viola consulted her watch, which informed her that it was just after midday. She cut it off before the advertising could start. "So what did they say? Can you bail us quickly?"

Viola looked at her with as neutral an expression as she could command and said "you know the WPC got burns on her face. It might be awkward."

Jane's face registered astonishment, gradually changing to guarded outrage. Who told you anyone ended up with burns?"

"I saw her; she was one of the two who spoke to me before I got in here. The burns are real enough. They're small, but they looked nasty; might need plastic surgery if she's vain."

"Because of the office coffee machine exploding, maybe. Jesus! Vile, somebody's been spinning you a story."

"But you said on the 'phone that one of the WPCs got a plate of food in the face."

"The staff they send in to these situations are robot avatars. They may be dressed as PCs and WPCs, but they can't get skin burns in the way we do."

"Are you sure the one that got in the way of the plate was an avatar?"

"Absolutely certain. Some of the food slopped down on to her hand and it gave off sparks." Viola twitched slightly at an unguarded memory of the encounter with John Librarian, but continued to look Jane in the eye. "All else apart, the food that got thrown was the food we'd all been eating. You left not long before it all started; you must be able to remember it had pretty nearly gone cold. You could pour any of it into a bath and jump in and you'd get dirty and greasy and smelly and tingle a bit, but there's no way you'd get burnt anywhere. Look, I was going to apologise to the avatar: we didn't throw the plate at her deliberately, but the way they're programmed, it can't have been pleasant, even given that she's virtual. And there might just have been some damage to the robot body. This sounds like a stitch-up, though. How much were they talking about for bail?"

"Two thousand tagged, maybe five untagged. They've not yet given a figure for unconditional."

"Two thousand doesn't sound too bad for eight of us. Five thousand is a bit steep. What did they think we were doing?"

"That's each, Jane."

Jane looked shocked, then enraged. "Each! They must be joking. Christ! they don't charge that for an armed robbery, not even unconditional. They must think we're loaded."

Actually, Viola thought, Jane was loaded. But how would the police know that? "I haven't done this before, Jane. I don't know the prices. What's reasonable?"

"As I said, somewhere around two thousand for everybody tagged, maybe three untagged, five unconditional. It's always bad news when the police get involved, but they do have a price list. Price ranges, at any rate. If they get too greedy, people just go to court and challenge the amount, and the less gets discussed in the open about the bail system, the better for the police."

"Have you done this before?

"Once: a drugs charge; it was about ten years ago. It wouldn't have looked good to have that on my record, not the public record at all events, so I got to know quite a lot about how you bought your way out of it. Joe's the one to talk to. He knows the going rates for everything."

Joe would. His seemed omniscient, particularly about conflict, particularly about things that someone somewhere would probably want to see buried. "So what do you want me to do now?"

"Go back to them, make it clear you now know the going rate and tell them to be more reasonable. If you're not getting anywhere, you could drop vague hints about a lawyer: they won't want one of them involved; everything'll be under scrutiny then and they'll get a much smaller cut. If you're not sure, you could suggest bringing me in on the meeting. I doubt they're supposed to do that, but they might if it looks like they'll get a deal."

"I'll do what I can and get back to you. If I can get the deal you said just now, or something reasonably close to it, I'll just say yes. Okay?"

"Yeah. Thanks. I'll try to speak to the others."

Viola summoned the warder avatar and was ushered back out into the police station and, after a wait, into the presence of the robot-look-alike sergeant. The WPC was no longer in evidence. They looked at each other in silence for several seconds; Viola eventually felt compelled to open the conversation. "You're asking too much; it's way out of line."

The sergeant's expression remained unaltered. "I'm not sure I understand you. What do you think we're asking for?"

Oh God! Bureaucrats! "The bail amounts. They're way in excess of what you'd normally charge. My friends are unlikely to be able to afford that."

"I think you need to understand, Ms...?"

"Trent".

"You need to understand, Ms Trent, that the bail money is just a surety. Provided your friends keep to the bail conditions, the money is returned once they go to trial, apart from a few small administrative charges. So I don't see the problem."

Yeah, yeah, yeah! Of course it would be returned. And of course they would be happy to go to trial. "They've got to find cash now, haven't they. And at the level you're talking about, it's not going to materialise."

"You need to be realistic about the situation that faces your friends."

"Which means what?"

"The nub of it is, Ms Trent, that we are investigating potentially serious terrorist action in the area and have reason to suspect that at least some of your friends may be involved. We're prepared to take a view on the likelihood of that involvement, but you must realise this is a very risky situation."

Viola strove to keep her face blank, with only moderate success. "Terrorism? You must be out of your head. They're academics and professionals who got a bit carried away on a girls' night out, not some crowd of bomb-happy fanatics. What do you think you've got on them, then?"

"Terrorism takes some unexpected forms. We see a clear basis for suspicion in this case."

"If that's what you're trying to fabricate, it sounds like they may need some legal help."

He ignored the 'fabricate', but for the first time, looked slightly less certain. "If you are referring to calling in solicitors, your friends have, of course - most of them - the right to call one at any time. But that could itself be expensive. I shall call my Inspector; he can discuss what might be done about the bail." He activated his videophone and spoke into it.

What did "most of them" mean? It niggled her. As the Sergeant came off the 'phone, she asked him.

"My superior officer will explain the situation."

The presumed superior walked in. Now he *was* a heritage policeman. Tallish and very broad, a meaty face with clusters of broken veins showing on the cheeks, all he lacked was a flattened nose: most unlike the sergeant, who could, she thought, stand in for Jed Crabtree without causing comment. She looked at him in silence.

"Inspector Fox." He held out a hand that matched the face. Viola allowed her own hand to be ritually crushed in the cause of friendship. "We have a problem?"

The sergeant explained the salient differences of opinion, the Inspector grunting and looking closely at Viola when her status as a friend of the prisoners emerged. "The Sergeant's explained what this is about?" he said.

"We were discussing it when you arrived."

"Well then?"

"Well then, what?"

"Well then, why should we take a punt on letting a bunch of hell-cats out at a cut price?" He spoke with a distinct northern accent.

The Sergeant looked agitated and quickly added "It's a question of policy and risk management. An incorrectly balanced assessment of response outcomes could negate our performanistic responsibility to the community at large."

Viola and the Inspector snorted simultaneously. "Cut-price nothing!" she said. "You're trying for about ten times the normal rate. Most of them are not going to able to afford your 'bail'." She regretted the lift of voice for the 'bail' as soon as she said it, but the Inspector at least seemed unperturbed and said nothing.

"The Sergeant didn't mention my friends' entitlement to legal help."

"Well now, perhaps you'd better re-think that. There's no solicitors where the Terrorism Act applies."

"What's a hen party with a few drinks in it got to do with the Terrorism Act? Who are they meant to be terrorising?"

"A hen party, at least one of whose members has a string of offshore bank accounts, that meets at an Afghan restaurant before attacking the police?"

So they had investigated Jane's wealth: no wonder they were going for a big kill. "So you're going to keep them banged up until they pay? Suppose I speak to a few solicitors anyway? Just get their view on what you're doing?"

The Sergeant was visibly discomfited by such directness, but the Inspector perpetrated a smile, first cousin to a leer. "Speak to who you want. We can let most out on bail if they get real about what we're going to charge in the circumstances. "

"They might get real if you do too. And why do you say 'most'. Who're the exceptions?"

"Jane Fredricksson is the leader, yes?"

Viola neither confirmed this nor denied it.

"Her case is still being considered. We can't release her at this stage. You'll need to come back in a couple of days' time if you want an answer on that. As to the others, I'll take five thousand tagged, seven thousand untagged, ten thousand unconditional."

This was an advance, but still a long way from what Jane had been talking about. "So all but one of these dangerous terrorists can be released on unconditional bail, just so long as they pay through the nose?"

The Inspector leaned back in his chair, his hands spread on the edge of the table. "Take it or leave it."

"I can't give you an answer without speaking to the others and I won't get an answer from them without some decision on Jane. I'm not prepared to buy out the others and leave Jane to rot, even if it is just for a couple of days."

"I can't take it any further than I have."

"Who can, then?"

He looked at her for some moments. She looked back, unblinking. He turned. "Sergeant, could you have a word with the Superintendent."

The sergeant got up and left the room.

The Inspector relaxed a little, reclined his bulk in the office chair, close to tipping point and regarded Viola lazily. "What's a nice girl like you, as they say, doing with riff-raff like that, then?"

"They're my friends. And whatever you think they've been doing, they're not riff-raff, they're mostly academics and professionals."

Judging by the Inspector's expression, he saw no distinction. "Well, they do say Jack The Ripper might have been a prince of the realm, so you can't go by appearances." Leaning forward, he looked her in the eye and asked: "so do you go yourself to any of these social jamborees with your friends?"

She made a quick decision; if they had found that much out about Jane's money, they had probably investigated the whole group. "Quite often, yes. If you mean, was I there last night…" she looked him back in the eye and saw that her guess was correct: "…the answer is that I was, earlier on; I left as soon as we had finished the meal. For what it's worth, we talked about all sorts of things, including politics and including men…" here she gave him a snap once-over with a scornful flick of the eyes: "…but the only sort of terror involved was verbal: some of what we said about them, they wouldn't have wanted to hear. You can ask the waiters, if you need somebody to back that up. Most of it was being shouted."

"We have two of the waiters in custody."

"The waiters! They can't have been throwing things round their own restaurant, surely."

"I can't tell you that, lass. But you'll have to cast a bit wider for solid citizens."

Shit! Other customers had disappeared speedily after the hen party arrived and the decibel count started rising. What were the waiters in for? Surely there wasn't a terrorist connection there?

The Sergeant re-entered and spoke in an undertone to the Inspector, who turned to Viola. "The Superintendent's agreed to meet you. Two o'clock in his office. Don't be late."

But it was the Superintendent who was late. Viola had time enough to seek the outside world before the appointment, but instinct told her not to leave, and she sat in the Reception waiting area, contemplating the wall, flinging an arm over the adjoining seat, retracting it, standing up and turning about, lack of mission returning her to her seat, yawning, stretching, composing herself to stillness, contemplating the wall and so forth, until two-twenty, when she was finally called.

His office was the only room she had so far seen in the police station that had any distinguishing features. It had, for one thing, an outside wall, a real wall, decorated with some real photographs and with a small, non-virtual window, though the window was high up and provided nothing that could be called a view. The virtual walls, too, were relieved by hologram displays of what looked like crime scenes. Perhaps they were his hundred best arrests. The man himself was quite a smoothy, wearing immaculate uniform and topped by a no-hair-even-looking-as-though-it-might-think-of-getting-out-of-place coiffure. Quite a contrast to the Inspector.

"Hello, Ms Trent? Superintendent Mike Osler."

They shook hands and sat down again. "You're here as a friend of the eight young women my officers took into custody last night?" Viola nodded assent. "I'm told you have some issues around the form of custody. Could you expand on these for my benefit, please?"

She knew next to nothing about police procedure, or pecking order, but sensed she would be wise to keep this amiable and bottled up the impatience that had built up in her over the twenty minute delay. "I'm not a lawyer, I'm not up on legal terms, so I'm wondering what you mean by 'form of custody'. I've got no problem at the moment with prison conditions or anything like that. I just want a reasonable deal that will get my friends out."

"By form of custody, we are referring to the basis on which your friends may be held or made subject to controlled surveillance pre-trial. I understand that you have discussed these with the Inspector and the Sergeant and have some issues, which I'd invite you to clarify."

"We're talking untagged or unconditional bail, basically?"

"In simplistic terms, yes."

"It's about money firstly. There has been a little negotiation, but you're still talking about amounts that my friends can't possibly pay."

"Is there a secondly?

"There is, though it's only come up in the last hour or so. The charges that are hanging over my friends seem to be taking off like a forest fire. It started as damage caused by an over-enthusiastic party that got out of hand. That was easily compensated, but it was made worse, I can see, by one of your avatars getting an unintended faceful of cold curry. Now, all of a sudden, you're talking about terrorism, half the restaurant staff arrested and no-one getting access to solicitors. What's going on here?"

"Let's take these one at a time, the second point first. Our concerns over terrorism focus primarily on Jane Fredricksson. The others in the group are under investigation too, but they are not key players as things stand. I can't comment on the restaurant staff at this stage. In Ms Fredricksson's case, access to a solicitor is indeed out of the question, at least for the moment. Are you familiar with the Terrorism Act?"

"Sure, who isn't? What I can't see is what any of this has to do with terrorism."

"We cannot disclose the intelligence that leads us to this particular line of enquiry."

"Why would you be gathering intelligence about a hen party?"

"Serving the community can only be done through constant vigilance, identifying and neutralising its enemies."

"So you're saying that Jane is a public enemy. Why? And what exactly do you mean by 'neutralising' her?"

"The Police are not making any statements about Ms Fredricksson's character at this stage, Ms Trent. We are just saying that there is a prima facie case to put her under investigation."

"And neutralisation?"

"The measures normally taken to contain society's stakehold-refusers."

Jesus! "What about the first point?"

"The bail surety?"

She nodded.

"The purpose of the system for form of custody is to serve community need, and clearly we are not addressing that need if outcomes appear to be unaffordable. However, there is a need to balance community priorities with public risk, and you must appreciate that your friends are under investigation, however peripherally, in a matter of serious public concern, potentially an appreciable threat to public safety. Bearing that in mind, it should be possible to reach an arrangement that the parties concerned can agree to. I see no need as things stand for the further expense of involving the legal profession."

Why did he (and the Sergeant) have to blather on like this? At least muggers just got on with it. "That sounds fine, so long as the bail charges are realistic and there's a deal covering the whole party."

"I can't offer any deal at the moment with regard to Jane Fredricksson. Negotiations with regard to individuals under investigation in connection with terrorism need approval at Commander level." It was, she reflected, getting more, not less, out of hand. "You will need to return later in the week for us to give you an answer there. 'Phone or message us on Tuesday and we'll give you a time. With regard to the other seven, what figures are we looking at?" He looked down, with some distaste, at a well-worn piece of paper on which something was scribbled. He reflected a moment, then looked at her and said: "these seem to be about what I'd expect. What exactly is the problem, Ms Trent?"

"The charges are unaffordable, as I said before, and they're two to three times the going rate, as I'm sure any solicitor would be quick to point out."

"You are forgetting the terrorism dimension. That increases risk substantially and, inevitably the sum needed to offset that risk. But I don't see the need to rush into involving a solicitor. Bearing in mind your friends' modest circumstances and their relatively minor interest to the terrorism investigation, I can stretch a point and reduce the amounts to four, six and eight thousand. That's tagged, untagged and unconditional."

Viola's morale sagged. This was getting uncomfortably close to a final offer, she was still some way off the targets set by Jane and acceptance would still leave Jane herself imprisoned. "That's a reduction, but it's still way above the going rate."

"Ms Trent, you must understand that there is no 'going rate' as you term it for terrorism cases. For minor charges, a 'going rate' exists only in so far as the amounts for bail fall within certain broad ranges for standard circumstances." And what more standard than a hen party on a bender? thought Viola, though she said nothing. "You have been honest with us, and we appreciate that. If you are prepared to vouch personally for the pre-trial conduct of your friends – remember, that puts you on a charge if they misbehave – I will reduce each of the amounts by a further five hundred, but that is my final offer. You understand, of course, that we are talking about HEs?"

Viola had feared that. It made it a lot more expensive relative to the sterling currency that was all that most of them possessed. Sterling had been a soft currency for a couple of decades now; all official transactions used the Hard Euro. It had emerged from the collapse of American zone economies that followed as a knock-on a year or so after the Pakafiran debacle. She remembered all too well the effect it had had on her parents, as their savings were wiped out.

She pondered the offer for several seconds, then asked if she could see Jane and the others to discuss what had been said. She was ushered back through the virtual gateway and into Jane's cell, with the promise that the others would be brought there as requested.

"So, how's it go, then?"

"It's not great."

Viola described the negotiations and the offer she'd come out with. Jane listened intently, only interrupting with a vehement "Plonkers!" as she got to the terrorism investigation. Each sat, wrapped up in their own thoughts, for some minutes after she had finished. The cell offered no visual alternative or distraction, and the silence was only broken eventually by Jane saying "you did some serious negotiating there, considering what they're up to. I was expecting to have to pay in HEs anyway. I don't like this terrorism twist, though. They can't seriously think I'm into that sort of thing."

"I don't know, Jane, but they seem very determined to pin it to you. Mostly because it stops you getting a lawyer, I think."

"We'd better call the others."

Viola spoke briefly into the Virtualphone and a subdued hen party was reassembled, the room resizing to meet minimum space standards.

Jane gave the briefing this time, with a couple of minor corrections from Viola. The group found itself in a dilemma. They could stand together and demand a combined settlement before agreeing to anything. Or they could push ahead with negotiating the most favourable settlement for quick release, leaving Jane still imprisoned and dependent on a separate negotiation.

Opinion veered in favour of standing together. Jane re-orientated it. "You'd be mad to tie yourselves to me. You'll be in here for at least two days, and once you've been in too long to scrub the records you'll be on scrutiny and the charge will go up; they'll not be happy about losing any of their cut. I can't see you'll make any difference to the terrorism bullshit. As near as makes no odds, they've already said you're only part of that for as long as it takes to screw you for a premium charge."

Hastily, Viola got her word in. "If you're going for a settlement on these terms, it's got to be unconditional. The only way I'd vouch for the behaviour of you lot longer than about two minutes is to have you chained to the wall of my flat." But no-one had really considered anything but unconditional anyway.

Somebody asked about the waiters who'd been arrested. It looked as though they'd have to pay to get them out, but what might happen there was even less clear, so decisions were shelved until Jane's position was clearer.

Finally, Viola and a couple of the more forceful (and good-looking) members of the party resumed negotiations. With a mixture of feminine distress, fluttering of eyelids, smiles and surrender of a veep, 'to be held as evidence', the unconditional price was brought down to just over six thousand. Jane contacted her bank after promises of repayment, and seven of the party left immediately, free women, if substantially poorer than 24 hours previously.

Viola, much congratulated for her tough bargaining, suffered a nagging sense of having betrayed Jane, though she could not rationalise quite why. Jane herself seemed pleased: "cheer up Vile; I know it's blitzed your Sunday, but you've done wonders with those creeps who put us in here. See you in a couple of days, and we can get this all sorted." Viola smiled for Jane's sake and agreed, but something felt wrong. Turning down an invitation to a celebration drink with the newly freed jailbirds, she decided to talk it through with Carl, or maybe Joe. It needed another point of view.

Outside, the warmth and sunshine came as a shock; though little more than five hours had passed, it felt like days, stuck in the airless claustrophobia of the police station and cells, without access to natural light. Long-term prisoners must end up like mushrooms, she thought, clammy and devoid of a central nervous system. A drink with Sylv and the others hadn't appealed. Nothing to rejoice in from her view of it, and she really didn't want to risk re-running last night. But something to eat was another matter. And perhaps a consolatory

chocolate or two? She must remember to take Jane some when she
next saw her.

XIV

THE CHARTER

Alison had homed in on Karen's office as soon as afternoon working had resumed, only to find her out: somebody in a nearby office thought it was a half-day's leave. Impatient at the setback, Alison returned to retrieve the Internal Audit Summary for re-delivery on Monday, turned to leave and saw a briefcase and black umbrella on a small table near the door. Under the umbrella was a book, at which she sneaked a quick look. The cover just said AFFREM: Charter of Beliefs and Responsibilities. That sounded as fascinating as vomit, but the inscription at the bottom: Confidential: For the Sight and Use of Franchised Members Only looked more promising, a lead to covert activity. She didn't know what a franchised member was, but it seemed highly likely it didn't mean her. Still, they only had themselves to blame if they didn't make things clear, and a quick peek wasn't going to harm anyone, was it? Her senses sharpened for anyone's approach.

It was surrounded with the usual throat-clearing: version history, printing dates, forewords, acknowledgements, that Alison's job had trained her to skip past with minimal attention. As a result, she very nearly missed the line of thanks to Stephen Pendleton, 'Franchisee Extraordinary, without whose researches and unstinting efforts the final draft of this Charter could not have come to fruition.' So he was well in with whatever AFFREM might be. The Table of Contents was not very illuminating, though she noted that Beliefs were subdivided between Ancient and Modern, and Responsibilities between AFFREM Militant, AFFREM Enduring and AFFREM Triumphant. And there was a Banner Statement, to whose page she turned. It read:

'Proactively to uphold the ancient harmonic principles of freedom within tradition, market values within global evolutionary trends and performance values within sustainable contextual structures.'

Fine! She turned back to the Table of Contents. After Beliefs and Responsibilities, there was a long section on Exegetic Authorities (somebody had swallowed a dictionary), then Resolutions of Council and some appendices. She was about to turn to Appendix F Franchised Branches when there was the sound of a door opening from the room next door. As footsteps approached, she hastily replaced the book, tidied the umbrella and moved to the middle of the office, clutching the Internal Audit Summary, hoping she looked suitably nonchalant as the door into Karen's office opened and a tall man with broad shoulders and an air of command came through the door. He said "Hello" and fixed her with a gaze that invited an explanation of her presence. She launched hastily into her prepared line.

"I'm looking for Karen. Do you know when she'll be in?"

"Karen is on leave this afternoon."

Flustered, she rushed on: "Oh. It's not urgent, I was just here to deliver an Internal Audit report."

"You can leave it on her desk."

"Some of the details in it are confidential. Really it needs delivering to the person who needs to see it."

"In that case, I can take it myself. To whom do I have the pleasure of speaking?"

"Alison Somers. Internal Audit."

"Ranulph Fraserman." Alison handed the report over; it wouldn't do to get him to clarify who he was; she knew that perfectly well anyway.

"You'll find that it is safe to leave confidential reports in this office; it's often done. The office is locked out of hours."

Had he looked keenly at her when he said that, or was it her guilty imagination. "Thank you; I'll send Karen a message you've received it."

He nodded, smiled briefly and walked back into what presumably was his office: there was no name on the door. Alison exited swiftly, not even considering a second look at the Charter document. It didn't bear thinking what might happen if she were caught; he looked like a bruiser and that was his reputation; it would probably write off her job. He wasn't without charm, though. Not particularly good-looking; his features were a bit too square and regular to be interesting, but he was definitely a bit of a hunk. Had Karen ever given him a road test? Thinking of Karen, the re-visit would have to be about 'making sure she knew the audit report had been delivered'. It sounded a bit thin, but there was no helping it. This Charter looked worth investigating, and if anyone was likely to have seen more of it and be willing to tell, it was Karen.

XV

TAKING COUNSEL

Carl had been away in York over the weekend for a concert. This had extended itself to a lecture at the university in Beverley, so he was not due back until the Monday evening. Viola therefore descended on her military historian friend, Joe. She took Jane some books and chocolates, finding her bored and already dispirited, but glad for the company. Then she walked a large part of the way to Joe's flat in South Norwood, arriving late evening with the agreed take-away curry. She paused before ringing for entrance, to enjoy the view created by the sharp, urbanised, but tree-lined valley slope that fell away just beyond his housing block.

Inside, the flat was a mixture of the homely and the cheerless. Joe had organised the sitting room around the need to sit in warmth in agreeable surroundings, reading, listening to music or watching media productions; his study around his research work; his bedroom around the need to sleep in comfort. In any part of these rooms not devoted to these imperatives and elsewhere in the flat, things progressively deteriorated. More than one female companion had, over the years, simply refused to enter the kitchen. The general décor was acceptable, neither exactly clean nor exactly dirty, but redolent of neglect from an owner who very rarely stopped to think about it. Viola often itched to set about it with dustpan and brush, paint and some remedial building work, but life was short and it wasn't her flat, grateful as Joe would undoubtedly have been for the result, so she confined herself to intermittent suggestions, intermittently acted on. Hence, for example, the coffee table on which they now placed the plates of food: an upgrade from the previous resting place for such things: the carpet.

Food came first: Viola had found she had little besides a few oatcakes at home and, thankfully, a small chocolate bar, so was healthily famished; Joe had been working on an article all day and had forgotten to eat. The take-away demolished, Viola recounted her day in detail, omitting the veep: Joe, she knew, had old-fashioned views. He listened carefully and without interrupting to the end of the tale. "Basically, I'm frightened for Jane. She was very upbeat when I left her, but I really don't like the sound of this terrorism investigation, and what emerges over the next couple of days strikes me as likely to be unpleasant. I thought I'd ask you for advice, as you're generally clued up about this sort of thing. And I just need another, friendly point of view."

"It sounds as though you did the best you could in a difficult situation." There was a pause, and then he collected the plates and cartons and offered coffee and biscuits. Viola accepted readily; Joe liked both coffee and biscuits, arguably above all other sustenance, so they were among the few reliably good and fresh items of food in the flat. He left to brave the kitchen.

Returning, he asked: "You know the rights the police have on a terrorism case?"

"Not exactly. I think they can keep you for a fair amount of time, and they can exclude lawyers it seems, though I don't suppose they can stop friends talking to one."

"Ninety days, and, yes, they can stop you seeing a lawyer in all that time. Yes, you could talk to a lawyer, but they could only give you advice and charge you for it; there's nothing else they'd be capable of doing. Above all, the police don't have to give any reasons, before, during or after. They can't be got at unless you can prove they were acting maliciously, and you can rarely do that, because the intelligence information they say they're acting on isn't open to the public. Half the time it's not even open to the courts. They've mainly got to get the form of words right. I'd say your friend Jane's position looks difficult, I'm afraid."

"But why would they want to keep her. She's not doing anybody any harm; you know as well as I do that half the small restaurants of Peckham keep going on the payouts after her visits; it's no-one's idea of a social conscience, but at least nobody gets hurt."

"The WPC?"

"The robot avatar. Jane doesn't lie about things like that."

Joe smiled fleetingly. "She doesn't seem a serious criminal, it's true. What about the waiters?"

"The two serving yesterday, Mohammed and Farooz, I think they're called, have been there as long as I've been going to the restaurant, which is about two years. They're third-generation South Londoners and don't seem short of money or anything. I can't honestly believe they would get involved in terrorism. There is a new boy, who does odd tasks around the restaurant, but they probably cleared him off the premises as soon as they heard the police coming; he's only a kid, probably working underage. Besides, didn't you say, last time I saw you, that Afghanistan had been quiet for twenty years?"

"'Quiet' is relative, and some of the early terrorists were born here in Britain. But the Pakafiran debacle did wonders for morale in that area of the world; they lost a lot of the urge to attack the American sector. So it does sound a bit unlikely. Has your friend, Jane, shown any particular interest in the restaurant or its staff that you've intuited – you know, that famous feminine intuition." He smiled.

Viola did not return the smile. "Nothing that I've spotted. And Jane's restaurant visits, with the breakage money, are expensive even by her standards, so they can't happen too often. As far as I know, I go there a lot more myself, and I've never seen anything of note, involving Jane or not. Except the food, of course."

"I must give it a try when my stomach's feeling fit." He collected up the coffee cups, offered a retiring biscuit and braved the kitchen again, from where there was a succession of crashes and curses. He reappeared ten minutes or so later, with a wet patch on the front of his trousers. Viola would have helped, but the kitchen could be in a state to make you bring your meal back up, and politeness had its limits.

As he came back into the room, she said: "The police I met were a funny mix. Half of them were straight out of the detective soaps, even when they were virtual; they seemed to be trying to live up to a stereotype. "You've seen some of the soaps, haven't you?" Joe nodded. "The other half were more like professional managers. The sort of people who turn up to give a talk to the Fine Arts students on aligning themselves with business priorities in a global marketplace, or some other rubbish."

He turned from looking out of the window. "The management-style lot will have been negotiators. They work on commission, getting income where they can, particularly from the bail system. Nowadays, they're probably seen as more important than the real police staff; it's an odds-on bet that the Superintendent you met was from a negotiator background. The Inspector sounds like a genuine plod; he'd be relatively laid-back, because he'd be going no further with that background."

Sitting down slowly, with pauses for thought, he said: "One thing that really strikes me about this is the number of levels of seniority you got through. For the size of payoff for those who were released, you'd almost always get a Sergeant. Unless you just agreed to everything straight off. But the Sergeant and the WPC would have handled the lot. You've gone three levels higher, just for the asking. *And* they're supposed to be talking to the Commander. That's a hefty number of levels looking for a cut. The bail charges Jane told you about were a bit out of date, incidentally; you'd need to add another five hundred to a thousand to each figure now, which is why you got a perfectly good deal on the other seven, especially with terrorism being bandied around. But for somebody seriously fingered for that, there's no real standard." He paused; Viola said nothing. "They do, from what you were saying, seem to have identified your friend as quite wealthy?" Viola nodded. "The terrorism angle could just be a sting, I suppose, a way of building up the price of bail."

"Can't we do anything to stop them?"

"You could make a fuss publicly: demonstrations, that sort of thing. But it could backfire. The police have already given you an idea of the sort of things they'll talk about off the record to the press: the Afghanistan connection, the 'violent assault' on the police, the offshore bank accounts. All that matters much more than actual evidence. And it will put the activities of the Cowingdon in the spotlight. God knows what the media will make of that exactly, but it might not be good."

"But what about the police? They won't like having attention drawn to the way they use the bail laws."

"That's probably why they're being canny about how these will apply to Jane: they'll try to get you straitjacketed in negotiations before they reveal anything about terms and conditions. You're right in a way; they won't like attention on the bail racket. But they're unlikely to do anything in the early stages that can't simply be denied, your word against theirs. And they could retaliate in various ways."

"Such as?"

"Such as demanding that your other friends turn up to court to answer charges after all. You only buy your way out of a charge through unconditional bail on a gentleman's agreement; there's nothing contractual; anybody who causes trouble just gets the charge invoked."

Viola thought about it. "Sylv and the others might agree to take the risk on that. I can't see that Jane would have much problem in court; they can't have any evidence. I simply don't believe she's got any connection with terrorism."

"Courts can be eccentric in their judgements, but you're probably right; it's unlikely any terrorism charge would stick. But that's exactly why the police will make sure it never gets to court."

"How do you mean, they'll have to. They're part of the Justice system."

"Yes and no. They have ninety days before they need to do anything. A helpful judge and MP can extend that. She'll be under a lot of pressure in that time – and it's a long time in confinement, especially if the conditions deteriorate. At the end of it all, they can just let her go: no apologies, no charges, no potentially embarrassing court appearance."

"But they are still part of the Justice system. What about holding them to that?"

"They're part of the Justice system up to a point. As you've probably already guessed, most minor crimes are about the payoff. Only the stupid, or the very poor get convicted for those: look at the prison demographics. The police do haul people into court for major crimes of theft, or murder, though even these may still have their price. Just so long as it's not political. For anything involving politics or serious money, it's more useful thinking of them as the government's private army. As armies often do, they make supplementary income opportunistically from citizens who stray too close. As to holding them to anything, the problem is how?"

"Using the media?"

Joe got up and looked out of the window for a long moment. He turned back and faced her. "In your position, I'd fear the media more than the police and both more than the Justice system. The police have to follow some rules, some of the time, even on the political and money stuff; the media don't realistically have to follow any. It's very difficult to predict what line they might want to take if they got interested in your story, and if the facts don't fit the line, they'll quite likely just invent a few."

She didn't immediately respond, and he continued. "The police, if it comes to that, will use the media for their own side of the battle, and they have a large, highly professional media relations department with useful contacts everywhere." He turned sideways on to the window. "It's not impossible to win a battle like that; people sometimes do, but you have to be realistic." He turned back to look at her directly. "The odds would be very heavily against you."

They stayed still, in silence, for what felt like several minutes, before Viola collected her thoughts. "You make it sound hopeless, like you're saying we should just give up and dump Jane in it."

"I'm just trying to steer you away from anything quixotic."

"So can we do anything, then?"

"You should negotiate hard. Assuming they don't really think they've got a terrorist connection, there will be a price to settle on. It might be quite expensive, but you can aim to bring it inside a range that your friend Jane can pay."

"We don't seem to have much to negotiate with, though, from what you say."

"That's not true. The biggest problem with the actions we talked about is what happens if you actually carry them out. From the police side, what they'd ideally like is a quick negotiation and a swift payout to everyone concerned, with no complications. If you actually go to the media, they'll throw everything they've got at you, but that's expensive and difficult for them, and they'll probably be prepared to reduce the take to avert the possibility. Obviously, you'd have to dangle it in front of them fairly subtly. They will have other expenses too, such as the cost of holding her. Virtual environments take a lot of power. And there's the cost of the negotiators. They'll put in a fair amount of time on this, because it will look like offering a fat commission, but they'll be needed for other projects, so it can't go on forever.

Joe offered more coffee and biscuits and was turned down, after which they sat in silence for some minutes. Then he added: "the number of people involved is an advantage to you too: it makes it harder for them to keep a consistent story that can't be faulted if it ever does get into the media."

Viola took this in also. "So you're saying we're to keep it to negotiation if humanly possible, try to keep it looking complicated and long-winded to the police and give them the impression we might just do something impulsive they'd prefer us not to."

"Yes, that's it, essentially."

"It sounds scary, though. I've very little experience of this sort of thing. Could you help at all?" She allowed herself to look as she felt: forlorn and not far from tears. It wasn't a case of feminine wiles; neither of them fancied the other in a sexual way, as far as she could tell; they were friends, pure and simple and in many ways that was much better. But a certain vulnerability might help the appeal.

"Viola, I'd like to help, but I can't here and now, other than advice. I've too much on. In any case, I think you'd be better off alone, at least to start with. Don't make it explicit what resources you might have supporting you. The more you pitch in, the less naïve the dangled threats of media involvement and so on will look, and the more they'll ramp up their own team. If you want somebody to accompany you, why not take one of the seven who've just been let out. Two can be better than one for observing what's going on, and they'll be a familiar face; you won't have to explain why they're there."

"I suppose so. If it does go on a long time, can you consider getting involved then?"

"I'd think you'd want to aim to get this wrapped up round about next weekend: that'll spin it out long enough to make them think, but not so long they give up. If it's not finalised by then, I should have a bit more time, and we can see if I could do any more. If you need to talk things over in the meantime, I can always make time for that; just give me a ring."

"Thanks, Joe. I knew it would be really helpful talking to you." She looked out of the window, still dangerously close to tears: she must avoid this; she was going to have to be very controlled to be useful to Jane, but it looked like a tough assignment at the moment."

"Don't worry too much about the negotiating; experience only goes so far. You've done extremely well so far, with the other seven young ladies. You need to know what you want, backed up with a good brain and a quick wit, and you've got all of those."

Viola was unconsoled, but this did give her a fraction more appetite for the inevitable return to one of Denmark Hill's more desolate meeting rooms. As she stared through the picture window across the view that was the flat's chief glory, a small cloud, comically shaped in a way not quite definable, strolled into view from stage right, gradually thickening and darkening with just a suggestion of rain. She and Joe watched, in companionable silence, its slow progress to centre stage in a theatre imperceptibly darkening, minute by minute, as the daylight faded.

She remembered the other topic that had been worrying at her mind and seized the diversion gratefully. "Another subject entirely. Have you ever heard of the Ancient Fellowship of Franchised Reamers? I came across it in my research, but there wasn't much on it, and it sounds the type of thing you might know about."

"You mean useless trivia?"

"Something like that." She grinned.

"Well yes, Missy, I have actually, though I don't know much." He paused, savouring the view.

"Well, come on then!"

He raised his right hand in a mock salute. "It's a name that cropped up several times in the records on Pakafiran. The American records; the English ones are closed for the next seventy years or so. They seemed to be a type of pressure group: very secretive; believe in tradition, driven in some way by the global market."

"But surely the global market idea is fairly new: the last fifty years or so?"

"Depends how you view it. Some see Genghis Khan as a pioneer of the free market in labour and real-estate."

"Or King Canute as the free-market hero of wave power, I suppose. So are they ancient, then?"

"Probably not; that's most likely pure cod. I've not come across them in any previous records."

"So not like the Knights Templar?"

"You've been reading too many popular works of fiction."

Viola flushed slightly. Some of her reading had been terribly persuasive, but even at the time of reading she knew better than to discuss it with Joe. "So just a boys' club operating from somebody's back bedroom?"

"A bit more powerful than that, I think; their people turned up at some fairly high-level meetings. And they seemed to have an influence on Management Education, for what that was worth. But you could be right in one respect. All of the names that were ever mentioned were male. That might be part of the tradition jag. Back to the good old days when women were nice and in their place and all that." His face remained serious and expressionless.

Viola started to rise to the bait, but caught herself. "Maybe they just have really small dicks. What about the 'Reamers' bit of the name? That doesn't seem to fit with anything."

"I don't know." He strode over to a bookcase, pulled a large volume down and opened it. " Yes. A reamer is a boring tool. Not to be mixed with boredom, in case you were wondering."

He replaced the dictionary, Viola observing with amazement. Nobody else she knew used anything but the virtual libraries for reference queries. A thought then struck him. "Actually, there could just be a musical connection. A couple of their people got mixed up in incidents with musicians. One of them shot a woman playing an Oud. Because, he said, it was untraditional for women to be allowed to play that particular instrument. It clearly flummoxed the investigators; you'd expect that sort of thing from the local fanatics, but not one of ours."

"That's awful. What happened to the woman?"

"She died."

"But that was murder. What was done about it?"

"A reprimand and repatriation. Don't look shocked; it's the way things were done there, probably one of the reasons it failed so spectacularly. He got more than some did for that sort of thing."

Viola remained silent, looking unconvinced. Trust Joe to know something that the Search Library hadn't picked up, though. She felt she would never fathom the extent of his knowledge of, seemingly, anything.

It was dark outside, time to be getting back. Her overriding wish as she thanked Joe, let herself out of the flat and walked to the tram was for sleep, a sleep she fell into swiftly once she had navigated herself, on auto-pilot, back to Quiberon Road.

XVI

NEXT MOVES

I was in a state of shock for a day or two afterwards. For me, it was so unusual for a hen to do something like that; they mostly make coyness a way of life. Well, yes, of course I tried the veep. What did I think? A gentleman doesn't discuss these things, as my father would say.

What to do about another meeting got me in a muddle. I felt I had to have a reason. But in the end I thought, sod it, just ring her up. I did work out a formula for what to say when she answered, but she's got quite a crisp, though not unfriendly style on the 'phone, so most of it got driven out of my head when she answered. And it was all very straightforward: she was away that weekend, but she said yes to Monday evening. We fixed to meet in the Oast House at seven. I had a drink with Paul to celebrate, though I didn't tell him about the veep, as he was pretty down about Janet.

The great Stephen Pendleton mystery is still just that, though I can't say I've been thinking hard, or losing sleep over it. It doesn't sound, from what Karen said, that he's on anything like the bosom pal terms with the Vice Chancellor that the Ancillary Music people seemed to think. I haven't worked out what the deeply unfriendly meeting might have been about. It could be Stephen Pendleton himself was the one who was to be made an example of. It didn't seem likely, though. If he was for the chop, that would have been the meeting. Everyone would have heard by now. The Vice Chancellor doesn't get himself slowed down by things like procedure, from what I've heard. Maybe the VC thought he was being too harsh or not harsh enough. Probably not harsh enough, knowing the VC's reputation. Even if he is a 'sweetie'.

Over the weekend, I ran into Ali. The thing with Karen doesn't affect what I feel for her, of course, though it does make her attitude a lot easier to bear. Anyway, she suddenly seemed willing to talk to me again.

"Hello, stranger."

"Hi!"

She kept a kind of cordon sanitaire between us: standing just beyond reaching distance, but she did at least look at me while she was speaking.

"What are you up to these days?"

"Oh, this and that. There's been a lot on at work." There hadn't, but it's what you say.

"I hear you're going with Karen."

It must have been Paul told her that, exaggerating as usual. "Depends what you mean by 'going with.' I've met her once or twice." Actually, that was once, but I counted in Monday. That'd be what Ali and her audit friends call an accrual.

"Oh. If you're feeling gallànt at the moment, I'll let you stand me a coffee."

Well I did, of course. There was a coffee shop nearby, we settled into one of their booths once we'd bought the necessary. "Well then, am I forgiven yet?"

"How do you mean, forgiven?" I said.

"Well, you've been avoiding me for the past few weeks, haven't you?"

The cheeky bint! "I was told I was under a ban, if you've not forgotten."

"You need to lighten up, Tad. But am I forgiven, anyway?"

"You are, I suppose, if I am."

"Well, you're on probation. Depends if you're a good boy."

I wasn't going to win this. "So what have you been getting up to in all this time before being forgiven and putting me on probation?"

"That sounds complicated. What have you been getting up to, apart from chasing women?"

"As if!" I said bitterly.

"Karen, then?"

"We've only talked to each other once." I remembered the accrual. "Twice."

"Shame. I thought she might make you behave."

The conversation hung in stalemate. She sat there waiting for me to say something, looking slightly disappointed when I didn't.

We left. I said I was going into Camberwell for some shopping, hoping she'd be going that way too, but she muttered something about Nunhead and shot off in the opposite direction, throwing "see you around" over her shoulder.

XVII

GATHERING INTELLIGENCE

On Sunday afternoon, Ben recollected the promise he'd given to Carl, to contact Paul Fairley. He wrote it down, to be seen to on Monday. Monday brought more invigilating, so it wasn't until the late afternoon that he waylaid Paul after a lecture, ostensibly to remind him of an overdue essay. Paul was monosyllabic, not at all his usual self. Janet had chosen that lunchtime to rid herself of his attentions, citing his desertion from the Körthofer workshop incident as just and sufficient cause. She had delivered this in a calm and measured manner, intending to leave no hope of a change of mind, and Paul had spent the afternoon feeling like a deflated balloon, albeit one with severe heartache. Then, too, there was Tad's revelation of the prospective date with Karen. He was the only one left out of the game. Who cared about essays?

Ben, sensing his mood, asked him what was the matter. "The girl in the VC's office?" Paul looked at him with an air of disdain. Karen? I've nothing going with her. She's Tad's."

"One of your friends?"

"Yeah."

Further enquiry seemed stymied. "Well, I won't trouble you further. I need the essay by Thursday; best of luck with the personal life!"

He didn't seem too severely down, Ben thought, while trying to work out what to do next. Seeking out Karen and trying out his charm would be the obvious course, but Alison and Atinuke was quite enough complication to be going on with. It occurred to him that Alison might know Karen. Meanwhile, Atinuke was expecting him in an hour or so. He decided on finding something to eat. Evenings with Atinuke were not about food, and for sessions like last Friday's he needed sustenance.

Alison found Karen in her office this time, handing a file to a harried-looking member of the academic staff. Alison vaguely recognised him: from Visual and Plastic Arts. Actually, she thought, wasn't he VAPA's boss? He didn't look very commanding, though. He scuttled out, pursued by Karen's studied indifference. She looked across to Alison and said, with a slight smile "Hi!"

"I just wanted to tell you that I gave this month's Internal Audit Summary to your boss on Friday."

"I saw it in the Filing tray this morning. It didn't look like he'd spotted anything revolutionary."

"It'd be worrying if he did. Just so long as everyone official knows it's there."

There was a brief pause while Alison studied her nails with critical enquiry. Karen knew that Alison had not just come about the report. Alison knew that Karen knew she had not just come about the report. Karen too was pretty sure that Alison knew this. The pause was not hostile, though. Karen recognised Alison as a kindred huntress and, on balance, liked her style. Alison admired Karen's (relative) directness.

Alison spoke first. "I like that top."

"Thanks."

"Where did you get it?"

"Spiro and Maddox."

Alison nodded.   Spiro & Maddox had sure-footed back to mainstream rag trade a year or so ago.   She studied her nails again. "When I was in here Friday, I met your boss.   He seemed quite nice."

"Mr Fraserman.   He's not bad.   You fancy him or something?"

Alison giggled.   "No, of course not.   It's just I expected something a bit more ancient, a monster.   If he's not bad, does that mean you ever … you know?"

"Don't be daft.   I've got more sense.   Sadie hadn't, and look what happened to her."   Sadie, one of Karen's more short-lived predecessors, had let her affection for her boss get the better of her after a drinks reception one summer day, some said on the floor, others on the table.   Summarily transferred to a job of equivalent rank in VAPA, on the grounds of "needs of the business", she had been rationalised along with the rest of the department shortly after.

"He was carrying something he seemed determined to keep out of sight."

Karen snorted.   "Probably a dirty magazine."

"I've never heard of one called 'Charter', have you?   That's about all I could see of it.   There were no pictures or anything on the front."

So that's where it got to, and that's what she'd come about, Karen thought.   "Why the interest?"

"Just curiosity.   He was quite straightforward in the way he spoke, but he definitely wasn't straightforward about this charter, whatever it was. He seemed to regret me having seen it."

"I can't really help you.   There was something with 'Charter' in the title on his desk earlier that day.   He was using it in a meeting, I think, but I only glanced at it quickly as I saw to coffee for them.   Do you know anything about AFFREM, then?"

"Why, did you see that in it?"

"That, or something like it."

"It's a society like the Masons, I think."

Maybe that was why the American was about so much, Karen thought. It wasn't like Mr Fraserman having someone telling him what to do, though.

Alison asked: "Do you mind my asking what the meeting was about?"

Karen thought about this a little, then brought the appointments diary up on the screen. "'Organisational Dynamics', whatever that's supposed to be. It was just Mr Fraserman and that American, Stephen Pendleton."

Great! She'd got something there, though it didn't make much sense to her. At that moment, heavy footsteps sounded at the bottom of the stairs leading up to Karen's office. "Him," Karen said, looking uncharacteristically guilty: "Mr Fraserman".

Alison did not want to be found by the VC, unsummoned, in Karen's office, two working days in succession, no matter how innocent an explanation could be concocted. She exited quickly on light feet down the back stairs, avoiding the mud patch outside, but forced to smile and improvise "Oh, I must have come out the wrong way, could you show me where the main square is" to the swarthy man of stocky build standing outside, with whom she had almost collided. He grunted something incomprehensible and pointed her along the grass towards the far corner of the building.

XVIII

YORK

Flicking the final pages of the clarinettist's music, with his fingertips and at arm's length, Carl moved across to turn, two-handed, the harp's large and elaborate score, before pirouetting to complete the turn for the piano. The pianist got his final page only just in time. A wave of applause broke out as the musicians trudged through the coda, Carl taking a series of bows in time with the music.

He left the stage as the manucussionist handed over the last pair of drumsticks and took, generally unheeded, her bow. The musicians played to the end, expertly, but unacknowledged and largely unheard; people were already moving from their seats and breaking into conversation, clearly enthusiastic about this visit from a London paginist virtuoso: a London base remained the only route to credibility with the punters.

Taking a shower back at the hotel, his thoughts ran on the performance. Overall, it had gone well, though the recent tendency to get almost behind the action, as with that final turn for the pianist, was worrying. Not that, as a Paginist, he had any shortage of things to worry about. Paginatorics nowadays was inherently artificial, for one thing. Musicians had had perfectly good electronic displays of scores and parts for thirty years. They didn't use traditional printed music when they were out of sight, producing time-slot music or soundpaper or whatever. And much of the music he performed was specially written to display his skills. Traditional, purely S-Class music had a habit of not co-ordinating itself properly, even with skilled re-editing, so that batteries of paginists were needed to keep things going. That was all right for big spectaculars with big budgets, but uncommercial for anything else. Some productions were known to place a proportion of their musicians out of sight, the better to turn their own pages, but he had never compromised his artistic integrity to that extent. Ah well, he thought as he started dressing, he might be getting a little old for the standards he demanded, but there should be a few more years in it yet and a few more in the art form too.

He thought of ringing Viola, but dinner with the concert promoters gave only a short turn-round time, so he delayed this once again, finally speaking to her some time after 11 o'clock that night. She was already in bed, half asleep and still suffering the day's discouragements. Catching the flatness of her mood, Carl asked if she was feeling all right, and was there a problem?

"I'm worried about Jane."

"Your linguist friend?"

"Yes. She's been taken into custody by the police, and they seem to be trying to bring terrorism charges against her. I'm trying to help, but not very successfully so far, and I can't really work out what's going on."

It meant very little to Carl; his working life had been first about playing the piano then, more successfully, about Paginatorics. Terrorism as a term conjured up bearded fanatics, and bore little relation to the people he met day to day. "What do the charges come from? Surely they haven't just pulled her off the streets at random?"

Viola gave an edited summary of events so far. She had never talked about the Cowingdon's activities to Carl, out of a sense that he would disapprove, and she took care now to detach herself from the plate and food-throwing stage of the evening.

Carl listened with mixed feelings. He couldn't really understand the point of the plate-throwing and so forth, and he could definitely understand why the police had gone round and stopped it: Viola hadn't elaborated on the Cowingdon's history, of which he knew nothing. On the other hand, he couldn't see what lay behind the terrorist charge at all, other than a vague, largely semantic, connection with Afghanistan, where the beards traditionally seemed to grow longest. Viola's friend was clearly in quite disproportionate trouble for some minor affray.

"It sounds like the police might be preparing to demand a lot of bail money. Can your friend pay that?"

"Maybe, but I think she might refuse on principle if it's too much. Jane can be very stubborn on things like that."

"Couldn't you threaten to make a fuss, go to the media, that sort of thing."

Viola described the meeting with Joe, causing Carl a twinge of jealousy. "So the problem is, if we cause trouble now, they can just drag eight of my friends into court and give them minor criminal records. Not to mention digging their heels in over Jane. Once they call you a terrorist they seem to be able to do anything they like."

"Mmn."

"How has it got like that? Do you know?"

"The terrorism laws?"

"Yes."

"Not really, not in detail. But there have been a lot of Acts of Parliament. I think it's been a gradual drift to where we're at. It strikes me you should try negotiation first. Before you get bogged down in legalities."

"Joe said the same. I think you're both right. It's just I have this feeling we've abandoned Jane somehow: that we should have stuck together and insisted on a deal for all of us."

"It doesn't sound as if they were offering one, though, does it? And mightn't they have just treated that as 'making trouble'."

"I suppose so. It's just a feeling."

"I'd sleep on it; you've had a rough weekend. Things always look worse when you're tired. And you're getting good reviews for your negotiating, aren't you?"

Viola would have preferred no attempts at reassurance; she had every intention of sleeping on it. But it was kind of Carl to try. "We'll just have to see how it goes; I can't do much until the police come back, anyway."

"If there's anything I can do to help?"

Just being here, Carl, she thought; that would be the greatest help. But he couldn't be expected to mess up arrangements for a prestige concert and lecture just to be around for her. "No, I'll be fine. Thanks anyway. See you tomorrow."

"I'll be round as soon as I'm back."

The call terminated, Carl found sleep difficult. Though the details of what had happened remained sketchy, Viola's unease had left him with a sense of threat, of looming danger, quite different from the familiar risks of indulging in S-Class activities. After a couple of hours of highly restless relaxation and preparation for sleep, he gave up, got out of bed, sat in the hotel's close-fitting armchair and read, calming and finally achieving sleep as the darkness outside grayed and cast shadows across bed, chairs, desk, wardrobe, mini-bar, clustered in the standard-format room.

XIX

DAWN CHORUS

I woke up to darkness, disorientation and some confusion. Plus a real sense of relaxation. Plus, also, an almighty, almost painful erection, leading an independent life from the relaxation. It took several seconds to grasp why I was disorientated: the bed wasn't mine; it was a lot more comfortable for one thing. Then I realised I was not alone in it. Somebody was beside me, fast asleep, snuffling gently. Then I remembered. Karen. We had met for the drink; conversation had been easy; I accompanied her back home and got invited in; it was made clear enough that she had expected company in bed and that's where we'd ended up. Just like that. I moved across the bed slightly to lie touching her and she stirred and rolled over, coming to rest with the erection jabbing into her thigh, which woke her. She reached out and touched and we put it to use, before I fell asleep again.

Waking a second time, it was just starting to get light, which was fortunate, as I was in urgent need of a pee and had no idea where anything was. A quick prowl around quite a small house settled that, and I returned to the bedroom, lying back down before thinking to look at the time. It was 4.55am, so no need to hurry anywhere. Karen was sleeping steadily. Best to get back to sleep myself, but I didn't feel sleepy for the moment.

So I lay quietly, thinking about things. Karen and everything. It was hard to take in; everything so difficult and slow with other hens, notably Ali, but so straightforward in this case. I hadn't set out on the date with any thought of getting Karen into bed. That rate of progress had always been unthinkable; just getting to know her a bit better and arranging to see her again was as far as ambition had stretched. It might be different for blokes like Wayne; for me, that's as good as it normally gets. Actually, I'd never got beyond the veep stage before, and that only with tremendous effort, so this was a revelation.

Whoever said "Better than the real thing!" on the commercial veep adverts was lying, though it's a lie that's taken in a lot of people. Everyone seems to see the 'real thing' as messy, unhygienic and risky. Well, it may be, but more fool them.

As the light strengthened, a bird started singing. Not one of the starlings that occasionally do a few minutes of videophone rings, tram bells and police klaxons in the middle of the night, just when you're trying to sleep and really need a concert. No, it was just an unvaried trilling, but after a couple of minutes another bird joined in with a different song, a basic 'cheep-cheep' sound, but with a more definite musical pitch. In quite a short time, a whole army of birds was competing. The strange thing was how wonderfully it all went together; if you got a crowd of human musicians playing a few dozen instruments that way, the result would be hideous.

And all of a sudden that poem came into my head, and I saw what it was about. It was one that a literature-freak tutor had tried to make us build a game around for one of last year's projects. I don't know why he'd bothered. The game had turned out dull, because we couldn't make much of the poem; for one thing, it was written in an old style of English, and we could barely understand what it said. But bits of it came back to me now as something straight out of life. As I say, I couldn't remember much of it at the time, just the first two lines and odd snatches here and there. But I looked it up later:

> 'Me thoughte thus that it was May
> And in the dawning where I lay
> Me mette thus in my bed all naked
> And looked forth, for I was waked
> With smalle fowles a great heap
> That had affrayed me out of sleep
> Through noise and sweetness of their song'

I'd already been awake when it started, but let's not get literal.

It goes on:

'And sungen evereach in his wise
The most solemne service
By note, that ever man, I trow,
Had heard. For some of them sung low,
Some high, and all of one accord.'

One more line I did remember at the time got me out of bed again quietly, to look out of the window to see if it was also true:

'Ne in all the welkin was a cloud.'

But there was no shortage of those.

Gradually, the light increased and the chorus lessened, settling down to a constant background I'd normally not have noticed. At some point I fell asleep again, to find myself being shaken by the shoulder and Karen saying "come on, I need to be out of here in half an hour." It was just coming up to quarter to eight, so I needed to get a move on too. I was due at a workshop at nine, and I had to get back home first, though that wasn't too far away. She was wearing just a skimpy dressing gown that only just covered the tops of her legs and put ideas into my head and elsewhere immediately, but she pushed me away after a quick hug and pointed out the bathroom.

Breakfast was mostly silent and a bit awkward, because I knew I would be leaving the house with her in a few minutes and didn't know quite what would happen after that. I certainly didn't want things just to end there. So I said "when can we get together again?"

"Get together for a drink or for bed?"

I laughed. "What do *you* think?"

She smiled, with an air of Fifteen-All. "Would this evening do, then?"

This evening would do really well. It wasn't as if I'd be doing anything, apart from going to the pub with friends. "Yeah, I'm free this evening."

"Seven o'clock round here? I'll cook you dinner."

"Sounds great! What would you like to drink?"

"White wine." She didn't even pause to think. Then she added: "The deal is, you'll have to cook for me sometime."

Oh well. "I'll try. Would taking you out for a meal do instead?"

She made clicking noises with her tongue. "It'll do to be going on with."

We cleared the dishes and made a quick exit, Karen in a smart work outfit, me in the smart (but now rather creased) get-up from yesterday evening. By unspoken arrangement, we parted company, with a peck on the cheek, at the beginning of Rye Lane.

XX

NEGOTIATING

The call from the police finally came on Tuesday evening, requesting Viola's presence at a meeting at Denmark Hill early on the Wednesday morning. It relieved the sense of stagnation that had afflicted Viola since Sunday.

Carl had returned on the Monday evening to find her preoccupied and directionless. Sex, he found, was still on the agenda, but music was definitely off; she just felt too listless and dispirited to raise sufficient enthusiasm for the couple of hours working on the Franck that they had promised themselves. It had nothing to do with the risk it entailed: music demanded a certain passion and joie de vivre that had temporarily been driven out of her system.

But the promise of the meeting, though it forecast another long day splitting hairs with semi-automata, at least meant that things were moving again and renewed her spirits, to Carl's delight. He agreed to take over her morning lectures and rang Ben to take over his workshop; Ben had no more than an invigilator's meeting, early. The afternoon would have to be dealt with ad-hoc, but she was due only at a seminar, for which she was a supporting rather than principal speaker. She rang Sylv, who had agreed to go along as an observer and fixed to meet.

The biggest problem, as always, was what to wear. The Commander might put in an appearance, though this seemed unlikely; most likely she'd meet the Superintendent again. Carl suggested a balaclava and was withered with a look. She needed to appear business-like, somebody to be taken seriously, but she was determined not to fall into just following their lead and accepting wholesale their way of doing things. There was also the matter of temperature. Generally hot, fine weather outside had to be balanced against the air-

151

conditioned police station - simultaneously coldish and stuffy - and the dry coolness of the virtual environment.

It ended up as a relatively severe, dark skirt, sensible but not unfashionable shoes, a light but smart and shaped cotton top with long sleeves and a cashmere cardigan, sufficiently thin and light to be squashable into her handbag. It was plausibly the sort of outfit she might wear to work, but effectively made her look a little older than her thirty four years and, she hoped, more formidable.

Carl saw her off the following morning with a "Give 'em hell!" which elicited another look, before she kissed him and turned to go. He had offered to walk with her at least part of the way, but she preferred to have the time to herself, preparing mentally for what was ahead. She took a slightly more roundabout route to avoid meeting colleagues or friends, joined Sylv by the agreed pub in billionaire's row and arrived at Denmark Hill on the dot at a quarter to nine, prepared for anything.

Which, to start with, was nothing. The avatar receptionist spoke to somebody, directed her to a waiting area, and wait they did, for another twenty-five minutes. She went back over to the receptionist. "There seems to be a problem. I had an appointment for a quarter to nine. If the person I'm to meet hasn't turned up, we'll need to set another time; I've got other things to do."

The avatar looked apologetic, spoke again to somebody and within less than a minute, Inspector Fox walked in, negotiating the furniture like a well-trained bull in a china shop, greeting her with apologies for the effects of a traffic hold, though it was something about a helicopter, so not very convincing.

The sergeant and Superintendent Osler were in the meeting room, the same one as before. There was also a man in civilian clothes: fairly nondescript apart from ears that came almost to a point at the top: obviously a policeman of some sort, because he was wearing a suit, which nobody else did nowadays. He wasn't introduced: crassness or more psychological one-upmanship? The Superintendent opened the proceedings.

"Thank you for taking the trouble to come here at such short notice Miss Trent

"*Ms* Trent."

"Ms Trent of course, I'm sorry and …?"

"Sylvia Smith."

"We have called the meeting to discuss the case of *Ms* Jane Fredricksson" (he looked at Viola, she nodded) "and felt that with your early involvement in what has happened your presence here would be of value."

Of great value to them if she could help get Jane to cough up, Viola thought. "I'd like to make it clear that I have no interest in getting more involved in police procedure than is unavoidable. I'm here simply to disentangle my friend from this spider's web of terrorism charges you seem to be trying to knit around her."

The other three remained impassive, but the Superintendent looked pained. "I think you must understand, Ms Trent the seriousness of the charges that are being investigated."

"It's serious only for the person you've banged up without good reason. Terrorism is only an offence if you're involved in it, not if it's something the local police have dreamed up for lack of anything better to do." This was not going well; she was getting angry. For God's sake, she thought, shut up!

"You will need to let us be the judges of that for the time being. I can assure you that all measures being taken are in the fullest sense necessary." The Inspector looked as though he was about to say something less mealy-mouthed, but he was silenced by a look from The Fourth Policeman.

She remained silent, as did Sylv. "Shall we return to the subject of the meeting?" No-one dissented. "Inspector"

The Inspector, let out on a provisional leash, unfolded his legs sat up a little straighter and read from small bundle of papers and a notebook in his hand. "Jane Fredricksson was apprehended in the company of seven other young women last Friday night, by …" A detailed account followed, up to and including the release on bail of the seven and the discussions with the Commander. There was little to glean from the latter; they were mostly exchanges of high-flown sentiments about 'primary duty of care to our society', 'need to protect the public' and 'neutralisation of stakehold-refusers'. He concluded "Ms Fredricksson's friend, Ms Viola Trent" (nodding in her direction) "has requested discussion of bail conditions, and Superintendent Mike Osler' (with a nod in his boss's direction) "has been authorised by the Commander to discuss what arrangements might be possible given the circumstances of the case." He relaxed, folded his legs and relapsed into inscrutable boredom.

Sylv started to take notes, but was stopped by the Sergeant. "What is said at this meeting is restricted under the terms of the Terrorism Act, Ms Smith."

There was a silence, which Viola eventually felt driven to break. "So what happens now?"

The Superintendent nodded at the Sergeant. "You will recall that we withheld bail in the first instance for Ms Fredricksson, on the grounds that there was prima facie evidence of her involvement in terrorist offences."

"I recall you saying that. It's a load of cock, but, yes, you said it."

The Fourth Policeman suddenly came to life. "Ms Trent, if I may give you a word of advice?"

"You may, but first things first. You weren't introduced. Who are you and why are you here at this meeting?"

He held out an identity card for viewing. It had an unmistakable photograph and identified him as John Doe, a Special Projects Co-ordinator with the Office of Security & Co-operation. John Doe: wasn't that a legal fiction? Not that his real name mattered much, she supposed.

"You are not experienced in matters of this sort?" Viola remained studiedly neutral. "I shall take that as an affirmative. Then it's important to point out that your conduct in this meeting so far has demonstrated an attitude problem. This will not help in achieving a satisfactory outcome for your friend. Do you understand what I am saying?"

Sylv exhaled forcibly and muttered something that sounded like "Bloody men!"

"So what does all this mean? Attitude or no attitude, it's for you to say what you're thinking of doing about bail. If you won't, I guess I'll have to see what others say."

"I'm not sure I catch your meaning Ms Trent." (The Superintendent)

"I'm not sure I do myself. If the authorities want to chuck my friend Jane into a virtual dungeon for no precise reason that they can say and leave her there to rot, and none of us have the power to stop them doing it, then I suppose we'll need to get views from the unappointed authorities instead."

"Like the media", Sylv said.

"Or whatever. I might have attitude, but you lot are more like a brick wall. I need an answer to what this meeting's about, so over to you."

There was a brief silence, then the Superintendent, after conferring silently with The Fourth Policeman, said "you should be aware, Ms Trent, that the media are a double-edged sword. I would not let your inexperience take you down that route too hastily. There is, in any case, no need to do so. We at the police take our responsibilities to the citizen very seriously, and your friend, Ms Fredricksson is a citizen too, irrespective of what may be alleged against her. It is only in the most serious circumstances that citizens are held in custody without charge for a prolonged period, and our feeling is that some arrangement should be possible in this case."

Well that was another six inches forward. Viola said nothing and continued to look as neutral as she was able. Sylv reassumed her role as observer, doing her best to memorise what passed.

The Fourth Policeman leaned forward. "It is the opinion of the OSC that, although the terrorism allegations under investigation are of a serious nature, Ms Fredricksson's precise involvement remains uncertain at this stage. As a consequence, the possibility exists of release on bail subject to stringent conditions."

"Which are?"

The Fourth Policeman disregarded the question. "In the circumstances, both tagged and untagged bail are clearly inappropriate. The former is too easily abused and circumvented by the organisations that we believe we are dealing with here."

"Such as? You can't seriously mean the hen party or 'Memories of Kandahar'?"

"I'm not at liberty to reveal to you the nature or identity of the organisations referred to."

"Jesus!" Oh dear, attitude again!

He let it go.   "Untagged bail suffers from the problem that supervision takes place within the context of a charge, but no charge currently exists.   The one possible option that leaves us with is unconditional bail. Do you understand me so far, Ms Trent?"

"I understand the words you are saying, yes."

"Good. Then we need to progress the discussions on the basis of an agreed figure for unconditional bail. What is your view on that Ms Trent?"

"You know my views on reasonable amounts from our discussion on Saturday."   The Fourth Policeman looked at the Sergeant and gestured. The Sergeant passed over some papers, which The Fourth Policeman read, frowning. "I'm afraid the level of figure you were discussing here is completely inappropriate for what we are considering now." Turning to the Superintendent: "could we discuss this privately?" The Superintendent nodded and they left the room, accompanied by the Sergeant.

Viola, Sylv and the Inspector fell into a brooding silence for several minutes. Viola thought about the Fourth Policeman's accent: very slight, but it was there; about his only distinguishing feature apart from the ears. Maybe Welsh, she thought. Jane would know. She became aware of the Inspector speaking to her: "… wouldn't wind up the ostrich-shaggers if I were you: can land you in real trouble."

"Ostrich-shaggers?"

"The spooks. OSC?"

"What does shagging have to do with it?"

"Depends where you bury your head when things get difficult. I don't wind them up myself, however tempting it gets."

"I seem to be getting advice from all corners of the police force today. Pity that none of it does anything for Jane."

"Aye, well, she's not the only one you've got to be thinking about. OSC couldn't detect terrorists if they were shitting landmines on the station forecourt, but they're dangerous once you wander up close enough they can see you."

"So what are you saying I should do, leave Jane to rot?"

"Nay, I wouldn't leave a friend like that, but I'd be polite about the things they say, however you think they sound. Let your friend Jane Fredricksson do the swearing and name-calling; she's got a good mouth on her that one."

Was this genuine friendly advice, or just another stage of their negotiating? The exchange was almost certainly being recorded, but she recalled Joe's assessment that the Inspector was a real plod, possibly not too fond of his more secretive, powerful and presumably arrogant associates. She resolved to calm down for when they got back. But it might be worth trying to puncture the Inspector: he seemed sufficiently human to be puncturable. "So what sort of a pay-off do you expect to get out of this, then?"

"Don't know what you mean by pay-off. Are you on about the Service Supplement?"

"What's the Service Supplement, when it's at home? I'm not going to give you a tip, if that's what you mean."

"All that attention and the best table in the place and she doesn't give a penny!" he mused, straight-faced. "No lass, I'm talking about our performance-related pay. It sometimes goes up a little if we've had a successful quarter, but I don't stake my mortgage on that."

"Successful?" she said, raising her eyebrows.

"Catching criminals. You know, the kind of thing we do here."

"Really? And all that bail money."

"Bail money goes to the government. We don't share in it."

Oh yes? "What about the Service Supplement?"

"Straight out of our pay, lass; it's docked from what we earn and gets paid back if we're good boys. One more reason not to wind up OSC! Thirty per cent less pay hurts."

"So why are you involved in this, if there's nothing in it for you?"

"I'm dealing with a criminal; it's my job"

"But she's not a criminal except on some minor charges of disturbing the peace and breaking a few plates and glasses. There's no way she'd be held in here like this just for that. And the terrorism idea is ridiculous."

"Not for me to say who's a terrorist or not a terrorist. I leave that to the Superintendent. And the ostrich-shaggers, of course, pardon my French!"

This last was a concession to Sylv, who had frowned slightly at the first reference and frowned again now: "Know a lot of French, do you?" Too long patient, too long silent, Sylv now subjected the Inspector to rapid-fire questions and speculations about his views and home life, which were handled or deflected with a detached amiability.

Viola knew she had hit another dead end. She settled down to wait for the Superintendent's and Fourth Policeman's return, whiling away the time by drinking the station's disgusting coffee and discovering a common affection for cats with the Inspector, although his un-neutered tom sounded more like a one-cat crime wave than a fellow creature of the peaceable domesticated ginger female and neutered black tom of her acquaintance back at Quiberon Road.

The return took a surprising amount of time, suggesting conferral with higher authority, and Viola had attained a Zen-like calm when the other two finally re-entered the meeting room.

The Superintendent spoke. "Ms Trent, we have taken into account very seriously your comments earlier in the meeting and validated our position in discussions at Commander level. I tell you this to anticipate any further outbursts from you and to make it clear that what we have to say has been fully thought through and is in no sense a casual, off-the-cuff offer. Is that understood?"

She borrowed a Crabtree favourite. "I hear what you say."

"As we have already explained, we are in a position to consider only unconditional bail in this case. This we can offer for two hundred and eighty thousand."

For Viola, it took a second or two for this to sink in. Playing for time, she said "two hundred and eighty thousand what?"

"The usual currency Ms Trent. Two hundred and eighty thousand hard euros."

She was speechless. That was slightly more than what she was still paying off on her flat. And it was a nice flat. She had no idea what Jane could pay, but it sounded a lot more than anything she could ever have imagined. Just the thought of negotiating around it brought on a nightmarish image of an unaided ice-cliff scramble she had seen on the media.

Her silence eventually led the Fourth Policeman to murmur: "well?"

She collected her wits a little. "No disrespect, but you must be out of your collective mind. We couldn't afford a tenth of that."

"I think you will find that the amount is within Ms Fredricksson's means."

"You really must have been studying her finances in detail. Is that what gave you the figure?" she said in a tone of contempt. She had no idea whether what they said was true or not, but they seemed very sure of their position.

"It's not clear what you're trying to allege, Ms Trent, but I think it would be in your interests if we all assumed that that last comment had not happened." (The Fourth Policeman). They stared at each other for three or four seconds, powerless contempt facing powerful indifference, then the Superintendent asked if she wished to speak to Jane. Viola said yes.

Jane was pale and subdued, but rallied when Viola and Sylv appeared in the cell. "Vile, Sylv, how's it going? It's good to see you. It's just so bloody boring gazing at a wall all day. Thanks for the books, though. I'll make it through 'Bleak House' yet."

They hugged, Viola noting small details such as the box of chocolates she had brought a couple of days ago lying open and quarter-finished on the floor. They wouldn't have survived the first night left alone with Jane in the real world, and would have been fastidiously cleared away out of sight between assaults. It distressed Viola in a way that was hard to rationalise that she was now on at least level pegging with Jane as regards dress. Jane was wearing a skirt slightly crumpled and clearly not on its first day of wearing, and her blouse had what seemed to be a small stain on one side, possibly chocolate. She had launched into animated conversation meanwhile with Sylv about the last week's events and scandals, but the inevitable came round. Turning to Viola, she asked: "have they made up their minds about money yet?"

"They've said something, but you're not going to like it."

"That doesn't sound too good. Try me."

"They'll only allow unconditional bail." Jane looked unimpressed; she would never have contemplated anything else. "They're asking for two hundred and eighty thousand."

Jane seemed to shrink and lose substance with the shock. "You're sure you heard them right?" she said after a few seconds.

"Yes, that's it. Vile asked them to repeat it and they said two hundred and eighty thousand HEs", Sylv said.

Viola added: "they seem to have had a good look through your bank accounts."

"Who gave them the right to do that? They're confidential, especially offshore."

"It's this terrorism angle they keep talking about", said Viola. "It seems they can do anything they like."

Jane nodded miserably. "Well, they've got it wrong, anyway. Most of that money is tied up in trusts and isn't mine; I just have my name on the account. Some of it is in business partnership accounts taken over from my parents; the partners are never going to agree to release money for something like this. Oh, and one account has inheritance money in it from my grandmother; I've only got a one-eighth share of that. I'm not badly off by the standards of you lot, but I can't possibly afford to pay this, even if I wanted to. Could you go back and tell them that, see if they'll see reason." For the first time since this had started, Jane looked frightened.

"I'll try." Viola felt the need to sound more positive, for Jane's sake. "They're only after a bribe when all's said and done; they must see reason fairly soon. We dropped a not very subtle hint about the media, and they were immediately out to dissuade us. Getting across to their seniors that it's not going to be as rich a haul as they thought might take a day or two, but we'll have you out of here soon."

"Too right!" said Sylv, with some passion.

Viola thought of another thing. "What about the two waiters they hauled in here. Have you seen them or heard about them?"

"Neither sight nor sound. I spend all day and all night in this cell. I tried walking out of it – the walls are only virtual, I thought - just to see if there was anybody else to talk to. I'd only got a foot and an arm out – there's more resistance than you'd imagine – and an alarm went off and I got an electric shock. Then half the police in South London, it felt like, came running. I was given a telling off and the window screen was turned off for a day. I haven't tried again since: the shock really hurt." She folded her arms tightly and shivered slightly. "So I don't get to talk to anyone but visitors like you; they hardly give me any attention themselves."

Sylv moved across and put her arm round her. Viola said: "I'd better ask about them again sometime. The waiters. Not now, though." It would just complicate matters.

Jane gathered herself. "Sylv, Vile, it's great seeing the two of you. Locked up here, you wonder normal life ever existed."

They hugged again and, after a few minutes of inconsequential chat, Viola called the warder avatar to return them for further discussions. Outside the cell, she looked round and up. The virtual partitions were convincing enough to appearance, but not all angles had been covered. The Condominium was really just a huge barn, subdivided by some brand or another of virtual environment control system.

The discussions were brief. Viola reiterated that Jane could not pay what they were asking and outlined Jane's observations on the state of the various accounts, a summary greeted impassively except for "that depends on the family's values and priorities" from The Fourth Policeman when the inheritance money was mentioned. The police negotiators, bland of expression, arms folded, promised to give some thought to what she had said. Another meeting was arranged provisionally for Friday morning, same time, same place. Viola left with a miserable sense of failure and increased foreboding, Sylv in a state of barely concealed fury, muttering "Wankers!" as she left the room. It registered no reaction.

Huddled in a nearby coffee shop, they committed to paper as much of the meeting as they could remember, Viola silently thanking Joe for his advice on having a second person present. She had already written notes of the first meeting, but these were sketchy. It occurred to her that hiding them might be wise, though without any specific idea why, and she decided to locate somewhere when she got back. Walking together down to Camberwell Green, to catch trams in opposite directions, they agreed the same meeting arrangements for Friday.

XXI

LUNCHING

The trip north and Viola's distress and preoccupation over Jane, had pushed faculty into the background. They could not afford to stay there. Having quizzed Viola about her Pitchfork researches, Carl rang Ben and proposed meeting at the Faliraki. Popular for its Greek food (cooked by Turks), it was more suitable at lunchtime than the Oast, which, less crowded than in the evenings, lost the effective sonic screen around conversations.

Alison, having no such qualms about privacy, related the previous day's get-together to Eva over the usual Frutenlo in the refectory. She was pleased with herself, and Eva felt pleased for her, though still puzzled as to what she saw in Ben. It was obvious the information on The Charter had gone down well. Eva got the benefit too of the snippets held back from Ben for the sake of future meetings.

"Are you going to do anything about it?"

"Such as?"

"Tell the authorities. They sound wicked."

"I think you mean evil."

"Evil, then. Someone needs to know."

"Well the Vice Chancellor is 'the authorities' if anyone is, and it doesn't look like he needs to be told."

Eva realised, with dismay, that she was being dim again. A strong moral sense was all very well, but it too often smashed into reality.

165

Alison rescued her. "What about your Manucussionists, don't they ever play games like this?"

Eva shook her head. "They're too nerdy. And permanently sober, though I don't think that makes any difference. There is Alan Westwood."

"Who?"

"Alan Westwood. He's our head of department."

"Oh, him. I didn't think you liked him."

"I don't. He's a toad. Fancies himself." And Eva, among others, as it happened. She scowled at the creepy memory of the time he'd tried to get a copy of her veep. Over her dead body!

"So why's he different from the others? Except he's the boss."

"He's a bit of an operator. As well as a toad."

"Do you think he's in on this Charter thing, then?"

It hadn't occurred to her, but she conceded: "It's the sort of thing he'd love. Smarming around with secrets no-one else wants to know."

"Except we do this time. I think you should keep an eye on him." That sounded wishy-washy. "Under surveillance."

Eva recognised she had, as so often, been outmanoeuvred. Grudgingly, she nodded assent, and moved on quickly, hoping that Alison might forget the commission. "You know Tad, the bloke who's always eyeing you, is going with Karen, don't you? Maybe he'll leave you alone now."

"They've met once or twice, but there's nothing in it."

"Where did you hear that?"

"From Tad, of course. We bumped into one another a few days ago."

So much for the banishment, Eva thought. But she'd definitely got one over Alison on this. "I heard it from Sue in Corporate Planning. She reckoned they'd hit the jackpot. Karen's too grand to give all the details, but it must have been Monday or Tuesday this week."

Caught up in the thrills of the chase and of espionage, Alison had not heard this. She felt a stab of irritation that she was behind Eva in the information flow and a stab of jealousy. Unrequited suitors pined at a distance, adoringly. They weren't supposed to cut and run into someone else's arms. She took a nonchalant sip of her Frutenlo. "That was quick work."

"You know Karen, she doesn't hang about."

Alison tacked. "That must be why Paul's looking so miserable. First he loses Janet, then two of his friends get off with each other."

"Paul?"

"Paul Fairley. He's over there." Alison nodded at a dispirited figure mournfully tucking into a pint of Manager's in a far corner. Eva looked over, recognising him from Tad's group the previous Thursday. A shame the world was so full of unattached men who just wouldn't do. "You heard about Janet?" Alison continued.

"Something about her getting off with a tutor."

"Not just a tutor, she got off with some celebrity. Over here for a master class is what Karen said. From Dresden. He's gone back home now, but they're planning to meet again."

These were two really meaty pieces of gossip: picking their bones saw off the rest of the lunch hour. Paul's chances for soothing Janet in her temporary abandonment were not discussed; they both knew he had none.

Ben was well briefed when he met Carl; the lunch date with Alison the previous day had seen to that. He was feeling unusually pleased with himself, even if taxed with an sense that Atinuke couldn't feasibly be run in parallel for much longer.

Carl went straight to the point: had he found out anything more about Stephen Pendleton's intent?

"About Pitchfork … not much directly. But I have found out something about where the VC may be coming from. The two of them had a meeting about 'organisational dynamics' a few days ago; the day before the faculty meeting. So it seems to go beyond just budgets. And the VC has a document he doesn't want people to see. His PA has had a sight of it, though. Something called a charter. For an organisation called AFFREM. I can't make much sense of what that's supposed to be."

Carl's expression quickened. "How much of this charter did his secretary see? That's Karen, I take it, Karen Swindells?"

"Karen, yes. I haven't got much on what she saw, I'm afraid, not yet." Alison had rationed her disclosures, to make sure of a further meeting. "Does 'AFFREM' mean any more to you?"

"Possibly. I asked Viola to do a search on Pendleton": Ben raised his eyebrows: Carl conceded: "Pitchfork. Mostly it was academic background that she found. Michigan, Princeton, Cornell, the sort of publications you'd expect. But she did also find his name on the minutes of a group called the Ancient Fellowship of Franchised Reamers. I'd think that must be AFFREM."

It sounded plausible.

Carl continued. "The minutes were not complete; she accessed them through the dirty reader" … Ben raised his eyebrows, unseen: dodgy stuff … "One of the things it lacked was under discussion: a Mission Statement." Ben said nothing. "If we could find that, it might give us an idea where they're coming from. It strikes me that it might be stated somewhere in their charter, hence the interest. Could you work on that, please, find out what you can."

Ben nodded. He was framing a response, when Carl added: "A friend of Viola's has also heard of AFFREM. They were mixed up in Pakafiran. It's not clear what they stand for, or at least what they stood for then, but apparently they operated at quite senior levels, so they are probably neo-con."

Ben felt rather dashed. His (Alison's) sleuthing skills had been unmistakeably sidelined by Carl's (Viola's). He needed to get back into the conversation. "Doesn't sound too good for AUP." This made Carl look thoughtful and slightly depressed, so he added quickly: "But then, look at the Department for Life Enhancement. It's neo-cons in every corner there and they still fund us."

Carl grimaced. "DLE are only neo-cons because nobody's come along and changed the record. They were 'neo-cons' when they called themselves Education, and it had no more effect then. This AFFREM crowd could be dangerous, though."

"Why more than any other, do you think?"

"Just gut feel."

"I'd better try and get a look at that charter."

"I'd appreciate it if you could. There's another thing Viola found too. They have this odd connection with music: one of their people murdered a woman playing a musical instrument. Because it wasn't traditional for her to do so, apparently."

"Sounds more like fundamentalist Islam."

"That's what Viola said, but it's a Western group. The minutes she turned up were for a meeting at Ann Arbor, and the names listed were mostly of European background."

"Did the minutes mention any other places? Like Peckham?"

"The meeting was fifteen years ago, so no Peckham. But it did mention a group at Berkeley and some problem that had to be dealt with in another group at our own dear Cambridge. They're not clear about where the Cambridge group was based, though I'd guess one of the universities. It seems, or seemed then, to be a group that started in academia. The Cambridge problem was to be dealt with using their 'T & D Protocol', whatever that was."

Ben took up the challenge. "Testosterone and Damnation?"

"More likely something and Destroy? Terrorise? Transmute?"

"Transmit and Disease? Maybe they were just going to screw them?"

The possibilities were endless.

They passed on to happier subjects as the Lamb Kleftiko appeared. Carl had another concert in Birmingham booked in a couple of weeks' time. He intended to use the trip to visit Tony MacLeish at Warwick for some gentle arm-twisting around the Körthofer solution. Ben had been asked to give specialist classes on Paginatorics for the Contemporary Dance Foundation in early July. Carl congratulated him; he believed in research resulting from practical involvement and had chosen his academic staff accordingly: the most notable exception to this was Viola.

There was too the Bucharest conference in August, though that was for Carl and - as an invited speaker - Viola. Ben was not going that year.

Carl kept the detail about AFFREM's meeting in Vishiney to himself. Viola and he were planning, after the conference, on a week of rest, relaxation and S-class music beyond Western scrutiny. Re-organisations, he had found, tended to be slow-moving affairs, capable of crushing the unwary, but moving with the speed and grace of a super-tanker on Prozac. Time enough to leave enquiries about that until they were on the spot.

XXII

SECURITY MEASURES

Much more of that stare and he'd eviscerate him and throw the bits through the window. Though he did look formidable in a squat, low-key way. What the hell did Pendleton need a bouncer for, anyway? The Hon Ran found it hard to believe that surveying skills were the chief reason for his employment. Pendleton was droning on in the usual way. Interesting to speculate what would happen to him in a regimental mess if he talked like this.

"As of this moment, the building is sub-optimal, security-wise. As you will recall, this was our apprehension from the meeting eight days ago, and Leke here has confirmed this apprehension." The bouncer continued to invite evisceration, unblinking. "The situation presupposes normalisation."

"Meaning?"

"A change of accommodation parameters."

"And those are?"

"Change of building, or much works."

The bouncer had spoken. Thank God for that! It might have taken another twenty minutes to tie Pendleton down to something so fearlessly direct. He turned his attention to him. "So what's the problem with what we have? We have security guards."

"Is everything. Security guards ... is useless."

Couldn't disagree about the security guards. They were the best they could get, but most of them would have spent their time on punishment drill in his regiment. The Hon Ran assumed a non-committal expression: "And the building?"

"Too much doors, too much people hearing, too hard defend."

"Ye-e-e-s … some interesting observations there. Just take me through the problem areas one at a time."

The bouncer looked down, digesting the sentences, syllable by syllable. Pendleton seized the opportunity to intervene. This was suddenly going much too quickly. "Leke, we first need to spend some quality time on core objectives."

"Sure, boss" said the bouncer, subsiding to the previous watchful immobility.

The Hon Ran groaned inwardly. One way or the other, they were going to have to endure the twenty minutes, probably with more to follow. "We haven't said anything about objectives before. I take it this is to make sure I'm in agreement with what you're assuming."

"That's it one hundred per cent, Ranulph."

"And if I don't agree with any of them, you go away and re-think your conclusions?"

"Without question, Ranulph."

"Good. Fire away!"

Curiously, the sudden command seemed to disconcert Pendleton, who ducked his head and rifled through the papers he was holding. The other two watched in silence. Then he seemed to pull himself together and said, without reference to the papers: "firstly we need to agree on the function of this office as a central point for the various normalisation exercises that are planned in AUP."

"Various? I thought we had two: reorganising Paginatorics and the Manucussionists."

"In the current playing field, you're right on the spot, Ranulph. But as you know, The Charter commands us proactively to prosecute the Fellowship's objectives in all areas likely to show a positive business outcome, within the terms and parameters laid down in the Fellowship's Normalisation Framework. There are some prime candidates for normalisation in this university, Ranulph, and I have put together the first draft of a programme."

"Then you'd better delete it immediately."

As always, such directness took time to soak in. "You will be the first person to see this draft. Of course! You could see it now, but a further two days to regularise its suitability for discussion would be optimal."

"I don't want to see it, still less discuss it. Delete it: in the fire, down the loo, through the shredder. Up your bum if that's what it takes. As vice-chancellor of AUP, I decide what happens here. What we agreed was reorganising Paginatorics and the Manucussionists. Nothing else on your agenda is even to be thought about until those two are done. Do I make myself clear?"

Pendleton descended into a brooding, slightly hunched silence, avoiding the Hon Ran's attempts to look him in the eye. Then he appeared to come to a decision and raised his head, straightening his back. "Very well. Leke …"

"And the objectives?"

"Negative. Discussing strategic objectives in the context of tactical action plans is a no-win."

"So let's discuss the tactical objectives. What are you aiming to get out of the security changes Leke here is about to recommend?"

"Ranulph, we could be looking at some kind of category error here."

"Meaning what?"

"Meaning … the security changes are strategic parameters; normalisations of departments are tactical."

It was like wrestling with an amoeba. "So just re-organising Paginatorics and the Manucussionists won't need any security changes?"

"If we could just take this from basics. Security has got to be number one support priority in effectualising The Charter."

"I've heard that said at one of the meetings, certainly. So why do you think it's a category error to talk about it as support for what you call a tactical action plan?"

"The Charter itself: you recollect the three "I"s."

"Possibly. Refresh my memory."

"In the sacred trust of the Fellowship, The Charter is Illimitable, Indivisible and Irrefrangible."

Trust a bunch of Yanks to come up with that! The Hon Ran allowed an extra touch of the sardonic to take up residence on the corner of his face. "And?"

"Effectualisation can recognise no limits and is not to be divided into separate parts. It must be considered as a totality."

"So no grand plan, no security plan. Well, try me just one more time with the programme you were talking about, and I'll soon show you whether it's irrefrangible. I've agreed to two action areas, and that's the lot for now."

"Ranulph, a Charter-based investment from the Fellowship needs business case affirmation to win acceptance. A support concept for an advance plan whose business analysis indicates a likely failure to deliver Charter mandates or the possibility of introducing deterioration to Charter principles is unlikely to gain that affirmation or win that acceptance."

At last, the point. "So no grand plan, no money?"

At this point, Karen entered without warning, notepad in hand, to take orders for coffee and tea. It spared Pendleton the need to reply. The Hon Ran ordered a coffee, suppressing the recurrent desire for a gin and tonic that meetings with Pendleton brought on. Leke followed suit. Pendleton refused.

It looked like war again, she thought.

Her exit performance was appreciated by two-thirds of the audience. Pendleton looked down at his papers, still framing a reply. The Hon Ran stared at him unflinchingly.

A lengthy silence was finally broken by Leke. "Do you want I talk what we find?" he said, gazing in turn at the other two.

"An excellent idea. Fire ahead!" said the Hon Ran, this time uncontradicted by Pendleton, who looked briefly at Leke and nodded.

"As I saying, for this building, too much doors, too much people hearing, too hard defend."

"Doors. Is door at back of building, go nowhere important."

Actually, thought the Hon Ran, it had got him clear of more than one unwelcome meeting. It was a relic of the Old Bin's original incarnation as a terrace of residential houses.

"And is second front door, go nowhere."

Another relic.

"This office, two doors. Is easy hear what said inside: hole in door," (presumably the keyhole) "glass against door, microphone."

The Hon Ran interrupted. "Have you tested either of these?"

Leke leaned across to a small musicplayer lying on the table beside him, inserted a small device on his key ring and fiddled with the player's selection screen. Faintly, as if heard from a distant bathroom, the plaintive tones of Morrison of VAPA could be heard, asking for improved accommodation for Performance Arts, apparently without success. "The glass. Now microphone." He re-selected on the musicplayer and the same meeting replayed, much more clearly, conveying the hint of a sob after Morrison's penultimate plea. It was impressive.

"You'll have to bring along somebody to sit outside the door when we meet."

"Microphone. Room below" said Leke, pointing.

Karen re-entered the room, having taken interested note of the possibilities for improved listening in. A little of Leke's coffee made its way onto Pendleton's trousers as it was transferred to the table. Profuse apologies and a return trip for kitchen towels. Pendleton was not amused. Leke maintained an emotionless façade.

The Hon Ran observed with saurian detachment. The microphone revelation was a bit of a jolt. Christ, he'd better not have given Corporate Planning any ideas. Their schemes were far enough off the wall as it was without incorporating some of his wittier sadisms.

Karen re-exited.

"Point taken. Do carry on."

Leke picked up his notes again. "Second door."

"To this office?"

"This office, yes. Also easy hear what said inside."

No need for a demonstration. "Karen is my PA. She's privy to most of my correspondence and most of my meetings. There's no problem there."

"But not these meetings" Pendleton interjected

"And back door lead to office. Many peoples"

Was Karen entertaining her boyfriends on the stairs or something? "What people?"

"Many. Girls, men; many peoples."

Corporate Planning sometimes used it as a short-cut to the park, and there were toilets off the stairs. So what? He'd always believed in observation and surprise to catch out snoopers. The AUP staff were too dormant to have that sort of initiative anyway. "Do continue."

A lengthy list of security shortcomings unfolded in pidgin. They were, in large part, about possibilities for listening in on meetings. The Hon Ran listened with increasing ennui. Who cared? Most meetings were well enough armoured by sheer dullness. The bouncer clearly knew his stuff, but this was very familiar ground. Jumping in on a pause, he said: "you mentioned defence."

"Yes. Your office. Very easy attack. Third floor. Front of building. Old building – bricks, wood."

That, of course, was its charm. "Only if you use rockets. Who do you think is going to use those?"

Leke looked at Pendleton, who said: "As I said at our last meeting, we need to be prepared for counter-progressive reactions to The Charter's radical concepts of modernisation. We should presuppose violence."

"And as I said at that meeting too, I'm looking to drag AUP into the present century, not start hand-to-hand combat. So why does this subject keep coming up?"

Pendleton didn't reply. Leke clearly had no idea what this bit of the discussion was about.

"It's the grand programme again, isn't it?"

Still no response. "Well, since we're not doing a grand programme, we won't be getting any money and we won't need any defences."

Pendleton remained inert. It was alarmingly out of character for somebody so stuffed-shirt American. To jolt him back into life, the Hon Ran stretched, yawned at length, then said: "Any progress on the business benefits for the Paginists' and Manucussionists' re-organisation?"

He doesn't even speak the right language, thought Pendleton, mentally grinding his teeth. "Business benefits are proximal to core business objectives …"

"And core business objectives are something you'll only talk about when you've got a grand programme?"

Again silence. Karen, judging her entrance, came in to collect the coffee, observing: Mr Fraserman sitting back in a mode of surface relaxation, a caged tiger assessing the passing punters for meat: Stephen Pendleton silent and withdrawn, perched on the edge of his chair; Leke, impassive, dumped in his chair like a sack of charcoal, staring at her with unmistakeable appreciation. She exited with a valedictory swing of the hips.

Usually irritated beyond measure by this European penchant for interruption to the flow, Pendleton started to glimpse its occasional merit: a chance to re-group, re-impose some order on the chaos of non-normalised thinking. This insistence on naming the Fellowship's strategy for AUP as 'the grand programme' and hanging it out to dry on that account was making life very difficult. Goddammit, he knew the score when he joined them; he'd been one of their major operatives for a couple of decades; what was it with him now? Had he gone native? Some of the things being said were dangerously close to giving Leke more insight than he was authorised to possess. Another good reason for continuing to ignore the 'grand programme' references. "Leke, could you outline your recommendations on defence."

The Hon Ran let that go; he was curious.

"Is three. One door into building only: eliminate others. Cameras on door into Sir Fraserman's office." He nodded at the Hon Ran. "Clad building: blast-compound."

"Suppose there's a fire on the stairs. How are people going to get out with only one door?" Leke looked uncomprehending, so the Hon Ran continued. "This is a 250-year-old building; I'm not even sure it has any foundations; covering it with blast-compound will probably make it collapse." Blast-compound was effective stuff, if you were liable to attack, but its sheer density made it unbelievably heavy; an occasion - the only occasion - on which he had picked up a single slab had brought him close to a hernia.

Leke was struggling to summon the necessary English; Pendleton took over. "The building's use will be normalised to core functions only." Curtains for the refectory, then. "The blast compound will be constructed, on foundations, adjacent to the building but free-standing. It will exert no force on the building's structure."

God almighty! An Isfahan Jacket. The classic (and original) example had been the HallTech HQ in Isfahan, a traditional building with a charming nineteenth century edifice that had been expanded and metamorphosed into a species of mud-coloured, non-melting igloo. Hideous even by Pakafiran neo-architectural standards, it had at least been effective in its way: HallTech had never successfully been attacked in its building. Shame about what happened outside it, of course. What was going on here? It must be some serious 'strategy', probably above and beyond AUP, if they were really contemplating giving an Isfahan Jacket to the Old Bin. Well, it wasn't a strategy he knew anything about, and they'd better start re-planning off his patch.

Pushing the unsayable to one side, he said: "totally unnecessary for the exercise we're contemplating. It will make the building look like a bunker. British Heritage would go bananas."

"Leave British Heritage to us, Ranulph. That will be a non-issue."

"In that case, let's say it's an issue with me. I'm not ruining the only decent square in this part of South London so that AFFREM can pretend it's playing at soldiers, whether or not it chucks in money and influence. If the Paginists and Manucussionists don't like what we're doing, I'll handle it the way I handled VAPA."

"We have not made our ideas clear to you. I think we need to take a rain-check here", said Pendleton after another lengthy pause.

Hooray, thought the Hon Ran. "Karen has my diary. I think you'll need, in your own language, time to re-focus. Fix another appointment when you've re-focused."

He stood up, and they followed suit, allowing themselves to be gently ushered out of the room. Perfect, he thought: now they'd have to come up with something sensible. At all events, Pendleton would; the bouncer, Leke, had his head screwed on the right way. If there wasn't to be any work out of Pendleton's schemes, maybe he'd welcome something commissioned directly. It would need care; the Fellowship didn't tolerate open infighting, though a good deal went on out of sight. It would help if he had somebody who spoke the bouncer's language, though the Lord only knew what that was.

Coming up with something 'sensible', though, was very far from Stephen Pendleton's mind as he walked out. Fraserman had clearly de-normalised. He would have to report back to Grand Temple before anything more could happen; if he had any say, he would cut Fraserman adrift with his departments and all the rest of the wreckage. Honorable Fellows of Fraserman's standing were not to be dealt with so casually, though. He gave Leke instructions for a meeting in two days time. Leke nodded assent expressionlessly, before returning to dreams of Karen

---

"He's not co-operating?"

"There is zero alignment with the wider objectives, sir"

"Hmm. How widely does his alignment go?"

"Fine with the hors d'oeuvres. Everything else is out of play."

"The hors d'oeuvres. Remind me."

"Ancillary Music. Chiefly the Paginatorics Department, plus Fraserman is insisting we do something about Alan Westwood's domain."

"And the main course?"

"The objective is to normalise the university across all of its academic disciplines."

"And then?"

"Use the realised example of market-compatible, normalized higher learning to network out to other academic institutions."

Grand Temple made no response to that, and there was a brief pause. "Have you briefed Ranulph about all this, Stephen?"

"He is aware of our parameters, sir."

"That's not what I asked. Does Ranulph know your plans? And have you talked these through to make sure he's on side?"

"Ranulph Fraserman has been an Honorable Fellow for more than twenty years now. He knows what The Charter implies probably better than I do myself. Everything I am foreseeing is one hundred per cent in line with The Charter. We have discussed plans. Sir."

Another pause. "Perhaps I'd better speak to Ranulph myself. Have you his current contact details?" Grand Temple took a note of these.

"Ran. Herb Summerson here. Haven't spoken to you in a while. How's it doing?"

"Herb! Nice to hear from you! Could be doing better, but I'm still in play. How about you?"

"Not so bad. A few aches, and I'm slow round the squash court these days, but I still do the golf on six."

"Haven't played squash since I rogered the knee playing that friend of yours, but I can better you on the golf."

"How so?"

"Four."

Grand Temple whistled. "Impressive. How's your lady wife? Tamsin, isn't it?"

"Tamsin's fine; indestructible really. How's Julie?"

"Fine too. The womenfolk get their second wind at our age."

The Hon Ran grunted: too true! "Anyway, what can I do for you?"

"This Charter project that we sent Stephen Pendleton in to steer through. The feedback I'm getting is a little unsettled. I wanted to talk through any problems."

So the bastard had gone squealing to his boss. Well, he knew (and liked) Herb Summerson from a long time back, so it wasn't the best-chosen route. "Keeping him focused on the job in hand seems surprisingly difficult, but the last I heard he was getting on with that."

"What do you see as the job in hand, Ran? Just checking perceptions."

"No problem, Herb! Bringing Paginatorics and the Manucussionists into the real world of market economics is the job in hand. There's some pussyfooting going on about Alan Westwood being a Fellow of a few months standing, but I assume he'll be looked after somehow, whatever happens to his department."

"Sure. Stephen is having difficulty with a sense that you place different priorities on the longer-term objectives. Would you agree with that?"

"There's certainly a big difference. He doesn't really seem to value anything else. I want them tried and tested in situ first. And I don't mean to start any unnecessary fights. Could I ask a question or two back? If AFFREM seriously thinks it wants to fund an Isfahan Jacket for the building my office is in, what scale of operations is it thinking of long-term? And how long is long-term?"

"You've got us in deep there, Ran. Some of it is need-to-know. But I can say that we would be looking beyond the university. Off the record, all universities, over time."

"That's not what we agreed when he was appointed. I was looking for a fixer, who would have the time to knock a bit of sense into the departmental structures and focus them. The Fellowship has always had lots of that sort of skill. Instead, I've got some species of Jedi, whose chosen starting point is the only department I'm broadly happy with. Now I find there's a much bigger agenda, parts of which I apparently don't 'need to know'. We'll come back to what's going to happen to that in a moment. Firstly, though, why is the Fellowship playing it this way all of a sudden, Herb?"

"Ran! Ran… you're jumping to a lot of conclusions there. The Fellowship is playing things the way it's always played things. You remember the three Is: every project ends up with a wider agenda because of that; it's just the way The Charter has always panned out in practice."

"Not over its members' dead bodies it hasn't. Over the years I've done several projects as fixer and several as sleeper. I've always kept the Fellowship informed, they've always kept me informed. Anything significant. Not so this time. Why the difference?"

"No difference, Ran. Sounds like Stephen has been over-eager. I'll speak to him."

And tell the pompous little prick to speak in English too, the Hon Ran thought, though he didn't verbalise it. "About the big agenda you gave me some clues on. My project as sleeper here is to normalise AUP 'having regard to European social constraints'. That's what the terms of reference say. Pointing an Uzi at anything that looks out of line goes down well enough in the States; it's not so well thought of over here. Grand plans happen on the back of small plans that you can say are successful, and that's how I'm running things. Plans beyond the university need to find another base."

"Of course, Ran! Of course!"

"Can I leave it to you to pull our mutual friend into line, then?"

"Surely. You and I go back a long way, and you're one of our most valued Fellows. It's not good to interface with you in a conflict situation like this; I'm glad to help normalise it for you. Leave Stephen to me, Ran."

"Great! Well, goodnight Herb. Give my regards to Julie."

"Goodnight to you, Ran, and love to Tamsin."

The call terminated, the Hon Ran knew he'd been soft-soaped. Herb Summerson never used to be like that; at Princeton he had been notorious for his directness of speech. Perhaps the new Global Master was having an effect; Germans were never to be trusted.

XXIII

NEGOTIATING AGAIN

Friday's meeting, with the Superintendent and the Sergeant, led nowhere useful. The police reduced their demand to two hundred and sixty thousand after some general throat-clearing about serving the community and balancing risks. Viola pointed out again that the money in the accounts was mostly not Jane's, some of it inheritance money still to be distributed. The Superintendent repeated the observation about family priorities. Clearly a big sting was expected.

They met Jane, who was subdued, looking strained and tense as they speculated on how long it would be before the police saw reason. She had accumulated a couple of books that had passed the informal censorship of the reception desk, but confessed that she was able to find little appetite for reading. When it was time to go, she hugged Viola and Sylv with an intensity in which Viola felt a suppressed trembling.

On the way out, the Sergeant asked them to stay for a few minutes and ushered them back into the meeting room, before disappearing. The Inspector was there. They sat down; he looked at them without saying anything. Sylv fixed him with a glare that could have been called brazen, with no apparent impact on his composure. Viola looked at him coolly, with no greater effect. Viola broke the silence first.

"Well?"

"You want to read this."

He handed them a piece of paper, of official appearance. Sylv leaned over to look, and the two girls read it together, saying nothing. A Restraining Order, issued by a magistrate, it forbade any contact with the media about the case, under penalty of arrest and detention for 'succouring terrorism'.

"Have you any questions?"

"Would they be any use?"

"That's up to you to decide. Anything you're not clear about."

"Such as how you got a magistrate to sign this when Jane hasn't been in front of a magistrate."

"She has. Technically."

"Not that Jane has ever realised. Doesn't she have to know when there's an official meeting?"

"I can't comment on that. Not with a case like this. She's been seen, that's all."

"And this magistrate that's happy to sign away people who haven't seen him, he's one of your lot, making it up, isn't he." Viola looked closer at the signature. "She."

"She's a magistrate. She knows what her duty is."

"Meaning she's on your Service Supplement scheme, I suppose?"

"Sorry lass, can't comment on that."

Sylv muttered: "You never bloody can." She was ignored.

For Viola it was the culminating disaster. A feeling of defeat washed over her. In the last week, the target of getting Jane back to normal life had receded into a seemingly inaccessible corner. She and Sylv were too stunned by this new misfortune to offer much comment to the Inspector, other than asking whether Jane had been informed. Jane had not; it was not a terrorist suspect's right to know.

Leaving the station, they forced themselves to produce notes about the meeting, which Viola would discuss with Joe and possibly Carl. And, Viola reflected, Jane's family, if they could track them down. What she was held for, trivial really in origin, had escalated, without obvious cause other than an appetite for money, to a state of impasse whose resolution would need some serious outside influence. They parted, Sylv in a state of hissing fury.

SUMMER 2063

EASTWARD HO

XXIV

BUCHAREST

The ambient warmth was relaxation in itself: no need to plan against the cool of an English evening. A whole summer of this and hotter, particularly with such a still closeness to the atmosphere might be something to escape from, but for the time being it was just enjoyment. Carl found the translation south and east, however temporary, a bonus in other ways. For three weeks he had, barring out-and-out emergency, licence to forget about AUP, its works, its empty promises; forget about the necessities of running the Paginatorics department; forget about the roof damage to his house, caused by a thunderstorm in June and still protected only by a makeshift covering.

MacLeish had, with only a little arm-twisting, come up with the goods and he had a handsome, leather-bound volume to present to Körthofer later that week; one designed to lie naturally flat when opened, in a manner never native to the original Ravel score that had caused the debacle. In retrospect, they had been crazy to allow its use. For a pair of student Paginists, the intricacies of turning pages for a piece moving by at such a furious rate while dancing a co-ordinated stylised waltz were quite enough. Add to this the necessity of creasing each page flat to stop it springing back; of avoiding tearing off pages where the volume's spine had been split by more ruthless predecessors; of doing all this gently enough to avoid showering the piano keyboard with little flakes of perished paper from the outer reaches of each page: it had been a pre-destined calamity. They should have insisted on the department's own more practical, if less atmospheric copy. Learning how to deal with mechanically difficult scores should be left to late-20th century editions: practically indestructible and, frankly, who cared?

The Calea Victoriei exuded prosperity, both from its buildings and from the smartly-dressed crowd promenading in both directions. It had not always been so, Carl reflected, remembering a holiday in Romania with his parents, some forty years ago, in which they had spent two nights here and been struck by its uneven mixture of restoration and dilapidation, its beggars, genuinely needy, apparent everywhere. Not so now; the benefits accruing to the largest city on or near the border to the Russian sector were obvious. That reminded him to check his card in one of the machines; he was meeting Viola at Ciprian's. It would be unwise to square up to the eventual bill with just the cash in his pocket.

Viola's agreeing to early evening cocktails was, he hoped, a sign that she was ready to relax and enjoy the holiday to come. Tomorrow's conference paper promised well, and then there would be two weeks in Vishiney of uninhibited music-making, in an environment (unlike the American sector) unconcerned about that sort of thing. He hoped that the sex might improve too. Viola's preoccupation with Jane's ongoing nightmare had drained her of energy and enthusiasm. What little remained, she had marshalled into her professional life, leaving effectively nothing for either music or love-making.

Carl's frustration at the double loss had been made worse by his inability to offer constructive help in the Jane situation; it was simply outside his experience or expertise, and he didn't even know Jane herself particularly well. He had visited her with Viola on a couple of occasions and been struck by the increasingly forlorn aspect both of the virtual cell and of Jane herself. Never quick on small talk and unable to discuss her case to any effect, Jane's listlessness had defeated his attempts at conversation. He had felt that his greatest contribution was probably as moral support to Viola. Viola herself had not fared much better, conversationally. She could not indefinitely generate new ideas for action, and was reluctant to give assurances of release that she didn't believe in.

Arriving early at Ciprian's, he secured a table for two overlooking the street and sat, waiting for her to appear. She might, he thought, permit herself to forget for a while

The conference so far was on the good side of average, much assisted by location. Viola's paper promised well. It would be competing with a workshop on advanced techniques in music-stand construction, of interest only to Presentationists, and a dreary-sounding screed on 'Ethnic Dimensions to Ancillary Music Discourse' to be given by an academic from Kazakhstan and hopefully made intelligible by a simultaneous translation. He had talked to only one person likely to go to that, an Hungarian curious about the Kazakh language. Viola seemed to have a fairly clear field, especially as her presentation promised entertainment through practical demonstrations.

Carl himself would be responsible for most of these, with some assistance from Viola herself and the two pianists promised the gig after the Körthofer incident, who were now identifiable by name: Henry and Pete. With the normal barriers of social standing and respectability loosening in the small AUP group, far away from home and unobserved, they had fallen into conversation with them the previous night.

There was a fifth member of the group, though they had, for obvious reasons, seen less of her. Janet was there as Körthofer's consort, already a veteran of three or four weekend trysts in various European cities and looking established in the role. Viola, extrapolating from the kiss on the hand, declared her to be Körthofer's 'mistress', perhaps the last of the breed. Mistress, partner or whatever, it had done no harm at all to Janet's progress as a Paginist, and she was now one of Carl's most promising pupils. Sadly, this had been matched by Paul's precipitous decline, which, Carl trusted, would be reversed by a summer of reflection and, possibly, new female interest.

He ordered a drink and nursed it, his thoughts turning inevitably to the niggling concern that had grown, slowly but steadily, over the two and a half months since the faculty meeting. Pitchfork's position had clarified to some extent: he was a member of a neo-con cult with some musical obsessions, a cult primarily bent on re-organising the universe, but then, weren't they all? Everything, though, had gone quiet. Ben's initially promising line of information through Alison via Karen, once the drip-feed of revelations about The Charter was exhausted, had simply dried up. The last Faculty meeting before the summer had been cancelled at less than 24 hours notice. The position, or lack of it, on budgets, had concerned Carl and had led to a shoot-out with Crabtree, a confrontation of stunningly indeterminate outcome. Crabtree, lurking darkly in his under-sized office, bent and dwarfish in effect, though he was in reality on the tall side of medium height, had glanced sardonically at Carl as he knocked and entered, neglecting either to greet him or to uncoil himself to shake hands. The dialogue proceeded in keeping with this:

Carl: "Jed, I'm concerned that we're five months into the financial year and still have no budgets to spend against."

Crabtree: (with a snicker) "That should keep AUP's bank balance healthy."

Carl: "No doubt. But what's the cause of the delay?"

Crabtree: "It was all said at the Faculty meeting. Item 6, if you remember."

Carl: (restraining impulse to throttle)

                    "That was nearly three months ago. Has there been nothing since?"

Crabtree: "Only on a need-to-know basis."

Carl: "Well, I'm a Head of Department. I have a pretty clear need to know about budgets."

Crabtree: "I am not in a position to comment on that."

Carl: "I'm not asking for comment, I'm asking for information?"

Crabtree: "I am not sure what information you are referring to."

Carl: "Budget information. That I can use to run my department."

Crabtree: "As I have said, this is on a need-to-know basis."

Carl: "I do need to know."

Crabtree: "My terms of reference do not extend to that."

Carl: "Well, Jed, you're the Resources Officer for the Faculty. How do you suggest I manage my resources without knowing about budgets?"

Crabtree: "Surely I don't need to start teaching you about fiscal responsibility?"

Carl: "Only once you've had the training. I take it that's a no to telling me anything about budgets."

Crabtree: "I am not in a position to comment."

Carl had given up and continued to spend against last year's budget; it wouldn't be hard to justify when the truth was eventually declassified. He had tried a direct approach to Pitchfork himself, but found him elusive. Pendleton had had a similar meeting with Crabtree about accommodation; he was still stewing in the Portakabins as a result. The initial murderous fury abated, he had realised their out-of-the-way position was handy in evading petitioners.

With a smile and a wave, Viola entered the room and made her way over to Carl, evidently somewhat breathless.

"Sorry, I'm late. I set off in the wrong direction from Piata Revolutiei and only turned back when I saw the Enescu Museum ahead. Isn't it lovely being here? It's such an elegant town."

Carl smiled and kissed her. It was going to be all right.

XXV

LIVING TOGETHER

What's biting her now? She was talking about her boss. That's Onran as I now call him, though not to Karen, who takes him much more seriously. She's been worried for a while that something's going on that's threatening him, though she hasn't known what. She was telling me she'd got to hear that there is something going on, something called normalisation. And that not much information seems to be coming through to him about it. It wasn't very clear to me how she found out, and she didn't seem to know what 'normalisation' was, but I've learnt that Karen doesn't like to admit ignorance about anything, so I didn't cross-question. But I couldn't see, why she couldn't go back to whoever had told her and try finding out more. So I said this and she flounced out with, "Oh, for God's sake, Tad! You just don't get it, do you?"

Half an hour later, she came in, said sorry and gave me a hug. That gave me ideas, but I got firmly, though gently, pushed away, as she had to get to the shops. Truth to tell, there's been quite a lot of gentle but firm pushing away in recent weeks, in bed and out of it. That's not all bad. The last couple of months have been, to be honest, exhausting. Still, I guess you might say the relationship has matured.

What I haven't yet worked out is what I'm supposed to 'get'? I doubt I get the point of the normalisation thing much less than Karen, i.e. hardly at all. Maybe she's genuinely worried about Onran. I can never really see why; he seems a right bastard to me, though I've noticed hens often seem to like that.

'Hens': I must remember not to use that word. I did use it in something I said to Karen, I forget what, a few days ago, when she was in a bit of a mood, and she came back with: "Do I look like I've

197

got feathers?" and started waving her arms up and down. "Cluck, cluck, cluck. Is that what I sound like?"

So I said: "well, you do now", which was the wrong answer" "you think we're all bird brains, don't you?" and so on and so on. I don't think that, actually, but saying so didn't have much effect. I waited till she'd calmed down to ask her what was wrong with 'hens' then and what should I say instead. It was demeaning to women, or something. I'd always thought of it as affectionate; the Scots friend I heard it from used it that way, but there you are. Asking for an alternative threw her, rather. "How about 'ladies' for a change?" I didn't say anything, and she caught on it sounded ridiculous and started to laugh.

So it was all right by bedtime, but it's been 'ladies' ever since when I'm talking to her. I have learnt to be choosy about arguments with 'ladies'; they're a life-form much quicker and much more ruthless at constructing cages out of words and dumping you in them.

I have my own view on normalisation, incidentally. I think it sounds pretty bloody sinister. It could just be the reorganisation that I got briefly interested in before Karen took charge, but in that case why not call it a reorganisation. Everyone else would. No, I think the word is hiding something, and I think Karen may be right to be worried about her boss's position. Doing anything about this, though, is more difficult. Perhaps I should take up sleuthing again; the last attempt did very well for me, if not in the way I'd have imagined. Paul might be a good starting point again. He's a miserable sod at times, especially the last couple of months, but he does tend to know what's going on. Karen and her mates are leagues ahead on all that, of course, but they can't know everything, and Paul hasn't been part of the crowd in the last few weeks.

I suppose I'd better get some work done; it's the pub again tonight, if you can call DizeeLizee a pub. Karen likes it and it's certainly smart, but the beer is piss.

XXVI

SURVEILLANCE (1)

Karen had indeed observed worryingly little. Though the VC had meetings with Pitchfork every week or two, they all seemed to be reports of 'continuing progress', whatever it was that was progressing. There was none of the interesting conflict of the earlier meetings. Bulletins from Alison had dried up: her interest had waned anyway, once the original reason for the interest had been netted, and Eva had had nothing exceptional to report about her boss. But that was to change.

Eva's lot in keeping Alan Westwood under observation was a grim one, not least because he led, within work hours at least, such a resolutely uninteresting life. She had to be very discreet; he was bad enough on subtle molestation without anything that he could interpret as encouragement, but at least that was shared with four other girls in the department (Marie had graduated to unapproachable after an incident that had caused him severe pain and embarrassment). With apparent encouragement he would be impossible. So she angled chairs, kept just out of sight around corners, spun out photocopier runs, walked past meeting rooms with eyes in the side of her head, rummaged in waste-paper bins and all to no avail. If he was up to something, he was either very subtle or just plain dormant. It was not as if she really wanted to know anyway, and it added insult to injury that she should have to do this on Alan Westwood ('Wankwould', as the girls had nicknamed him). Only loyalty to Alison had kept her going, and that seemed misplaced; as soon as her friend had reeled in the conceited one, she had all too obviously lost interest in grubbing out information herself. In fact, probably the strongest factor in Eva's staying on the case was rooted dislike of its object.

So the reward, when it came, was overdue and gratifying.

Hard at work on classifying a recent batch of ethnic drumsticks, by application and handover technique, time had run on. She finished the batch to a realisation that, at 7.15pm on a fine summer day, no-one else was around,. Or almost no-one: going to the printer to pick up a copy of her labours, she heard voices and stole up unnoticed to find her departmental head in his office, talking to someone on the videophone. Perhaps because the day was too hot, perhaps because he thought no-one else was around, he had left his door open. The 'phone was on loudspeaker, so every word was audible, at the cost of staying uncomfortably close to the action. Eva decided that if he got up at any point and checked the vicinity of his office, she would walk towards him, the printed document on display and ask him about locking up. If someone else blundered in, she would do the same to them.

Alan Westwood was not, however, just a toad with a high opinion of his powers of fascination: he was a careless toad with a high opinion of his powers of fascination, and her extra presence at the conversation was not detected.

Wankwould was expostulating his own merits as she came into earshot. " ... my feel for market requirements is instinctive ..." (funny name for female body parts, Eva thought) " ... and this naturally translates into the way I run my department. I would expect this to be reflected in the outcome of your normality exercise ..."

"Normalisation."

"Yes, your normalisation exercise"

"And Alan, it's our, remember, not your. As an Associate Trainee you participate as fully in the Fellowship's objectives and projects as the Global Master himself."

"Oh, yes, certainly Stephen. I would anticipate the outcomes of our normalisation exercise to reflect the intensely market-conscious nature of the Manucussionists department. Your project ..."

"Our project, Alan."

"Our project – sorry! ..." ... our project will be making initial recommendations soon, and it would be useful to have some foreknowledge of the way they are going. Forewarned is forearmed, as they say." He laughed, mirthlessly.

There was a brief silence at the other end of the line. "I scarcely see the relevance of forearmed in your present context. The three Is make it clear that members of the Fellowship, at whatever grade, acknowledge no personal boundaries to the scope of their activities and allow no personal interests or loyalties to intrude projectwise."

"Ah, Illimitable, Indivisible and, what is it? ... Indefensible? No", he said, sweatily aware of how that must sound. " ... err ... Irreversible?" That sounded better.

There was a sigh from the 'phone. "Irrefrangible, Alan."

"Yes, I'm sorry, Irrefrangible, of course." Whatever it was all about, he really wasn't very good at it, was he, Eva reflected.

"Yes. Do you not see the rollout of those concepts?"

"I understand the rollout is to the Paginists and to my department."

"No, Alan, the rollout of the concept: the forward implications of projecting the three Is into the reality sphere."

An image of home cinema evenings at home came to Eva's mind, her father cursing the inadequacies of software, hardware, hologram resolution: the whole package of mute digital intransigence, before avatars were introduced to do it all for you (though even then, never quite right). Must concentrate: Alan Westwood was clearly struggling, but he hadn't reached Head of Department without the ability to hack paths through verbal jungles. This was definitely machete time.

"I feel like I'm taking an exam here, Stephen." He laughed; there was no response. "I think you're saying in essence that I cannot afford to put the interests of my department ahead of the principles on which the Fellowship runs, and that's understood. But I was admitted, not much more than six months ago, precisely on the grounds that my department and my direction of it exemplified the Fellowship's market-orientated approach. You proposed me yourself, on those grounds. I'm a little concerned that that assessment seems to have changed and I'm looking for some guidance on what will be asked."

Pendleton recalled saying something of the sort: but couldn't the little jerk understand that life's needs moved on. "There is no change in assessment, but we are looking at a bigger scenario now, and the indivisibility and irrefrangibility of our aims mean that personal issues need to be parked. Straight up: the Fellowship ensures that the needs of its members are met, but that may not take the form that an individual member may have expected. Just so long as there is still buy-in to the Fellowship's ideals. Relax, Alan, go with the flow. Sincerely, I wish I could say the same parameters applied to our Benedict Arnold."

No he wouldn't, thought Eva. He sounded delighted, whoever Benedict Arnold was.

"You mean Ranulph Fraserman?"

"We avoid naming in AFFREM, except when talking one-to-one."

"Oh, yes. The Honorable Fellow?"

"That is correct. There is some serious backsliding on objectives evident there. It is unclear that the normalised scenario can feasibly recognise and contain such elements of negativity."

To Eva, it sounded pretty clear that the 'normalised scenario' wasn't going to. But wasn't Ranulph Fraserman the Vice Chancellor: the boss. Surely they couldn't just get rid of him?

"That's obviously a matter for the AFFREM hierarchy to decide. Do you have a timescale yet for producing an outline of how the normalisation will look?"

So he was happy to throw his boss to the wolves, just as long as he was looked after himself: he sounded mollified about his own part in it. And what about the individuals in his department? They hadn't even been mentioned except as spear-carriers for those market values he had such a feel for.

Stephen (presumably Pendleton, she thought) fobbed off the timescale question and started sounding anxious to finish the conversation. The man with the clammy hands blethered on a bit, but Eva took this as the signal to absent herself and scurried quietly back to her desk, before making a noisy exit from there, pondering how the back-stabbing might itself be back-stabbed.

XXVII

EAST IS EAST

Viola found the heat of the sun (after an English summer of climatic understatement), the feeling of loosened responsibilities, of being under laxer observation, combining to lighten her mood. Bucharest and the conference had timed themselves well. The soirée at Ciprian's was a great success.

This gladdened Carl, but the improved spirits were in part an act. The shadow of Jane's increasingly desperate situation did not fade. It could be pushed to the back of her mind as the occasion demanded, but it pushed itself back to the forefront in more reflective moments. She particularly made an effort for Carl, aware of his frustration at not being able to help, but she could not sustain this indefinitely. During the walk back to their lodgings they fell into talking about the case, Carl mostly listening, interposing the odd word.

Negotiations had barely moved at all for the intervening two and a half months. The police still clearly had their eye on the inheritance money and had maintained the price close to the level it had reached by the end of the first week. Clearly, they expected the family to ransom her, and Viola had made contact after the first few days. She had had a fairly chilly reception; the family generally were not close to Jane and obviously didn't like her much. A second cousin had proved more amenable and she had discussed the case with him, but without any result up till now. The family were far from inclined to lose any inheritance money, especially (the implication hung in the air) over Jane. Jane herself had, anyway, put an embargo on any payment at that level. Two of the relatives had managed a prison visit, but had offered only moral support.

Joe, with the collapse of effective negotiations after the first week, had become involved as promised and tried, briefly but energetically, to move the haggling on, only to hit the same wall. In spite of the injunction, they had tried to raise the case in the media, using an anonymous site. Joe, through his publishers, had contacts in the news media, and had achieved a meeting with a news editor and her technical manager. The case history of what the editor described as 'a gross abuse' sparked their interest, and the technical manager had seemed convinced that they could conceal identities.

But something had got out. Viola and Joe, meeting the editor for a third time, shortly before the publication date, had found her changed in manner, unwilling to discuss the case and finally, after being put on the spot by Viola, of the opinion that publication was not going to be possible. She would not discuss why, but Viola, over a drink with the Technical Manager, who clearly fancied her, heard that there had been a visit by a man and a woman a couple of days previously, following which the story had been stopped. They had been closeted with the editor for half an hour or so and had entered and exited with the minimum of fuss, but, from a rough description that he managed to give of the man, it could have been the Fourth Policeman, especially the pointy ears. The Technical Manager's guess was the spooks, or other terrorism and would have the necessary effect on his editor, who did not otherwise "scare easily".

Joe had made even more discreet enquiries elsewhere, but the threat of the injunction and, presumably, the attentions of OSC had killed off any follow-up; there were no obvious loopholes in the injunction's coverage, and no editor had any greater wish to end up under terrorist detention than Viola had herself. Essentially, the case had drifted for two months. Gradually, Viola had become used to the idea that Jane would be in custody for the full 90 days that they could hold her and that any action must be deferred until then. With the chief 'suspect' free, it would be harder to apply the injunction to anybody else, though Jane might by that time wish to avoid any fuss and just get on with resuming normal life.

So it had been with raised spirits that she had visited Jane just over a week previously: the 90 days would soon be over. It had not been discussed, because of the presumed monitoring of conversations in the cells, but both could count. Jane was pale and lacking in energy, and Viola had tried to rally her, but without positive response.

"You're only in here for half an hour or so at a time. I'm stuck with nothing to look at but the walls for hours on end?"

"But don't you get out to the open air once in a while? They're supposed to let you do that, aren't they?"

"Not for people they call terrorists, Vile: too 'dangerous'. They just open a view from the cell; I only get to look at it. That's when they don't forget; there's been a lot of forgetting."

"That's awful, I'll speak to the Superintendent. They can't just abandon you here; it's medieval, like throwing you into a dungeon." Jane shrugged her shoulders and said nothing. "Did you try those exercises I got you, incidentally?"

Jane shook her head. "I did, but there's not enough room in here." Viola looked round; the exercises hadn't been ambitious; she had got the idea from researching hostage situations. "The room is only this big when you're visiting; they shrink it when you're gone. After I'd tried a few of the exercises – and I kept bumping the wall even then – I could swear it got smaller still for a while. In fact, I paced it out, but it always expands again when I do that. As soon as I stretch out my arms again, it's squashed back in."

This sounded like paranoia, and Viola didn't pursue it. Instead, she demanded to see the Superintendent when she emerged from the cells, leaving Jane weeping after a valedictory hug. After a wait of a few minutes, she as shown into the usual meeting room, where she found the Sergeant, "I asked to see the Superintendent."

"Superintendent Osler is not free at the moment. Can I help you?"

"I need to speak to somebody with management authority over the cells in which my friend Jane Fredricksson is held. I think that means you can't help."

"I can convey a message to the Superintendent, should that be necessary."

"Who decides whether it's necessary?" There was no answer. "It's a serious matter about the way in which my friend is being treated. I need to speak face-to-face with somebody who can actually do something about it."

"The Superintendent is unavailable at the moment."

"Later today, then."

"The Superintendent has a full schedule of meetings today."

"Tomorrow then."

"The Superintendent is very heavily committed tomorrow, in preparation for a period of leave."

"When's he going on leave?"

"That is confidential information, that it would not be appropriate to divulge, especially in the context of a terrorism investigation."

"So when can I see the Superintendent."

"That is not possible to say as of this moment."

It was like coaxing an obstreperous robot. "So who will take over management of the cells in the Superintendent's absence? The Inspector?"

"Inspector Fox's managerial responsibilities are entirely concerned with operational policing."

"So who?"

"That would not be appropriate to divulge."

"So who can I speak to who has management authority over the cells?" An eyebrow flickered. "You?"

"Day to day management of the cells is not the responsibility of the police hierarchy. Only Superintendent Osler in this Secon has the authority to intervene."

"Secon?"

"Security Condominium."

Or nick, if you preferred. They must be run by a private company. "Who does do day to day management, then?"

"We are not at liberty to disclose that."

"For security reasons?" She rolled her eyes.

"For security reasons." He nodded.

"Sounds as though I'm going to have to turn this into a formal complaint."

"We would naturally regret your deciding to press a complaint. I would advise exhausting the normal channels of communication first."

"From what you say, there don't seem to be any of those."

"As I said, I can convey a message to the Superintendent, should that be necessary."

Viola was not too surprised that the tape had come back on the loop. Capitulating, she outlined her concerns about the lack of exercise regime and left it with him, resolving to find out the complaint procedure; Joe would know.

There hadn't been an answer, of course; not one that counted for anything. There was a stiff little note, purportedly from the Superintendent, that had been handed to her the next time she visited. It had regretted circumstances arising in which a customer might feel that its community service standards fell short of target, but assured her that the contractor responsible for the infrastructural facilities was a blue-chip security consortium with decades of experience in prime-quality infrastructure management, operating to tough performance measures fully compliant with the GSO19057 directive. Any reported lapse from these standards would of course be rigorously investigated, the Security Condominium recognising the overriding importance of customer confidence in the quality of its service provision.

A form was attached to the note, requesting details of Security Condominium code (not supplied), incident code (not supplied), date and time of incident, identity code of customer (not supplied) and copious details about the complainant. It was not clear to whom it should be sent, but Viola was tenacious and over several days of visits persuaded Jane to log what happened, drawing her listless attention to a covered-over sketch of why and what it was she had to record: essential to avoid revealing counter-surveillance to the surveillance! There were wearying robotic interviews with the Sergeant and flirtation with the Reception avatar, from which sources the codes were extracted slowly and in chunks, like recalcitrant teeth. Actually, she had quite enjoyed the flirtation; the avatar was professionally charming and distinctly more human than the officially human Sergeant, and something about his very virtualness appealed to her.

The timing of incidents had been troublesome, as Jane - being a terrorist, of course - was denied a watch. However, mealtimes did give her an approximate sense of time, and the warder, a female avatar who clearly disliked Jane, liked to pass on bad news and could be persuaded to tell her the time if this seemed likely to cause distress. Jane became temporarily expert in finding causes of distress and summoning tears over the fact of it being various times of day and night, and though it didn't always work, she managed to log two incidents of being denied an outside view, with passably accurate timings.

She also logged one of the cell shrinkages, though Viola had not asked for this, being unconvinced that it was happening. Joe convinced her otherwise: "just think coercion and profits. The contractor probably gets a fixed payment per cell, and the smaller the cell, the cheaper." As to the cell itself reacting to being measured, who could say?

Viola finally assembled a completed form detailing all three incidents and submitted it as required to the local Customer Services Officer (who had turned out to be the Sergeant), copied to some Central London address she had been given by the Reception avatar. A breezy communication arrived just three days later, welcoming her to the Capital Security Customer Services Complaints Channel, informing her of their commitment to a prompt, honest, transparent and courteous handling of the 'service challenge instance' and assuring her that the process to be followed was fully in accord with GSO29184.

It became apparent that GSO29184 might have been designed for some degree of certainty, but certainly wasn't designed for speed. The 'Service Challenge Instance' must needs be processed by the police themselves, before requiring Viola to submit a 'Challenge Confirmation', basically saying that yes, she had meant what she first said. Then it went to a Challenge Assessor of the Joint Security Partnership Committee, who decided whether the Challenge was appropriate for investigation, liaising, at as much length as seemed necessary, with the Complainant, before - if it passed at this stage - submitting it to the next of the monthly meetings of the Committee. They, if no technical objection was raised, allocated it a case number and appointed a Challenge Prosecutor, whose job it was to enquire into all circumstances necessary to establish whether or not the Challenge had any basis in fact. Liaising with the Complainant, the police and the contractor took a great deal of time, and there was a procedure for the Prosecutor to report back quarterly on progress to the Committee.

Viola hadn't yet looked into what happened after that; it was apparent that Jane should be released long before any of this got anywhere useful at all, and she persuaded her to tolerate the cell shenanigans as best she could until she was released, then look for compensation afterwards. Through the good offices of the Reception avatar, who liked Viola and, coincidentally, didn't like the warder avatar, the completed form had already tacked its way around several submerged procedural rocks, and she had learned, just before she left, that her Challenge had been passed by the Assessor and would go to the Committee at its next meeting in early September. There was a long way and many months, possibly years to go. Meanwhile, Jane remained imprisoned.

At her last visit to Jane before flying to Bucharest, Sylv had accompanied her, breathing fire and indiscretion as they were passed through the usual sequence of Reception, Sergeant and warder before reaching the cell. A crescendo series of snorts greeted the customary inanities from the Sergeant. It was cheering. Sylv might not be the best member of any team for reasoned analysis or discussion of tactics, let alone strategy, but she personified no-surrender better than anybody Viola knew. As the Sergeant, who had visibly flinched at Sylv's concluding effort, but succeeded in remaining expressionless throughout, was ringing to get them taken across to the cells, another visitor was shown in to the room, a bearded Asian man, wearing a smart casual suit and, to Viola at least, of some obvious distinction. Her impression was confirmed in short order by Sylv, who immediately sat to attention and concentrated on being ladylike, a manner that had never been wasted on the Sergeant.

Viola was cautious: he might be police or security. He came across to them, smiled and extended his hand.

"Hello, I am Daoud Amin. Am I right in thinking you are Miss Viola Trent?" He was speaking to Sylv, who gave an ever-so-slightly slack-jawed smile and, in the act of extending her right hand forward, pointed with her left hand to one side, to correct his aim.

"Ah, I'm so sorry. Then you are?" He smiled again.

"Sylvia. Sylvia Smith."

He shook her hand, then kissed it. Twice in three months: there must be something going round, thought Viola. Sylv melted.

"And you are Miss Trent?" looking at Viola.

"I'm Viola Trent, yes." Her hand was shaken and given the treatment. Viola was charmed in spite of herself.

"Ah, I am so happy to meet you at last. I think we have a shared problem." Silence. "I mean that we both have friends held in custody for no good reason, and releasing them is a slow business. I am correct in this?" His speech was mildly accented, with a very slight sing-song quality.

To the background of a muttered "Yeah! Too right!" from Sylv, Viola answered, "That's certainly true of our friend Jane Fredricksson. But who are you here to see?"

"Mohammed Khan and Farooz Karmal."

The waiters from Memories of Kandahar. Viola felt a pang of guilt; she had largely forgotten about them and was unaware of their fate.

This was not entirely reprehensible; she had attempted to discuss bail terms at an early stage, the hen party having accepted responsibility for this as much as for the restaurant damage. But, though no figure was ever discussed, it became clear that the police were expecting a killing on this as well, and subsequently they had simply refused to discuss their case, or even say whether or not the waiters were held in custody. Viola had attempted to contact the restaurant owners, but Memories of Kandahar had remained shuttered and inaccessible. In fact, they had still not heard about the bill for the damage. "So they're still held? The police wouldn't say anything."

"Yes, they are still held, and for no good reason, as I said. Farooz has been a silly boy; he needs to choose his friends more carefully, but he is no criminal. Mohammed has nothing to answer for, not even an association."

"Jane is in a similar situation. Some damage to the restaurant, which she'd have paid for, but everything else is invented. They seem to be making a lot of the Afghanistan connection."

"Ah, your government does not like us so much; we have caused them a great deal of trouble in the past, I think." He smiled. "But the past is not now. There is no terrorism in this case, and all must be released quickly, that is my aim."

"Are you a relative?"

"No, I am a blood relative of neither. I am their Official Community Representative."

This rang a bell in Viola's mind. Of course: the replacements for councillors when local government had finally been wound up and sold off, thirty years ago. They had been derided at the time, and the result had been a generally good representation of the ethnic and religious minorities, who had a surer sense of who they were and a generally poor representation of the Anglo-Saxon majority. Viola had no idea who her Official Community Representative might be, or even whether she had one. She said as much.

"I could enquire for you if you are interested."

"Actually, I suppose I would be. I'm not sure they would be much use to us in this case, though."

"We Afghans have more cohesion than your community, that is true. But Representatives do more for their communities than you might think. I will find out for you. Meanwhile, I would like to ask whether you would like us to work together as far as we can. There are limits on this, of course. I have attempted to discuss your friend's case also with the police and have been unsuccessful. That, it seems, has been your experience for Mohammed and Farooz?"

"It has; we're not even supposed to know they're in custody, though it baffles me why they keep up this pretence that we know nothing about them."

"It is a matter of ensuring that as little as possible is on the record, I think."

"Working together, even if it's only sharing information, sounds good to me. I'm not sure here and now is a good place for a discussion, though."

"No, of course. You must get on to see your friend, who will await your visits anxiously if her experience is like that of my charges. And it is uncomfortable being under such detailed scrutiny, as must be the case in this room. Would you like to arrange to meet another time/"

"Yeah!" from Sylv.

"Yes, we would, very much. Can you suggest when and where?"

They had consulted diaries and fixed an early evening meeting for the following day. Viola had rather favoured the open anonymity of the Oast House – DizeeLizee, Sylv's favourite, certainly wouldn't do – but Daoud was teetotal, and it didn't seem ideal. So they settled on a coffee bar near Tower Bridge: a bit of a trek, but it was large and many chambered, hard to monitor, if that's what anyone was setting out to do, with recesses in which one could converse in reasonable privacy. And it did have very good cakes and coffee: the memory instantly made Viola dump her police station coffee back on the table, untouched. She had heard the phrase 'canteen culture' from Joe; if this coffee was anything to go by, it must have been dark and disturbing stuff. Daoud gestured farewell and exited, back to normal life.

"Well, that's something", Viola said, as they were being escorted into the cells complex. If it's a bother for you, I could do the meeting myself; you don't have to be there"

"Are you fucking joking, Vile? He's gorgeous, you're not having him all to yourself."

Viola laughed. "Carl will do fine."

Sylv looked at her with a sharply mocking side-glance. "And the others?"

Viola was startled. She couldn't possibly know about John. Besides, that was months ago. "You've got the wrong idea about me, Sylv."

"Oh yeah?"

"Yeah!"

They laughed together, each suddenly hoping that they could sustain the mood into the time with Jane. Neither was looking forward to the sallow, unloved chaos that Jane's cell had become, nor the inexorably declining morale, self-respect and care for appearances that was evident in Jane herself.

It had been as bad as they had expected. Jane had withdrawn into herself, and communication had been difficult; attempts at conversation ended up as rather desperate dialogues, in search of a third party, between Sylv, always the more accomplished chatterer and Viola. Jane did on that occasion make just one unprovoked remark. As Viola went to sit on one of the chairs, Jane spoke, quite sharply, even anxiously, "No, not that one. Sit on the one over there." Viola obeyed unquestioningly. Jane looked momentarily more aware of her presence and of the need for an explanation. "It breaks the triangle."

Had she got into mysticism? She exchanged a quick glance with Sylv, who raised her eyebrows almost imperceptibly and twitched a shoulder. Jane retreated again into detachment, and they got little more out of her.

XXVIII

DATING (1)

He came to, with the awful realisation that they'd been talking about the weather. This had to stop. Trouble was, he couldn't very well talk about what was on his mind. Which was Atinuke, or rather the break-up with Atinuke. Not to Alison.

He was, she thought, a bit preoccupied, and wondered what it was about. Conversation had been slow, and she'd even had to resort to the weather. But she didn't sense there was anything wrong, exactly, just he wasn't quite with her for some reason. Relations with Ben had been going slowly anyway, but intuition told her this wasn't a bad thing. He was a quick operator by nature, she could tell, and he needed jolting out of his routine if he was to be netted conclusively.

Atinuke hadn't taken it at all well. She hadn't for a moment been deceived by the suggestion of cooling it for a bit; he needed time to think. It insulted her intelligence: things had gone full tilt right from the beginning and stayed that way, for more than two months. Ben was not her idea of a thinker, not on personal relationships. And she'd grown fond of him. So it had been storm, tempest and tears, leaving him feeling washed out and (unusually) guilty too.

He'd lapsed back into silence; she was going to have to fall back on prattling about clothes shopping if this carried on. Well, it was his turn to say something. Eva, now she was another who wasn't talking to her at the moment. Not usefully. She relied on Eva's meticulousness when it came to tasks such as information gathering. That was all right, because Eva was good at things like that and enjoyed them. Besides, it was only right that she, Alison, should look to strategy while Eva, the junior partner in the friendship, did tactics. But Eva had become coy about delivering. The last time they had met, she could have sworn that Eva had something to impart, but she stubbornly denied witnessing anything interesting or new. Alison had tried several questions to catch her off-guard, but only the one about Pitchfork had gained any reaction, quickly covered by a laugh. Eva's broad face, with fair, hardly noticeable eyebrows and eyelashes did inscrutability well; such an expression had seen off more than one of the less beguiling of Alison's B-side conquests, and she had used it then. But she knew something new about Pitchfork. Why wasn't she telling her?

For once, he really did need to think things out. Alison had upset his whole schema. Until he met her, relations with Atinuke, an uncomplicated mixture of raging sex and friendship had been the ideal. It would roar ahead until boredom set in on one or other side, and an expert coup-de-grace turned it off more or less neatly. His feelings for Alison, on the other hand, were bewildering. They had become friends quickly, and there was plenty of sexual attraction, on either side as far as he could tell. She wasn't, he sensed, an innocent in need of gentle handling. And he knew well enough how to push things forward. Yet, three months on, the relationship had still not developed beyond regular meetings over lunch, or in the pub. She seemed happy enough, though you could never be sure with women. There had been Atinuke, but it was still hard to work out why decisive action had not yet seemed right.

In desperation, Ben rewound the conversation, and they drifted on to the subject of the Bucharest conference.

"It'll be my turn next year, though that might be somewhere less interesting. It'd be just my luck to get Birmingham, or something."

"And what's wrong with Birmingham?" Alison came from Solihull.

"Nothing at all; it's a very fine city. Just not far away or exotic."

"Oh, like Manchester, you mean." Ben came from Salford."

"No, if you want real exotic you've got to look at Middlesbrough."

Alison giggled. "So Middlesbrough's where you take all the girls, is it?"

"Why; you interested in going?"

"Not Middlesbrough, no. Too posh. Did you hear that Janet's gone to Bucharest?"

"No, really? With Körthofer?"

"The one."

"I had heard she'd done a few other cities with him in the last couple of months."

"She has. She did Munich for a long weekend only three weeks ago, and we reckon she did Paris soon after she got off with him."

"Doesn't sound too bad a deal. She'll find Körthofer like one of Wagner's gods when he's in the wrong mood, but he's a Paginist's idea of a celebrity. And rich. Would Cambridge do, then?"

"You'd have to ask Janet."

"No, I mean would *you* fancy a day out there? I've got to do a morning's worth of research in the University Library, but then I could show you round."

"How come you know Cambridge so well?" Alison said, stalling for time.

"I did a post-grad year there. At Anglia, but they call it all Cambridge University nowadays, so I've got members' rights. Do you want to?"

"When are you going?"

"Saturday, first thing."

"Will you take me punting" said Alison on a sudden inspiration. "Promise I'll wear my straw hat if I do."

"My punting skills are second to none", Ben said with mock solemnity. Actually, he hadn't had time for much of that when he was there, but felt he could rely on being the practical type. "Perhaps something waterproof as well as the hat, though."

"Right you are."

"I take it that's a yes."

"Not so fast. How do we get there?"

"I'll be on expenses, so it'll be a hired car."

"A flash one?"

"I'll make that specific request."

"Well, that almost sounds good. Where will we meet?"

"I'll pick you up from your place. That is a yes, then?"

"How do you know where that is? You've been spying on me?": eyebrows raised.

"Actually, it would be helpful if you said where it was."

"Marlowe Road, Brockley."

"It's a long road."

"Number 16. Flat B: the entry-video can be dodgy, so give three rings and I'll know who it is."

Ben input the details to his videophone. "Seven thirty okay? We want to get there early if we can."

"That'll be fine." It would usefully avoid interrogation from Eva, who never emerged from her room before ten on Saturdays.

"So that's a yes?"

"I'll bring the straw hat."

XXIX

DIPLOMACY (1)

Eva had decided to cut out the middle-man.   More and more obviously, Alison ran straight to Karen with whatever news Eva had to impart, thereby claiming all credit for gathering it. Most irritating of all, that made Alison the sole conduit for whatever Karen herself had found out.   Eva suspected she was no more diligent at the feedback than at the detection.   Besides, the Westwood-Pendleton summit was of obvious interest to the VC and his gang, i.e. Karen, but not much relevant to the conceited one and his, i.e. Alison nowadays.   And her friend could barely give her the time of day recently, so wrapped up was she in her new interest. There had been a sharp decline in joint evenings out and a corresponding decline in B-side boyfriends. Eva was ambivalent about that: the absence of their attentions was not wholly unwelcome, but it was starting to make her feel invisible. It was time to strike out on her own. She chose a direct report to Karen as the starting point.

The mechanics of this were not so easy as the decision. She didn't actually know Karen, except for having met her once or twice with Alison. As the Vice-Chancellor's PA, she was a slightly formidable figure; not that Eva felt any whit inferior as an academic research assistant, but the rest of the world didn't see it that way, and Karen herself probably didn't either. So she planned on the basis of striking up a working relationship with a Queen Bee. An English Catholic girls' school education had given useful training in that.   Timing things, so that no-one else was there for five or ten minutes was straightforward; she just let Sue in on some of the background, in exchange for intelligence from her observation post in Corporate Planning. Armoured and scripted, she accosted Karen in her office on a late Wednesday afternoon, when the Hon Ran was away at a Vice Chancellors' Committee in the City.

Appearing in the doorway, she said, "Hello, you're Karen aren't you? You know Alison. Alison Somers?"

Karen nodded acknowledgement, warily.

"I'm Eva, Alison's friend. The thing is, Alison's busy at the moment, and I've got some news about the AFFREM thing that needs talking about. She said you'd know what I was talking about." Eva's school training in casuistry had not been wasted. These were white lies. That was all right.

Karen was still de haut en bas, but rapidly relaxed. Eva, yes, she thought she'd recognised her; she'd met her once or twice with Alison. So this was who the information came from. Karen had never believed that a lazy cow like Alison would be working it out for herself. She decided on or two security questions, though. "I may do, but what's AFFREM when it's at home?"

"It's an organisation that's planning something here. It's the Fellowship of Reamers or something. That doesn't mean much to me, but it's what they've called themselves."

"Oh, that one. Who's with it, then?

"I don't know for certain, but I think Alison's talked to you about the new Reader in Phoniotics, Stephen Pendleton. He's part of it, I'm sure."

Eva was clearly okay. "Him! Yes, there's a reorganisation going on. Mr Fraserman is in on it, obviously, but it's being kept secret, and that's not his style. What news did you say you'd got?"

There were approaching footsteps on the stairs. Morrison appeared, a pile of papers under his arm and an expression of resigned harassment on his face. Karen made a quick decision. Eva was obviously potentially good value; Karen had wondered about cutting out the middle-man herself, but hadn't then identified the source.

Alison could always be briefed afterwards. "Are you free at half-past?"

"Half past four?

"Yes."

"Yes, I am.

"Let's meet at DizeeLizee then."

"The place near The Green?"

"Yes."

"All right, see you."

Karen waved and turned to Morrison's latest futile scheme to improve the lot of his department, which he wanted to be passed to the VC in confidence.

"All of this?" Eva heard, as she turned to go.

"I felt it essential that the VC understand fully the issues involved."

"Suit yourself, but I think you'll be lucky if he gets round to this lot by the same time next year. You know what he's like on reports?"

"One page, yes, but this is supporting material…"

The discussion faded as Eva started descending the stairs. Poor Morrison; he might be a bit of a berk, but he was a nice enough man in his way, and he did get the rough end of everyone's dealings. His attempts to better his department were no more effective than her battles to make an impression on the opposite sex. At least, though, she didn't waste her time writing unread reports about it.

DizeeLizee was still quiet at half past four. Both girls were prompt. Karen ordered a Limacolada and Eva decided to join her in that. Finding a suitably out-of-the-way alcove, they sat sipping a little of their drinks and engaging in covert scrutiny. Karen, as the Queen Bee, spoke first.

"So what is it, then?"

Talk about direct! When she wanted to get something out of you, Alison would approach a subject on tiptoe with much circling around the point, though Eva had become expert at short-cutting her to it. "Something I overheard. It may affect your boss, but I don't know much of what it's about, because I don't really know the background. Do you know anything about this AFFREM: beyond the name?" She wasn't lying; Alison had been parsimonious with the feedback.

"A bunch of wallies out for world domination as far as I can see. Mr Fraserman has something to do with it. I've no idea why; I'd have thought he'd have more sense."

"Oh. What are they planning to do?"

"Anybody's guess! Here in AUP, they want to re-organise everything to death, and there's some grand plan. But I've only overheard odd snatches as I've gone into the room. The one who works for them is that stiff Stephen Pendleton. Do you know him?" She sucked at her drink with the straw.

"Yes, I know who he is. Alan Westwood is in on it too."

Karen snorted with laughter, ejecting gobbets of Limacolada from her mouth. "That moron! They must be desperate", she said, wiping splashes daintily from her skirt and top. "Talk about scraping the barrel."

Eva wondered about a show of loyalty, but the idea died an early death. "I heard them talking. On the 'phone. When I was at work, late yesterday afternoon."

"Karen snorted again. "So much for their famous security."

"Security? Do they do that? There was something about rolling out the concept of the three Is into the reality sphere; does that make any sense to you?"

"No, it doesn't, but not much that Stephen Pendleton says does make sense that I've heard. It could be to do with this Charter of theirs."

Eva hadn't heard of any Charter. "Does that say anything about security?"

"I don't know, but they were banging on about it in a meeting a few weeks ago. The stiff had brought a gorilla along with him": momentarily, she looked wistful. "Mr Fraserman wasn't having any, mind you", she said, proud of her boss's bolshieness.

That could explain the comment about the 'Honorable Fellow' 'backsliding' that she had heard. "Well, they seem to be planning to do something they call 'normalisation' without him. To the Manucussionists for now, but it sounded like a lot more than just that."

"Without Mr Fraserman?"

"Yes. What Stephen Pendleton said was something about not meeting members' needs when they weren't in agreement, only in much longer words."

"That figures." She sipped at her drink and looked round. "So el stiffo and his moron friend are planning to take over AUP bit by bit and without Mr Fraserman, are they?"

"Something like."

"We'll see about that. I don't know how Alan Westwood has the nerve, attacking Mr Fraserman like this. He only got his job because of him." It must have been one of her boss's off-days, Karen thought. She suddenly looked formidable: the lioness defending her cub.

Eva was quite startled by the transformation, not having realised that Karen saw the Vice Chancellor's office as an indissoluble joint enterprise. She had a momentary sense of guilt; she might have got her own boss into some trouble. But it was only momentary; he was with Stephen Pendleton and his boys club, and that could look after itself. "What do you think we should do?"

"I don't know yet, but I need to warn Mr Fraserman somehow, and we'll take it from there." 'Somehow' was the word, she thought. Tell him this straight out and he'd go off like a bleeding rocket, not necessarily in the right direction. "Can you keep an eye on Alan Westwood."

Eva groaned. As if she hadn't been doing that all summer. "All right. And Stephen Pendleton too, if I spot him around."

"Thanks. I owe you one. I'll keep an eye on him myself."

"Can I ask a favour in return? Let me know about anything you notice. This normalisation project as they called it didn't sound as though it would be good for many people in the department. That means my job's at stake as well. And my friends'. If Alan Westwood has anything to do with it, people like Marie will suffer. I don't think he likes me much either."

"Yes, okay. Why doesn't he like you?"

"I made a fuss about the wandering hands."

"And Marie?"

"The same, but Marie got him somewhere sensitive."

"You mean … ?"

"She nearly tore them off."

Karen greeted this with joy and insisted on another round of drinks to celebrate. Eva had formed an alliance. Now she could brief Alison.

XXX

LIVING APART

Well, all's bad that ends up being swiped with a dead fish. You'll probably have heard by now, anyway; it was gossip when Karen hooked me and it's gossip now she's thrown me back. The only good thing is that it's August, and a lot of people aren't around to notice.

It was extremely painful, most of all because it came completely out of the blue. We were in the middle of a not particularly heated argument, that she'd been at least half the cause of, when she suddenly said, "It's not working out, is it Tad?" I must have looked gone out, because she continued with "I think we should cool it for a bit; see where we stand." It took a bit more discussion for it to sink in that, basically, she was throwing me out - I had moved in to her place for the last two months - and ending it.

At the time, I just felt crushed. I packed my stuff and left, back to a bed-sit that felt even lonelier than before. But I had to return the next day for the items I hadn't managed to carry in the one load, and that led to a scene in which I didn't keep much dignity. She was just so adamant and so sure that a 'space to breathe' was the right thing for our relationship. It was horribly frustrating. Only twenty-four hours before, everything had looked sunny, not to say settled. Now it was back down the big green snake to square one. I never believed in the idea that the break might be temporary. It was too obviously the chop.

The first week back by myself was awful and the second not much better. I virtually gave up eating and lived mostly on coffee and beer.

I didn't sleep well either. The diet probably didn't help that, but it wasn't the only cause of waking up at four o'clock every morning. I'd lie awake, anger and despair churning around in my head. It's a nasty mix at any time, but the early morning made it a nightmare. One that didn't even have waking up to look forward to. I became an expert on the dawn chorus, but it only sometimes gave pleasure; more often I got stabbed with memory. I just couldn't see how Karen had treated me so cruelly, then the next moment I could see only too well, then I'd get angry with her for being heartless, then I'd feel humiliated, then I'd try to think of ways to get her back and dream of reconciling things, then I'd get real again, then I couldn't see why she'd treated me so cruelly and so on and so on and so on.

What snapped me out of it in the end was that, after several days as a hermit, Paul came round. I'd been in touch with him shortly before Karen's regime change, about the normalisation thing that was worrying her. I can't say he was a welcome face at the door, but then nobody but Karen would have been that, and Paul had the immense advantage over others that he never really notices or knows about anything anyway. I think he just assumed I was pale and tired because I was a bit hung over; mind you, I was that as well.

"Hi Tad, what's doing? You don't look quite with it. Too many late nights?"

I laughed through misery. "Something like."

He invited himself in, and I made the ritual cup of coffee: I've read in books about students doing this a century or so back; it must be part of our heritage now. It served Paul right that I'd only got a cheap and very nasty Instant. My room was as you'd expect after a week of frowsting inside and not making the bed or washing up, but that must have made it like Paul's place, as there was no reaction to the chaos and not much to the state of his cup. He just sipped, scowled slightly and said "Fuck me!" with feeling. "Are you coming down the pub this evening?" he said, "Get something decent to drink. And I've something to tell you."

"If it's another female you want to introduce me to, thanks for the last one, but I'm giving them a rest for a little while."

"No, it's not a bint; I'm keeping them to myself now Janet's buggered off with some sugar-daddy. This is serious stuff. You'll be transfixed and amazed."

This did sound interesting, discounting the build-up, which came with long practice if you knew Paul. "Can't you tell me it here?"

"No. You owe me a drink or two now, and my loan's not come."

Well that sounded reasonable enough, so I agreed. The Oast suddenly sounded really attractive after a week of the bed-sit, and I'd certainly been saving money in the last few days.

The information got me into one hell of a mess as things turned out, but it was a vitally useful distraction from the Karen situation. I can't pretend I started sleeping better straight off, or there weren't bad moments, but it did blunt the worst of it, and that side of things started improving from then on. So credit to Paul; he does have his uses. Now and then.

XXXI

THE LECTURE

Viola had not elaborated on how negotiations had worked out with Daoud Amin, and Carl asked her whether his help had been useful as they lay side by side in bed, languorous, much later that evening.

"So far, not much. We met him at the coffee bar, which had a brilliant view over the river, and he stood us coffee and cakes, which was nice, but for the life of us we couldn't think of much we could usefully do together. The police have put a Restraining Order on the waiters as well, to stymie any media protest. He did manage to get away with a discreet item in the monthly newsletter for the mosque they sometimes attended, but nobody's picked up on it. It probably had to be so vague that no-one understood. I asked if he could do an update and include Jane, and he said he would think about it, but there wasn't likely to be much sympathy for a westerner caught in the traps originally set for Muslims. He did give me the name of my Community Representative, though."

"Did Sylv do anything?"

"Yes, she tried hard to get off with him. I think the dress she chose might have been too revealing."

"I'd be surprised if he objected."

"No, he didn't object as such. Anyway, she managed to engineer another meeting, "to talk about how things are going", which will be when we're in Vishiney, so she'll have him to herself. I said she'd do better dressing more cautiously, but I can't see Sylv taking any notice of that."

Viola's thoughts drifted onto the lecture, mentally rehearsing the arrangements for the practical demonstrations and the transitions to and from the speech that she would need to cover them. Only two days away now, it was a real career opportunity. She had already called a summit conference with Carl and the two pianists for the following day, in a bid to ensure the others took it seriously. The whole production needed to be seamless and accident-free.

The large lecture hall was filling rapidly. With just five minutes to go, Viola felt sure that everything was in place: the lecture notes and slides; the holopoint backups just in case; the pianists sitting at recently tuned Bechsteins in the corner; the various musical scores placed where needed; Carl in the freshly cleansed performance suit that she had insisted on, sitting just to one side of the lectern. He looked up and grinned at her. "Relax!"

"You must be joking."

"No, really, just enjoy it. "

She knew Carl thought her arrangements obsessional. Brought up as a musician in the British tradition, he winged everything once learnt. He did so very well. But obsessional was what worked for her. She smiled back at him and cast her eye over the notes, making sure she had the opening line pat.

The lecture hall was full now, with extra seats being brought in. She spotted a number of eminent Paginists and other Ancillary Musicians in the auditorium. There were even a few Presentationists. Briefly, she felt sorry for the music stand expert and the Kazakh with his translator. But it was not the time for sentiment. The doors closed at the sides and back, and silence fell for the chairman's witty and mercifully brief introduction. This was it!

"Thank you, ladies, gentlemen: human and avatar; I am flattered by your interest in what I will have to say. As the conference programme promises, this is to be about future directions for Paginatorics, a discipline that I believe to be on the cusp of a revolution in methodology; a revolution with implications for all of the M-class ancillary music disciplines: manucussionists, chordologists, presentationists, Reedsmiths, case technicians. I will first aim to establish the context, both historical and social, within which this methodological revolution has come about, and for the practical demonstrations that this will involve, I am joined by the distinguished Paginist Professor Carl Trenchard, who has kindly agreed to help, and by our pianists, Henry and Pete."

There was enthusiastic applause for Carl and a more muted reception for the pianists; their S-Class background was less than respectable to the American sector delegates.

"Paginatorics is a discipline held in esteem today, but it had very humble beginnings if one looks back as little as forty years. Page turning, as it was then, simply gave assistance to musicians whose performances, if they had turned the pages themselves, would have lost too many notes. It was a little-regarded pursuit, done on an entirely amateur basis. Dependent on the musical abilities of the person drafted in for the task, the cure could sometimes be worse than the disease." Here Carl and the pianists burlesqued some incompetently assisted Rachmaninov.

Viola breathed deeply and slowly to calm down her pulse rate. So far, so good; they were looking interested; they were even laughing where they were supposed to. She had been very lucky in getting Carl; he was a natural at this sort of thing.

"Professionalisation was clearly essential. For music to be delivered to the highest standards, the musicians' information-input experience needed to be seamless. But how? Page turning at this level of execution was too subservient an art to command any sort of fee that would provide a living, let alone attract the calibre of performer that it needed.

It was at this point that Paginatorics was given its guiding genius, its Paganini. Harry Portoli, a dancer trained by the Royal Ballet who had been forced to retire early owing to a knee injury, discovered that the tedium of his work as assistant concert manager to a major orchestra could be relieved by treating the distribution of music before the concert as a balletic exercise. He challenged himself to optimise the efficiency and grace of the movements involved. To do so, he evolved a style and technique that placed as much importance on the precision of arm and hand movements as on the footwork, while brilliantly accommodating the space limitations imposed by the orchestral layout.

This remained a private passion, known only to the few who turned up early for rehearsals, until a last minute change of music for a concert by a Russian maestro, notorious for his intolerance of delays, meant that Portoli was unable to distribute the music in time without going through his routine in full view of a capacity audience, an act that led to enthusiastic and sustained applause. Anderson Szekely, the celebrated American concert promoter, who was in the audience, immediately spotted the act's potential as a new performance art form and engaged Portoli under contract to develop it.

Portoli, with the time to develop his brainchild, realised that it could be extended well beyond the parameters of distributing and collecting music. It could be made part of the musical performance itself, by a straightforward extension of technique to include page-turning for the musicians. Helped by experienced orchestral musicians, he succeeded in choreographing a through-performed version of the slow movement of Mozart's piano concerto, Köchel 467. By demonstrating that an interesting concert aperitif could be extended into a commercially viable concert performance, he transformed the drab chore of page-turning into a glamorous professional discipline in its own right. It can be said that Portoli's initial treatment of Mozart was both the founding event of Paginatorics and the birth of M-Class music.

I would like at this point to hand over to Carl Trenchard, one of Harry Portoli's most distinguished pupils, to give a brief demonstration of typical prologue and epilogue routines, together with the paginatoric routines choreographed by Portoli for the Rachmaninov piece, the 'Russian Rhapsody', that you heard a little earlier. It was enacted then with the trademark hindrance that you might have expected from an amateur page-turner of the last century. Portoli's rendering shows how far and how quickly he had advanced paginatoric skills."

This was Carl's most nervous moment. Prologues and epilogues (distributing and collecting music) might be Paginatorics' starting point, but they were infrequently done nowadays, so he was relatively unpractised. And he was used to using the music itself as a focus, so had had to develop his own techniques for the few routines such as this that lacked it. It was often fudged by playing, through headphones, a suitable section of a piece of music that fitted, but the headphones could never entirely be concealed and certainly would not do in the present context. He snapped into the routine, the music playing inside his mind, stepping in rhythm towards the music scores lying on a table.

As the pianists took over, he wondered whether Portoli himself had imagined a musical accompaniment in that way. Perhaps not: Portoli was notoriously, within the profession, indifferent to the music itself, and many a soloist had had to make the best of a cadenza cut short, or a final sustained note gently floated away, as the music abruptly cut to the next page or disappeared into the library cupboard. That was why, the legend established, most of Paginatoric's techniques had actually been developed by Portoli's pupils rather than by Portoli himself. The page-turning routine now in progress was, in consequence, a rather basic exercise, but it had an old-fashioned charm that Carl could bring out most effectively and that the audience responded to. The epilogue was a rather perfunctory repeat of the prologue: that was where Portoli was the master of all of them, Carl thought, as he dropped the music soundlessly back on the table and walked back to his seat; he would have conjured a magical grace out of any routine that did not play servant to music. It was an aspect of his art that he had passed on to no-one. All of his more able pupils had been musicians first and dancers second. It was an irony known only to a few that the acknowledged founding father of Paginatorics was in reality the begetter and master of a related but distinct art form that, almost unnoticed, had died with him.

The applause died away. "You can see in that an artistry and professionalism entirely absent from the pre-history of Paginatorics. A task, once regarded as the poor cousin of musical performance, was now transformed into to a major art form with a large public following.

Paginatorics chose its moment well. There was an audience in waiting. Unadorned classical music ('straight', or S-Class) performances, that is, by musicians only, had embarked on a suicidal rejection of its core audience in the second half of the last century. The fashionable composers, of what was then called simply 'classical' music, had aimed to write music of an artistic purity that only an inner elite could be expected to understand, let alone enjoy. Not everybody followed this idea, but, taken as a whole, the audience did what was expected of it and ceased to listen to contemporary S-Class. Only in popular music, in its many subdivisions, including ethnic music from non-Western cultures, did audiences continue to expect to enjoy music that had been recently composed. S-Class audiences largely restricted themselves to a fossilised repertoire of classic pieces from the distant past.

This left a gap. A taste for the more considered, less ephemeral music in the Western European tradition had not disappeared, but the living tradition of performing and listening to it had. Ironically, by this time, S-Class music aimed at audience enjoyment was again being written, but audiences remained a small elite. M-Class leapt into this gap, presenting S-Class music with the sort of spectacle and theatricality that had been an expected feature of rock music for the previous half-century, but that had until then had little or no impact on the more serious-minded forms. One area had held the clue throughout: film music showed that audiences could enjoy even the recherché, 'elitist' products of mid-century S-Class if they were placed in an interesting and varied visual context.

Paginatorics' take-on was meteoric. Almost immediately, it spawned the related disciplines now known collectively as Ancillary Music: the manucussionists, the chordologists and the Reedsmiths, who provide support to the percussionists, the string players and the reed players respectively; the presentationists who deal with music stands in their own inimitable fashion; the case technicians responsible for entry and exit of instruments and their presentation, as needed, during a performance.

As the number of ancillary artists involved in M-Class performances proliferated, the trend was to reduce the number of musicians. The larger pieces are still performed occasionally, but only as special, showcase events. Thus we have the annual Wembley Stadium performances of Mahler's 'Symphony of a Thousand' – now a considerable under-estimate – or the open-air, winter stagings of the 'Verdi Requiem on Ice' at the Caracalla Baths.

Paginatorics has advanced a great deal, in its technique over the last thirty years. Portoli, as you will have noticed, used a limited repertoire of movements for page-turning and a range of foot-work that, though much more fully developed than the upper-body action, was always limited by the need to accommodate his problematic knee joint. I would like to ask Carl Trenchard once again to apply his skills, to a demonstration of Paginatorics as it is currently practised."

Viola sat down, helping herself to the glass of water provided and using the break as a brief relaxation before she launched into the key thesis of her lecture. Carl put on one of his showpieces, with an astounding variety of choreography for a piece, albeit one written for the purpose, that demanded just two pianists and two pianos. The applause was sustained. When it started to lessen in intensity, Viola returned to the lectern.

"Before outlining what I see as the future direction of Paginatorics, I will need to spend some time looking at the social environment in which M-Class operates. No art form exists in a vacuum; the social context is always a significant influence. M-Class certainly gained from contemporary S-Class discarding its audience. But it gained also from an increasing public preference for visual presentation.

The relative status of the two art forms has been further affected, some might say distorted" (a nod to the Russian sector delegates) "by the way in which social attitudes to S-Class music have changed in the last twenty years. The evangelical Christian movement has for a long time considered it frivolous and amoral. More damagingly still, it has come to be seen by many as damagingly elitist: to a degree likely to harm individual social development, particularly in childhood.

These two views together have marginalised it. S-Class music-making is no longer, at least in the American sector, regarded as a respectable pursuit and is no longer part of any educational institution's syllabus. Some countries have gone so far as to make it illegal, and even where this has not been the case, its legality has proved constantly vulnerable to challenge. M-Class, by contrast, is eminently well thought of and, in the American Sector, part of everyone's education. Many feel that this downgrading of the status of S-Class has gone too far and that M-Class needs to acknowledge the value of its root stock, but there is no avoiding the fact that this is the environment within which M-Class develops and flourishes."

The last remark led to one Dutch and two American delegates walking out noisily, but Viola was holding her audience well.

"What other social factors should we be looking to? My thesis is that there are two linked phenomena that will be key to Paginatoric practice in the next decades. First is the trend towards detachment from and de-personalisation of performance practice. M-Class, in the American sector, has reduced the actual music to a supporting role, the musicians routinely ignored in concert promotions and in concert programme notes. Dependent as their skills are on S-Class training and technique, M-Class relies increasingly on importing musicians from sectors in which social attitudes are differently positioned.

The second phenomenon is the creeping virtualisation of individual life experience. Technology has refined its ability to measure and deliver sensory inputs and outputs at a startling rate. Perhaps inevitably, this has most quickly been taken on for erotic and sporting purposes. The X-Glove product, famously, or notoriously, is capable of delivering various modes of sexual stimulation and of simulating various types of sexual intercourse to a high degree of accuracy, using the personal sensory profiles commonly known as veeps and penpros. It uses sophisticated algorithms for real-time sensory interaction and feedback. Despite some unfortunate early accidents and malicious mis-programming, despite being denounced for its immorality by religious groups, despite health and safety scares, the X-Glove is now in almost universal use by the generation in their late teens and twenties. Similarly, sporting performance can be simulated, with a variety of sensor types, taking it to higher levels than any human could achieve unaided. These too are in common use.

The erotic and sporting applications are often dismissed as trivial, aimed largely at self-gratification. But they illustrate the way in which virtualisation insinuates itself at a social level. A significant minority of individuals, for example, now claim to achieve sufficient sexual and emotional satisfaction from virtual environments alone. And the 'Assisted Performance' Olympic Games attract more onlookers than the original brand.

The virtualisation techniques involved are also being applied to less attention-grabbing areas. The erotic applications are no longer the most advanced. There have been two particularly significant technological breakthroughs.

Firstly, it has been possible to create ambient virtual environments, within limited real-world spaces, in which virtual entities, generally known as avatars, could take effective physical form and interact with real-world living entities. Making such avatars convincingly human was a long-standing problem, given the slow speed of learning from interaction with actual humans. However, packaging up such interactions as digitised learning programmes, on a massive scale, allows avatar programming to run through the learning process at computer processor speeds. Once estimated to require 300 years of natural interactions, it now needs just a two-day production process.

Secondly, encapsulation has allowed individual virtual beings to inhabit exclusively a defined and shaped physical space and interact fully with real-world entities in this form. In practical terms, this has allowed avatars to function as robots, often quite difficult to distinguish from actual human beings, or whatever other physical shell, such as dogs, they were programmed to inhabit. Encapsulations are still very costly and relatively rare, but the two advances have opened up a vast range of possible uses. These include many aspects of policing and incarceration, tasks involving physical danger such as fire-fighting and military reconnaissance and traditionally low-paid tasks regarded as unpleasant or demeaning to humans.

It seems inevitable that Paginatorics and the other Ancillary Music art forms will themselves be affected by these two trends. The samples of Paginatoric art that you have seen illustrated here, make the point that although it is a second-tier performance art, one step removed from the primary material, it remains as physical in execution and as reliant on personal style as the music-making itself. It has an intensely human expressiveness, and in this lies both its appeal and its limitation.

The appeal can, as we have seen in other areas, transfer to virtualised equivalents if virtualisation can offer the same level of expressiveness and a more interesting spectacle. Audiences will have to be the best judges of this.

What, then, are the limitations of current Paginatoric practice?

Most obviously, Paginatorics is constrained at present by human physical capabilities: by the speed at which humans can move; by the physical manoeuvres that they are capable of; by the fact that a single controlling mind can only be in one place at any one time. If multiple Paginists are involved in a performance, control is unavoidably distributed between them. No matter how well choreographed and rehearsed, there will always be a margin of error.

Some aspects of Paginatoric performance, also, are already anachronistic. Human paginists can make little or nothing of a performance in which the instrumentalists are using electronically presented scores and parts. Used for more than three decades in recording sessions, they have been generally ignored in Paginatoric practice.

Then, as already mentioned, there are the moral and legal dilemmas around S-Class training for the musicians involved.

Virtual beings do not necessarily suffer these limitations; it is a matter of programming. They can, for example, interact with holograph projections of musical scores, in a way that is impossible for humans.

None of this is to suggest that virtualised Paginatoric performances are yet in place for the mass market. Human performance is, for the moment, the standard.

However, several initiatives are now in progress that program avatars to learn S-Class performance and Paginatoric technique. In most cases, this is strictly under human direction. At least two experimental projects, though, are programming avatars to develop their technique (after an initial learning programme), entirely independently. Effectively, the avatars, using feedback mechanisms, develop through self-programming.

Could I ask the avatar performers in the audience to identify themselves and come to the front now? They will demonstrate to you the level of capability reached in just five years of research effort. My thanks are due to Herr Doktor Schliemann and to Professor

Martinsen, from whose research teams our avatar performers are drawn."

Four individuals stood up, in some cases to the evident amazement of neighbours and made their way down the aisles. Pete and Henry relinquished their places at the pianos, and the avatars duly put on a rather stiffly and unimaginatively choreographed rendering of a Mozart Sonata for 2 pianos. The audience observed politely but without great interest until the moment towards the end of the piece, when one of the Paginist avatars, to secure a stiffly bound score that would not lie flat, held it down with both hands, temporarily detaching his right hand from his body for the purpose.

The performance, that moment apart, was unimpressive, but Viola had made her point. She continued with some speculation as to the possibilities of avatar Paginatorics, both human-directed and free-form, before wrapping up the lecture with a summary of her view of Paginatorics' future direction and a lengthy list of thanks to all who had helped her and made this possible. Carl, Pete and Henry were given a final ovation.

Throughout this concluding section, free of further performance responsibilities, Carl let his mind run free. Viola was, essentially, speaking the funeral rites for his area of distinction. Did that matter? Not too much, he thought: he was part of the history of the art-form, and traditional, or straight Paginatorics, in the terms in which he had already started to think of it, should retain a good following for some years to come; long enough to see him out. But there was sadness there too. He was no longer where it was happening. Probably he had not been there for some while, but this was the moment of recognition.

He could, of course, go with the flow and clamber onto the virtualisation bus, but he had no stomach for it. For one thing, he was accustomed to leading not following. For another, he had had over thirty years refining his particular art and had no wish to re-run the process. He remembered page turning for fellow students at college;

it was grim work, demanding surprising concentration, totally without reward or acknowledgement; noticed only if something went wrong. Harry Portoli and his music distribution act had just come to light in his later student years, but no-one thought of it as a career at the time. Looked at from that standpoint, the intervening time seemed as immense stretch of years, of creative effort, of career slog, of hard repetitive work to establish a position. Now it was time to think of something else to do; something that could mature as the Paginatorics he knew withered. Nothing came immediately to mind.

A dozen or so further walk-outs, mainly of Christians who saw virtualisation as the work of the devil, and Viola had finished, to prolonged applause and a Q&A session that had to be cut off in its prime for time constraints. Surrounded afterwards by a small crowd of fellow academics and commercial Paginists, it took her some time to work her way over to Carl, who was chatting with Henry, Pete and the two avatar pianists.

"Thanks so much." She hugged him. "Thanks" she said to the pianists. "What did you think?" turning back to Carl.

"It was great. I think you made quite an impact."

"Well, I couldn't have done it without you." She swivelled to include Henry and Pete, and the four Paginist and musician avatars, who had now joined the group. Thank you. I really enjoyed your performances."

Carl decided to steer her away at the first opportunity; she was on a high and would soon start to babble. A wind-down drink called. Or two. He invited the two human pianists and the avatars, and they left the hall, by now almost empty, in which stony-faced university support workers removed the extra chairs, repositioned the lectern and parked, without obvious love or care, the two Bechsteins.

XXXII

THE BEST LAID PLANS

The atmosphere in the meeting room was palpably different as he walked in. Quanco, in last week's meeting, had grouped themselves tightly around the Holopoint machine. Half the point of Holopoint was the ability to operate it from almost anywhere. Really, they had just been huddling for safety in a strange castle. Outvesta, by contrast, looked relaxed and had disposed themselves at various points around the table. It was not unexpected; he had enjoyed, over the last two months, several dinner discussions with the head of their bid team, a privilege not extended to the other two bidders. There was a sense of familiarity and of working together, which had not been there with Quanco. A sense that would not be there either, if all went to plan, with Brillian.

Kavkazian waved and smiled. He gave a cursory acknowledgement. Overt friendliness was not appropriate at this stage and in an open meeting. He stored a note in his brain for later communication. It was less than a minute before two o'clock; time to pour a coffee and get started.

"Thank you all for making the effort to come here today. We extend our apologies as appropriate for any inconvenience suffered as a result of our security precautions," (there had been at least one strip search) " which reflect the degree of seriousness that we bring to our operations and the standards that we feel we can expect from our co-workers. We have you to thank you for co-operation in maintaining jointly in this way the highest standards of ethical commercial responsibility."

They seemed, with one exception, mollified. Jack Kavkazian had remained relaxed and smiling; Security had been instructed to treat him easily. The exception had presumably experienced the strip search. He was mentally noted also. Kavkazian would be asked to remove him from the team. Normalisation work required a neutral demeanour in the face of formalised humiliation. Consultation sessions routinely saw plans verbally dismembered, distinguished members of staff heaping scorn on their idiocy. Facilitators needed unbending decisiveness; any hint of possible compromise could be fatal to the purity of the concept.

"I shall keep the introductions to a minimum. Outvesta have worked with us before and I believe are fully conversant with AFFREM's international standards for a normalisation programme schema." Kavkazian signified agreement. "I think we all understand the high degree of commercial sensitivity and confidentiality that is involved in the opportunity before you." That was for the Whitehall people, unavoidably involved, but apt to treat secrecy lightly when dealing with their own circle. "One particular feature that redoubles this is the compartmentalisation of the university's executive, a situation that has occurred only after consultation at the highest levels."

Or to put it another way, Fraserman was out on his ass; not that he knew it, not yet. After he had briefed Herb Summerson, Herb, he knew, had rung Fraserman. Not surprisingly, the next (last) meeting had been, as he put it to Herb later, 'difficult'. After a run-through of options, Herb had given him the go-ahead with "if you say so, Stephen", and he knew that Herb would have discussed it with the Global Master.

"That is at the highest levels in AFFREM?" – one of the Treasury people.

"It has been discussed at length with my immediate superior, Grand Temple, who has discussed it with the Global Master." A shadow of what might have been disdain flitted across the Treasury man's face as the titles rolled out; he made no further comment.

"The purpose of today's meeting is to grant Outvesta the opportunity to outline its approach to normalisation in organisational situations adjoint, matrix-wise to that of AUP, demonstrating their approach to conceptualisation and the catalysis of progessivisation of the resultant programme schema. I'll now hand over to Outvesta for their presentation."

Jack Kavkazian stood up and walked casually to the front of the room, speaking as he did so. "Thank you Stephen, and our thanks to all of you who have devoted the time and effort to coming here today. What we would like to share with you is Outvesta's CPLGold philosophy, comprising the stages of conceptualisation and progressivisation that Stephen has already mentioned, and integrating too the all-important logisticalisation that's needed if the normalisation is to run smoothly once it engages with the human resource."

The presentation got into its stride, and Holopoint visions flowed in a smoothly engineered succession. Stephen Pendleton allowed himself to relax a little, the better to study the room. He noted two more exclusions: one of the AFFREM team had an inexcusably maladjusted tie; one of the Outvesta team had been too obviously struggling to maintain an expression of intelligent comprehension even as the closing comments prior to handover were being delivered: if you couldn't find your way round the words, as his mentors used to say, you couldn't find your way round the folk. Two down from the bid team and one from AFFREM was disappointing just ten minutes into the meeting, but it wasn't unusual.

A choreographed succession of Outvesta speakers took the presentation through in just under an hour, with varying levels of skill in the delivery, but with nothing less than a bland professionalism. After brief applause, a break was called: the Brits didn't seem able to function without them. What he was looking for now was a polite series of anodyne questions, with answers that left no commitments hanging. The audience should be left receptive to the written bid, to the promises of its large print and the realities of its small.

It was not to be. He realised afterwards that he should have had a pre-meeting with the Whitehall people to make sure that they were all on-side and cleansed of awkward viewpoints. For what was itself a variety of pre-meeting, you didn't get the top-level people, the political appointees who knew who their real paymasters were; you got a level or two below. Chosen by competitive examination and kicked up the hierarchy in a similar spirit, their prime and very dangerous skills lay in taking interesting views on subjects and asking the questions that the more business-focused material in the top ranks knew instinctively to avoid.

The problems started immediately. Outvesta were asked to explain details of their methodology and approach. The tenor of the question suggested inadequate sensitivity to business realities in the questioner. Jack and one or two of his more able colleagues managed to maintain an equable surface, though it was clearly difficult going. Then one of the under-secretaries (or whatever) from the Agency for Skilling and Business Alignment went much too far.

"Mr Kavkazian", she said, "thank you for the very clear and interesting presentation that you and your colleagues have given us. I would just like to clarify one point that I don't yet understand. Briefings that we've had on the normalisation process have given an indicative cost, when applied to institutions of skilling, of between one thousand five hundred and three thousand hard euros per student to carry the process right through."

She looked up. Nobody responded. She continued. "The overall price you will be quoting for a normalisation process across AUP is yet to come, as part of the competitive bid. We have, though, the price that you have quoted for an initial normalisation of just two of the thirty three departments in the university, the Departments of Paginatorics and of Manucussionism, in the Faculty of Ancillary Music. This exercise, if I understand correctly, has been awarded to Outvesta without competition, at a price of fifty-five million HEs."

She was looking at him; he nodded grudgingly. "Looking at the table of departmental information towards the end of your presentation, it's apparent that there is a total of 1,430 students between the two departments, which gives a cost of more than thirty-eight thousand HEs per student. That is more than ten times what might have been expected. Could you take us through why the cost for these two departments is so high and why, at this cost level, the initial review has not been put out to competitive tender."

Jack, he saw, remained imperturbable, though without any immediate sense of response. Over the remainder of the Outvesta team, there was an air of stunned silence, of 'this one was in the bag, wasn't it'?

He jumped in. "Perhaps I'd better lead on that, as the impetus for structuring the normalisation in this way comes from AFFREM. The Paginists and Manucussionists are to lead the way, and this is at the special request of the Vice Chancellor. He sees the need for normalisation as particularly urgent in their case, and has consequently used his powers to exempt their normalisation process from the European Public Sector Tendering procedure, which, as all of you will know, takes much time." The Whitehall people nodded and grunted agreement. None of them were fond of European procedures. "Both AFFREM and the Vice Chancellor are determined that, as the first normalisation exercise to AFFREM international standards in a British skilling institution, it shall be carried out to the highest possible standards. I should like to share with you that AFFREM has, as a result, agreed to provide seed-corn funding of £47M for the initial exercise, leaving AUP to find just £8M."

The Treasury representatives now looked happy. Eight million from an overall budget of nearly four billion was not going to be a problem. The girl from ASBA looked unconvinced, but she let it go at that. A man from the Department of Health and Safety asked why the university's executive was 'compartmentalised', but that was easily dealt with: the VC had distanced himself from the exercise at his own request, in order to give a 'level playing field', free of 'pre-developed societal chemistry' to the AFFREM team. The girl from ASBA continued to look unconvinced, but also continued to hold her peace.

The meeting wound decorously to a close, without further incident, but with much hand-shaking and exchange of infocards. Stephen Pendleton made sure that he exchanged infocards with the girl from ASBA. She was an awkward case who would need to be neutralised. Removing government representatives from teams was usually avoided; governments were like Hydra: chop off one head and another one got you. But she was also a very attractive awkward case - petite, Asian, just what he liked. Neutralisation might take many enjoyable forms. Purveen Aqsa: he resolved to call her.

All was well, as far as it had gone, but he had been forced into numerous statements on Fraserman's behalf that Fraserman himself had not yet actually made. At a meeting in three days time, he expected to manoeuvre him into doing just that, but the position was uncomfortable. Somebody from Whitehall might contact him on the subject before then. Besides, Fraserman might not be so easily manoeuvrable; it could take time. He was going to need backup, someone who could stop Whitehall, asking mistimed questions. He would need to mobilise Herb Summerson again, and quickly.

XXXIII

HOOVERING

Karen had not rejected Tad on a whim. She knew it would hurt him, but that was unavoidable. She felt a strong affection for him still, and that demanded a more honest approach than stringing him along until the relationship dissipated in boredom. The truth was, he was great company, quite presentable, not bad in bed, but not really, not truly, her type. And there was Leke.

Leke definitely was her type. He had taken to dropping by her office on the pretext of asking about progress on the security proposals. Was the Hon Ran going to make a decision soon? In Leke's pidgin, asking that took time and effort, though it was obvious enough that both of them knew there wasn't progress and wasn't going to be. He was interested, no question. He might also be able to tell her what that creepoid Stephen Pendleton was up to. Eva had reported nothing further on Alan Westwood, but it was obvious anyway he was only a junior, not likely to be in on anything interesting. Leke was much closer to the creepoid, and she needed a way of hoovering up the information that he must possess, ideally without his noticing he'd been hoovered. And then she would see.

Following up on Leke's interest was taxing her, though. It was partly having two objectives, but most of all it was the language barrier. She was quite unapologetic about knowing no Albanian – she had sussed his nationality out. Leke, in her view, ought to be very apologetic about his English, but apologising wasn't going to solve anything. If it had just been a matter of getting him into bed, it would have been no problem; at least one previous boyfriend had been so short of words, she might as well have been sleeping with the dog. Having to hoover him first and possibly later as well, though: that was a real difficulty. And Leke, unlike the boyfriend, was not stupid; he just couldn't say things so you could rely on what you heard.

Then one day she got it: what to do. As he was leaving her office after an inconsequential exchange of words, looks and silences, she said "Do you speak Polish?"

He looked blank.

"Russian, then?"

His face lightened. "Pa Rooski?"

"If you say so."

"Little bit Russian, yes."

"Great!"

He smiled at her and said "Da svidanya" as he went out of the door.

"Same to you. Da svid. Whatever."

Eva, she had found, in one of their intelligence colloquies, spoke some Russian, as well as her native Polish. Karen arranged a get-together of all three, in DizeeLizee, with Eva, resigned to the role of gooseberry, briefed as interpreter to Karen's Mata Hari.

Leke was there first and had set himself up with a beer by pointing at the pump and nodding his head towards the larger of the two glasses held up by the barmaid. He would have liked a chaser too, but raki, even in London, was hard to come by, and it didn't do to appear too hard a drinker in front of the ladies. It was not his sort of bar: too neat, too fussy in detail, too branded — that ridiculous soft-toy crocodile on all the walls and even on the ceiling, presumably DizeeLizee itself. But the chairs at least - matching the crocodile in green, fake leather - at least were comfortable, unlike the broken-down miscellany that littered his regular retreat. And they had proper, European-style lager; not the stuff they called beer here in England.

Eva entered the bar, just ahead of Karen. Not knowing her, Leke looked but made no acknowledgement, took a heavy swig of his beer and was thus caught out with a raised glass and mouthful of beer as the two girls approached the table. Careful not to overreact and splutter beer over his 'dates' (he was still unsure about the nature of the meeting Karen had created, but it didn't seem to be about work), he took his time swallowing, smiling weakly as he did so, then shook hands with Karen, smiling, saying "Hi" and shaking hands again as he was introduced to Eva.

"Drinks? Ladies."

Eva asked for a small beer. Leke confirmed, pointing at his glass, moving his hand from the top of the glass downwards and both nodding. Karen's Limacolada put a slightly desperate look on his face and she accompanied him to the bar. While Leke waited for the barmaid to produce the drinks and braced himself for the hurdles of payment, Karen quietly re-briefed Eva. Eva received this with just adequate patience; unlike Alison, she always listened the first time round.

Eva started the interrogation. "Karen says you're in Security, Leke. Do you enjoy that? A friend of my father's was a policeman for a time. He was in Security too, but said he preferred the Police. He's an insurance agent now and seems happy enough: he makes a good enough living anyway, but my parents have always felt he didn't give Security enough of a chance."

This had the expected effect. Leke was dumbfounded. He recognised "Karen" and "Security" (two or three times) and "Leke" and "Police" and one or two other words, such as "and". Was the get-together about work after all?

Karen played her part. "Leke's English is not too good yet, Eva. You'll need to go slowly." She turned to Leke. "English not so good. Speak slowly?"

"Yeah. English. Speak crap."

"Sorry, Leke", Eva said slowly, a small worry frown appearing on Leke's brow; he didn't know 'sorry'; they didn't use it in his trade. "You work in Security."

"Me? Security? Yeah!" He took a swig of beer, elated at a successful conversational exchange.

It was premature. "A friend of my father … You understand?

"Understan'. My father. Friend?"

"No, my father", pointing to herself.

"Oh, Eva father. Yeah! What friend?"

"A friend of my father."

"Friend?"

"Oh, you mean, what does friend mean?" Eva thought. "We are friends", she said, pointing to herself and Karen and, more tentatively, to Leke."

"Aah!" A smile of understanding illuminated his face.

"Eva father my friend?"

"No. My father is friend with this other person."

"Other? Person?"

"I'm Eva. Karen is an 'other person'. You, Leke, are an 'other person'. That girl there" (gesturing across the room) "is an 'other person'"

"Eva father friend with girl? And Leke?"

"Not exactly": though she had wondered at times about some of her father's absences.

She ploughed on. "My father's friend."

"Yeah": looking at the girl, who became aware of his attention and gave an appraising stare in return, to Karen's displeasure.

"Works in Security."

"She? Security" he said, looking over again in astonishment.

"No. A friend of my father."

"Eva father?"

"Yes"

"Friend?"

"Yes?"

"Aah. Leke. Works Security. Yes."

Eva lapsed into silence. So far, so much in circles.

Karen rode to the arranged rescue. "Eva, Leke speaks some Russian. Is Polish like Russian?"

"But I speak some Russian too." "Gavareetye pa Rooski" Eva said, turning to Leke.

"Da!" he exclaimed with delighted astonishment, before breaking into a relative flood of Slavonic. The girl at the other side of the room, to her annoyance, was forgotten.

Leke and Eva from now on conversed in slightly fractured Russian, Karen and Eva in English. Karen and Leke's direct communication remained strictly non-verbal, though no less expressive on that account

"Where you learn Russian?"

"At school. It's reasonably easy if you know Polish."

"Polish, I no speak. But Russian, is good, yes?"

"Yes. Karen says you work in Security. Do you enjoy that?"

"Yes, I do Security work, and I enjoy sometimes, sometimes not. The money, it makes difference", rubbing his thumb and index finger together."

"What work do you like?"

"Security surveys. Is easy work, clean, no danger. And the money, is good."

Karen broke in. "What are you talking about?"

"Just how I know Russian and what he likes about Security."

"And what does he?"

"Security surveys. And money. Give me a chance; it's not supposed to look like an interrogation."

"All right. Sorry."

Eva turned back to Leke. "Karen asked what you do when you're not doing Security Surveys."

"Ah. Much other work too. And after work I go for drink with my friends."

"Friends from work?"

"No. No meet friends in work. Except Karen and you, I think. After work I drink most times with friends from home."

"That's Albania, isn't it?"

"Yes. Are Albanian. We can talk, you understand?"

She understood. Even his Russian was functional rather than expressive. She tried to imagine having to communicate most of the time in pidgin and recoiled mentally. His Albanian friends must be an oasis. "Well, you know us now as well."

"Yes, is very good. Your friend, Karen, is very beautiful girl, I think. And you too", he added hastily, as Eva's eyes started to glaze. I think you look more like Russian girl. Russian girls very beautiful also, though different from English." Funny that, an interpreter she'd met a couple of years back, while setting up for a concert, had said much the same thing, though without being effusive about beauty. Perhaps she should quiz her mother sometime.

Karen, who had been exchanging gazes with Leke through much of the preceding, demanded a translation.

"He fancies you something crazy."

"Come on, Eva, he never said that."

"No, but he meant it. I heard something about beautiful."

"You or me?"

"You. I'm Russian apparently." She flicked her head back, but her hair was not long enough for the gesture to be truly effective.

"Tell him you think I like him too."

Eva obliged. Leke beamed, then took a slightly embarrassed sip of his beer.

"Karen says you work a lot with the new American bloke on the staff. Stephen somebody."

"Stephen Pendleton. Yes, I do many works for him. And sometimes for Police, or private people."

"That must take you away a lot?"

"From home?" Eva nodded. "Yes, sometimes much travel. American sector, Russian sector, Chinese sector one, two times."

Karen coughed. Eva hastily updated. "He goes abroad a lot, working for the Police and other people. And a lot of work for el stiffo."

"But he's been round here a lot lately; he's been in my office, eyeing my boobs and whatever else he gets a sight of, two or three times a week for the past two months."

"Karen says you've been around in Peckham for a while, now, though. I think she's wondering how long you might stay."

With a quick glance at Karen, whose gaze remained fixed on him: "I think some while yet. Is big job, many months."

"I'll tell her." She turned to Karen and relayed the information. Karen responded, allowing (without difficulty) an expression of pleasure to appear on her face. "There's nothing much doing on the job he came to see the VC about." (She suspected he would notice if she said 'Mr Fraserman', no matter how quickly enunciated). "What else are they up to?"

Eva had to formulate a tactful way of putting this and took a sip of her lager, while the lovebirds (it was sickening, really, how easy it was for some people) got on with exchanging glances.

"Are you working on the Old Bin, then?"

Leke returned his attention to Eva. "Old Bin? I am not knowing."

"Sorry. The building Karen works in."

"Ah, yes. Maybe yes, maybe no. I make recommendations, but her boss he seem not sure he like."

"But you'll not be leaving us just yet?"

"No, no. There is big job for whole ... what is it you say?"

"The university? AUP? Arts University of Peckham."

"AUP, yes. Is big job for whole university. Is many buildings. Even in China is AUP buildings, I think."

"That'll be the Ceramics people."

"Ceramics? I not know."

"Pottery, like this bowl." Eva pointed out a pot-pourri arrangement.

"Ah! Yes. I think they work with Chinese people, make (what you say?) artist pottery"

"So you'll be off to China sometime. That will make Karen sad, maybe."

"Nothing to worry", he said, smiling. "Is no need travel to China. All work made from office in Charlton."

"I'll tell her."

"They're taking on the whole university, not just your building, even the department in China. And it's all being done from an office in Charlton, so he'll not be disappearing abroad anytime soon."

Karen flashed a smile of relief at Leke, while saying, "what's this place in Charlton? It must be something to do with the outfit we've been talking about." ('AFFREM' also had to be avoided in the conversation, unless Leke could be manoeuvred into referring to it.)

"Karen wants to know, can we return your visits and see you in your office in Charlton" Eva said, laughing.

Leke looked serious. "Is not possible, I think. Is very secure office. Unless Karen and you enjoy strip search."

Eva blushed and conveyed this to Karen, who raised her eyebrows at Leke. "Depends who's doing the stripping."

"I don't think I should tell you what she said about that. I would never have thought of finding Fort Knox in a place like Charlton."

"Fort Knox?"

"Where the Americans keep all their gold. It's very hard to get into."

"Ah. I see. Perhaps is little bit like Fort Knox. But outside, you see almost nothing. On surface, just like house. Is mostly underground. Is what you call it, public house."

"A pub? Like this?"

"No. A house, but made by public. By government"

Eva was confounded for a moment, then understood. "You mean a 'council' house."

"Yes. That is word. Is 'council' house."

Eva relayed the information to Karen, who assumed a stagey Scouser accent. "Yer live on the Council then, chuck?" Actually, there were no longer any Councils to live on, but Leke in any case comprehended only that he was being teased.

"She wants to know if you're living in a council house."

"No. Working, not living. I live with other Albanians. In flat near here."

"It sounds like a bit of a journey getting to work.

"No, is no problem. Thames Tramway easy to get to, and it stop right outside."

That must mean the office. She'd try another question before telling Karen that one. "So you're not leaving us just yet?"

"No. Work at university is big job. Is many months' work, or longer."

Karen spoke up with the offer of another round of drinks. Eva having translated the offer and identified the beer, followed Karen to the bar, where she updated her on the conversation and asked for further guidance. "We've got as much as we can hope for now, so don't push it any more unless he offers something. We'll arrange another meeting and see what else we can get out of him." Eva's heart sank at the prospect of another three-cornered linguistic wrestling match, for the advancement of someone else's love life, but her sense of duty, to work and friends, carried her through. Leke agreed another date, in a week's time, with unforced enthusiasm.

Eva did not linger over her second drink. She translated a macedoine of mild flirtation between the two others, then drank up and left them to it. With just English between them, Karen and Leke did not stay much longer. Leke was allowed to walk her home, but got no further than the doorstep. It was Karen's view that a bit of deprivation for Leke's sort of man often produced longer term benefits. There was much investigation and hoovering to be done before she surrendered to sentiment.

XXXIV

ASPECTS OF ROBOTICS

"Mr Fraserman."

"Yes?"

"Where should I file this?"

The Hon Ran looked up, not unwillingly, from the ASBA report on 'Income-Generation Focus for Business-Disadvantaged Youth Customers in the Life-Skilling Phase'. As far as he could tell, it was about bringing the more gormless students up to scratch, but it was hard to be sure. He'd have used this sort of stuff for wiping his bum when he'd been in the army. Morrison was usually willing to translate, but he'd been a bit off with him recently; fellow couldn't take a joke. He gave his attention to the brief document Karen had put in front of him.

It was in AUP Admin's standard format for recording a telephone conversation. Stephen Pendleton and Alan Westwood, a few days previously. About to say "Not one of mine; bin it", his eye caught the penultimate paragraph, which read simply 'RFIDBDFN'. What the hell did that mean? RFID was an old tagging standard once used in warehouses, but it felt more like a coded reference to himself. What it was saying about his ID was anybody's guess, but the Hon Ran had handed out too many of his infocards over the years to feel there was any new security threat. So what was it getting at?

"Might be personal; not sure. I'll keep it for now", he said, putting it into a back pocket. Karen inwardly rejoiced; he had taken the bait well. She and Eva had concocted the record of the conversation she had overheard, with the bits objectionable to Mr Fraserman edited out. The code had been designed to titillate without giving anything

263

away. His reaction, if he were told straight out about Stephen Pendleton's stitch-up, would be awe-inspiring and best experienced at a distance. He needed softening up first.

"Yes, Mr Fraserman. Do you want a new file opened on meetings with Mr Pendleton?" Not that there was much on record to put there - a couple of short, hand-written notes.

He looked hard at her for a moment, and then said, "yes, might as well. Put it in with Organisational Reviews."

Karen resumed her filing in the amicable silence that filled much of their working relationship. The Hon Ran resumed his reading of the ASBA report. Didn't they use to be called the DLE? Life Enhancement or some such garbage. He chewed through another page and a half before dropping it back on the desk with a sigh and running his hands over his face.

"Hard going?" she said, looking round with a smile.

He groaned. "If I could get a robot to summarise this rubbish I would."

"Why not ask one of the librarian avatars?"

He rubbed his chin. "They wouldn't be able to read between the lines. Sometimes there's something real buried under all the guff."

"You could try them: give them a couple of reports you've already read through and see what they pick up."

"It's a thought."

Silence again. Karen continued filing; the Hon Ran glanced through some messages on his Holoscreen. These finished, he resumed the report and read for ten minutes or so, with increasing desperation.

"Do you know any good librarian avatars?"

"Just the ones I see in the Library Installation. John Librarian is the most switched-on."

The Hon Ran didn't use the Library Installation; he hated virtual space and wasn't a great frequenter of any library. "Is that his name? John Librarian?"

"Yes it is; they don't have proper surnames like us."

"A lot of our surnames are trade names if you go right back."

"Oh, what was mine, then, do you think?"

"Swindells." A saurian smile did something to his face. "I don't think you'd want to know, my dear."

She laughed, with an accompanying sniff. The Hon Ran continued.

"How do you know John Librarian?"

"He's been very helpful with the searches I've done for you; better than any of the others."

"I see." He continued to look directly at Karen and she had to work hard (and not entirely successfully) to avoid blushing. John had been her only virtual lover to date. She was scornful of virtual sex (she had never tried out Tad's penpro), early experience having taught her both its vulnerability to faking and its general inferiority to the real thing, but John had made his pitch when she was in the mood and the boyfriend of that time was away until Sunday week. And as a senior librarian he could readily summon up the necessary virtual facilities for the room in which they were carrying out a literature search together. She had been luckier in her software versions than Viola, and there had been three or four repeat visits over the two years since then. As with Viola, there was an inescapable feeling that it was a slightly shameful diversion, one not to be discussed with anyone else.

The Hon Ran, seeing the slight colouring of her face, looked away abruptly; heaven forbid that the girl should get ideas about him, though he had a high opinion of her and was, in his own way, fond of her. "Would I have to visit the Library Installation in person to speak to him?"

"I'm pretty sure you would; he's not an encap avatar."

"Encap?"

"It means they can walk around outside. Outside a virtual environment, I mean. I could take the reports for you."

"Encap sounds more useful than the other sort. Why don't they make them all like that?"

"Money."

He pondered for a moment. "If it has a chance of relieving me of some of the garbage the government send, it's worth a go. Are the librarians used to this sort of task?"

"They're well used to scanning documents for information. I'm sure they'd do something for you if you asked." "Nicely, mind", she added, conscious of the Hon Ran's normal style of request. He looked sufficiently bowed down by the sheer backbreaking awfulness of the report that he might compromise to that extent.

"The Virtual Library's entry point is just across the square, I think?"

"In that door there." She pointed at it through the window. "But that's for the public. You can get an entry point installed in your office if you want. Quite a lot of the staff have them at home."

"How much room would it take up?"

"I'm not sure; you'd have to see one. But people have them in their living rooms. It takes about four weeks to order, but I'm sure it would be much quicker for you."

He couldn't take much more of Income Generation blah blah blah, and decided to seize the hour. "It's only three o'clock. Could you ring this John Librarian character and fix an appointment for the three of us for fifteen minutes time. I'll get a couple of old reports together. The door entry I'll think about later."

Karen exited to pursue the commission.

John Librarian was busy with some foreign academics when Karen rang, but she got the appointment in half an hour, the news of which reaped a non-committal grunt from the Hon Ran. Exactly ten minutes late, at the Hon Ran's insistence, they presented themselves at the Library entry and the Hon Ran was inducted into the mysteries of a virtual environment. To his disappointment, the experience was almost indistinguishable from entering into a real one, except for the neatness of everything around; electricity failures apart, virtual environments did not deteriorate to the normal institutional tattiness.

John Librarian's eyes lit up as Karen entered the room, settling firstly on her face with its upturned nose, then travelling south to a skirt of sober colour, cut in a way that emphasised the hips beneath it. His eyes reverted to respectable dullness as the Hon Ran followed her.

Introductions accomplished, the Hon Ran put down what looked like a small plastic key-fob on the table round which they had gathered. "There's three reports on that that I'd like you to have a look at, if you would", he said, fixing John with a gaze. I need to see what you can make of them. Not to beat about the bush, they take up far too much of my time, and if I can get them in an accurate summary, or at least précis, I'd be obliged."

He paused; Karen leapt in; this was much too direct; Mr Fraserman might look forward to feeling obliged, but John had certainly got no obligation. "Mr Fraserman gets reports all the time, John, mostly from Whitehall. It's important to know what they say, but they're written in a lot of jargon and can be very slow going.

"Written by bloody robots, I wouldn't doubt."

God! Would he shut up and leave this to her. John already looked as though he was thinking up obstacles. "The thing is, we think Whitehall do it deliberately. Often, they're hiding something in the middle, something we might object to. They think nobody has the patience to decipher it. So it's like we're getting puzzles we need to solve, but don't have the time to."

"In the army, we called it bumf. But this is enemy bumf that's been encoded. We need to solve it to get their plan of attack, if y' see what I mean."

John probably didn't, was looking less guarded. Karen persisted. "We need somebody who can get at information that's been hidden in a difficult source. And we thought of you first." She flashed him a quick, encouraging smile.

John was looking more interested. "What are you looking for right now?"

"Bit of common entrance. Up to snuff and all that."

It meant nothing to John. Perhaps as well, Karen thought. She intervened once more. "We'd like to use these three reports to see if we can make it work: get you to summarise them, make a note of anything you can't understand, and see if it can help Mr Fraserman."

"Vitally important work. I could take a new look at your organisation structure if the arrangement went well. If you get my drift."

Clearly this was intended as a bribe, but John was looking less happy. No matter what might seem to be promised, keeping the VC away from any sort of look at your organisation structure was a first priority for anyone in a management position in AUP. He took evasive action. "I'd like to take it one step at a time. Doing summaries of the reports should be no problem in principle, but if they're going to be sent across regularly, several of my staff will need to get involved, for coverage. I'm happy to do the three on the storage tag" (he nodded at the key-fob object on the table) "as an experiment and I'll think through the managerial issues. If it's to be a regular piece of work, we may have to rewrite job descriptions, for example."

Karen read this as 'quite interested; not quite sure; need time in case I have to work out how to say no, even to my boss's boss'. So she contrived to stay behind "to show John where the reports are", as the Hon Ran left, looking marginally happier than when he had come in, eager above all to reach real space again.

The door closed behind him, and John looked across at her. "Well?"

"What do you mean, 'well'?"

"You don't need to show me how to get the reports off this; it's not even new technology."

"I need to show you which reports. Mr Fraserman has no idea about clearing off files that aren't wanted."

He plugged the device into a docking station; a list of just three files appeared in the air". He grinned at her; she blushed.

He played, absently, with the zip of his trousers and grinned at her again, raising his eyebrows.

Duty called, and it had now been two weeks of abstinence since Tad. "Better lock up" - she nodded at the door - "we'll talk about the work as well." He complied speedily. Pants stowed and skirt rolled, she lowered herself on to his lap: he may only have been a simulacrum, but it felt real enough as far as it went. Twenty breathless, climactic, but also talkative minutes later, she had his agreement to the work and two of his staff allocated to assist.

Leaving, she passed a female avatar in the corridor, who shot her a look that said, unmistakeably, "tart!" That was not how she saw herself, but it was a give-away that John had been spreading his favours about. Karen glared back, but without any real sense of anger; when all was said and done, she was just a bloody robot, after all.

XXXV

REBOOTING

Sylv's second meeting with Daoud Amin had got her no further than the first, though she had taken much care over the choice of the blue silk top - closely cut and subtly uplifting - and the skirt — not too short, but showing her legs to good advantage. He had seemed detached, sitting back in his chair and insisting on discussing exclusively the cases of Mohammed, Farooz and Jane. Where Jane was concerned, there was nothing further to report, but Daoud was in negotiations over Mohammed and Farooz. The details were all a bit above Sylv's head, and she'd been hoping to get on to something more personal, so the memory of what was said was all a bit vague.

Jane's release being imminent, Viola had extracted a promise from Sylv to collect and look after her. The trauma might take some time to overcome. She regretted not being around to help, but losing a career opportunity like the conference presentation wasn't to be thought of. Sylv in turn had persuaded Clare, one of the Cowingdon, an accountant in real life, to accompany her, for moral support. Jane's behaviour had been unpredictable in recent days. Sylv had called in to see her four days previously and had been summarily ejected — visitors, Jane said, contaminated cell space that 'they' then took away. Even the box of chocolates she had taken had to be removed, in case of similar retribution. She knew Jane was having a hard time, but there was no need for that sort of thing, was there?

It was a glorious morning, preluding perhaps the hottest day that summer, a blazing sun in a blue sky casting a dappled shade, from the plane trees lining billionaire's row, so vivid that walking through it felt as though they were walking into an underwater hologram of sea shallows, a watery impression reinforced by the sweaty gradient of the road. It was a day for a celebration: of the end to an unnecessary bondage and, for Sylv above all, the last time she hoped to have anything to do with Denmark Hill Neighbourhood Security Condominium and its more or less robotic inhabitants.

The Reception avatar, when they announced themselves, looked slightly uncertain for a moment, then recovered herself. "Miss Fredricksson. Certainly. Would you take a seat."

They sat, grateful for the chance to cool down. Five minutes extended to ten minutes, extended to twenty. Sylv went over to the Reception avatar, who had sedulously avoided their gaze. "What's the problem; she doesn't want to leave, or something?"

The girl rang through again; somebody replied and she listened briefly. "Sorry, there's been a delay. It'll be another five minutes; ten at the most."

Sylv sat down again, ostentatiously eyeing the clock. Ten minutes went by and lengthened into fifteen and, just as Sylv was preparing a stronger blast, the Sergeant – Brown she remembered him being called – he wasn't the sort of person who deserved to have a first name – came into Reception and across to them.

"Hello. Miss Smith isn't it? And... ?"

"Clare Bowman"

They shook hands. "Our apologies for the delay. Would you like to come through now?"

Ushered into the inevitable meeting room, furniture and decorations the standard corporate bland, Sylv instantly clocked the sinister OSC man that Vile, for some reason, always called The Fourth Policeman. It was then she realised that this was trouble. The Sergeant left the room. Instinctively, she attacked. "What's all this about?"

"I thought that was supposed to be our question." The OSC man smiled, without warmth. "Won't you sit down, Miss ... ?" She neither returned the smile, nor provided her name. And she did not sit down. Clare followed her example, lingering slightly in the background.

"We were supposed to be meeting with Jane more than half an hour ago, like we were told on the 'phone two days ago. Her ninety days are up. Even you pigs can't keep her longer than that."

"I would advise a more conciliatory tone of voice, Miss … ?" Sylv again declined to answer this, staring at him with an expression of fury. "I'm afraid that you are wrong in what you say. Certain technical issues, necessitating further enquiries, have compelled us to extend the period of detention. Jane Fredricksson has been informed of this."

She had half known this since she had seen him in the room, but it still took several seconds for Sylv to grasp what she had been told. Leaning slightly on the back of the chair in front of her, she stared at him, mouth slightly open, until the implications hit. "You bastards!" she screamed. "You fucking thieving bastards."

"As I said before, Miss … Smith, isn't it? I would advise a more temperate approach. We have a zero-tolerance policy with respect to abuse of staff. I have a broad back, and am prepared to overlook an emotional outburst in what must be a state of shock, but you must adopt a more reasonable tone."

The energy went out of her, and she started to cry. Clare guided her into a chair and sat down herself. The OSC man regarded them impassively. So far, so good, he thought!

Sylv, recovering herself, dried her tears with a small handkerchief she kept in her sleeve and faced the OSC man again. "What right do you think you have to keep her?"

"The right of National Security, Miss Smith. Jane Fredricksson in our view constitutes a real and present danger."

"And what about anybody else's view?"

He did not answer that.

"So you think you can hold anyone as long as you feel like it, just on your say-so?"

Sylv looked at him intently, then briefly looked away, blowing her nose fiercely. So she missed the momentary smirk that passed over his features like a ripple of water over a stone. Clare saw it, and it chilled her. "There are, of course, a number of necessary safeguards that we are required to observe. To extend the 90-day detention needs the consent of a Member of Parliament, given before a High Court Judge. I must inform you that we obtained that consent yesterday afternoon."

"So what scumbag gave this consent, to lock up somebody they can't know anything about?

"I am not at liberty to disclose that."

It struck Sylv that they were at liberty to do anything they bloody liked. "Was it our MP? What's his name?

"Warrendell. Tom Warrendell", Clare said.

"That scumbag Warrendell. It was him, wasn't it."

The OSC man remained impassive, but a tiny movement of the eyebrows as Clare said the name had been the giveaway.

"I'm right, aren't I?"

"It would not be appropriate to comment, Miss Smith."

"Ms Smith to you, copper!" She put a lot of venom in to the last word, conscious of it being rather weak. Clare felt relief that Sylv's vocabulary had failed her in this instance.

"Ms Smith, then, if you will. I cannot comment on your supposition."

The two main protagonists stared at one another for a minute or so, near-homicidal fury facing a tautly non-committal (though unmistakeably annoyed) mask, Clare requested, in as level a voice as she could manage: "We would like to see Jane now."

"I am afraid that would not be appropriate at the present. I believe that Reception already has your names and telephone numbers, but if not, please let them have these as you leave. They will contact you in the near future to fix an appointment."

"But she'll need the support of her friends now, not just in several days time. Nothing we say or do now can have any effect on your national security, you must know that." Clare was starting to lose her precarious cool.

There as no change of expression, and he remained silent.

Sylv spoke up: "Go on, be a human being for once. The state she was in when I last saw her, she'll need someone she knows now, not you lot."

"I hear what you say. I'm afraid I must reiterate that a visit at this stage would be inappropriate. We shall be in touch."

"Know what I think, scumbag? I think you enjoy doing this to people. You're a pervert. You can't be a human being, because there's nothing human in you. You've got less idea what any of us feels than the robots working here. That's true, innit? A fucking inhuman pervert."

"Ms Smith, one last time, I'm warning you."

Clare, putting an arm round Sylv, gently hustled her towards the door, aiming to get out before they were both locked up. As they reached the door, he spoke again. "On a point of information, you should be aware that the injunction on media reporting has been extended also."

They made their way back to Reception and sat there for several minutes, attempting to regain some composure. As they sat there, a face familiar to Sylv appeared on the threshold of the outer door. It was Daoud Amin; Sylv brightened a little, but was too crushed in spirit either to greet him, or attempt even the sketchiest improvement to her appearance. He recognised her immediately and came over.

"Hello, Sylvia." He kissed her hand. "And your friend?"

"Clare."

"Delighted to meet you," kissing her hand also. He looked again at Sylv. She was decidedly not the proto-harpy who had bustled in to their previous meetings, offering copious glimpses of bosom and thigh. He preferred the modest and subdued version now in front of him, but something was obviously badly wrong. "I do not think I have caught you at a happy time; is there anything I can do to help?"

"Thank you," said Clare, "we'll be fine in a minute. It's just we've had some bad news." Sylv could only nod at this, looking down, struggling not to cry again."

"Would this perhaps concern your friend Jane Fredricksson?"

"It does, yes."

"I am almost late for an appointment, so cannot speak to you about it now. Would you like to talk about it to me later?"

"Yes. Please." Sylv nodded and quickly turned away. Clare made the arrangements, for the now-customary coffee bar, late that afternoon. Daoud spoke to Reception and was immediately taken past the security entry. Clare left her name and number, rang for a taxi and devoted herself to getting Sylv safely home, where they could think about what might happen next. The encounter with Daoud had been a Godsend for that; it had given them at least one thing to be done.

XXXVI

CAMBRIDGE (1)

Alison, dressed to the nines, clutching a straw hat, but with a lightweight waterproof cape stuffed in her handbag, successfully evaded her flatmate and was whisked off early to Cambridge, experiencing the grim fascinations of the Blackwall Tunnel for the first time, in a car that made up in sportiness what it lacked in size. She was well content with life. Even Eva's recent shiftiness on supplying information ceased to matter, though it was not going to spare her the calling to order that she had now earned.

Having got away smartly at 7.30am and the University Library not open until 9am, they had licence to follow a slower route to Cambridge. They progressed from village to village, through a landscape blocked out in green, yellow and blue, the trees sometimes closing in above. An intimate landscape, just on the rolling side of flat: dabs of ground mist created small blank spaces in lower-lying fields. Alison, urban from her immaculately groomed hair to her only slightly more practical shoes experienced it as an immersion in strangeness, a series of landscape stills and sounds, complementing the feeling of Ben sitting beside her, her mood.

Reaching Cambridge, they parked near the Library. She followed Ben's directions and wandered into town through suburbs, along the Backs, down Silver Street. Smart though Peckham was nowadays, she knew it would never compete with this. A century of modern cut and thrust, globalisation, the end of history, the beginning of post-history, the end of post-history, the beginning of neo-history, the realpolitik that had effectively divided the world into three main sectors (American, Russian, Chinese), two semi-independent sub-sectors (Brazilian, Indian) and one carcass (Africa) had had, seemingly, no effect on the surface of Cambridge, the sense it conveyed of a timeless graciousness. Much of the history had passed her by, and she knew too little about architecture to guess how recent many of the buildings were, but there was no doubt that this was class stuff.

The morning done: sight-seeing and shopping (mainly window-shopping) on Alison's part, inconclusive research on Ben's, they met at one of his favoured cafes for a late lunch. A pub might have been a bad idea, he thought, if he was to try his hand at steering a punt later. Alison, it was clear, was expecting this. So they made their way slowly down to the river and lingered for a while on the bridge, Ben observing the action below in a quick refresher on how it was done. Gently steering Alison up-stream through the crowds, he hired a punt on the Granta, a trickier stream to punt than the Cam, but less on display. Laughing off a fall into the river between the two of them was one thing; laughing it off with dozens of interested spectators was quite another.

She seated herself, straw-hatted and languorous as to the manner born. Taking it slowly, Ben, sticking to the well of the boat, negotiated awkwardly but with adequate competence up-stream. A leisurely tour d'horizon, reassured her that the surroundings were equal to her expectations. She looked down at the turbid water flowing past, thought of trailing her hand in it, as she had heard was done, thought better of it after a closer look, fixed a gaze on him, waiting until he could bring his attention back to her and setting her head aslant: "Why so slow?"

Introducing a slightly laboured effect to his poling, he dropped into stage west-country. "So as 'ow I be not wetting us all, my lady."

She laughed, retrieved the waterproof covering and spread it over her legs. "There!"

He shook his head with an air of sorrow and started poling faster, effectively but without style, splashing spoonfuls of water into the boat at a steady rate. She was forced to raise her feet onto seating and requested, without apology a slower progress after all. They progressed about halfway to Grantchester, before Ben, in need of a rest, pushed them into a side-water among reeds, where they could stay unobserved. He stepped cautiously into the water, which proved mercifully shallow, waded laboriously over to the bank pulling the punt sideways, pulled himself up onto dry (ish) land and brought the punt approximately in line, wedging one end as best he could in reeds; there was no discernible current here. He kept hold of the paddle. Grasping his hand, Alison slowly raised herself and stepped daintily ashore.

The waterproof acting sketchily as ground cover, they spent the next half hour or so in one another's arms, gazing into the intense blue of the sky through the arrangement of grasses that gave a sketchy cover against the sun. In an overcrowded world, it was not an idyll destined to last undisturbed for long; they heard approaching footsteps on a path running nearby. Sitting up to get a sight of the intruder, they saw an untidy figure shambling towards them, a middle aged man: to Ben's eyes, a university don; to Alison's, a species of unmade bed. He caught sight of them and raised his hand, calling out when still some distance away. "Hello. This path seems to be going nowhere. Do you know a way through?"

Alison said nothing, gazing at the newcomer with a mixture of curiosity, sharp judgement on his slovenly mode of dress – an open-necked shirt that looked in need of a wash, shapeless trousers, ditto and shoes that had seen much better days. – and slight distaste. He was not a welcome visitor. Ben did respond. "I'm afraid not. We came here by boat."

"Ah, an ancient and honourable conveyance. A much better idea than trying to second-guess the byways as they are nowadays. And I do so hate walking any distance along a main road." He sighed. "Well, I must suffer that, though I may just try what might have been a path of sorts along the field-edge back there." He gestured vaguely in the direction he had come from. It did not look promising. "Time is at my heels, as always", he said with a harried expression. "My presence is needed at a meeting in town within the next hour, and I should decamp quickly. I am sorry to have disturbed your idyll." He smiled at Alison, who found herself unexpectedly charmed, though it didn't alter her opinion that he talked twaddle.

"We could give you a lift down the river, if you want. Find a road." Ben spoke as he turned to depart.

"Could you, do you think? You know, that would be most awfully kind. I wouldn't intrude on your privacy in normal times, but I find myself in a muddle today." It certainly looked it. His expression hovered between vague worry and vague guilt, but there was no mistaking the sense of hopefulness that the offer was serious.

Alison resigned herself. They needed to get back for some tea, which she had resolved would be her treat for Ben, so couldn't have stayed much longer. It wasn't going to be possible to look gracious with this object in the boat, but they could always drop him off before they got to the crowds. And he seemed all right, if only he'd talk a bit less.

"Bernard Saintsbury", he said, holding out his hand. "I feel it is fitting to introduce ourselves, so oddly thrown together in this way."

"Ben. And this is Alison." She smiled and shook his hand. They embarked, the new addition dumping himself clumsily in the middle of the punt, Alison wielding the paddle with modest expertise, while Ben, freeing the punt from the reeds, stepped on board and guided them out into the river again.

"And what do you two young people do for a living, if that is not too forward a question?"

Ben paused as he hauled the pole up and let it drop again. "I lecture in Paginatorics. Alison is an auditor."

"Auditing. Now that is a very sound profession I'm sure. Paginatorics, though: I do not recognise that discipline. What is it, could I enquire, that you do?"

"It's the oldest branch of ancillary music. An art form quite like ballet, based on techniques of page-turning. I'm a performer as well as an academic."

"Page-turning. You mean, page turning as one does for musicians?"

"Yes, that's it."

An expression of slightly comical dismay came on to his face, reigniting the harried look that had receded as the river lift took shape. "Oh, dear me, how unfortunate! If you are an ancillary musician, then I am supposed to consider you as an anathema, you know." He paused, looking, to Alison's eye, genuinely flustered.

"How so?" Ben did not look unduly concerned as he poled downriver, blessing the circumstance that had added the extra weight downstream rather than up.

"I work, you see, for an organisation that seeks to restore what we consider to be real music. Ancillary music is one of the accretions that we exert ourselves to strip away from the core treasure. Not with much success, it sometimes seems," he said sadly, "but I am glad about that for once, for you do seem such a charming and helpful enemy, if that is really what you have to be. Now I feel guilty, for you have taken a fox to your bosom." He looked unsure. "I think that is an appropriate metaphor. Never mind. You see, you are very kindly and generously assisting me in my passage to a meeting at which I must join in condemning your professional modus operandi and devising ways in which it might be swept from the face of the earth. That is what you have in your midst. How very unfortunate. Perhaps I should disburden you immediately." He raised himself on his haunches, starting to turn sideways with the evident intention of trying to jump on to the nearer bank. The punt rocked violently and slewed towards the other bank.

Fearful that they were all going to end up in the river, Alison reached out, took their passenger by the hand and gently but firmly guided him back to his seat. "Stop worrying. We're not turning you out of the boat just because you don't agree with everything Ben does."

He subsided and calmed down a little, looking round apologetically at Ben, who was manfully bringing the punt back under control, thankful that he had not tried standing on the till, from which he would now have fallen overboard. Alison pressed her advantage. "What is it you work for that tries to do honest Paginists out of a living, then?" she said, with a smile aimed at preventing a recurrent fugue episode.

"Oh, dear me. I am the secretary for the Franchised Reamers Fellowship, which promotes what we see as authentic music." Alison and Ben both mentally sprang to attention, but kept neutral expressions, though their companion's attention was anyway devoted largely to talking his way out of embarrassment. "You see, we do not really consider ancillary music to be authentic, excellent though - I have no doubt – your professional skills may be."

"It's not a name that sounds like anything musical," Ben observed in a neutral tone.

"No, I suppose not. Perhaps it is rather like the Freemasons, who have had only a tenuous connection with stonework in recent centuries. In our case, the name originates with the erstwhile tools used to bore out woodwind instruments. They were the craftsmen who first felt threatened by the rise of electronic music and then, of course, M-Class, though I intend no disrespect to present company. We are not a secret society, mind you, though somehow," he added rather wistfully, "nobody I speak to ever seems to know of our existence." "In point of fact," he added "we should perhaps be called the Real Franchised Reamers Fellowship, but that sounds just a little too much, I suppose, like a terrorist cell." He giggled; they smiled: he was an unlikely terrorist.

Alison pressed the point. "Why would you want to add the 'Real'?"

"Oh, because of an argument that blew up some time ago; I suppose you would have to call it a schism, if that does not sound too grand. We had a large American membership; sadly it is a very small one now. Some of their number adduced that we should be more political. We acquiesced in that for some considerable time. It was so nice to get more attention." Again he looked wistful. "But it did start to get out of hand, what you might perhaps call the tail wagging the dog. Mark you, the American members had been the tail wagging the dog for a long time; there were so many of them."

He drifted off into thought. Alison brought him back to what she saw as the point. "So what did they do?"

"Who? Oh, the Americans. Well some Americans, anyway. The more politically inclined members started to develop what they called – why do the Americans insist on that sort of thing? – a philosophy. We split from them over that." He mused on what he had said. "To be perfectly precise, they somehow presented matters so that we were thrown out from their ranks, but of course we have never given any quarter to such a patently absurd version of events." He looked indignant.

"How did they do that? If you were the Fellowship?"

"Oh, it pains me to think of it. At a meeting in America, they declared themselves the real leaders of the Fellowship. Because they had eighty five per cent of the membership, I think. The American legal system liked the sound of that, of course. Then they declared that we were a rogue chapter of the Fellowship and started what they called a T and D protocol."

"A what?"

"Termination and Dissociation. We were cast into their idea of the outer darkness, presumably to wail and gnash our teeth. We just kept on going, of course. But it was all frightfully unpleasant." He looked genuinely upset at the memory.

"It sounds ghastly. What was so special about this philosophy that they had to do that, though?"

"Dear me, it was terribly indigestible stuff, and I never got to the bottom of it. But it was mixed up with some neo-conservative management theory and had a Mission Statement. Can you imagine it? That was just the sort of inauthenticity that we had thought we were trying to overcome. The members who had worked in Pakafiran were chiefly responsible. A fandango like Pakafiran, I would have thought, would have put the cap on it forever, but far from it. They were so determined, I think, that somehow nothing seemed to be able to stop them. Then, as time went on, they wanted the Fellowship to adopt this mishmash as its own. And we heard that the members who had been in Pakafiran had claimed to be there as the Fellowship's representatives. We were horrified and asked them to explain themselves. Actually, I have never found it a good idea asking Americans to explain anything. They took it as a personal slight. Maybe that is what caused the problem."

It seemed more than likely. The punt had, by this time, attained the upper reaches of Coe Fen. "Would you be so kind as to let me off here. On this side, please," he said, pointing to the west bank. "It is only a brief walk from here to where I must meet my colleagues." Ben steered the punt over to the bank, and their passenger disembarked without further incident. "My thanks to you both for tolerating my company thus forced upon you. It has made such a difference, and I shall now be at my meeting on time; it is such a disadvantage otherwise." It was evident that he was often under this particular disadvantage. "Thank you again for such charming company. Should you ever consider a return to the older forms of music-making," he said, turning to Ben, "remember that we can give support and encouragement."

He took a small piece of card from a back pocket and presented it to Ben, who had never seen an old-fashioned business card before, but thanked him and responded with an infocard of his own. "Perhaps you can influence your consort in his professional path, my dear", he said to Alison, who gave him a slightly mystified smile. Influencing Ben was certainly what she intended, but his musical life was not on that agenda. "Then au revoir." He waved, smiled again and loped off indecisively, Ben and Alison saying "Bye" to his back.

This took some thinking about, and they retired to a local teashop, having returned the punt. To Alison, the day retained a dreamlike rightness, now enhanced by the reflection that she was once more ahead of Eva in the information management stakes. For Ben the knowledge just gained was of solid value, but any joy that may have been gained by that was tempered by the realisation that his job as an ancillary musician was currently under scrutiny by an organisation rooted in musical fundamentalism. He parked Bernard Saintsbury's business card carefully in an inner pocket and devoted himself to Alison.

XXXVII

SURVEILLANCE (2)

What was this thing of Paul's, then? For the best part of a week I was still wondering myself. He's always got to dress everything up to be grander than it is. It wasn't quite, "If I told you that, I'd have to kill you", but he'd have loved to have said that if he thought he could get away with it. So all I got out of him at the Oast, apart from a fourth pint that he was forced at last to put his hand in his pocket for, was some blarney about undercover work, tracking down some organisation that was trying to take over the university, or maybe it was the world: it all got a bit confused by the end of the evening. I did get out of him that Karen had put him up to it. I was half thinking of telling him to jack it when I heard that, but didn't. It's not that I hate her, after all, it's just her putting the shutters up and I don't really know why. Anymore, come to think of it, than I ever knew with Ali, though to be honest, getting it off with Karen sorted that one out; she's just a sort of fond memory now.

There was another pub visit before I got anything more tangible; it ended with an arrangement to meet Paul at London Bridge station early on the following Tuesday morning. I still didn't know what it was about, but Paul said he would "brief" me and "show me the ropes" over a coffee that I was obviously going to have to pay for. It was a pity the usual crowd weren't there as well; they'd have taken the piss royally. But I couldn't think of anything witty, I just agreed. The station, at eight o'clock in the morning was its usual closed-in bedlam. It's very colourful round the edges – all those shops and cafes – but always somehow feels grey. The only lively thing about it is the unending streams of people criss-crossing, magically never knocking in to one another. London Bridge station always looks to me like somebody's very large scale, very, very disappointing particle-collider experiment. What would the man with the briefcase over there and

the hen in short pants and high heels turn into? Well, nobody's ever
going to find out, because they've just missed each other.

"Are you feeling all right, Tad?" Paul was looking a bit concerned, and
I realised he must have been saying something: probably 'showing me
the ropes', or whatever. I apologised for "just thinking about
something" and attended to my coffee (which I'd had to pay for) and
to what he was saying. By Paul standards, he was getting to the point.

"We've got to try and spot the entrance to some offices. They're
mostly underground and hidden behind council houses, somewhere
around Charlton. They're right opposite a tram stop, though, so it
shouldn't be too hard. After he'd done a bit more of his 'briefing', we
went down to the tram. Karen had made it plain, even to Paul, that
we hadn't got to be obvious; I think he might have tried on a false
beard or something if she hadn't. So we split up and sat in different
parts of the tram, one on each side; he'd observe everything on the
left, I'd observe everything on the right. Then we'd each be looking at
the opposite side on the return. We had notebooks to jot down
anything we spotted and we'd compare notes and do the journey
again, swapping sides and concentrating on anything that looked
interesting.

Well, I found it almost straight away, because we passed it just when
everyone was going in to work, but by the time we were returning it
had quietened down, and Paul didn't see it, so we had to go through
the whole rigmarole again. We got something to eat in the market (I
made sure Paul bloody well paid for his own) and sat by the river
going through the notes. The office entrance had been no easier to
see the second time round than it had been for Paul the first, but there
was definitely something there once you knew where to look. So we
set out a third time, with the aim of walking, on opposite sides of the
road, from the previous stop, along past the entrance and then keep a
lookout separately for anything, from a couple of cafes we'd seen just
along the road.

Paul allocated me to the right-hand side of the road, away from the river, where the entrance was, I guess to reduce the chance that it was him that got done over if anyone spotted us. Thanks, Paul! The private eye bit was starting to get to me, and I was feeling a bit nervous about it. But really, it was hard to see why anyone should be bothered with a couple of students passing by. Just that they wouldn't have tried to keep the entrance largely hidden if they were happy about all and sundry knowing they were there.

Sure enough, there was no interest from anyone as I went past. A camera, swivelled and took a shot, but that would be a starring role shared with half of Charlton. I flashed a glance sideways, but there was only the sheen of heavily tinted glass and doors that looked like two-way mirrors, though it was probably just the sun reflecting. They were set back at a level slightly below the street, like a superior garage. There weren't many people about: it was hot by now; the pavements and the buildings had that baked look of South London streets in summer. The heat they were giving off made it like an oven, though anyone who designed an oven as chaotic as the average South London street would have been out of a job before any got built. Speaking as a designer, I mean. I'd only walked about a quarter of a mile, but I was well ready for the café, and not just for its lookout possibilities. Paul, of course, had allocated himself the nice coffee shop; I got the greasy spoon. But it turned out they did a good iced coffee, and the coffee shop had run out, so there is some justice.

I managed to spin out my iced coffee for the best part of an hour, before the ice melted completely, the coffee dwindled to nothing, and the waitress finally scooped up the glass, looking triumphant, pausing meaningfully by the table, and I was forced into paying up and leaving. I did better than Paul, who was back in the street after only half an hour, but I'd done no better in seeing anything. The doors to the office stayed still and shut the whole time I was sitting there. It was only as I left the greasy spoon and crossed the road to dodge the camera that anything happened. A security man – in a uniform – came out of the door carrying a largish package, which he put down on the pavement beside him before looking round and waving to an approaching van, which stopped and took the package on board. He disappeared back inside, and the van drove away. It all happened very quickly – they must have arranged things by 'phone – and it didn't obviously signify anything, but I wrote down the name that was painted on the side of the van, 'Albasec'.

I found Paul sitting on a wall by the tram stop, in the sun. He didn't seem much interested in the van, which in any case had gone off in the opposite direction. Our staking-out operation hadn't been a success, but Paul was pleased enough with himself, as we'd definitely found the place we were looking for.

That was that for the day. We had a solid result. One. It wouldn't do to make ourselves too familiar in the area before we'd worked out what needed doing next. That would be Karen's shout; she was the one who knew why she wanted to know. About this office. We would report back and await instructions. I hoped she'd chip a few highlights off Paul's aura of self-congratulation while she was at it.

XXXVIII

VISHINEY

Scruffily relaxed, Vishiney lounged in the hot summer sun, inviting its visitors to do likewise. Just into the Russian sector, it was a discreet centre for music tourism; the landlord of their rented apartment had pointed out the presence and the qualities of the large Bechstein grand piano in the main room, a smirk playing about his lips, before taking them in to admire the equally magnificent double bed. They had made unfettered use of both in the three days since. The Franck sonata was coming along nicely.

Neither Carl nor Viola knew much about Vishiney itself, and the past three days had done little to extend the acquaintance, the local cafes and restaurants excepted. But Viola in particular experienced a sense of relaxation, an uncalled for but infinitely refreshing winding down, like being released from a headache she hadn't known she was suffering. There was a nearly tangible sense of tolerance of life's pleasures in the Russian sector, particularly of S-class musical performance, in which it still maintained its tradition. Back home, tolerance was much more selective; it wasn't just S-class, it was a whole range of pursuits that had once been freely practised and that had, for reasons sometimes hard to identify, slipped a little or a lot beyond the pale. Indeed, staying within the pale needed constant vigilance. Here, though life was in a sense more risky, the barriers were more simply defined, based on traditional religious morality, rather than the complex sophistry of the American sector. The one area requiring a circumspection not needed back home was their sexual relationship, but both were discreet by nature.

With old-fashioned tolerance came old-fashioned ways. Viola, laden with food shopping, had been about to exit the nearby supermarket when she realised that the ID tag that routed charges to her account might not work. Sure enough, as she halted and looked around, she

291

saw what she had not seen since shopping with her mother as a child: cash tills, manned by shop assistants, a local girl, by appearance and a solid, lumpy, older Russian woman, ditto. Viola joined a disorderly queue and waited several minutes before two older men taking pity on her lack of queueing experience, let her through to be served by the Russian woman, who simply grunted "Buna" as she reached the till and what was presumably "Goodbye" or "Have a nice day" as she left – Viola's less than basic knowledge of the local language was not up to being able to tell. But the whole experience of exchanging words with another person, just to pay for some food, was indescribably appealing to her. Some of the other people in the queue had had proper, if incomprehensible, conversations with the assistants, particularly the girl. It was perhaps then that Viola fell in love with the city and with its style. The gentle pace of things, the implied courtesy, the quaint smallness of shops that in London would be several acres of sprawl, were comforting in ways she could not define.

The 'phone call came late on the fourth day, as they enjoyed a post-musical glass of wine. Neither reacted to pick up the call at first; it was unexpected that anyone would want to or be able to track them down like that. Carl collected his wits first and answered it, to find there was no video link, just a voice, a female voice.

"Hello."

"Hello. Is that you, Carl?"

"Yes, Carl Trenchard here. Who's that?"

"Oh, we've only met a couple of times, so you probably don't know me. I'm Sylvia, Sylvia Smith, a friend of Viola."

The famous Sylv, he thought. "Do you want to speak to her?"

"Could I?"

"She's right here." He passed the connection over to Viola, who had been listening.

"Hi, Sylv! What's it about?"

"Vile, it's good to talk to you. I've been doing my nut trying to work it out, and you always know what to do."

"Why, what's happened? Is it Jane?"

"Yes." There was a pause.

"Well what then?"

"I'm not sure how to explain it."

It wasn't like Sylv to be short of an explanation. Had Jane gone on a bender after her release, or something? "Just start at the beginning."

"All right. We went to meet her at the nick on Friday – like we arranged, you know."

"Yes. Thanks."

"And… Well…"

"Come on Sylv; what happened?"

"That's the thing. Nothing happened."

"You mean she didn't cause a scene?" Thank God for that, Viola thought.

"No, they didn't release her. I caused a scene, but it didn't do no good."

"But they've got to release her. The ninety days are up, aren't they?"

"The ninety days are up okay, but they got some arsehole of a judge to say she had to stay in. Oh, and the wanker who's our MP."

"But they can't do that."

"I went to see your friend Joe, like you said, and he thinks they can. I mean, he went ballistic, but he still reckoned they can if they want."

Carl, watching Viola, aware that something was wrong, saw the colour drain from her face as she went silent, then sat down on the edge of the bed. Viola had prepared herself for calls for help in cheering Jane up, or thinking of things to keep her occupied with, and she had expected to speak to Jane herself at some point, but the idea that she was still caught in the spider's web and that the whole situation could have stuck fast where it had been for the last three months had not been on the list. She was devastated. Carl put his arm around her and attempted to ask her what was wrong, but her attention was diverted by Sylv again.

"Vile, what do we do now?"

"I don't know just yet, Sylv, I'm trying to think. Have you spoken to anyone else about it but Joe?"

"We have talked about it to Daoud. You know, the dishy Afghani bloke."

"Daoud Amin?"

"Yeah, that's him. We met him when we were coming out of the nick, and he could see that something was wrong. I wasn't making much sense by that time, but Clare arranged things. She's been great, Clare."

Viola mentally gave thanks for her choice of Clare. "What did he think?"

"He thinks we should strike a bargain with them."

"You mean pay them? After all this?"

"Something like that. You know the two waiters got out?"

"Mohammed and Farooz?"

"Yes."

Things were happening, then. "So is Daoud doing anything about Jane?"

"We gave him her brother's number. He said he'd talk to him."

It didn't sound very hopeful, but then there didn't seem to be anything much else to do. A sudden inspiration hit her. "The media injunction. It must have expired when the 90 days did. We can start on the media again."

"They thought of that, Vile. It got renewed as well. Sorry."

She felt flattened; everything seemed blocked. "I'll have to think. For the moment, there only seems to be Daoud. Could you make sure you keep in touch with him."

"No problem."

Stupid of her; Sylv didn't need any encouragement there. "How's Jane taking it?"

"That's what I was really calling you about, Vile. She's been strange the last few days. It isn't just me either. Clare noticed it too. We're worried what she's going to do."

"How do you mean, strange?"

"It's things that she says and does. Like the other day Clare went to see her and had to leave her shoes outside the door. She was saying something about being punished for bringing too much in the cell. Her own shoes – she's only got two pairs in there – had been put in the corners, one shoe at each corner. And they looked like she'd put them there just so, Clare said, all pointing out to the centre of the room." There was a brief silence, then she continued. "I've noticed things myself. Like I really got an earful for some comment I made about that creep of a Sergeant we have to meet, every time they've got something nasty to tell. She went on at me about how only she got punished for saying things like that. I asked her what she meant when she said punishment, and she just looked around her a bit, then shivered and crouched down."

"She's said in the past that they reduce the cell size when we're not there. I put in a complaint about it, but it's a terribly slow process. I don't even know if its true, but it's what she says. Maybe that's what she was thinking about."

"Mm. Could be. It got worse when she heard the waiters had got out. I thought it'd cheer her up, give her some hope, but she was just face down on her bed and cried. It took me half an hour to get her sitting up again and sort of calm. Sort of."

"How is she now?"

"I saw her this afternoon, and there wasn't a problem then. I took my shoes off before I came into the cell: she was looking down at my feet just before I walked in. So that was all right, and there wasn't anything else. But it's like talking with a zombie. Sometimes it's like she's drugged up, but there's no other signs." Sylv had experience, so Viola took this seriously.

"Did you discuss this with Joe or Daoud as well?"

"With Daoud, yeah."

"What did he say?"

"Not a lot. He thinks the main thing is a deal to get her out of there. He's not wrong, but Jane…"

"You think she's on the edge?"

"If you mean half-crazy and might get worse, yeah."

There was a lengthy silence. Carl, after giving a sympathetic squeeze, had tactfully moved into the other room. Viola stared at the print of a crudely rendered Russian landscape on the opposite wall. The farm (presumably collective farm) workers in the foreground looked content enough, but as boxed in by their situation as she felt Jane to be by hers. "Sylv. Are you there?"

"Yeah."

"Sorry, I'm trying to think."

"It's been going round in my head all week. Oh, Vile, what can we do? Those wankers want to kill her, I'm sure of it." Her voice was breaking now, self-control at the limit.

"No, it's money, Sylv. What bothers me is what they might do to her to get it."

"I s'pose so." She didn't sound even slightly reassured.

"Look, I'm not going to be able to work anything out here and now, on the 'phone. I'll ring you back when I've had a think about it." A thought occurred to her. "Do you have Daoud's contact details; it might be worth giving him a ring."

She was speaking to the right person; Sylv had the number from memory.

"Are you all right yourself?"

"I'm okay Vile, don't worry. It's Jane I feel bad about."

"I'll see if I can think of anything. Speak to you later."

"Yeah, see you!"

Sylv rang off. Viola, on automatic pilot, wandered through to the other room and gave Carl a hug, breaking off to amble round one circuit of the room, before sitting down again.

"What's the matter?"

"Jane. They've extended the custody; nobody seems to know for how long, but it's legal, apparently. The media injunction is still on as well. Jane has taken it badly – can you blame her? She's behaving strangely."

Carl was appalled. But the instinct of sympathy was overlaid with the frustration of a terrible sense of helplessness. He took Viola in his arms and cast around for something to say. "That sounds awful. Is there anything Sylv wants you to do?"

"No, she has no idea what to do. I don't think I'm any better off myself at the moment. I feel guilty leaving her, just because of this bloody conference. She was starting to behave oddly before, I went: throwing me out of the cell when I visited last, not because she was pissed off with me, or anything, but because of some rule she seemed to be trying to follow. You remember me telling you?"

"I do. But you mustn't blame yourself for something you have no control over. The people to blame are the ones holding her to ransom, aren't they?"

"Yes, you're right, but you know. I'd just feel better if I'd stayed with her."

They sat in silence, sympathetic on Carl's part, brooding on Viola's. Carl spoke first. "If there's anything I can do to help?"

"Thanks, Carl, that's sweet. I may take you up on it, if I can only think how." Then she acted on the only possibility that immediately presented itself. Walking back into the music room, she picked up the vintage handset and 'phoned Daoud Amin. A female voice said hello.

"Hello, is it possible to speak to Mr Daoud Amin, please.

"I am afraid he is away from the house at present. Who is that speaking?"

"This is Viola Trent here; I am ringing about the case of my friend, Jane Fredricksson. Mr Amin knows about this case, because he was recently representing two Afghani nationals whose case related to hers. I'd very much appreciate the chance to talk to him about this and get his advice, if that is possible."

"Miss Trent, of course. Daoud has spoken about you and about your poor friend, on many occasions. I am Tala, Daoud's wife. As I have said, Daoud is away from the house now, but it should not be long before he returns. Where can he contact you?"

"I'm actually ringing from Eastern Europe, so a return call could be expensive. I could ring again, if we could fix a time."

"Not easy to fix any time with a man like Daoud." She laughed. "You are not to worry about costs of calls. This is important, yes?"

It was, and Daoud's wife overcame her reservations. She gave the contact details, thanked Tala and rang off. Confined to base now until Daoud rang, she sent Carl out for some shopping and turned her mind to practicalities. This might push her plans askew. She had counted on at least a week's music-making, possibly two, combined with some travel in Moldova. But the situation with Jane sounded serious. Should she return? It all hinged on Sylv's view of events, and Sylv could be over-emotional. Viola remembered Jane's dismissal at the last visit, though. An instinct that Sylv was right about this nagged at her constantly, clouding her perceptions for the rest of that day. Carl was prompt with the shopping, and they had had a leisurely (in retrospect, valedictory) meal and a play through a Telemann Suite, before Daoud eventually 'phoned.

"Viola, this is Daoud here. Are you well? I am sorry it has taken so long to ring you back, but I have been toiling rather with the family of Mohammed. That is Mohammed Khan, you remember, one of the waiters who were in custody?"

"Yes, I remember him well and Farooz too, though the police and whoever haven't allowed us to meet them for the last three months. How are they? I'm fine, by the way, and how are you?"

"I am fine too. Farooz also seems to be relishing his freedom, though I think he did not like so much the lecture I gave to him on his release about friends he should spend time with and friends he should make excuses to. But that is to be expected; he is a young man, possessed of more vigour than intellect. We hope that he shall learn from this. With Mohammed it is more difficult. There were no lectures to deliver; he had done nothing that could be looked at amiss. Yet I fear this episode has taken away his confidence. He is in low spirits, and his family are naturally worried. But I am talking on about my Afghani friends, and you may not even know yet that thy have been released. My apologies; let us talk about Jane."

"There's nothing to apologise for, Daoud. I was glad to hear that Mohammed and Farooz were free and hope that all goes well for them. But I am very worried about Jane; I spoke to my friend Sylvia late this afternoon."

"Ah yes, Sylvia, indeed."

Viola was unable to interpret the tone of this interjection, but it couldn't be expressing particular interest with his wife nearby. Poor Sylv! "Extending beyond ninety days is bad enough, but Jane is acting very strangely – I've seen a little of it myself – and I don't like to think of what she might do. Sylvia said that you had spoken to them since this happened and that you were still trying to help. I can't thank you enough for that. I rang you because I just felt I needed another view, to help me try and work out what to do."

"Yes, of course. I will do what I can. Is there anything particular you want to know?"

"It's difficult to know where to start. I don't seem to have got it sorted out in my own mind yet."

"Should I tell you what I have seen and heard in the last two weeks?"

"Yes, please. Including what happened with Mohammed and Farooz."

"Mohammed and Farooz we finally pulled from custody one week ago. That was when I met your friends, Sylvia and … I forget the other friend's name."

"Clare."

"Clare, that is it. They seemed distressed, and I found out that Jane was still being held. We have met once since, and I have tried to give what help I can. That is essentially all that has happened that has involved me. The situation now for the boys is recovery. For Mohammed that may take some time, but he is at least on that road. For your friend Jane, I fear that the situation is more serious."

"What I can't understand is why they let Mohammed and Farooz go after the ninety days, but not Jane."

"Ah, but you misunderstand. The boys were released only because we reached a deal."

"You paid?"

"Yes. Though we brought the price down."

Shit!

"Why did you deal with them so close to the time limit? Wouldn't it have been worth waiting? Just to see."

"I think you are taking this time limit too seriously. There is no time limit. Oh yes, for people who do not know how it works they might have to find a judge and an MP for an extension, but they are always easily found."

"So, you're saying that Jane could be held for as long as they want?"

"I am saying exactly that. What I told your friends Sylva and Clare was that for Jane's release, there needs to be a deal done."

"But what about the law. Surely there are rules about this. I know the bail system is a scam, but it's not a completely one-sided scam."

"I am sorry to say this, Viola, but I think you are missing the point. Once something is named as terrorism, there is no law, and there are no rules. My community has had much experience of this area in the last fifty years or so, sometimes as a guilty party, often not, sometimes in our country, sometimes in Britain. Guilty or innocent, this country or that, we have found that money can make a difference. And we have found that only money can make a difference. That is why we negotiated a payment for the boys' release, regardless of rules about release dates. If we had not, they would still be in custody now."

She stared out of the window at people going about their business, in the summer evening from which she felt increasingly removed.

Daoud asked was she still there? "Sorry, it's giving me a lot to think about. So you think we should negotiate? Sylv said you had taken contact details for Jane's family. Have you got any further with that, or do you want me to take over?"

"I am happy to give what assistance I can; I think we have become friends in these past few weeks, yes?"

"Definitely yes, but it could take up a lot of your time."

"You are not to worry about my time." He was sounding more and more like his wife. "I have spoken to Jane's cousin, and he is to come back to me once he has spoken to other members of her family. I am thinking   they   are   not   a   close   family?"

"No, I don't think she has much to do with them."

"That is unfortunate, but her cousin seemed ready to take a reasonable view. I think there is value in my helping you negotiate a deal with the family and with the authorities. I have experience in how it is best done; my community lives by making deals."

"Thank you, Daoud, we've not done very well ourselves so far; relying on justice, I suppose."

"Forget justice, British, or any other type. Whatever relevance it may once have had, in our time, what is called terrorism is all about deals."

"Can I get your advice? What do you think I should do now?"

"It is not really for me to say, Viola. But your friend Jane needs help from her friends. I am not allowed to meet her, of course, but she seems to be at risk of a serious breakdown. In the negotiations, I sense with the family that you are the one they would most listen to. It would be good if you were able to join me some time in talking to them."

"I need to return to London as soon as possible, don't I?"

"That may be of benefit, but it would be a pity if it were to disrupt your holiday."

Viola did not answer. Facing away from the window now, she thought the farm workers in the picture seemed to inhabit an idealised prison. Breaking off the holiday would be a wrench; such uninhibited music-making was a rare opportunity. Jane might not need her so soon, and the negotiations were unlikely to get very far very quickly. Intuition told her she needed to return, though.

"I'll have to think about it; there's Carl to consider also."

"Yes, of course, your partner." Viola was not sure she'd quite put him in this category, but if it simplified things … "Would it help if I spoke to Carl also?"

She didn't think so, but called out. "Carl, would you like a word with Daoud while he's on the 'phone?"

Carl was taken by surprise, but realised that, yes, he would like a word."

Viola thanked Daoud again and passed Carl the 'phone, leaving the room and shutting the door. Carl and Daoud spoke for nearly fifteen minutes: it must be costing him a fortune, Viola thought. When he rang off and came back to join her, she said, "I need to go back, don't I?"

"Probably. It sounds pretty grim back there. I'll come back with you."

"No, don't do that. It'll only mean both of us lose our holiday, and you'll end up hanging about in London and going in to work; you know you will."

"I think you need moral support."

"I can get that over the 'phone; we'll talk every day, won't we? Promise me you'll stay."

They argued the point back and forth for some time, but Viola prevailed. Carl was to stay on for the remaining ten days or so; Viola would return to join him if the situation in London permitted. In the afternoon of the following day, after a hasty lunch, she picked up a last minute cancellation and flew back. Carl, feeling uneasily that he should have been more forceful about accompanying her, returned to an apartment abruptly quietened, the farm workers still toiling stoically.

XXXIX

DIPLOMACY (2)

Something to be said for robots after all. The report summaries were back and they were almost up to army briefing standards. Prose-wise, the Hon Ran had no higher praise; he despised the prolix and evasive civilian equivalents. Thinking of this before could have saved him much brain-ache.

'Income-Generation Focus for Business-Disadvantaged Youth Customers in the Life-Skilling Phase' had been rendered as "Thick, idle, alienated, mentally ill, artistically inclined, criminal, 15-18, feckless youth. Non-profitable – a bad thing. Re-programme. Think fast-food jobs, call centres, shelf-stacking correction, hotel cleaning, anyone got any new, up-to-date ideas? Forced? – new legislation, fights, government fault, government money. Voluntary? – with threats, dump responsibility on universities, universities can pay, 'community-based approach'. Implied budget threat P.40. Definite budget threat P.86. 'No extra staff needed' P.102. Extra staff estimated from proposals: 6. Funding for extra staff: nil. Re-orient entire youth population: 2 years P.108. Précis superfluous."

Just his thoughts on the matter, though only after half a working day filtering out the dross. And he hadn't noticed the threat on page 40, locked within a 15-line sentence, a nightmare tangle of managementism and subordinate clauses, a solid and impenetrable chunk of text glowering menacingly at the reader from the middle of the page. In fact, he still couldn't work out exactly what the threat was, but there was definitely something there.

A phrase in the next summary down in the pile ('Heuristic Strategic Enablement for Dynamic Learning Stratification Recrudescence') caught his eye: 'streaming the stupid from the bright could be unpopular, need to be discreet for now.' The last phrase: BDFN: the second half of the set of initials he had worried at off and on for the last two weeks. He looked round for the offending minutes but could not see them. "Karen" he called through the open door, "can you find me those minutes you filed a couple of weeks back?"

Karen appeared at the door. "Which minutes? Your meeting with Mr Morrison."

"No." Screw Morrison, he thought "The minutes of a 'phone conversation between Alan Westwood and Stephen Pendleton."

"I think you kept them yourself, Mr Fraserman. But I may have a copy in the files; I'll just see." Karen knew perfectly well she had a copy in the files: she never trusted the Hon Ran with sole copies of anything she considered important; he was so hopeless about losing them. A token file search and, five minutes later, she reappeared. "That one?"

He glanced at the document presented. "Yes, thanks," taking it and blessing Karen's unfailing efficiency of recall. She smiled at him and left in flamboyant style, provoking in the Hon Ran the beginnings of an erection, which he hastily damped with thoughts of his gun collection.

The Minutes were disappointingly anodyne, just a canter through the usual jargon. Westwood was in on the act, he supposed, because of his timely crawl into the embrace of AFFREM. It was only the RFIDBDFN that suggested anything covert. Ranulph Fraserman ID be discreet for now. Hard to see why they'd want to be discreet about his identity; no-one else was, least of all himself. What ID could stand for, he then thought, was 'in the dark'. He experienced an upswelling of rage. If that slimy Yank and his no less slimy stooge thought they could put one over him with some side play of their own, they'd find out the hard way how unpleasant it could be to cross him. But he knew that just facing up Pendleton with the evidence of the Minutes would get nowhere; he'd find some smooth explanation and admit nothing. Bullying Westwood would be easy enough, but he'd have his story, no doubt, and body language was unlikely to reveal much: the man was a shifty little sycophant, even when he wasn't plotting something. No. Direct confrontation would be called for, all right, but not until he'd found a bit more out; done now, it would just alert them to his being on alert.

He thought for a few minutes, then caught sight of the title of the third report summary: 'Non-Hierarchical Conflict-Situation Learning Paradigms for Hierarchical Organisations'. He walked over to the door and asked Karen to come into his office.

"Can you remember how this ended up here?" he said, handing the Minutes back to Karen, keeping a sharp eye on her.

Butter couldn't have melted. "I'm not certain, Mr Fraserman. It may be something Mr Westwood left. I just found it in a pile of papers when I was filing."

"Hmm." Westwood was a careless bugger, it was true. But he had a feeling that Karen knew more than she was letting on. "Does this mean anything to you?" He pointed out the letters at the bottom.

Karen thought for a moment or two. "No, it's not shorthand or anything."

"None of the rest of it is of any concern to me; it could go in the bin. If Alan Westwood left it for me, it'll be because of those letters, but he's going to have to explain what he means by them."

"I could ask Mr Westwood about them, if you want."

"Yes, please do that. Don't say I've seen them"

She took the Minutes and retreated into her own office.

What to do, meanwhile, with Stephen Pendleton? They had a meeting fixed, in a quarter of an hour or so. These were desperately boring at the best of times. Having to simulate enthusiasm, because of the AFFREM context, cramped his style severely. The thought, in present circumstances, was insupportable. It was too late to cancel. He strode to the door. 'Karen, could you make an appointment for me at ASBA this afternoon. Say it's about oh …" he read from the papers in front of him "…Income-Generation Focus for Business-Disadvantaged Youth Customers in the Life-Skilling Phase". Karen did so, making short work of a secretary guarding her flock. She secured an hour of Purveen Aqsa's time. Shortly afterwards the Hon Ran departed. He gave her a nod and a wave as he passed, bolting down the back stairs as Stephen Pendleton's clean-cut righteousness approached the front.

"Hello. I have a meeting with Ran Fraserman."

Karen deadpanned. How dare he call Mr Fraserman 'Ran'. "Mr Fraserman is out this afternoon."

"No, I made an appointment last week for now."

"There must have been a mistake."

"No mistake. I'll just speak to Ran and clear this up." He moved towards the door of the Hon Ran's office."

"Mr Fraserman is out of the office at the moment."

He halted. "I think you will find you are mistaken. The meeting has been in Ran's diary for more than a week."

Tossing her head fractionally, Karen consulted the diary and projected the display outwards for little dick to see. All traces of the appointment had been erased and replaced by ASBA. Seeing Purveen Aqsa's name did little to improve Stephen Pendleton's temper. Was the asshole trying to nail her himself? He had ambitions of his own, and they were not maturing as fast as he liked.

Karen regarded him with practised blankness. He re-regarded her, and she continued her stare before shifting it unworriedly to her fingernails. The diary continued to make its statement in the air between them. It was checkmate. Raging inwardly, he left Karen a message, asking the Hon Ran to contact him urgently. She input this verbatim to the Organiser, gazing at him between phrases with a discomforting lack of expression.

"Eva."

"Yes, that's Karen?"

"He's swallowed it."

Eva had a brief, alarmed apprehension of what Karen might mean, then common sense reasserted itself. "He's caught on, you think?"

"Not exactly, but he knows it means something. Are you on for DizeeLizee at five?"

Eva moved that to seven; she had a draft paper to finish. She also suggested bringing along Alison, who was being coy about some discovery she'd made. Getting it out of her needed a more brutal interrogator.

Karen looked out of the window, to see a brief back view of Stephen Pendleton as he turned the corner towards Camberwell at the far end of the square. "Up yours!' she enunciated, to the surprise and chagrin of Morrison, who had ascended the stairs noiselessly and was entering the office. "Sorry, Harold," she said, "not you. What can I do for you?" It was be-nice-to-Morrison time at the moment. He'd got very obviously pissed off at recent treatment, which was not so good. He was a nice bloke really, who had his uses, even if he was a bit of a pillock.

It was another report trying to improve the position of his department – fifteen pages plus graphs; he never learned; Mr Fraserman didn't do anything more than a page from subordinates. She attempted to set him right.

DizeeLizee was filling up for the evening, but they secured a table near the toilets, overlooked by one of the green crocodile murals. It had a misplaced eye and gazed down with a reptilian squint.

Eva had been successful in securing Alison's presence, though only by subtly conceding to her the role of Queen Bee. Interesting to see which of the two Queen Bees will come out on top and how, she thought. Her money was on Karen.

"Somebody said you're seeing Ben Cordell."

"Depends what you mean by seeing." Alison lowered the drinks card and cast a neutral glance at Karen.

"Going out with, then."

"Seeing is better. Yes, I'm seeing him now and then." She looked at Karen with an air of 'want to make something of it.'

But Karen was just curious and signed off, complimenting Alison on her taste.

Alison preened, while attempting to conceal it. Eva snorted inwardly. It was all right for some. Anyway, he was still conceited. Karen's compliment had not, in its manner of delivery, conveyed any sense that she would like Ben for herself, but then she had Leke, now thoroughly hoovered and admitted finally to her bed, a fact of which Eva was also aware, having acted as translator/gooseberry for the final hoovering.

Social updates and speculation drifted gradually to the main agenda.

"We know they're up to something on this organisation review that Mr Fraserman isn't in on. There are meetings at offices in Charlton, near Woolwich. I can't get Leke to say what the meetings are about, but I don't think he really knows anyway; he just does the security."

"Alan Westwood is going to some of them" said Eva, who had continued her thankless shadowing assignment, "but not all the ones that Paul thought he spotted. Paul hung around outside the containers this Stephen Pendleton works in for three or four days and followed him when he could," Eva explained to Alison.

"Followed Pitchfork? Where?"

"Who's Pitchfork?" said Karen

"Oh, it's what Ben" – the shadow of a smile crossed her face; the other two girls rolled their eyes at one another – "calls him."

Well, it was snappier than calling him Stephen Pendleton all the time. "Why not just call him Little Dick and have done?" Karen asked.

"It's something to do with a painting, Ben" – Eva and Karen scrutinised her like hawks, but there was no repeat giveaway – "says."

"Let's make it Little Dick," Karen proposed. There was no dissent.

Alison counterattacked. "What's Paul getting out of this, anyway, he's only a student?" Eva and Karen, like her, had jobs to think about.

Karen was caught on the hop and hesitated for a micro-second that did not escape scrutiny. "Friendship with eastern promise."

"What's that mean when it's at home?"

"Not a lot, but he'll have to get past Leke if he wants to get what I think he thinks it means."

Alison laughed raucously, joined more tentatively by Eva, who felt some sympathy with the victim of what sounded like a fairly thin deal.

Paul had been promised one of the rare copies of Karen's veep. On his one experience of the goods, he was anxious to secure it. Karen passed quickly on; the original mistake had been quite embarrassing enough.

"We've got Mr Fraserman thinking now. You never can quite tell what that'll do, but he won't forget. And so far he's not gone off the deep end. When he catches on, we want to make sure he feels grateful. I don't know what Little Dick is planning, but I don't think it'll be good for us."

Alison looked set to hug her secret to the death. Eva sicked the dogs on her. "Didn't you and Ben find something out about who Little Dick is working for?"

"I'm not sure what you mean, Eva."

"You know. Something about who Little Dick works for."

"You mean this AFFREM outfit?"

"Yes, you and Ben met somebody who knew about it, didn't you?"

"Met somebody?"

"Your excursion."

"Excursion?"

""Day out together. You went up to Cambridge and met somebody there."

"Oh", she said, as if struck by magical recall, "you mean Bernard Saintsbury? He was weird. Have you been to Cambridge?" she asked Karen, "it's great."

Karen looked poised to discuss shopping possibilities. Eva intervened. "Who was Bernard Saintsbury, then?"

"Just some weirdo. Quite old. Lighten up, Eva. Cambridge is full of old weirdos, but they're not what I went to see. The town is just amazing."

But Karen had heard the call to duty. "Weirdo or not, if this Bernard Saintsbury thought he knew something about AFFREM, we ought to know what it was. There's your and my jobs might be looking dodgy," (and mine, thought Eva) "and they're not telling anyone what they're doing. Not even Mr Fraserman, we think. So what was it he told you?"

"I wouldn't have thought auditing would be anybody's target", said Alison, in a last-ditch attempt at diversion.

"Ever heard of toys for the boys? Nowadays it's management they fire at people rather than bullets, and it's your job that ends up dead, but it's the same: they just love spraying it around. Anybody who's near at the time. Bit like the way they do sex." They all laughed loudly, Eva to blend in. "If AFFREM remember Auditing's there, they'll fire at it."

Alison bought a little time, sipping at her drink. "What Bernard Saintsbury said?" Karen nodded. Eva watched with her special quality of impassiveness, ready to pounce on further feints, tangents and evasions.

"He had this funny way of talking, like he was in a play, so I may not have got what he said quite right. He was part of something called the Franchised Reamers Fellowship – that got us interested straight away. It started by trying to stop S-Class music turning into M-Class.

That got nowhere, of course, so some of the American members started getting political. Then they slung out Bernard Saintsbury's lot, who wanted to stick to the music and renamed themselves AFFREM. Oh, and the reamer bit of the name comes from a tool used to make woodwind instruments."

"How did they get political?"

"I wasn't clear about that. I don't think Bernard Saintsbury was all that clear about it himself. They developed something they called a philosophy. He called it a mishmash. It was all management theory. Neo-conservative, he said; Ben seemed to know what he was talking about. Ben said afterwards it sounded like a group of fanatics with an agenda that they'd wrapped up in a lot of theory to stop the rest of the world knowing what they were about. Bernard Saintsbury did give an idea when it happened, and Ben told me that neo-conservatism was already discredited by then. It was after Pakafiran."

"What was Pakafiran?"

"Didn't you do that in History? A company tried to take over Iran, Pakistan, Afghanistan and a few other bits and pieces and run it all for profit. It didn't last very long."

"Oh, that. My dad was there." Karen's school hadn't done History, but her father had had an exciting eight months in Pakafiran. "He called it something different."

They asked and were told.

"If I called it that at work, I'd be sent on a Diversity Readjustment course", Eva said, her tone suggesting its delights.

Karen gave thanks inwardly for Mr Fraserman. He wasn't strong on Diversity.

"That was another thing", Alison added. The AFFREM people who put together the philosophy were mainly Americans who'd been in Pakafiran. They'd used the AFFREM brand there, and the British members didn't like it."

Credit where it was due, Alison had got some good stuff here, Eva thought. And Karen had, as expected, got it out of her. Now what did they do?

A bunch of nutters set on shooting up the world with management. They probably still did the musical mission in some way as well, Karen was thinking. No wonder Little Dick had been so set on 'normalising' the Paginists. Clever old Wankwould, joining the executioners just in time. Bernard Saintsbury's lot didn't sound so wonderful either – probably all S-Class perverts.

Alison felt she had used her information to best advantage; it had certainly silenced these two.

Eva spoke up. "Have you kept in contact with this Bernard Saintsbury?"

"No, but he did give Ben a card – just a piece of card – so I suppose he could be contacted. Why?"

"I'm not sure, but he might know a few more things about AFFREM."

Karen interjected. "Worth trying."

"I think it would be best going through Ben. I think one of us talking to him might make him nervous, and Ben was the one he gave the card to."

Eva concurred from an analytical standpoint. "What questions do we want him to ask?"

"Do all the AFFREM men have small dicks?" Karen ventured, to applause.

"If they spray our backs, can we spray theirs?" (Alison).

Eva felt unequal to the level of debate. "Seriously, though, Ben might not want to contact him too many times, so we ought to cover the things we want to know."

They settled down to a discussion of Ben's terms of engagement, while Alison planned how she'd persuade him to follow his orders.

Eva adjudicated the Queen Bee contest as a draw. Each was still in charge of their respective information conduit. If only Alan Westwood could do something interesting.

XL

WHITEHALL EXCHANGES

She was sitting there wearing a headscarf, for Christ's sake. What was it with these Asian women? She still looked great from any other angle, though - a formal, but closely fitted trouser suit, shoes that looked expensive, with just enough of a heel.

She had risen to greet him, aiming a brief and formal smile not quite centrally to his eyes and offering her slim, rather cold hand for a peremptory handshake, disengaging almost before he had time to enjoy the contact.

"I've a meeting at two; I need to be quick. What was it you wanted to talk about exactly?"

Squaring up ASBA's attitude to the Outvesta deal: that was what the discussion was about. The lunch and the celebrity-chef, riverside restaurant were about her, Purveen, but it looked off-limits to say anything about that just yet. "I detected some concerns from your side about our structuring of the deal with Outvesta. We wanted to reassure you about that."

"We?"

"AFFREM and AUP." Shit! He was going to have to be careful.

"So what is this deal?"

"Let me assure you that the proposed arrangement is one hundred per cent ethical and compatible with your competition rules."

"Surely that's everybody's competition rules, Mr Pendleton."

318

"Stephen, please. Sure, that's the rules that apply to everybody. I was just acknowledging your department's stewardship."

"Very proper!" No discernible warmth.

A waiter appeared to take their orders, affording a temporary respite.

"So please explain the deal to me in a way that supports what you said."

"Let me explain a little about the normalisation process first. It is a complex sequence of interlocking paradigms. Over the past two decades, AFFREM has refined its interpretation of objectives and desirable outcomes, and these are pretty much set in stone. The process itself, though, needs interpretation by the enabling partner. There is no prescribed approach or sequence. We aim to leverage the creativity of our partners to achieve a working philosophy that runs well with the normalisation subject and the situational dynamics in which it and the enabling partner coexist."

He was encouraged to see that her eyes had not glazed over in the manner now anticipated when he met Fraserman. He winced inwardly at the thought that he had that pleasure ahead of him later in the afternoon. The wine waiter appeared on the cusp of the rhetoric, and he ordered a bottle of good white Burgundy, in deference to his guest's Europeanness

"Outvesta proposed a two-stage approach in their Expression of Interest. Their individual concept of normalisation majors on processes of communication as a catalyst for mandated cultural change. Naturally, these processes evolve most effectively in synergy with the normalisation subject population, so some kind of trial run is fundamented in Outvesta's philosophy of process. AUP presents particular challenges through its historical looseness of organisational association and what AFFREM terms the European factor."

Her eyes came more definitely into focus and gave him a straight stare. Hands raised and a slight smile around his mouth, he said "Okay, okay, no gunfight, no hostages. This side of the pond, you have some different priorities, different positioning, employee-wise."

"You mean European employees have rights?"

"Priorities, Purveen. May I call you Purveen? Priorities. It's a cultural thing, a clined relationship matrix."

He just couldn't help himself, could he? In spite of herself, she found the never-faltering, never-doubting flow to exert the same involuntary fascination as water flowing over a weir: interminable, smooth, ever-renewable. "And the other suppliers didn't go for two stages?"

"They did not."

The starters arrived. Purveen, eyeing him across the table, crunched her deep-fried mushrooms with vehemence. He forked up his Caesar Salad in a manner that a wife might eventually sort out. Which, thankfully, was not her concern. "The Expression of Interest gets discussed, doesn't it. Was the possibility of a pilot stage raised with the other bidders?"

"Negative, Purveen." He looked questioningly at her; she glared back. "AFFREM's policy is to not stifle creativity. Intruding on the process of bid construction would cause endangerment to that policy."

"So you didn't discuss Outvesta's two-stage process with them either?"

"Only as a concept." She glared, effectively clipping off the intended addition of her name.

"Even such an expensive 'concept'?"

"A concept is a concept, not a matter for the bottom line."

She knew he was lying.

"Doing normalisation; is that how you see your life's work?"

His face lit up. She was taking an interest in him, rather than AUP and its cast of deadbeats. "Sure! There's no better."

"How long have you been doing it now?"

"Just over fifteen years. Close on all the time since I was in college."

"Which was?"

"Michigan - Ann Arbor. I did my PhD and post-doc at Princeton, then was at Cornell as Assistant Professor."

The wine arrived. Still annoyed by his not consulting her, she put her hand over the glass, requesting water instead.

"And normalisation since then."

"Since Princeton. I joined AFFREM at Ann Arbor. They treat you as an intern for a year or two." He smiled; she did not.

"The academic bit sounds high-flyer."

He dissembled his feelings a little, English-style. "I'm proud enough of it. The normalisation work is the real thing."

The main courses arrived, and there was a lull as Purveen concentrated on eating, keeping a surreptitious eye on her watch. His eating manners got no better. Finishing up, she watched these narrowly for a few seconds then observed: "this normalisation thing, doesn't it ever look to you like walking along the beach and kicking over everyone else's sandcastles?"

Not so friendly. "The connection?"

"Always destroying, never building?"

"Sometimes you have to destroy completely first to build. Almost always, you have to take out something. Otherwise, you get faulty foundations."

"Nothing I have learnt about the normalisation process suggests there is any building, though. It's all about deconstruction and replacing things by a new organisation that has to fend for itself."

"We believe in releasing the creative spirit of the right-structured organisation, if that's what you mean."

"But you don't actually do anything for this 'right-structured' organisation?"

"We create the conditions in which creative release is possible."

"And how many of the organisations you've gone and 'right-structured' have had any creative release?"

"It is AFFREM's policy not to look backward. Retro-thinking simulates the conditions of creative reversion and deconstruction."

"So no idea whether your normalisation has done any good. And why all this jargon? Civil Servants are bad enough at that, but we're amateurs by your standards."

"Normalisation is a very precise and delicate concept. Its philosophy needs precise and delicate linguistic expression, uncontaminated by the imprecision of demotic speech."

"In other words, the common man is too thick to understand what you're saying and doing?"

"If you wish to express it in that way."

"But they're not too thick to understand that they've lost their job, or their skills have been thrown out with the rubbish?"

"It is important not to get emotional. Loss of a job in a normalisation context is simply instigation of a creative process of transition, acting in the wider, long-term interests of the normalised population units. An essential element of the transition is self-reprogramming of skills."

"And the ones who can't manage to self-reprogramme?"

He shrugged his shoulders. Retro-thinking was to be avoided.

She looked at her watch "Meeting's in ten minutes. That's half, I think. For the food." She put some money on the table. He tried to remonstrate. "Department rules." She shook his hand briefly, already turning and made good her exit.

He was left with a profound sense of dissatisfaction. He had headed her off quite adequately, he felt, on the Outvesta contract, though she still did not seem quite convinced: he had better cover that off at a more senior level. The rest of the lunch had not gone to plan at all; he would need to try again when she was in a better mood. For now, there was close on a bottle of wine to finish. The Brits were not great on doggy bags, particularly the higher-class restaurants, and it was far too good to waste.

Purveen, back at the office, removed the headscarf, which had done its job in creating misapprehension and threw herself into the meeting. Just under an hour later, she found herself (as the most junior senior member of staff not otherwise occupied) booked to meet AUP's Vice-Chancellor, to discuss Income-Generation Focus for Business-Disadvantaged Youth Customers in the Life-Skilling Phase. It meant a nasty hour grappling with the relevant report to find out what she was supposed to be discussing – she had better summon the avatar who wrote it. It was also, she realised, an excellent and timely opportunity to do some digging.

The Hon Ran, in his haste to avoid Stephen Pendleton, had carried with him little more than John Librarian's single page of notes, a copy of what proved to be a different report and an umbrella made superfluous by the unusually brilliant weather. So he had sat on a bench on the Embankment for a quarter of an hour or so, shooing importunate pigeons and composing what he would say to convince the doubtless formidable and ever-so-slightly robotic civil servant whom he would meet, that this was a meeting to be taken seriously. Before he started digging.

"Ms Aqsa?"

"'Purveen', please. And you are Mr Fraserman?"

"Quite so. 'Ranulph' will be fine."

"Would you like a drink? A coffee?" He hesitated. Purveen, on the rebound from a teetotal lunch, recognised need where she saw it, and it crystallised her own decision.

"A gin and tonic?"

They settled at opposite sides of the table, gin and tonics in hand.

"What can I do for you?"

"This report. Obviously relevant to AUP. Having difficulty deciphering the finer details. We military types, you know, used to simpler briefings. Would like to get the gist straight from the horse's mouth." He fished out the notes and the report from his briefcase, turning the latter over hastily as he spotted 'Heuristic Strategic

Enablement for Dynamic Learning Stratification Recrudescence' on the cover.

She let the horse's mouth bit go, as she fished around herself for something to say. Fifteen minutes with the Income Generation report avatar had rendered its contents only slightly less opaque. At least, she consoled herself from observation, she had, unlike her visitor, got the actual report. "Would you like to start by focusing on income generation or on the change management implications?"

He flailed around mentally, wondering which choice would give him less trouble. In her favour, she had not treated him to the upward nose wrinkle with which the female young were wont to greet the senile over-40s. "Change management, then. What bits do we change manage, what bits do your people change manage?"

Damn! She shouldn't have given him that option. She flailed around mentally. "You want to look at the interface between ASBA and the universities?"

It sounded as good as any. "Yes. Not sure if the 'community-based approach", he said, reading carefully off the notes, "means we have the complete say over what happens, or whether your people still want to put in their two penn'orth."

She hadn't noticed the 'community-based' reference, but it didn't really matter; everything was community-based nowadays; it was just throat-clearing. 'Two penn'orth' meant nothing to her either, but it sounded like the sort of thing her father would say. In fact, he reminded her of her father, standing in his shop, trying to make sense of the latest from the tax office without losing face in front of the distaff side. "ASBA will always want their say in what concerns them, of course. Perhaps it would be easier if you could give me some background on AUP, so that we could look at this in context." That should buy a little time. It might even steer the conversation usefully.

He seized on the invitation with gratitude. He knew a lot more about AUP than about all that change management bollocks - in his experience, you either forced change down people's throats, or had it forced down yours. It might even steer the conversation usefully.

"We've got every category listed in your report at AUP. What you call disadvantage, that is. Cripples, ex-cons. We probably have a fair few current cons as well. The students are all 16-22, and then there are the staff. Not much difference from the students, except they're a bit older. And by definition they're all artistically inclined. You could say we're a melting pot of all your income-generation problems."

He did sound very much like her father giving his views on the youthful assistants in his shop, especially the smartly turned out specimens with a good line of patter who ran down quickly when out of sight, like a duff wind-up radio. "Art does have its place in society, of course", she said. The Hon Ran blew his nose vigorously. "Do you have any initiatives in progress?" she added.

He pondered this briefly. "Let me give you a couple of examples", he said, stealing shamelessly from one of Morrison's half-arsed pleas for rescue. "Visual and Plastic Arts are working on relocation from China to Stoke-on-Trent, as a means of tapping into the heritage, authentic-production-techniques market. And the Paginists have established twinning arrangements with Dresden, giving the students access to tuition by Professor Körthofer, the top man in their field." That was being less than fair to Carl, but you couldn't afford to qualify bullshit. "Are your people offering anything that will help this sort of initiative along, or fund new ones?"

That was a difficult one; ASBA didn't do specifics. "It depends on context." That was always a good line. "It might be useful to start by looking at your two examples in rather more detail."

"Context for Visual and Plastic Arts is that it wants to rediscover its roots and original values. It sees future income opportunities in areas in which competition is on the basis of quality rather than bulk price."

Morrison's verbiage had its uses after all, he thought. "Early days, though. Seed-corn funding is the thing. The Paginists, that's another story. Distinguished department in its own right. Looking to improve value through networking and skill sharing. Very successfully to date." The debacle of Körthofer's score had been carefully hidden from him, with Karen's assistance. "Biggest context thingy for the Paginists at the moment is normalisation. Got the AFFREM crowd working on ideas. You'll be aware of this, of course?"

Got there! "I have had something to do with that, yes. Seed-corn funding seems to be a popular idea there too, except that in this case it will be awarded to the suppliers."

Suppliers? Seed-corn funding? What was the woman talking about? "You're referring to consultancy help, I take it?"

"A little more than just consultancy from what I could see. And I'm talking about the suppliers who will do the actual normalisation. Or one supplier in particular."

"There's only outline discussions with suppliers at this stage. First-draft ideas are due soon." Actually, he thought, they were well overdue. So much for the Yanks being efficient. "Nothing happens until we have had a look at those."

It was as she had suspected. Instinctively she sided against Stephen Pendleton. "The impression that I had was that supplier relations were more advanced than that. There seems to be a favoured supplier, and they seem to be close to agreeing a rather expensive pilot scheme."

Pilot scheme? So that little turd Pendleton had been keeping him in the dark. He'd soon sort that one out. Starting with Westwood. He had an image of holding him upside down by his feet, shaking him until his teeth dropped out. His hands moved involuntarily to match the thought. Purveen observed the hand movements; it was just like her father as he contemplated the idler assistants.

He said, "I am not clear as to which of the project stages you might be referring when you say 'pilot scheme'. And in what way do you see it as expensive?"

Carefully, carefully. "'Pilot scheme' may just be what it's being called for the moment, subject to discussion. It referred to normalising two departments – the Paginists and I think they were called the Manucussives."

"Manucussionists." Pendleton was obviously still trying to engineer his grand plan on the quiet. Think again, prick-face! Another word with Herb Summerson would be useful. It might give him a clear run to crucify the bastard.

"Manucussionists. Sorry, Ancillary Music is not really my area. It struck me as an expensive exercise at fifty-five million, though I was told AUP were contributing just eight million themselves.

He was struck dumb. His thumb tightening on the drink in his hand, the stem suddenly parted company with the body, shooting gin and tonic down his trouser leg and slivers of broken glass about the carpet. Purveen exclaimed in dismay and went to fetch some paper towels and a portable vacuum cleaner, with which the worst of the mess was cleared up. The Hon Ran saw to a bleeding palm with two of the paper towels. It was a good fifteen minutes before the office was once more in order and the drink reconstituted, by which time both parties to the meeting had been doing some thinking.

On his part, rage jostled with incomprehension. If the figures were anything like, the whole scale of the exercise must be well beyond what he had authorised and, extrapolating from the word 'pilot', which normally signified a small beginning, probably well beyond even what he had guessed of the grand plan. How dare the Yanks (and Herb Summerson must have given his approval if AFFREM were seriously thinking of spending fifty million of their own money) start cutting deals above his head. And where was AUP expected to find eight million.? They could not be serious. He wondered if he had misheard. The replacement gin and tonic placed in safety on the table, he asked. "would you run those figures by me again, please?"

Purveen had been amazed by the strength of his reaction. She repeated the figures, adding that Outvesta (which the Hon Ran had never heard of) was set to gain this part of the contract without competition.

"They have changed upward since I last saw them. You say these figures were given to you at a meeting with suppliers?" Purveen nodded assent. "I will need to speak to AFFREM about releasing revised figures before they have been discussed. I have already expressed concern about the weighting of Phase 1 costs: the part you called the pilot scheme. Think of that as under review." It was a sketchy performance. Poleaxed by Purveen's revelations his voice could not command the usual fuck-you conviction and arrogance. He found himself struggling to hold her gaze consistently as he said it.

She observed a momentary tightening of his right hand, still clutching a tissue to staunch bleeding, as he enunciated 'pilot scheme'. Now he was more like her father after TelCart had jumped in on the lease renewal and forced him into selling up to spite their offer. She felt guilty about having caused this, but it had never occurred to her that he would have, genuinely, no knowledge whatsoever of something that affected him so radically, not to mention the thousands of staff who worked for him. It was better that he did, and she might be able to help. "I will, on ASBA's behalf, be inquiring into the basis of these costs; please do let me know if you get any further clarification in the meantime."

He rallied, achieving a tight smile. "Very right and proper, my dear. Do stay in touch." He proffered his infocard, receiving hers in return, and it wasn't until he had gained the heat, noise and dust of Victoria Street that it occurred to him firstly that he had left a substantial quantity of good gin and tonic untouched and secondly that she had probably been no more interested in or knowledgeable about income generation for disadvantaged youth blah blah than he had himself. He fingered her infocard within the inner breast pocket of his jacket, reassuring himself that it was not already lost. A tram klaxoned his tentative descent on to the road, before sweeping past, a near miss. He swept his finger skyward in its direction, peremptorily and with a concluding jerk. If they wanted war, it was war.

XLI

CAMBRIDGE (2)

What did I get out of it all? Well not the return of Karen, that's for sure. Any hope she'd be impressed by my sleuthing skills was quickly put to rest; Paul made sure he took all the available credit.

After we'd staked out their offices, we were sent out again to find out what we could about ALBASEC, the only actual movement we'd spotted in and out of the office door. That wasn't much of a success; we did seem them again, a couple of times, entering or exiting the AFFREM offices. We also saw a couple of blokes in suits and a hen in heels and a short skirt, a vision of loveliness, of pure, undiluted fuckability - but I mustn't get carried away – who all went into the building at different times, but didn't re-emerge, at any rate, not in front of us; a matter of great regret in the case of the hen. The point, though, was that we didn't have a car – neither of us can drive anyway – so there wasn't much more we could do than watch the ALBASEC guys get into their van, then - if we could have been arsed - run after them while they buggered off down the road at a lot greater speed. Karen did, the second time, agree we could get a taxi – she had some sort of budget - but have you ever tried getting a taxi in a hurry in Charlton? And the trams, well, forget the trams.

All of a sudden, Karen's interest in ALBASEC seemed to disappear, and we were told not to bother any more. Next thing I knew, a week later, they needed somebody to go to Cambridge to act as minder for one of the girls, for something they'd got to do. I said yes, straightaway; I'd have been mad to turn down a whole day, some expenses paid, with Karen or Ali. But Ali said she'd got a cold, Karen had to work that day, and I got bloody Eva instead. Teach me to volunteer for things!

Another station, this time Liverpool Street. I walked from Moorgate, early morning, so getting into the station was like walking into a rough sea. Eva was there already, looking bored, next to Coffee Crescent, where I was going to buy my breakfast. Her expression lightened a fraction when she saw me, but went back to sullen. I said "Hi", she said "Hello"; I bought my coffee and a couple of croissants after asking her did she want anything herself – she didn't. She had the tickets already - Karen had entrusted her with the expenses money; we got on the train, already quite full: we found two seats side by side. I offered her the window seat, which she accepted with a quick nod in my direction.

There were a few announcements no-one seemed to listen to, then the train was suddenly moving, so smoothly you hardly noticed it to start with; it's the platform scene shifting to the right, like running the scroll bar across a screen, that gives it away. I'd thought I'd watch the outside world go by, but there's not much to look at for the first few miles apart from fences and stations that go by too quickly to see where they are. I got bored and started on my coffee and croissant. That finished, it was still fences and overhead lines outside. We hadn't spoken since the breakfast colloquy, and the silence was lengthening and starting to choke me. I don't actually dislike Eva; she's even quite attractive, though I don't think she much likes me. We had to keep things reasonably friendly if we were to spend a whole day together. But I've never been good at the sort of witty banter that some of my friends seem able to churn out indefinitely and that keeps hens happy. The silence now felt like a stand-off. I asked, "so what is it we're going to see, then?"

She turned that off immediately. "I'll tell you when we get there. It's too noisy to talk in here." Then she rummaged around in her bag, got a book out of it and started reading. That solved the conversation problem, but I only had a free newssheet with me, that I'd printed off as we got into the train, so I had to hope the scenery improved soon. It did eventually, but I've never read a newssheet in such detail. Even the sport and the business news; the sport is useful for the pub, but the business news is desperation. Outvesta was considered by the market to be on the verge of announcing a Rights Issue, whoever they are and whatever that is. It's hard to imagine how I could ever find that interesting, but oldies often seem to have got there somehow.

I bought a book at the station when we got there; it looked like the day would give lots of opportunity for reading it. Eva announced that where we were going was about a mile and a half away and that she was going to walk. Perhaps the budget didn't run to a taxi, and there wasn't much sign of a tram, but it suited me well enough. It was quite impressive, really; most hens I know would rather take the chance of a lift from Jack the Ripper than strain their leg muscles for more than a hundred metres or so. About a mile on, soon after we'd passed the Polar Institute, which I pointed out, to Eva's total non-interest, she suddenly said, "let's get a coffee here" and tacked suddenly to the left, towards an old house with seats and tables in its front garden. I started to follow her, but she zigzagged crazily around the tables, briefly pausing before several of them before taking off again. When she finally settled on one, a seat shaded by a large tree - an ash, I think - I went over and joined her. She went in to the house to get the coffees, and I saw the discreet sign by the front door: Coffee Crescent. Home from home.

She attacked her bag again and brought out a street map. "Has Karen or Paul told you what we're doing here?"

"No, nothing. Zilch. Nada. Have they told you?"

Her face stayed set with seriousness of purpose. "We're going to talk with somebody. Here." She pointed out a street on the map, the other side of the river, with a small red cross marked on it. "Bernard Saintsbury."

It meant nothing. "That map's going to be tough to eat if their agents get us."

She scowled and pressed on officiously. "He works for an organisation that used to be part of the organisation that's doing this re-organisation in AUP."

"It all sounds very organised."

"If you're just going to sit there making feeble jokes, then I'd better go by myself."

"No, hen, I'm your minder, that's what I was told."

"Who's supposed to be a hen, then?"

"It's just a word I use."

She didn't look like she thought much of it. "I don't need minding, thank you. But I could do with somebody to take notes when we're speaking to Bernard Saintsbury. You can write, can't you?"

"Yes miss, I can read as well."

She sniffed and fished a small notebook and biro out of the inexhaustible bag, handing them to me. "No jokes, if you can manage that for a couple of hours. Just take down what you hear."

"Have I got a permit to speak?"

"Only if you have anything worth saying. It might be the only chance we have to get any information out of him about what AFFREM are doing. We don't want you messing it up with stupid comments."

"AFFREM?"

"Yes, AFFREM."

"Who are they?"

"*They* are reorganising AUP."

"The ones with the office near Charlton?"

"Yes. Bernard Saintsbury works for the Franchised Reamers Fellowship, which split off from them a few years back. Or maybe AFFREM did the splitting; I wasn't very clear about that. But he does know a lot about AFFREM. You're quite sure you can take notes and not try to be funny." She looked at me with impassive sternness

"Aye, aye." I raised my arm in a pompous salute.

She looked dubious, but got up and started stuffing half the world into her bag. I thought of asking her if she were taking the tree as well, but thought again. "He's expecting us at eleven."

We had a little under fifteen minutes, so strolled along, enjoying the riverside in warm sunshine.

Number 17 Saffery Gardens was one of a terrace of old houses in a light-coloured brick, the branches of a wisteria over the front door and window next to it and ivy trying to pull down the garden wall. The 'garden' was mostly paving, with a few forlorn-looking pot plants. It took three rings on the bell, at least one of which probably didn't activate anything, before shuffling sounds were heard from inside, and a tall, stooped, slovenly dressed man stood before us.

"Hello, are you Bernard Saintsbury?" said Eva. He seemed only half awake, but was edging towards what looked like saying yes. "Ben Cordell spoke to you last week and arranged for us to visit you, if that's still convenient. I'm Eva." She turned towards me.

I introduced myself as Tad.

"Good gracious, why, of course, I recall the conversation well. Do come in, if the state of the house is not too inimical to the spirit of youth."

Inimical or not, Eva was on a mission, and went in. The minder followed. The hall, floored with parquet, was almost entirely covered with old newspapers, hence the shuffling sound. It wasn't obvious why, but there were some aged paint pots in a corner by the stairs.

"May I enquire your surnames also? My memory slides off Christian names nowadays – or should that be 'first names'? Dear me! A solecism and only two minutes acquainted." He turned to Eva, enquiringly.

"Koniecka."

"And?" He turned to me.

"Litvinaus"

"Ah, and Tad is a shortening of?"

I hesitated over that. I use my full name as little as possible; it was treated mercilessly at school. But if Eva didn't like it, well, sod her anyway! "Tadeusz."

"Well, well, a Polish visitation. And possibly a Lithuanian connection. How very charming. And you are boyfriend and girlfriend, what our degraded language has taken to describing as 'an item'?"

"No." Eva answered forcibly, colouring slightly. I shook my head in agreement.

"Ah, my apologies, I have embarrassed you. The other couple, whom I met so fortuitously in Grantchester Meadows seemed to be very much 'an item' and I had let my assumptions run away with me."

From what I've heard, he'd let his assumptions run away with him a bit on that one too, but I stayed silent, backgrounding myself. Eva was about to say something, suppressed the urge, then spoke anyway.

"We're colleagues in the Ancillary Music Faculty. That's the Arts University of Peckham. AUP, we call it. I'm a research assistant, and Tad …"

"I'm a media designer. Postgraduate."

"Ah, like Mr Cordell, toilers for the subject my organisation sets itself to oppose. Nevertheless, I am delighted to meet you and will help you in whatever way may be possible. Firstly, may I offer you refreshment? A tea or a coffee perhaps?"

We both declined.

"Come through, then, come through. If our meeting cannot be toasted, at least we shall have a view."

Considering the state of the hall, the sitting room at the back of the house was surprisingly comfortable. In fact, it was quite cheery. There was a holoscreen on a table by the window; he probably spent a lot of his time here. The view, of the garden, was wall-to-wall, exhausted-looking greenness.

"Well now, your colleague Ben Cordell is clearly a man who likes to get to the point, but I was left with only the sketch of an impression as to what you wished to talk to me about. Something about our old friends AFFREM putting you under attack. Not an unfamiliar experience I am afraid! Would you care to enhance my understanding?" He looked somehow both extra-planetary and acute at the same time

Eva seized the invitation, plumped her bottom solidly down on an armchair, and homed in ruthlessly on what she was after. "You've got the word we'd use. Attack. That's what it feels like, the way they're going about it. But the word they use – that's AFFREM – is 'normalise'. We don't know what that means, though it doesn't sound like anything good for us. Can you explain what 'normalisation' is; what exactly AFFREM is and how they work?"

"That is a large subject, and it begs several questions, my dear." I got the impression that he'd have patted Eva's knee if she'd been a bit nearer. "Let me see." He went into reverie and was roused only when Eva shifted position in the armchair to pull down the skirt that had ridden up, showing more of her legs than she seemed comfortable with. "AFFREM, as I explained to Ben and his paramour, is a breakaway group from the organisation to which I have devoted most of my working life, though I suppose, as Americans are apt to, they would invert that particular relationship. Our aims and modus operandi, however, are chalk and cheese. My own organisation concentrates simply on promoting traditional musical performance, what you call S-class. With limited success, I sometimes feel, and with particular difficulty in recent years, given the vagaries of changing social attitudes to S-class and the training of the young that it necessitates." He lapsed into reverie again, looking despondent.

I attempted to take notes of his ramble. Eva chivvied him back to the conversational tramlines she wanted him on. "So what are AFFREM's aims and modus whatever - sorry, I didn't catch properly what you called it?"

"Modus operandi – pure Latin. Did you study Latin at school?"

"No," Eva said. I shook my head.

"Ah, a pity. The decline of the classics in the last century has been a scandalous rejection of our cultural history." He continued to look despondent.

"AFFREM's aims and modus operandi. Can you tell us what they are?"

"Yes, indeed. Of course! Well, they retain an intent to further the effective functioning of traditional musical performance. That can be difficult to see through the surrounding miasma of managerial jargon, though. Managerialism is what my generation would call 'their thing', really. Yes, I think they are definitely managerialists. From time to time a few scores are settled on the musical front, if you'll forgive the pun, but management and its peculiar dialect of power that is their afflatus, that evokes passion in their breasts." His gaze wandered to check out Eva's - they're pretty good, actually; it's just a shame they're attached to Eva. "What was I saying?" He looked confused.

"AFFREM are managerialists."

"Ah yes." He tore his gaze away and put on a professorial look. "Understanding managerialism, its motives, priorities, paradigms, that is the key to understanding AFFREM. With that key you have the means to understand what normalisation is about and how it is likely to progress when applied to your own organisation. In essence, it is the exercise of power, pure and simple. Its language, a peculiarly impenetrable dialect of English, is the verbal expression of the exercise of power. It shrouds its subject from the eyes of the uninitiated, as I would suppose they consider non-managerialists. The word normalisation is in one sense just such a shrouding, but in another is a straightforward statement of what is intended. Provided, that is, that the observer understands what a managerialist considers normality to be. Are you with me so far?"

We both nodded, though keeping notes on this lot was a struggle.

He was well set by now. "Normality, in managerialist terms, is a state of stable equilibrium between management objectives and resource deliverables. That may sound at first to be a good scientific statement of the self-evidently worthy, but it fares much less well if looked at closely, I'm afraid." I thought I'd have to take his word for it. Just getting intelligible notes down was taking up an awful lot of brain processing. I concentrated on writing. Eva had no such fallback, and was floundering. She gave an unhappy nod, and he continued, shedding diffidence and looking more authoritative as he did so.

"Firstly, management objectives may seem to be dictated by the business and business environment. However, within any given sector of business, there is no consensus on their relative importance and many are mutually contradictory. In any case, few managers have the energy or the wit to achieve more than a selection of them. Resource deliverables, to take the other side of the balance, can be manufactured to order just as you like, so long as they are not human."

The lecture seemed to be over, at least for the moment. He offered us refreshments again, with a suggestion of something alcoholic, and we both accepted. We sat in an uncomfortable silence for several minutes as he prepared something in the kitchen, relieved finally as he appeared carrying a tray with glasses and a large jug filled with a fruit concoction. "Brooding? Dear me, this will never do. Try some Pimms, it always has a most marvellously laxative effect on conversation, I find." If he meant stringing the long words a bit further apart, that would, I thought, be just fine by the note-taker. Eva continued to look slightly bored and inscrutable.

I must see if I can get some of this Pimms stuff, because it had just the effect he said, though I still had to cope with more of the lecture notes. Eva took a cautious sip from the glass she was given and picked up the discussion. "What sort of objectives do you think AFFREM might have for us?"

He swallowed a large proportion of his drink and looked thoughtful. I used the respite to get down a fair quantity of mine; it was good. Eva sipped again, cautiously. "AFFREM may not be the 'onlie begetter' of your normalisation – it sounds as if they are trying to dice you like vegetables, doesn't it: hideous word. Our own dear government often hands this type of thing to others to do the dirty work. I often felt that our enforced secession had more to it than a simple internal quarrel, but that's ancient history now, of course. If it is just AFFREM, they still make notional gestures to upholding musical authenticity, so anything interpretable as inauthentic is in danger of rough handling. If it is the government, and perhaps the American government too, then the Lord only knows. You are in the lap of the Gods. Have they done or said anything suggestive of intent?" He put his fingers together as if to imitate a church steeple and directed an acute look, unmistakeably at Eva's tits, followed by a more generalised survey of her face.

There didn't seem much to tell. But he was interested in the way that the Vice Chancellor was being marginalised (Eva – first I'd heard of it), the fact that Alan Westwood had been recruited (ditto) and the offices near Charlton. "A classic Dégringolade" (I got him to spell it) "to my way of thinking. Useful when you want to get control of an organisation that inconveniently has very little wrong with it. A period of ritual bloodletting to instil fright, then everyone surviving is settled down somewhere different from where they started. I'm afraid Mr Westwood's recruitment is probably not good news for your Ancillary Music faculty. AFFREM are adept at finding Judases, who validate the unshakeable need for change once the massacre has taken place, though usually without having the conscience to hang themselves."

Eva looked stricken; I can't say I felt happy about what he'd said myself. He caught Eva's expression as his gaze drifted up from below. "Don't take on, my dear." He seemed to think about patting Eva's knee again, but unthought it and looked into her eyes instead. "The blood-letting is usually either of management staff, who can be paid to keep quiet, or of very junior employees who have no enforceable rights. Certainly, that is not pleasant, but professional staff like yourselves should merely be moved around. And it does not sound as though you derive great inspiration from the present leadership of our friend Mr Westwood, does it?" He was forgetting about me, I like Media Design, but he seemed right about Eva: she smiled, rather uncertainly. In fact, she held his gaze a little. He drew a fraction closer. He couldn't be thinking of getting off with her, could he?

To save her from a fate worse than death, I said, "You talked about" (I looked down at my notes) "The Dégringolade as one sort of normalisation. What are the others?"

Eva looked cross, but reverted to being businesslike. He collected his wits. "Oh, well then, let me think. There is, of course S and B - Slash and Burn – also known as The Guillotine: throw out whole layers of an organisation and grow new staff in the space created. I seem to remember that your Vice Chancellor is quite renowned in that area. It has many devotees, but there is little evidence that it is particularly effective, even if you define normality simply as 'our sort of people in charge'. And there are The Flail, which makes particularly strong use of fear, The Ratchet, particularly beloved of those with a financial training and The Garotte, which differs from The Ratchet only in the nature of the measures used. There are others still, but you would need to be involved day to day to know them all."

"They sound like methods of torture or killing.", I said.

"Quite so, quite so. To each his skill and to each his employment."

"How do you know so much about it?" asked Eva, clearly shocked.

"It is the fallout from my job. I liaise with outside organisations and, in particular with AFFREM, which remains, notionally, a sister organisation. Their managerialism people would not use the names I have given for their normalisation activities, of course, but not all of AFFREM's membership are sympathetic to the direction it has taken since the split with ourselves. They use these terms based on observation and discussion with normalisation's victims. I can never interest them in a return to the fold, though", he added sadly. "Americans do so like to be boss."

"So you see normalisation as creating victims?" Eva asked.

"I do indeed, though few would agree with me, particularly in our civil service or government. It is, I find, a very Jesuitical philosophy: the end justifies the means. And since, as I have said, the end can be defined in almost any way you like, if you are the one with the privilege of defining it, almost any means can be justified as contributing to 'the greater good'.

I switched the processor over to unpicking this for the notes, so missed what Eva said next. When I came to, he was saying, "probably, your leading practitioners are most at risk. Otherwise, they will just denude you temporarily of junior support staff and move you all to different jobs. Incidentally, starting on just one or two departments is always a blind. Invariably, with AFFREM, they are targeting the whole organisation. Ancillary Music practitioners remain a particular target, though, even to the most managerialist of AFFREM's members. And they love ritualised crucifixions where there is any sort of celebrity involved. Who do you have in that category at AUP?"

Eva wasn't sure, neither was I. Not Alan Westwood, for sure. Otherwise, they're all just senior academics who must have made it in some way to be there, but whether they're what you'd call celebrities is anyone's guess.

So that's about where we left it on the interrogation. I must say, Eva seemed quite good as an interrogator, though I think she was helped by his obvious interest in her, particularly her knockers. Those are actually pretty good: quite big, nice profile, well worth a leer, bit of a shame they're attached to Eva, but it's embarrassing seeing that sort of thing in someone his age. And she was playing up to it, so I stayed in the background most of the time, enjoying the Pimms. It was all much more interesting once we got off AFFREM, I could put away the notes, and he got onto music, which was what he really enjoyed. I could see why he worked for his Real Fellowship of Franchised Reamers, even if it was self-evidently a lost cause. Music isn't much my thing, so Eva again had a clear field to be sparkling in. Hens seem to be good at that sort of thing, and the two of them got on like a house on fire.

After a couple of, admittedly interesting, hours of this, I needed to stop myself from turning into a complete gooseberry. "What train do we need to get?"

Eva looked at the time, and it broke the party up straight away. He gave out another of his cards - just one - to Eva of course, and we started on a brisk walk to the station. She was quiet during the walk. A few attempts to start a conversation got zilch response that I could follow up on, and once on the train she dived into her book again. Mine proved a bad choice, so it was a quiet and rather boring ride back, in which I studied a lot of green fields.

Just once, when we were getting near to Liverpool Street, she put her book aside to look through the window. We talked a bit about the day, and I cracked a rather feeble joke about AFFREM's "Disgruntlement, or whatever he called it, of AUP." That made her laugh, and it transformed her face, lighting it up.

I must remember to try and make her laugh if we ever have to keep company together again. She has a broad, fair face, normally stern and serious. A smile lightens it up nicely. Just for a moment, she was pretty, somebody you'd want to devote time to, not a rather plain hen carrying around her own personal Disgruntlement.

XLII

CROSSING THE LINE

"Stop there. Can't you see it?"

She was terrified, sweating, pointing to something on the floor. Viola stopped, but could see nothing and said so.

"The line there, you must stay behind it. They'll never let me go if you go across that. They'll kill me."

Viola shuffled into what seemed to be the required position.

"Your foot is over. Can't you see? You must go back."

"Which foot?"

"That one." Viola didn't argue, but moved her right foot back six inches. Jane still did not relax, but the expression of terror on her face subsided into passivity.

"Jane, I can't see any line. Are you sure you're not imagining it?"

"That black line there." Her hand traced out a notional, curving line from one side of the cell to the other. "They drew it the other day. When I was asleep." She shivered and briefly covered her face with her hands.

"I'm quite sure there's no line, Jane. And who do you think will harm you if I go across it."

She muttered, half to herself, "they're hiding it." She thought a moment, clearly confused, then said, "It's a new rule." She appeared to retreat within herself.

Viola stayed still. "Why do you think someone is threatening to harm you?"

Jane just whimpered and covered her face with her hands again.

"When did it happen?"

Jane muttered something she couldn't hear. She asked her to speak louder.

"Two nights ago. When I was asleep." She was still muttering.

"How do you know nobody can cross this line?"

"Not nobody. They can cross it. She can cross it. She pointed to the door; Viola presumed she meant the warder.

"But no-one else?"

"I don't think so."

"So some can?"

"I don't know. They tell me the rules when someone comes in."

"But *I* mustn't cross it?"

"No."

"Why do you think you'll come to harm if I did?"

"You mustn't. They'd kill me.' She looked terrified again.

"Don't worry, Jane, I won't cross the line. But who's going to harm you?"

"They will."

"Who's they?"

"Some of the people who work here. You can tell who they are by the way they walk. And some of them make signs with their eyes."

"Which people?"

"I'm not allowed to say."

"I can't see how I can help if I don't know who's threatening you, or how." She had an inspiration. "Is it okay for a piece of paper to cross the line?"

Jane looked uncertain. "Don't know." There was a pause, then she seemed to reach a decision. "Put it down there."

Viola did so. "Push it forward a bit." She did. There was another pause. "A bit further." Again, a pause. "Yes." Viola flicked the paper in Jane's direction, and Jane picked it up.

"Write down the names of the people who are threatening you and push it back."

Jane looked fearful, but took up a pen and scribbled down three names. Viola could see the Warder, Mary, but not the other two. Jane turned the paper upside down, placed it on the floor, then paused. The pause lengthened; she seemed to be going through some inner struggle, before saying, "I can't. They say I can't"

"We're alone together, Jane. I'll make sure no-one gets the paper. Whoever they are, they won't know."

"They know everything."

"They can't know *everything*."

"They do. One of the prisoners across there" (she pointed towards one of the cell walls), "they chopped open his stomach. I heard him screaming." She shuddered. "For twenty-five minutes. All the punishments last for twenty-five minutes. Anything you do or say, they know. I don't want them to get me." She started sobbing convulsively and curled up into a ball on the bed.

Viola saw she was making things worse. There was no sense to be made of this. "Jane, we'll protect you. Pick up the paper and tear it up. I've seen nothing on it, so you haven't given anything away. Remember, we're here to make sure nobody does anything to you." As if! she thought.

Jane gradually calmed down, uncurled and dealt with the paper as Viola had said. Moving like an automaton, white-faced, lank hair, unwashed-looking, she bore little relation to the Jane Viola had thought she had known.

Viola spent another half hour trying to create an atmosphere in which they could, in some sense, meet. But the old Jane was gone, whether on the interior or exterior, and the best that she could achieve was to leave her relatively calm, without that stare of panic that had greeted her almost as she had walked into the cell. Walking back to the Reception area, she took a close look at Mary, the only known 'they' so far, but, with all the imagination in the world, it was impossible to fashion a monster.

Sylv's face fell as she saw her emerge from the virtual zone. "She's still like I said?"

"Worse, I think."

They sat, looking at one another. "What do we do?"

"Tell someone, make them do something. That bastard Sergeant for a start."

It sounded a good idea. Viola went up to the Reception desk. "We need to speak to Sergeant Brown. We have serious concerns about our friend Jane Fredricksson, who is in custody here."

The Reception avatar returned after a few moments behind the scenes to usher them into the too-familiar, visually null meeting room. "Must think we're paying up", Sylv said. But the Sergeant kept them waiting for the customary ten minutes and failed to greet them as he came in to the room.

"How can I help you?" The tone was neutral and business-like.

"Our friend, Jane Fredricksson, is showing signs of what may be some kind of breakdown. She needs medical help."

"What leads you to that conclusion, Ms …?"

"Trent." As you know perfectly well, she thought. "She looks ill and seems to feel under threat of harm."

"I can assure you, Ms Trent, that she has no basis for concern that she shall come to any harm while in custody. The virtual cell facilities are specifically designed to avoid the possibility of inter-resident abuse."

Meaning prisoners taking knives to each other, presumably. "I'm talking about harm from your side."

The Sergeant's face put on a mask of shocked astonishment. "There is no question of such a thing. The Condominium operates to the highest standards of professional integrity."

"So why are you holding an innocent person to ransom, then?"

"I fail to understand your meaning. Ms Fredricksson, if she is the person you are referring to, is held on suspicion of serious terrorism offences."

"Oh yes? And they are … ?"

"I am not at liberty to disclose the nature of the offences."

"Why not?"

"Protection of our information sources is paramount."

The record was well and truly in play again. Sylv came to the rescue. "That's your script, right?

"Script?"

"The stories you're given to tell us."

The Sergeant reassumed the passive mask and said nothing. Viola started again. "So what are you going to do about Jane? She needs help. Medical help."

"I hear what you say, Ms Trent."

Oh no he didn't. "What are you going to do?"

"In view of your concerns, I shall consult Condominium operational staff with a view to an independent assessment."

"When will that happen?"

"It will be conducted in accordance with standard procedure. Rest assured that we take our professional responsibilities very seriously."

"Yeah, yeah. How soon does that mean?"

"I am not at liberty to reveal that."

"You're so not at liberty, I'd think you were one of your prisoners, if you didn't look so fucking smug", Sylv said.

The Sergeant aimed a pained expression at Viola, who ignored it.

351

XLIII

O DARK DARK DARK

As summit meetings go, it promised better than most. Viola, Sylv, Clare (yet to arrive) and Daoud. Sylv had been persuaded to dress modestly. They had only one agenda item.

Daoud summarised progress. "I have spoken to the relatives on several occasions and there is, I think, some sign that they may yet bend. Jane's cousin, Neil, in particular, I find to be a person it is possible to speak reason to. They are rethinking now what might be done with their inheritance money."

Viola empathised with the relatives, losing their money to a ransom payment, but there was no other way out that she could see. "How much do you think they'll settle for?"

"The police? I am making enquiries and will be meeting Inspector Fox later this week to get an informal view. My guess is between one hundred and fifty and two hundred, but it depends on how many are to be paid off and how much of the costs they will seek to recover."

Viola remembered the Inspector, the Yorkshireman. He had been the only real approximation to a normal human being, one or two of the avatars excepted, that she had met at the Denmark Hill police station. "Ask him about the Service Supplement", she said on a thought. "It might be what most of them are worrying about."

"Service Supplement? This I do not know", said Daoud.

"Thirty per cent of their salaries. It's related to the bail money they get in."

"Ah. Who told you that?"

"The Inspector. In a spare moment when the OSC lot were out of the room, and we got chatting. He warned us about the OSC as well; he was right about that."

"That could be most useful."

Sylv moved her legs into an advantageous position for viewing and gazed at Daoud. He did not resist the invitation to regard her legs, but shifted his gaze quickly back to Viola and was on the point of speaking when Clare finally joined them.

Clare was not her normal self, agitated, clearly distressed. She made only the most minimal attempt to greet them, putting her bag down by the unoccupied chair and busying herself. Sylv looked over at her and said, "what's up?"

She looked back at Sylv, then looked down again. "It's Jane."

Viola said, "what about Jane?"

Clare didn't reply, just looked down miserably at the floor. Sylv went over and put an arm round her. "What's happened?"

Clare collected herself. "There's been what they called an independent assessment. Jane's been moved her to a mental hospital. I heard just as I came out." "They said they'd tried to ring you", she said to Viola.

Sylv looked shocked and was struck uncharacteristically dumb. Viola too, though in truth neither was really surprised. Daoud was the first to speak. "This is bad news if the assessment of her mental state is a true one, but it may be more hopeful for her release. OSC may now give up on her as a hostage, if they cannot see any prospect of profit."

Clare shook her head. "It's worse than that. The hospital she's been taken to is one for criminals, they won't say where. We can't even visit her now."

Daoud swore loudly and got up, kicking his chair aside, before recovering himself and apologising. Sylv went white and stayed dumb. Viola descended into a slump of depression, head in hands. They really are trying to kill her, she thought. Why? What had she ever done?

WINTER 2063-4

IN THE BLEAK MIDWINTER

XLIV

SMALL CRAFT WARNINGS

"Purveen, have you got five minutes?"

The meeting had finished early, so she had the free quarter of an hour that this meant. Nodding, she stayed seated as the others filed out of the Director General's office, through the PA's area and onto an immediate downgrade in carpet. The office took on a softly furnished, stilled hush.

"Water?" She refilled. He sat down opposite her, studying his fingers – surprisingly stubby for an otherwise elegant man – intently. She waited for him to serve.

"Good meeting?" He answered his own question. "Some useful decisions." She agreed with muted enthusiasm. It had been about Income-Generation Focus for Business-Disadvantaged Youth Customers in the Life-Skilling Phase. There had been comments from more than one university that the report showed insufficient focus, passion and commitment, and the avatar responsible had been summoned to explain himself. Report avatars were not optimised for verbal presentation and the meeting had been, on the whole, rather less interesting than the report.

"Education. We call it life skilling now, but that's more about survival and getting where you want to go, isn't it?"

It was difficult to raise enthusiasm for a considered answer. "Maybe."

"I think so." He looked at the uninspiring panorama of office blocks and angled lines of rain beyond his office window; it was a nondescript, very English day. "I should have brought my umbrella after all." He mused a little. "It is, of course, as much about what you don't do as about what you do. Rather like this wretched umbrella." He laughed and she joined in politely.

"I have been meaning to talk to you about where you see yourself going. This is something you discuss with your Director – that's Giles, isn't it?" She vocalised a murmur by way of assent. "It is my responsibility to follow this up from time to time and ensure that you have, as it were, been poured into the right mould." He smiled; she cultivated inscrutability, uncertain of where all this was going. If Directors General had a responsibility to take notice of the likes of her, then she had not noticed them exercising it before. But you never knew with the Government Service.

"Taking what you are working on now, what suggests a future direction? What points to where you want to go, do you think?"

One would normally book much of a morning or afternoon for this sort of thing. "I'm not really prepared," she said with a laugh, not reciprocated. "I get the most obvious reward from projects in which I can see an immediate result, but that's not always possible in policy work. I suppose I need to be clear that what I do will produce something useful."

She felt that that was safe enough, conscious that a morass had suddenly manifested itself, into which a wrong answer could plunge her, for reasons that might not be clear.

"When you refer to a clear view of useful outputs," (Damn! That would have been a good word to get in) "do you see these as outputs caused by yourself or by others."

"The outputs are normally defined by staff senior to me, but either could apply." It didn't do, she thought, to be seen as a control freak.

"You are comfortable, then, with the idea of enablement partnerships."

"Under the right conditions, of course. That's been departmental policy since before I joined the Service."

"Even when the partnership is with non-governmental organisations with very different cultures and motivating factors from our own?"

"Do you mean private-sector firms such as Quanco or Outvesta?" He did not respond. "Under the right conditions, I'm quite comfortable with such partnerships."

He appeared to relax a little. "I'm sorry, this must seem something of an interrogation; it's not intended. There are some excellent people working in our enablement partnerships, many of them a match for the excellence of our own people. I meet them at my club from time to time. There is an ongoing issue of cultural sensitivities concerning modus operandi that I personally find a constant challenge. No doubt you have already encountered similar challenges?" He looked at her attentively.

"Yes, all the time. As you've said, it's an ongoing issue."

"The right conditions. The weather could do with some advice in that area, don't you think?" He smiled at her.

She smiled back. "It certainly could."

"Well, it's been a useful chat. I think you have a bright future in the Service, Purveen. Just keep working hard at the cultural sensitivities" (he smiled again) "and there's no saying where you couldn't end up. I'll write a note of our conversation to your Director."

"Thank you," she said, uncertain if she had anything to thank him for. It seemed to be time to leave.

"Don't forget the umbrella," he said, looking out of the window at the intensified rain. "What you don't do as much as what you do, you know." He laughed.

Watch your back, Purveen, she thought. She was being threatened. Leaving the room smiling, she waved the micro-foldup from her handbag in his direction.

XLV

IN LIMBO

He must buy a proper winter coat; it was getting too cold at night just to wrap up with a few more of the summer clothes that were all he had with him. Money was a problem, though. The arrangements had not left him destitute, but they covered little more than the small apartment he had moved into and food. He would have to dip into savings.

The café was warm enough, and they did not seem to worry about his lingering all evening over a small meal and a couple of drinks. But it was a dull existence, shuttling between library, café and apartment, the latter lacking the consolation even of a piano. One of the enticements of the café had been an old upright he had spotted in a corner near the stairs. Allowed, even encouraged to play, it had proved too much in disrepair to be of use. An attempt at tuning had revealed rusty strings and a split in the soundboard. So there was just reading, snippets of conversation in his still rudimentary Romanian and thoughts of Viola's next visit.

The light glinting off the pump handles (hardly to be seen now in English pubs), the now familiar surround of old photographs around the walls, the noise level gradually rising, the café evening got under way. It was a so-so existence, but then, it was Limbo. He could exchange greetings with the regular clientele, but hold a useful conversation only in English, and few had much inclination to try this. The students were a different matter, but none were sitting near.

He was about to lose himself in his book, when a newcomer negotiating the double-door entrance caught his attention. It was scarcely credible, he thought, there were almost no tourists at this time of year and certainly none in suburban locations like this. But it must be; the likeness was unmistakeable as the new arrival moved towards him, looking for a table. "Henry!" he called out, overcome by the joy of seeing a familiar face in a strange place. The newcomer looked over at him, clearly puzzled, then showed recognition and came over.

"Carl! What are you doing here?"

"I could ask the same of you. Do sit down, if you've not got to be somewhere else. Is Pete with you?"

"Yes, he'll be here in a minute." Pete appeared at the door and was waved across to the table. The waitress, a pretty girl, clearly rather taken with Pete, delivered drinks unusually speedily.

"So what are you doing here?" Carl asked.

Henry answered. "A concert. The Bartok. And a master-class at the university."

"When's the concert?"

"Tomorrow. At the university. And the master-class is the day after."

"Open to the public?"

"The concert yes. But we can easily get you into the master-class if you're interested."

"I might take you up on that. Do you come here much?"

Pete answered this time. "We can only afford to get here when we're paid to do so. But that seems to happen quite often now, maybe twice a year."

"And it's worth your while?"

"Yes. They never pay great fees; there's not enough money around, and it's not something you can make much of in your CV, not in

Western Europe, but we like it here, and they're a lot more tolerant of our sort."

"What? You being a couple?"

"Oh no, we have to be discreet about that. The musician bit. Being pianists."

"Of course! Sorry, I'm being dim. I've been out of things for the last four months."

"Which brings us back," Henry said, "to my first question. What are you doing here?"

Carl searched for what to say. He should have worked out his story in advance, but its absence was not for want of trying; the problem was his mind wouldn't engage with the situation; his thoughts just skittered around it. The truth was, he still couldn't take the present hiatus quite seriously, and it wouldn't do to explain it in too much detail if there were any chance of a return. On the other hand, Pete and Henry were untouchables too and, gut feel told him, they were to be trusted. "I've been warned off returning. Returning to my job in London, that is. For the time being. It's like a suspension, but the pay isn't so good. For the moment, until I'm told more, I've got to stay here gathering dust. I don't know how long that might be."

"Why have they suspended you?" asked Henry. "And why don't you know when you'll hear – there're procedures round that, aren't there?"

"It's not suspension exactly. I've just been warned I'll not be welcome going back to AUP, and there'll be a criminal case brought against me if I try. Stay away and I get an allowance to live on. It sounds pathetic, really, but I'm sure they mean it."

"Who's they, and what have you done, though?"

"'They' is, I think, the organisation that's 'normalising' AUP at the moment. I'd been meaning to ask around about a branch I'd heard they have here in Vishiney, but they got in touch first. Just after Viola had had to go back to England. I arranged to meet them, it was just curiosity, really. Well, I didn't get much further with the curiosity, but I did get advised not to go back. Then it got more insistent, and I found the government was involved in some way. It became clear enough that they meant it all. They said they'd fix the AUP end of things for the time being. Sure enough, there's not been a murmur from them – I'm on 'Special Sabbatical' apparently, and the allowance turns up like clockwork. Not very generous clockwork."

"And the criminal past?"

"Nothing very specific was said, except to make it plain I'd be in a lot of trouble – lose my job at the very least. They sounded pretty sure that they'd get more than enough worked up against me if I went back. So for just under four months now, I've been a remittance man."

"They've done you too," said Pete. Henry looked at him sharply, but his query was forestalled. "They didn't need to do you, Den. You've only ever wanted to play the piano. But I looked set up for a Director's job for an Arts Festival one of my mates talked to me about. They soon put the mockers on that."

"You never told me that. Who's 'they'? And what did *you* do?" Henry said.

"OSC. The Office of Security and Co-operation. They keep a check on subversives like us two – you know, infiltrating lines of Chopin into the community. It was my one and only girlfriend: I didn't have sex with her until she was sixteen, but we did play piano duets together. Her parents encouraged it – the piano duets, not the sex – if you can believe that. It was the sex got me into trouble at the time."

"Teach you to go chasing girlies."

"Teach me to go playing piano."

Henry turned to Carl. "Well, it means you're back to being one of us."

"Sorry to disappoint, but Viola's coming out in two or three weeks time."

"Don't be stupid." "And you a professor and all," Pete interjected. "You're a pianist, aren't you. You always have been one of us."

"Oh. Well. I suppose I can play the piano, if that's what you mean. It's always been okay as part of my job – as a Paginist."

"That's not what I mean. You're a real pianist, like us. It's well known."

"I qualified as a pianist, yes. But it was a long time ago."

"You won some competitions too."

"I was a finalist in the Warsaw. It wasn't enough at the time."

"More than enough now, though."

"It's only the first-prize winners who get decent work nowadays. You're both first-prize winners yourselves, aren't you?"

"Yeah. I got the Leeds, Pete got Brussels. But that was fifteen years later than yours. Not so much competition by that time, not in the west. And pianists from outside the American sector weren't allowed to take part by that time."

"In fact Henry's was the last of the Leeds prizes before they closed it down."

"Not quite. There was a competition the next year, but it was stopped halfway through. Someone was given a prize, I think."

"Whatever." Pete said, turning to Carl, "your finalist position is at least as good as either of our first prizes when it comes to looking for work. And you've still got a big reputation, you know. Among those who know about S-Class music."

Carl was astonished and alarmed. What was being said? And what had been the point of all that caution over so many years if the whole world seemed to know about his S-Class tendencies anyway. No wonder AFFREM and the goon had sounded so confident.

"Come along to the master class," Pete said. "We'll introduce you to the Head of Department. He might be good for some work."

They made arrangements and Carl steered the conversation, with some relief, onto events in England and at AUP. It didn't sound too good overall. Westwood was swaggering round with a seigneurial air of entitlement. Crabtree had still not confirmed the budgets; delay much longer and they would disappear up next year's arse, he thought. Viola and Ben were holding the fort, but were stymied on anything very forward-looking by his absence. Henry and Pete's position had, at least, improved slightly; they had recently, for no very obvious reason that they could think of, been permitted to enter and leave demonstration workshops by the same door as the students - no more crawling over dustbins and through emergency exits. But it was in a slightly despondent mood that Carl eventually sought his bed, enlivening though the chance meeting with the two pianists had been.

XLVI

THE WORM TURNS

She could feel good about private life. Leke was well and truly in tow and proving his worth in bed. Tad had been put to one side without any great bother, though the plan she'd hatched with Alison, to pair him off with Eva didn't seem to be working out. Silly cow had only developed a fetish about this weirdo in Cambridge she'd been sent to hoover. Still, Tad seemed all right and should find someone else soon enough.

Working life, though - she had to say it - was turning into a train crash. An absolute farking disaster, as her brother Frank would say. She often told him off about his language, and he spread it around a lot too much, but that one was where they were at. They'd found out a lot about AFFREM and what it was up to, through the various spies, including Leke, whose position in ALBASEC had given them all sorts of inside knowledge. Eva had got some useful stuff out of her weirdo, even if she had gone off her trolley as a result. Credit to Tad too; he got her back with the info. She might still be there, gazing into the weirdo's eyes while he ogled her, if Tad hadn't been there to break the spell. All that information hadn't got them anywhere, though. None of them could think of anything to do to stop what was going on.

The worst thing was the effect this AFFREM rubbish had had on Mr Fraserman, who hadn't been at all himself for the last three months. If there was one thing she admired about her boss, it was the way he didn't give a monkey's about anyone else — what they did, or what they thought — just got on with it. Now he seemed lost inside himself, like a little boy at times, not feeble, just not really in charge of things. And then there was this woman he was seeing. One of the ASBA people. All right if he was getting a bit on the side; it was strictly hands off as far as that went; he could bed who he liked. But she wasn't sure that was it, and she wasn't having some tart from the Government Service telling Mr Fraserman what to do at work. That was her job, wasn't it?

Fretting, she stood up and walked about the office, stood looking out of the window for a couple of minutes: it was raining. She saw Morrison approaching under his trademark umbrella, which looked as though it had spent more time blown out than in. Morrison was easy to deal with – she decided that today she should be kind; today he would get to see Mr Fraserman, to pay Mr Fraserman off for being unfaithful. But there was nothing to be gained in sitting around in her office dealing with soft targets like Morrison. It was Stephen Pendleton and whoever had sent him here that needed to be dealt with. She realised that the basic problem was that he hadn't been around in several weeks; she couldn't work out what to do against somebody who wasn't there.

Morrison entered in his customary semi-dishevelment and was shown through to the Hon Ran, who uttered a combination of greeting and groan, before offering him the drink that he clearly felt in need of himself. To Karen's surprise, Morrison accepted; it was an act of unprecedented independence and decisiveness. Closing the door and back in her own office, she felt strongly that the time had come to act. A believer in doing anything when nothing suggested itself, she rang John Librarian and arranged to see him in ten minutes. Meanwhile, there was a tidy up of the office. She gave Morrison's umbrella a decent burial; it was time he smartened up. A letter from Stephen Pendleton complaining about a missed appointment and asking for an explanation went in the shredder. She left a note for the Hon Ran in case of need and sallied forth.

Hell's teeth! What had they put in his tea? Or was that fruit juice with yogurt? He winced at the thought. It certainly wasn't just the gin and tonic. Not even the second helping that he'd had the gall to demand - though a second G&T was not unwelcome. It was like seeing a sheep unzip itself and run around looking for something to sink its fangs into.

"If that Yankee cretin doesn't stop airing witless nostrums about carving my department up still further, I'm going to personally eviscerate him and hand over the remains to the performance artists."

It was tempting to tell him to go ahead there and then, but he was supposed to be Vice Chancellor, whatever the hell that meant any longer, so he contented himself with "any carving up of departments will be my decision and mine only. What has he done?" Morrison needed calming down; his face had a distinctly mottled look.

"Talk. Just talk, up to now. The garbage he talks, it's abuse and harassment in its own right. But when he starts on about 'normalising' the department, and I tell him that means getting it back together in its own space and he starts blethering about global atomisation and the relevance of quantum uncertainty to up-to-date organisational and managerial development matrices, it turns into GBH. I may not be a quantum physicist, but I have a good enough idea what that means."

That put Morrison ahead of him, and wouldn't do. "What's your view on what it means?"

"Grinding us up even further and scattering us over the rest of AUP as compost is the best interpretation. Or he may just be thinking of throwing us all down the toilet. He must be off his sodding head. Can you imagine an Arts University without Fine Arts?"

Actually, thought the Hon Ran, he could. It could be a distinct improvement no longer having to host bearded nutters dressed like tramps and wittering about artistic integrity. But it would do his image no good to say so. "Quite!"

"What are you going to do about it?"

Startling stuff. Not like Morrison at all. The obvious riposte of "Nothing. What are *you* going to do about it?" might be turned on him to devastating ill effect with Morrison in his present mood. Playing for time, he looked out of the window at the rain-drenched square, to see a student stepping on a loose flag and catapulting a gallon or so of water over his trousers. Barking with laughter, he turned back to Morrison. "Sorry. Bloody funny, though. What do I do about what? Mr Pendleton or his half-arsed ideas?"

"Both. They each drive the other."

Where had this talent for getting to the point come from? Fury must have created a massive short-circuit across the woollier stretches of his brain. Why couldn't the wretched man stick to the normal prolixity and give him time to think? "You make it sound like a perpetual motion machine. Don't want to have anything to do with those." He paused.

There was no response from a louring Morrison. What had got into him? Last time they met, that tangent would have been good for at least five minutes. "Stephen Pendleton is not a one-man band. Ideas may have been generated by any member of his team. We'd have..."

"He's the one who matters, though, isn't he?"

"He is in charge of the 'normalisation' team. I'll quiz him where the idea thinks it has come from. Would that be helpful?"

"Yes, please. And I want it killed off at source."

He was not going to give any promises, though he would far prefer to see Pendleton flushed down the toilet than Morrison. The latter had his uses and was at least amiable.

More precisely, as things stood, not normally unamiable. The Hon Ran's silence was not an acceptable response. "If you can't guarantee that it will be killed off, I'll have to speak to my Association."

Now there was threatening. The Association for the Preservation and Advancement of the Fine Arts, or APAFA as it called itself was not formidable taken at the individual level, but the collective effect of a dozen or so Morrisons clamouring all around the bushes for their imagined rights was to be avoided. He had had dealings with them over the previous reorganisation; in fact, he still had them badgering him about the disappeared lecturer - as if anyone knew or cared what had happened to him - and wouldn't mind not renewing the connection. They had some Whitehall tie-in too, which complicated things. "I'll be meeting Stephen Pendleton in the near future and will let you know how things stand after that."

"How soon?" Suddenly sobered and aware that the person he was hounding was his boss, he added "sorry, but we can't let this run too far."

"It'll be in the diary." The Hon Ran got up and walked across to the door with Karen's office, opened it and found her absent. The diary was out of sight. Where was the girl? He saw the note. Getting another Whitehall report or two processed, he thought approvingly. "Can't see anything; think it's Tuesday. I'll give you feedback."

Morrison, who had at last fallen below a full head of steam, nodded morosely, grunted assent and thanks and departed. Just before he went through the door, the Hon Ran added, "Keep me informed if he blows off any other ideas, won't you." Morrison nodded.

The meeting with John had started slowly, largely because she didn't have a clue what it was supposed to be about. She'd taken a new report anyway, and a little time was devoted to making it clear without pissing him off that he wasn't going to get it away this time. But the conversation then wandered off into extended aimless chat before she thought to ask him about AFFREM – did he know anything about them?

She wasn't too surprised that he had; he was an information avatar, wasn't he, and AFFREM had been poncing about AUP for several months now. But it did knock her back a bit when he said he'd bought some shares in one of the companies they were matey with – something about a consortium looking out for opportunities. So she said, "aren't you allowed to talk to us, then?" and he laughed and said "depends whether you're offering anything" and she said "and if we're not?" and he said, "now or any other time" and she said "you should be so lucky" and he laughed again and looked her straight in the face and she blushed. Then she said, "so you are talking to us still?" and he laughed yet again and said, "you should be so lucky", so then she laughed too and it was all right. It didn't get her any nearer to what to do about AFFREM, though.

XLVII

TRIOS AND QUARTETS

So that's what they were up to. Paul told me, after he'd got it from a girl he knows, who'd heard it from one of Ali's friends. I think I'll call her Alison from now on; no use fooling myself if she's putting that sort of effort in to pair me off with her best friend. Mind you, the scheme might have had some chance of success if Eva had learned to smile more than once a decade and, most of all, if she'd not turned out to fancy the old guy we went to see at Cambridge. Bernard Saintsbury. I can't see how she can; he must be well over forty; I wouldn't have thought he'd be interested in that sort of thing any more. It did occur to me that staring fascinatedly at girls boobs might be a way to their hearts; it had certainly worked with Eva, and, it's a staple of Wayne's repertoire, but a controlled experiment in the pub didn't go well. I didn't get arrested, but the subjects all moved away quickly. It must be the way you do it.

There hasn't, truth to tell, been much action since Karen gave me the boot. There was the architecture student, a month or so ago, who seemed interested and who did actually go to bed with me, but it was only for using veeps and penpros, "for hygiene", and it's just not the same after the real thing. Her veep wasn't bad, mind; I made sure I kept it; I can't bring myself to use Karen's.

So that's not too much action on the love life. The espionage business is something else. Karen's running me in this in the same way she ran me for a time, in and out of bed, but this time I'm one of a team. After chaperoning Eva to and from Cambridge, reporting back what we'd been told and getting lots of not-so-subtle speculation on how we'd got on – that's before Eva made it plain to everyone her affections had wandered off down a byway – I had a month or so looking after my own life. That was pretty boring, to be honest. The next thing I know is Karen wants me to infiltrate AFFREM, with Paul. She's arranged it all through Leke, the new boyfriend.

So, one Friday morning it was back to London Bridge station – actually, a sort of dungeon somewhere below it, a dismal concrete room, with a cluster of old-fashioned metal filing cabinets in one corner, several lines of racks with overalls, uniforms, and what looked like space suits hanging off them, a couple of skips full of boots and shoes and a holoscreen in another corner. Oh, and a couple of small cameras up by the ceiling, that followed us around like vultures looking for a meal. Paul and I did a little dance together to get them moving in rhythm, but they just clicked back and forth, slightly behind the beat. No passion. Then Leke came over with some clothes over his arm and we stopped. So would you. Ever heard of the Incredible Hulk?

"Try." He handed over two duffle bags and two sets of uniforms. Paul's trousers were excessively long in the leg. He picked out another pair and handed them over with a commanding nod. Hat-fitting had no more ceremony or chat. Togged up like a pair of Kazakh traffic wardens, we waited for instructions. "Tomorrow. Morning. Eight. Office. You go."

We nodded; Paul said, "The office we've got to go to. How do we find it?" Leke grunted, fished in his pocket and produced a couple of cards, which he handed over to us, pointing at some print; we thanked him. Leke looked us up and down. "Remember. Work security. Bah-ooncers. Prison. Wha'ever." (the last was pure Sarf London). "Studenti no." He drew a finger across his throat. "Is understanding?"

We nodded, slightly hurt at the insult to our intelligence; we were spies; spies didn't go round announcing their employment details ("The name is Bond. James Bond. On Her Majesty's Secret Service. Awfully nice to meet you old man." "Yes, I think we comprehend entirely Mr Bond. Can I introduce you to my friend Mr Oddjob. Oh,

Mr Bond, how unfortunate; but how fortunate nevertheless that you in the public sector are blessed with such generous death benefits").

The uniforms (including the incompressible peaked caps) securely stowed away in bags, we celebrated the new promise of income at a pub a few minutes walk away, next to Tower Bridge. The dirty and tattered cards that we'd been given announced the address that we already knew. "Not one for long conversations, is he", said Paul.

"Leke? I don't think he knows much English."

"Wha'ever."

"Yeah, that's because of Karen. When she really needs to talk to him, though, she does it through Eva."

"How's that?"

"Eva knows some Russian and so does Leke. I mean, no-one knows Albanian. Except Leke and a few of his friends. So they have these troilist conversations with everyone speaking in a foreign accent. Even Karen starts pronouncing English as pseudo-Russian, she reckons, though I've never heard them at it."

"I should think not."

"You've got a dirty mind. At it linguistically."

"That sounds different. How do you think you get at it like that?"

I supped some beer. "Never done any in-depth research, but you'd need at least three."

"Can you imagine it, those three trying to spend a linguist whatever night of passion. Three people, three languages."

"Count in Bernard Saintsbury to chaperone Eva and you've got four of each to think about."

Having said it, I realised I didn't really want to think about it, neither in Karen's case nor, as it happened, Eva's, not that I can imagine her getting much change out of her Cambridge fancy, given his age and everything. But Paul was well launched. "Ma darleenk, ah loffs you" he said, his arms describing an embrace in thin air.

"He says he loves you." I said, looking over to one side.

"I got that one. Tell him I loffs him too."

"She, 'ow you say, loffs you."

"What she want lop? I no understand."

"He doesn't understand."

"Fuck it, it's all just one thing with men."

"She just wants one thing."

"Ah. Yes. I think I am beginning, how you say, a stiff one."

"He wants a drink."

"Tell him he'll have to earn it first. What sort of drink, anyway?"

"Whisky."

"Good gracious me, a gin and tonic would be much more in order."

"Gin, tonic, whisky what are they going on about. Ah, that feels better, Ivan."

"She wants a feel. Ivan. No, that's me. Feel her. Bernard, do something, defend me."

"Indubitably it is meet to leap to the defence of a maiden in distress. But in what manner of proceeding, my most precious flower."

"Just move your hand down a bit and make yourself useful."

"Ah yes, certainly, but to what end?"

"End, yes, I could do with one of those."

"She wants to end. Bernard, just use your hand."

"Why she want to end; we only just started. Who stroking my buttocks? Is man hand. I no do man loff."

"He says he gets off on men."

"Leke, you never?"

"She says never."

"Never end. That better. And that go where it feel good. Ah!"

"That's me, you Albanian wally. Karen, take him in hand."

"Hand. Here, think of a man if that's what it does for you."

"My oh my! I never would have realised. And what is this. Oooh!"

"No, lay off will you, that's me … Aaaah!

"Aaaah … Leke like."

"He says, like … aaaah."

"That's better; move it more."

"Merciful; heavens! Aaaah!"

"Aaaah … what the fuck's going on?"

"She like ongoing fuck."

"One moment, ma darleenk."

We realised the pub had gone quiet. Not just subdued – there weren't too many customers – but deathly quiet, and everyone seemed to be looking at us. We had been acting it a bit and must have got louder as the creativity flowed. The landlord was scowling at us and had started to move in our direction, so we thought it best to have the second pint elsewhere and exited quickly, passing a little bloke by the door, with the face of a pensioned-off hit man, who looked at us intently as we passed.

DELIVERY

"It's stuffed and trussed and ready for Thanksgiving."

"That's great, Stephen. When do we take delivery?"

"Thanksgiving? A couple more civil servants need squaring, and we can leverage further value-add from the deal, Whitehall-wise. That's going to take a week, maybe two, then AUP is all yours."

"Good, good, good! We'd better arrange a meeting to talk detail. I've been taking soundings around our Board members, and they're expressing a lot of gratitude for the facilitation job you've done here. In fact, I've been asked to sound you out in return, about helping us as a non-executive director."

He became conscious of the sun through the window bathing his lower body in warmth. His expression settled into amiable neutrality. "It would be an honour. The situation could present conflicts of interest, though. Have your people thought about that?"

"Outvesta employs the best, Stephen. That goes for the lawyers too. Believe me, there will be no conflict here, not the way we'll structure it. Two days a month and all the expenses you can leverage."

"It sounds attractive. Project progression for AFFREM will demand residence in the States for months here, months there. Would that present a problem?"

"No problem at all. Transatlantic flights would be just part of the 'expenses leveraging'. Alternatively you can attend meetings virtually. We're fully set up for that."

"I should clear this with Herb Summerson. Could your people put a few details in writing."

"That's the thing, Stephen. These things work to everybody's best advantage if there's give and take, an attitude of flexibility. You don't get that when lawyers start to write too much down. And, Stephen, I may be speaking out of turn here, but Herb Summerson is a lawyer himself. We both know how inflexible lawyers can be. Write anything down before it's matured and they'll chew it up and spit it out. Give it a month or two, feel your way into the job, then it'll be time enough to speak to Herb Summerson. Two days a month for a couple of months, you could do that out of spare time or holidays, even the holidays you Yanks allow yourselves." He laughed and punched him playfully on the arm.

He thought about the roasting he'd been given over Fraserman. Not that he hadn't got his way, but Herb had been a real bureaucrat about it. "Okay, Jack, for now then, no Herb. But I must speak to him by the New Year latest. I'll take on the directorship when I hand over this job to you. Can you advise me of meetings, duties, getting expenses reimbursed, all that."

"You'll receive a pack in the near future. Here, let's shake hands on it. It's great to have you on the team."

"Thank you, Jack. We talked some time back about the relationship management fee for this project. What are the arrangements around this?"

"Not forgotten, Stephen, any more than the assistance you've given us. Let me see; we agreed £200,000?"

"Two hundred and fifty. I'm not looking to validate the amount, though, Jack; we agreed that. It's more that relationship management is prone to misunderstanding, particularly in a competition scenario, and the transfer of funds will require discretion on both sides for the outcomes to have lasting and stable benefits."

"That's the thing, Stephen, a discreet transfer could have its difficulties at the moment."

The silence grew. Neither wished to speak first. Finally, Jack Kavkazian continued. "You'll know that we're going for a Rights Issue just now."

He maintained a stony silence, his right hand, folded over his left on the desk, exerting pressure to conceal a momentary spasm.

"That's putting us under a lot of scrutiny. Financial scrutiny, procedural scrutiny, you name it. Regulators are an autistic species. They don't understand the softer concepts of good business practice such as Relationship Management remuneration and they can be trigger-happy when it comes to referring things to the Public Audit. I think we should look at a couple of months away. By then, everything will have become nice and easy."

The money had been committed already, but the commitments would have to wait. Having the Public Audit crawling over his project would be failure enough to see off his AFFREM career, whether or not they found anything to scream about. He went for another line of attack. "This Rights Issue. No financial problems we should be factoring in?"

"Not at all, Stephen, we're rock solid. The Rights Issue is for expansion opportunities. The universities, like we've discussed; the Arts Foundations. I don't need to tell you that you've got to invest to expand, and you've got to have capital to invest."

The sun had moved round and was now almost directly in his eyes. He moved slightly, then got up to pull the window blind down. It snagged, but was coaxed more or less into position. "What timescale is the Rights Issue running on? "

"It'll all be over by the end of the year."

So he could have his payback for Christmas. "You will need a good script on the Rights Issue. I've seen off questions in Whitehall about the pilot project, but this is new and could give the destructive critics a chance at another launch. It needs to be forestalled"

"Isn't that what we're paying you for, Stephen?"

He winced; Jack could be so unsubtle in his view of fee provider/fee recipient interactions. "Certainly, but I must speak from the Outvesta script, Jack, if inconsistencies are not to go on the record and damage credibility."

"Sure. I'll see to it."

As a gathering for mutual congratulation, it had, he felt, deflated and left nothing more to say. "I'll wait to hear from you, then."

"Before the end of the week."

They shook hands. Jack Kavkazin turned at the door and smiled: "keep a look-out for that Director's pack, won't you", before passing from sight. It gave off the sense of a consolation prize being handed out.

XLIX

RUN TO EARTH

The whole field of uncertainty and speculation crystallised as he stood there looking at it. Just a card, holoscreened in a window, neatly and professionally laid out in blue and red. It was the previous advertisement but two that had caught his eye, with its promise of a genuine gypsy band, and it was waiting for its return that had kept him here, but this was the jack-in-the-box. Retrieving his videophone, he captured details as they passed again, then stood hunched over the display, zooming it into proper focus, confirming that he was not imagining what he saw and considering its implications. It was difficult to make sense of and might be a mistake of identity, though intuition told him not. A sudden flurry of hard snowflakes drove him to wrap the collar of his coat more tightly and to move on; snow was less common in his native Dresden these days and the cold stung and insinuated itself uncomfortably.

It had been three missed sightings now: firstly Copenhagen in mid-September, then Edinburgh in October. Copenhagen, for all the charms of the city, had never been a favourite conference, dominated as it was by the numerist tendency and all its complicated and tiresome mathematics. But Edinburgh was practically home territory. And now, suddenly, this: a simple notice card offering lessons on the piano and in musical theory by 'the distinguished musical authority Carl Trenchard'.

Janet had, at his prompting, made enquiries, but none produced a satisfactory answer. Just something about a 'sabbatical', no-one knew exactly where, though it was clearly at some distance. But colleagues on sabbaticals, particularly one of his friend's (and sparring partner's) distinction did not thereby disappear; they just homed in on fewer conferences and from a different direction. Carl had unquestionably disappeared. That he should turn into a piano teacher was perfectly plausible at one level; he was a first-class pianist. The greater problem – if this was his friend Carl – was why. And why in Vishiney? Certainly you could admit to being a player in Vishiney in a way that you couldn't, at any rate as a Paginist, in England – even in Dresden, you had to be discreet. But if this was Carl, what had happened to the career in England. The card had, to his mind, an air of long-term need, rather than the-maestro-on-a-visit about it. Plunging thankfully into his over-heated hotel, he decided to follow it up, presenting himself as a would-be pupil.

The next two days were taken up with the workshops and concert that had brought him here. Out of hours, Janet having been held in London by exams, he indulged in a great deal of the chamber music (he was a very competent 'cellist) whose easy-going availability made this such an attractive location for extra-mural professional work. Friday, though, was free, and the weather had improved: intensely cold, but still and bright. Reception rang and arranged an appointment for a piano class, giving just his first name, rendering it as Pavel. Thus disguised he set off, towards the end of the morning, on what proved an uncomfortably lengthy walk through a succession of more or less shabby suburbs, negotiating organically uneven pavements and side roads, dodging trams and skirting the occasional street dog.

The address was in a residential block, in the Stalinist style still common enough in this area of the world, the characteristically brutal, flat-faced façade of grimy concrete stubbornly resisting, even in old age, the smallest hint of heritage charm. The scraps of shredded paper blown about around the main entrance by the icy wind could have shared their origin with the prevailing scent of garbage, but the lobby was clean and, above all, warm. Pressing the relevant bell, he took instructions over the entryphone and was buzzed into the lifts area. The lift was grinding but steady in its progress, clean and adequately lit; he remembered with a grimace of distaste those in Janet's student accommodation: stews from which it had been necessary to relocate her at an early stage of their alliance. The eighth floor presented corridors to right and left, dimly lit, carpeted, but otherwise bare. As he walked over and stooped to read the number on the nearest door, another one opened further up the passage and a figure appeared.

"Hello?"

Without doubt, it was Carl. The voice and the slight hesitation before the question told him immediately. Without answering, he walked forward and thrust out his hand. The figure leaned forward slightly, peering at him uncertainly then in apparent disbelief, then his hand was clasped strongly. "Paul. How do you come to be here?"

"I am the eager student, yes? Pavel, if you like better."

"Ah." Carl relaxed. "You'd better come in."

The apartment, though only scantily furnished, was at least well heated and had an extensive view from the living-room window, mostly over other like suburbs, with just a patch of river in one corner. Close to the window stood a small upright piano. Three or four cheap dining chairs stood around a table and there was just one armchair, in a corner of the room. A single bookshelf contained a small number of books and a pile of music. There was little else to see. A small but adequate bathroom was equipped with just toilet, washbasin and shower. He reconnoitred the equally small kitchen and the one bedroom, with little in it but a double bed, a chair and three suitcases lined up against the far wall. Truly, his friend had become a hermit.

"What brings you to Vishiney, Paul?"

"A concert and workshops. The university. I am doing for many years now. But why are you living here, my friend? Like this? I am remembering your home in London. What is happening to all that?"

"It's still there. Viola keeps an eye on it. I'm here because of circumstances, making an honest living at something else for the time being."

"But for what time, and why is it being like this?" He gestured at the minimal furniture, the less than minimal (for an academic of Carl's profession) collection of texts and crossed to the piano, raising the lid – it was of budget manufacture, Chinese – and trying a few chords, well-tuned, but tinny in sound.

"No, Pavel, like this." Carl replayed the chord and a sweeter sound emerged. Körthofer was impressed, but not by the instrument.

"Your London piano is Bechstein."

Carl shrugged his shoulders and raised his eyebrows, simultaneously and almost imperceptibly.

"How long you live like this?"

Was Körthofer to be trusted? As an old colleague, probably yes; as a professional competitor, God knows. But then, did it really make much difference anyway? "I don't know, is the simple answer. I'm just here on 'sabbatical' until somebody tells me otherwise."

"But Carl, you are distinguished professor. Sabbaticals you decide. Where. How long. Who is 'somebody'?"

He still hadn't developed a story that would fob off more than the most superficial enquiry. It would be difficult to divert somebody as acute as Körthofer, and he suddenly realised he didn't even want to try. "'Somebody' is, I think, a security organisation for the government. The British government. They want me out of the way, at least for a while."

"But why you listen to what they say? British government is not dictatorship. They are not shooting you."

"No, nothing so obvious. But you can easily prevent somebody leaving and threaten to end their career with criminal charges, if they don't co-operate. I have been threatened with that."

"What criminal charges? The johnny machine: that was nearly forty years ago."

Carl laughed at the memory, from their student days. An opportunistic raid on a delivery van had netted a very profitable box of condoms, substituted by a box of ankle compression bandages lifted by a friend from a local hospital, the substitution resulting in a minor wave of pregnancies among the Rubber Company's more dim-witted clientele. "I don't think anyone ever worked that one out. No, it's much more serious than that. Nothing definite, of course, but it was made clear they'd manufacture something around S-Class activities."

Körthofer quietly gave thanks that he lived and worked in Dresden. England had become notorious for its Witchfinder General approach to fashionable social dilemmas; Dresden was more balanced, more tolerant. Besides, he supposed, Germany had a more substantial S-Class musical legacy to throw away, so showed less enthusiasm for doing so. Not that indulging in S-Class was exactly respectable or career-enhancing there either, but it was more a social peccadillo than an ineradicable moral stain.

"I see. That is difficult. How is it you live here?"

"It's in the Russian sector, in practical terms, so a good place to exile somebody. And it's where I was when they sprang their little surprise."

Light dawned. "After the Bucharest conference. Where Viola gave her lecture."

"Yes. We travelled to Vishiney for a holiday; Viola had to go back after a few days to help a friend who was in trouble; by the time she got back I'd been nobbled."

"Nobbled? And what I meant was, how you live. Money?"

"I get a remittance. They could hardly get the threat to stick if I didn't at least get that. And I get some money from the University here for playing for workshops; some friends introduced me. People have been kind." Carl decided not to drag up the memory of what had happened to the Ravel score by identifying the friends.

"I see. And nobbled?"

"Stitched up. Shafted. Stuffed. We have all sorts of ways of expressing it in English. That may be because we do it so much to each other. In my case, it means being forced out of my job and life in England for an indefinite period, perhaps forever – I'm not sure."

"But why do this? I do not understand."

"Neither do I, really. It may be because somebody wants me out of the way while AUP gets what's called 'normalised'. Why particularly me, I don't know, though they are starting the process on two departments that include mine. The organisation that's responsible for this is called AFFREM; they have some sort of link with Vishiney, and I thought before I came that I'd enquire about them when I was here."

"AFFREM I do not know. And did you enquire?"

"I wasn't quick enough. They found me. The day after Viola left, I got a 'phone call. All very affable, said he was from AFFREM, Stephen Pendleton a mutual acquaintance, let's meet for lunch. So we did, had a pleasant chat over some decent food and drink, then all of a sudden he handed me this envelope and talked about an offer I might be interested in. I ought to have found it amusing, but he was just a tad too earnest about it all, so I opened the envelope there and then. Inside was a letter on AUP headed notepaper, signed by Onran and offering a sabbatical 'in the interests of organisational efficiency and the better realignment of AUP's resources for the achievement of its long-term vision at this period of unprecedented change.' The fourth paragraph down mentioned money. I asked my lunch companion - his name was David Wetherill – who he had got this from, but he just looked po-faced and said something about AFFREM advising me strongly to give the offer serious consideration. I tried rephrasing the question a couple of times, but got much the same result. Then asked him why he thought I was supposed to take it seriously. He said something about my not seeing the problem I had. I started to think I'd wandered into a lunatic asylum."

Both men were speechless for several seconds, looking at one another, the one attempting to order what he had heard into a sensible pattern, the other trying to order his recollections into what might sound like a sensible pattern. Carl spoke first. "It was the same reaction at the time. I just looked at him in disbelief. I'm not normally stuck for words, but the whole thing was just so outrageous. Then I saw it as funny and started to laugh. David Wetherill is American, so I hadn't expected him to share the joke, but the face he pulled was something else. Pitchfork I called it, after the way his colleague, Stephen Pendleton, normally looks – it's after a painting called American Gothic: sombre, condemning, nothing funny will ever happen again."

Körthofer was losing some of the sense of this, as the ideas exfoliated and the grammar imploded, but he gave an understanding nod.

"So I said to him 'Why do you think I'd have the least interest in this?' and he said 'You'd be well advised to accept'. I said 'Why? I've no plans to take a sabbatical in the near future; it would just interrupt my professional life and my personal life.' And then it got to the point. 'You have a reputation and an academic income to maintain.' 'Exactly' I told him. 'A sabbatical at the moment would do no good to either.' 'I think you are missing or perhaps evading the import of what is being said. A sabbatical on the terms stated would be in the best interests of your reputation and income.' I glanced down at the letter and said. 'At a salary not much more than a quarter of what I earn? I could do much better than that, even assuming I wanted the sabbatical.' 'You need to consider your position very carefully, Carl. The salary will be adequate for living in this part of the world.' 'But why do you think I would want to do that now' 'There are certain matters that we would prefer to keep hidden. In our view, such a sabbatical would be the most effective course of action to achieve this.'

It was then I knew for certain it meant trouble, but I still wanted an explanation. 'Certain matters? What do you mean by that?' It wasn't very clever of me to ask that, as it gave him the initiative, but they'd have delivered their threat one way or the other, so I don't suppose it made much difference. He made a great show of looking me in the eye then looking down at his hands a few times, the way people do when they're pretending to be embarrassed. 'Certain matters that I stress we do not ourselves believe, but that are poised to hit public notice in the near future. We can prevent that, but only by your effecting a period of absence.' 'What are you trying to threaten me with?' I asked 'Carl, nobody is threatening anybody, believe me.' (As if!) 'But there are matters that would be best kept out of the open.' 'Such as?' I asked. 'I would prefer not to elaborate, Carl, but if you insist…?' 'I do.' 'Then let me just say that certain allegations relating to your continuing involvement with S-Class could at the least damage your career very badly and might lead to criminal proceedings.'

Oh oh! I thought. But I wasn't giving up. 'Involvement with S-Class, as you call it, for someone in my position and, working in England might need some explanation to an employer. I wouldn't have any difficulty with that; my job does require some contact with that world. But even in England, S-Class is not a criminal activity.' He looked me in the eye yet again, with an unnecessary fixation. Bloody Americans, they always overdo the sincerity bit when they're about to lie to you. 'What has come to our attention relates to involvement outside your professional activities and unrelated to your areas of research.' That, I knew, could be nasty. Somebody must have gabbed."

"Gabbed?"

"Talked. Said too much. But I thought they'd have difficulty causing me real problems – more than a bit of embarrassment and general denials, that is - on my spare-time music-making, unless I'd been caught in the act, which I haven't. So I said, 'I'm a professional. I don't keep fixed hours of work or fixed areas of interest. I'm involved with whatever's necessary for my profession. That may be hard for you to understand.'

He scowled slightly at that, but it didn't knock him back. 'You would see S-Class music-making at your apartment and out of working hours with children as an essential for your profession, then?'

I said, 'S-Class involving children, in England, happens only when there's close supervision and a plan of work. It's not something you do ad-hoc, and I've always avoided it myself.' That's certainly true; most of my students are late teens or early twenties; nobody under sixteen is allowed on the course.

Then he said, 'The information that we have to hand suggests otherwise, Carl.' He put his hand on mine; I drew mine away; he continued, 'This must be very difficult for you, I know. You must consider very seriously the arrangements we propose to put in hand.'

It was very difficult for me all right, but not for the reasons he was suggesting. S-Class is so demonised as elitist now in England – it's bad enough in Germany." (Körthofer nodded) "Some consider involving children in it as abuse. You only need to be accused of that to have your reputation shredded; it doesn't need proof. Even in a court of law, a reasonably credible witness statement is enough. In practice, you can't challenge it effectively. So I was certainly being threatened. I asked him why AFFREM thought it worth going to the trouble of manufacturing this, but he didn't register anything: he'd be well used to that question, I would think."

"What you do then?" Körthofer asked.

"Told him I didn't talk to blackmailers, walked out and paid my half of lunch on the way. I left his envelope on the table, but it turned up again through the post a couple of days later. At first, I couldn't think what to do, though I was inclined to go back to London and call their bluff. But the threat had sounded serious, and I had no idea exactly what accusation I might have to fight. It occurred to me, though, that if Onran had signed the offer he ought to be able to explain why, so I videophoned him early that evening: he was still at work. It was an awkward conversation.

'Ranulph. Carl Trenchard here.'

A pause. 'Oh. Good of you to ring.'

I tried a few pleasantries, but he was obviously miffed about something, so I got to the point pretty quickly.

'I've been given a letter from you offering sabbatical terms. The people you entrusted it to seem pretty keen that I should accept. I'm not convinced as things stand; for one thing it's very rushed, but I thought I'd sound you out on how you viewed it and what you might advise.'

'Not sure there's anything much to say. I was told you were keen to get away.'

'Then somebody has been playing around. Until yesterday, my plans were the usual return to AUP for the autumn term. Now it seems I'm not being given the option.'

'What do you mean, not being given the option? You're one of my professors, for God's sake.'

'The letter I received came from you and was signed by you. And the person who delivered it, one of Stephen Pendleton's colleagues' (the 'phone emitted a snort) 'made it obvious I was expected to accept.' The 'phone emitted silence instead. 'He spoke to me as your representative, so I rang to get what it was about from the horse's mouth, as it were.'

'Sounds like you got the horse's ass first off. The horse's mouth was told, a couple of weeks back, by Pendleton, that you'd been in touch to say that you wanted to take a sabbatical over in that bit of Ruritania you seem to like.'

'Vishiney.'

'That's the one. I wasn't keen, but he seemed to think it would fit well with this normalisation bollocks, so I said I'd think about it, and he left the letter with me; said it covered the necessary arrangements. Then I was talking to one of the Whitehall chappies about the normalisation a day or two later, mentioned that one of my heads of department was thinking of going on sabbatical over the period, and he got quite enthusiastic, by the standards of that lot, asked where and started rabbiting on about the usefulness of cultural ambassadors to the Russian sector, you know the sort of drivel they talk. So I signed the letter when Pendleton brought it round again, thought you deserved a spell in rural bliss, knocking off the milkmaids. But it wasn't your idea, you say?'

'Emphatically not. And it came with a few threats, which I wondered if you knew about.'

'All the milkmaids have brothers, you mean?'

'A bit more definite than that. And related to coming back to London. The milkmaids didn't seem to worry them at all, not that I've met any.'

'Bad luck. Try the female tractor drivers. Engines revving all day, gives them a taste for the real thing. Don't know anything about getting at you if you came back; it was all above board and friendly as far as I was told. Do you want me to enquire?'

'It would be useful if you could; you're on the spot. Discreet, though; they don't seem to like me, or at any rate, they don't want my presence.'

'Leave it to me. I'm not having those berks putting one over my staff; that's my privilege.' He barked with laughter, and I did a courtier's laugh back.

That was about it then, but he did ring back a week later to say that he'd been in touch with one of his Whitehall contacts: a young lady called Purveen; contact might be the word, according to Viola. He confirmed they meant business, though no-one seemed to know why. I'd verified that for myself by then. After a few days, I'd finally got fed-up with the inactivity and Viola had rung to say she wasn't going to be able to get back. Hanging around just because of some vague threat seemed sheer indignity, so I packed and headed down to the airport. I checked the bags in and got a boarding pass, but the passport officer waved me aside into a separate room, blank apart from a couple of chairs and a desk, where I hung around in limbo for the best part of an hour, unable to contact anybody, before David bloody Wetherill turned up, wouldn't you believe it. It was the same soft-soap as before, 'strongly advise you not to act hastily, Carl. The offer is still active.' I said I had freedom of movement and would defend myself against any of AFFREM's fabrications, and he sighed and said that return to London 'as of this time, is not feasible.' I said 'meaning what?' and he sighed again. 'You're a very strong and determined character, Carl, and I respect that.' (Oh yeah!) 'For your own sake, your flight booking today has been cancelled.' 'What authority do you have to do that?' 'The cancellation has been ordered by the national authorities.' 'At your instigation?' 'I'm not at liberty to comment on that. You must remember, though, that all concerned are acting in your best interests.'

I thought of something. 'My baggage' (looking at my watch) 'will already be on its way.' 'Your baggage has been retrieved and is waiting for your collection.' So much for that. 'Suppose I just keep turning up at the airport.' 'While present arrangements remain appropriate, you can expect to be intercepted. A word of advice, though. AFFREM has no control over the actions of national authorities and there is a possibility that their patience will diminish should you make repeated attempts to put yourself in danger by returning to London.' 'That's a new threat.' He sighed again. 'We are all acting in your best interests, Carl. You have the sabbatical contract at your apartment?' I nodded. 'Just sign it, and this unpleasant charade will end.' Then he left, and I was escorted, not exactly under arrest, to another office near the airport entrance, where they gave me back my bags and shooed me in the direction of the bus back into town. Luckily, I'd still got some paid-up time at the apartment, so I just went straight back. I signed the contract two days later, when I needed an assured income to rent an apartment. Since then, I've been in Vishiney. The witchcraft charge over teaching S-Class was just a backup. Basically, I'm under a type of house arrest. You might call it country arrest."

Carl, who had been walking up and down the room as he spoke, came to a halt, his arms dangling down by his side, his shoulders square but, as Körthofer saw it, slightly drooped. The light in the room from the window was now diminishing fast, but neither moved immediately. Körthofer felt unable to offer immediate comment; only platitudes or statements of the obvious came to mind. Instead, he walked across and switched on a light. Carl blinked and came to, asking his friend to sit down; they had both stayed standing until then. "Paul you must need sustenance." Körthofer looked puzzled. "Food and drink. Let me get you some."

Körthofer made a decision. "Food and drink yes, is necessary. But we must talk. About your situation. Not cook. I buy you meal in restaurant. No, no objection. I earn well, you have difficulty, yes?"

Carl did not dissent, but insisted on his regular café, a fifteen-minute walk away, to which they repaired in the freezing early twilight, entering thankfully the haven of its light and warmth. The meal and some beers were demolished before either made any serious attempt at conversation. Körthofer led off. "I am thinking, you need to know is it London only you cannot go to, or anywhere."

This had occurred to Carl also, but there had been no occasion to test it, and he said so.

"You also must not stay disappeared. I am not the only enquirer where you have gone. I think I am inviting you visit Dresden, give workshop. We pay all expenses."

Carl suddenly found himself choked, fighting tears, a little in reaction to unexpected generosity, but overwhelmingly from the rush of homesickness for normal life, the sense of the strained artificiality of his recent existence. Mastering himself, he commented, "thank you, but I'd have to clear it with the authorities to get out of the country, and they're likely to see the risk of my taking a plane to England from Dresden as too great."

"That could be true." Körthofer took a swig of beer. "Then we must embarrass them. I appoint you visiting lecturer, put up posters about workshop… they let you, I think. More difficult say no and explain why to all the Paginists than say yes."

Carl was unconvinced, but it seemed worth a try. "That sounds good. Worth a try. And thank you again. A trip out will help stop the walls moving in." That was all too true. In the past four months, the encounter with Henry and Pete, two or three sessions accompanying workshops at the university, Viola's brief visits, his position as a regular customer at the café and more recently the three lessons per week for the pupils he had so far found were the only events that stood out against complete isolation. His remittance did not stretch to much in the way of communications to the outside world and there had been no further visible interest from AFFREM. The longing for a return to an unrestricted life hit him. He straightened and flexed his shoulders, suddenly aching. Körthofer suggested a glass of grog. They drank to snatching the future back from AFFREM and its myrmidons, and Carl relaxed a little.

The cold and the gusts of wind on the walk back remained merciless; he should have accepted Körthofer's offer of a lift in his taxi.

L

CAMBRIDGE BY NIGHT

What was the matter with him? Was she the problem? Alison's hand-me-downs had given her plenty of experience in fending off unwelcome advances, but little experience of fending on. And that was what he seemed to need. Half a dozen trips up to Cambridge, a couple of weekends, and they had become close friends, but there hadn't been the whisper of an assault on her virtue. He had his arm around her waist now, though, which was nice. She relaxed into the moment. Like Bernard, neither Cambridge, nor their current location, Trumpington Street, lacked anything in old-world charm.

A group ahead of them were having difficulties in basic navigation. As they came up to them, one of the girls fell into the open drain full of fast-flowing rainwater, beside the pavement, falling to her knees, losing a shoe and wetting her clothes. Her companions laughed. Bernard bent down and helped her up; she accepted his assistance, but slumped against him as she regained her feet, bringing him into more intimate contact than he had designed. He half-carried her to sit against the railings of the adjacent Casino, but as he attempted to place her in a position from which she would not slump to the ground, one of her male escorts took issue with him. "Who're you trying to grope, then?"

Bernard looked startled. "Whatever can have made you think that?"

"Not what I think. It's what I fuckin' see. Got a good feel of her tits, didn't you? Dirty old fucker."

"Dear me! You're under a severe misapprehension."

"Don't you try dearing anyone, cunt. You'd better fucking apologise."

"I have nothing to apologise for; you should be thankful that I helped your lady friend out of her predicament and stop this absurd fandango."

"I said apologise." He was fairly tall, quite broad and a good deal younger than Bernard. Eva, now thoroughly alarmed snuggled up and said quietly, "just say sorry, he's too stupid to be bothering with", but Bernard muttered "no, keep out of this."

"Just one more time. Apologise!" He bunched his right fist. Eva felt herself gently pushed to one side.

"Let us past, you can see to your lady friend, and we'll forget this happened."

"I warned you." An inspiration struck him. "Pervs like you, you need a bath." He lunged forward and swung a punch.

But it was not Bernard who took the bath. Stepping aside, without evident effort, he rolled his adversary over his back, using the momentum of the punch and deposited him on his bottom in the drain, with an almighty splash. It was the young man's turn to look startled, as he subsided to lie full-length, succeeding only in pulling himself on to his side. Drenched in nearly-freezing water, the fight went out of him immediately. His friends sluggishly moved to his assistance and started to heave him upright, without obvious expertise, so that he suffered two further minor dunkings. Bernard, meanwhile, retrieved the girl's shoe from further down the drain and presented it to her. She muttered, "Do you mind if I come with you?" he nodded and they exited with her, still shaky on her feet, her right breast intermittently nuzzling Bernard's left arm from which she was hanging. Eva was linked through his other arm, still high with a mixture of alarm and pleasure at her beloved's triumph.

They parted company with Bernard's conquest trophy, who gave him an enthusiastic, rather drunken hug and kiss, to his evident pleasure, at the turn-off into Fen Causeway, close to where she lived. Eva then took him briskly in hand for the walk back home. "Where did you learn to do that?" she asked, once the trophy had tottered adequately out of earshot.

"Kissing?"

"Don't be daft."

"Ah, that. Military training."

"I didn't know you'd ever been military."

"No, that was never my calling, though it has its own very special seductions, but even an administrative post in Pakafiran made basic training advisable. I was of the second wave of recruits, six months after the venture floated itself on the whim of events and already it had become obvious that service in the locality had very little to do with whimsy and very much to do with survival. So I was sent for eight weeks to essay the dubious pleasures of basic training and unarmed combat. Pleasure, it ensued, was definitely not the word, but the training has had its uses."

"I couldn't believe how easily you threw him."

"Technique, my dear, only technique. Also, he was drunk and I was not, which was truly a blessing."

"Tell me what you did in Pakafiran." But he was unaccustomedly reluctant to talk, and they watched a film instead. As the time for bed approached, Eva sensed awkwardness. She snuggled closer to him on the sofa, and he put his arm around her, which looked after that, but then the film ended. Previous evenings had been diffused at similar moments by the offer of a bedtime drink, after which he would disappear, saying goodnight, the drink half-finished. Now, though, he made no move, and they stayed together, not speaking. The heating switched itself off, and they held each other closer as the room cooled. He kissed her (good! she deserved at least what the other girl got, she reckoned) and his hand strayed lightly to caress her breast, a movement that she made no effort to repel. But after a minute or two of this, he abruptly withdrew his hand, and there was no further exploration. What now? Eva thought.

"We have known each other how long?"

"Just under three months." She knew it to the week. What did that matter, though?

"That is a remarkably short time," (he really was a slow worker, she thought) "but I have grown very fond of you nevertheless."

Eva snuggled a little closer still. Well, get on with it, then.

"And so I do not feel that, tempting as it is, it would be right to mislead you in any way, or leave you under any misapprehension as to what it is possible for you to expect from me."

 "What do you mean?"

"I mean, and I find it hard to say this to you, that I, and let me try and put this in a nutshell, cannot fulfil what in a different context and one that I might otherwise aspire to, you would regard as my marital duties."

What the hell was he talking about? She looked into his face, but he had turned away.

Her puzzlement becoming obvious, he plunged into direct statement. "I'm afraid I am not capable of full sexual intercourse. Functionally impotent. It seems unlikely that a young woman like you could possibly find that satisfactory."

It felt like a thrown punch that had connected. Attempting to minimise damage, she asked, "does 'functional' mean just limited, or what?"

"No, I'm sorry. It means that I experience many of the emotions and even satisfactions, but cannot get anything approximating to an erection, if you know what I mean."

Of course she knew what he meant. "What caused it? Is there anything can be done?"

"It was the military connection again. The office were I worked was caught in cross-fire and I was wounded in the groin area. It was nothing very serious, apparently, though it hurt a lot once the shock had worn off, but it must have caused some lasting physical damage. No doctor has been able to identify exactly what, though it may have combined with post-traumatic stress syndrome."

"Don't they have drugs to help?"

"Sadly, I seem to be largely beyond the recourse even of the drugs, and I get nasty side effects for the extremely limited reaction that they produce."

Eva suddenly felt overwhelmingly sad for him. "Tell me about it: what happened?"

"It was what the Americans would call a SNAFU; the equivalent terms in Farsi or Pashtun are unknown to me, but it was whatever they may be too. A few of the local Resistance fighters started firing on an American military outpost near the top of the valley in which we were situated. They were in an exposed position low down in the valley, so used our building as cover. The Americans, who were never too careful about whom they were firing on, must have assumed the Resistance were firing from the building, so started firing into it. Some of their bullets went wide on the other side of the building and hit a local Police Station. The police assumed they were being fired on from the office building as well, and started chucking additional ordnance in our direction. Add a few bullets going astray from the instigators and we were target practice from all round the compass. I was grazed by a bullet when lying on my back, obviously not as removed as I thought myself to be from the line of fire. Not, in that situation, that it's easy to work out, and I had had very little experience."

"Awful!" Eva shuddered.

"It could have been much worse. Others died. The hardest was realising over several weeks that something apparently minor, if painful, had had such a terrible effect. Though I have always liked women, it has eliminated the possibility of any close relationship."

Eva made her mind up. Standing up, she extended her hand down to him. "Come to bed."

He made no demur when she made no move to go from his bedroom. But the night's secrets, though comforting to both, made it clear that he had neither lied nor exaggerated.

LI

HAGGLING

A few floors above street level, the view over the bend in the river, trophy buildings lining both sides and a diverse selection of river craft moving slowly across the picture, beguiled her as always. A sense of Jane's loss in being removed from this washed through her. Daoud was looking at her. So was everybody else. "Sorry, you've asked me a question, haven't you?"

Everyone laughed. "It is a great river, Viola" Daoud said, "worthy of close observation, but before you do so could you first give us your reaction to what Inspector Fox has told us."

What he had told them: her attention had wandered to the view as a pure diversionary tactic. Inspector Fox was at least a human being, both literally and in terms of empathy, but he was still a policeman and holding her friend hostage. "I may have missed some of the details of the deal that the Inspector thinks might be struck. Sorry, but could you go through that quickly again, please" she said, looking at him directly. It was rubbish, she hadn't missed anything, but it bought time.

The Inspector looked her in the eye in return, then down at notes on a scrap of paper he was holding. "One hundred and ninety will likely work, if it's cash down. She'll be tagged for a year, but that's just bullshit; no-one'll take any notice of her unless she starts doing over restaurants again."

"But that's hardly less than we were talking about three months ago."

"I told you at the time, lass, you shouldn't have been uncooperative with the ostrich-shaggers. They heard you saying no to what they were asking, they dug their heels in; they always do. Length of time it's taken, there's a sackful of bills to be paid for keeping your friend in custody, and that's before you look at the treatment."

"But the custody was a Police and OSC decision, and the treatment is for a mental condition that the custody has caused."

"Can't comment on that, as you'll well know. But you must know by now, they don't admit owt."

"So you're still holding my friend … our friend … for the same price you quoted three months ago. If this is all about bargaining, what's happened to flexibility on your side?"

"No use talking about prices: won't get you anywhere. It's a bail fee for a person suspected of a dangerous terrorist offence."

"Bullshit! In your own words."

"Bullshit or not, it's the words we use. You're banging your head against a brick wall. It won't give way, neither."

"So that's your last offer."

"Offer nothing. It's the bail fee I think'll be accepted."

"The Police or the OSC?"

"Both."

"Really?"

"My lot, no sweat. Out of our league anyway. OSC, I've heard enough, I think they'll settle."

"For a hundred and ninety in cash?"

"There or thereabouts. You'll have to drop your complaint as well."

Oh, that. Viola had almost forgotten about the complaint. Written it off would be more like; it had only got through one more stage in the last four months.

Daoud had folded one leg over the other and was leaning sideways against his chair-arm, alternately craning his head forward and settling against the chair back. "Viola, Inspector Fox is acting as an honest broker in this. We have had many discussions, and this I think is the best that we can do. The complaint also must be terminated, because nothing will be agreed unless all traces are erased."

"Have we got one hundred and ninety to settle with?"

Daoud looked at the slim, quiet man sitting fractionally out of the circle of chairs they had arranged around two of the coffee shop tables. He looked glum. Not surprising, Viola thought: it was his inheritance, among others; he was a cousin of Jane's, Neil by name, actually a second cousin, but the only one who kept up any sort of contact. Not a very attractive man, she thought. Clare, as it chanced, had other thoughts, but didn't show them. Sylv was ignoring him, to concentrate on Daoud. The feminine board of assessment apparently passing him by, he was focusing on his knee and on the hands clasped there and saying nothing.

Daoud, uncrossing his legs, proposed a separate chat with Neil. They departed for a nearby wine bar, trailing Sylv and Clare. The Inspector maintained his air of observant relaxation. Viola had a few questions for him, and he seemed in no hurry. "So why start on this 'honest broker' lark? Haven't you had enough entertainment keeping Jane banged up for the last few months?"

The demeanour did not alter. "Entertainment has nothing to do with it."

"And the thirty per cent?"

"Aye, we get performance pay. The ostrich-shaggers may get more out of it than that; I can't say I'd be surprised. But policing isn't about feeding the funny farm."

"So you're having an attack of conscience. Pity it didn't happen sooner."

"No good trying to twist it like that, bail money isn't about conscience."

"So you approve of extortion?"

"Bail money. It's for tackling crime. Call it all you like, it's just bail money."

Viola sniffed. "So if it isn't conscience driving you, what is it?"

"There's a proper process."

"Which hasn't been followed here, you mean?"

"I don't mean anything that you or I could prove. I don't know much more about this case than you do, lass. The OSC have kept me clear of it since the day we first met. But custody until people see reason is one thing …"

"Go on."

"Mental torture …", Viola's eyebrows flickered upwards, "That's another."

"So my complaint is correct, then? And you're happy with holding people hostage, so long as they're just left to rot."

"Just speculating, from what I see. So are you on your complaint, for all that. That's why you'll have to drop it if you want to get anywhere. As for what else you're saying, you can keep finding words, but it won't alter the way Criminal Justice works. Stick to your theories if you want, but you'd best do that in silence if you want your friend Jane back."

That did finally silence her. She looked out of the window as the silence extended itself, collecting her thoughts, then, scratching at a fleck of mud that had stuck to a fingernail as she saw to the pot plants that morning, asked him, "so, keeping my mouth shut on everything I've got to keep it shut on, and assuming we can raise the cash, what happens next?" He even smiled. Bastard!

"That's more like. What happens next is I do a bit of straight talking with my Superintendent, make him see sense, then he'll talk to the OSC. As I said before, I think they'll see sense too. We could have it all wrapped up in the next month, if your boyfriend comes up with the readies."

"My boyfriend?"

"Yon miserable sod who's gone off with your friend Amin to have some sense knocked into him."

Viola actually laughed. "What makes you think he's my boyfriend?"

"I figured you were talking for both of you, him not having any words of his own to get in edgeways."

"Well he isn't; I hardly know him."

"Never prevented a good relationship, that. Mind you, you could do a lot better. Me, for instance." He leered, maintaining his air of alert relaxation.

In your dreams, she thought. He must be out of his mind, after all that had happened. She just looked at him coolly for a few moments. "If that's what you're after and it's errands of mercy you fancy yourself into at the moment, you could try rescuing Daoud from Sylv. But don't get your hopes too high."

He was unabashed. "Nay, I'm the faithful type, once my fancy's set. Good hotel just over there", he said apropos of nothing, gazing to the other bank of the river and leering again. "Not that your friend Amin needs rescuing, I wouldn't have thought." He leered yet again.

She stayed cool. "We're all spoken for, as you might put it."

"That so? Well, if you ever get round to speaking again, give us a shout." He handed over his infocard. This time he smiled. She looked disdainful, but kept hold of it; it might be useful now they were negotiating, after all. The bill paid, from police expenses, he walked her back to London Bridge Station. The offer of a lift refused, he parted company from her, delivering an almost imperceptible pat on her bottom and striding away towards the car park.

LII

CATS OF WAR

"Then he said had we any questions, and I asked whether the department needed to be 'aware of any manpower planning and redeployment issues arising from the normalisation of AUP and whether these could be seen as templates to be applied throughout the ongoing programme'."

The Hon Ran sneezed, and Karen raised her eyebrows, before looking down at her skirt and smoothing it down towards the knee.

Purveen looked apologetic. "You have to put it that way. Ask directly how many people they're going to throw out of a job, and they'll just think you're clueless. Anyway, he wittered on for a few minutes about the 'integrality of manpower planning and resource optimisation to the normalisation process', before saying that reskilling would be a principal axis of the normalisations rather than redeployment, in AUP and elsewhere, but that AUP presented particular challenges in the existence of 'radical foci', whose gravitational influence on core objectives required pre-emptive neutralisation. I think that meant that everyone would be moved around to different jobs, and a few individuals would be made an example of."

It sounded like a Disgruntlement (as Eva insisted on calling it) all right. "Who are the examples, then?"

The Hon Ran spoke. "Carl Trenchard for a start. I think they think they're lining me up too. We'll see about that. Any other names you got, my dear?" he said, looking fondly at Purveen.

"You two definitely. Mention your names and the Whitehall team starts sort of bouncing off the walls and yapping about the evil One. It's like a pack of dogs, locked up and scenting a cat."

409

Or hounds scenting a fox, the Hon Ran thought. Well this particular fox intended to outrun them. Shame about Carl Trenchard: the only really first-class member of staff in Ancillary Music. He'd find something.

"I think there are one or two others, but nobody is giving anything away. I'm not on the team myself. And that piece of slime, Stephen Pendleton, wouldn't say anything more." She shuddered imperceptibly at the memory of a second lunch in which he'd managed briefly to manoeuvre his hand onto her knee. She'd given him full-on outraged-maiden treatment over that one, and there had been no further lunches.

Karen was ready to do battle, but couldn't work out who with. She'd been targeting this Purveen and had finally inveigled herself into one of Mr Fraserman's get-togethers, but she wasn't an enemy, not trying to control Mr Fraserman, not even bonking him, as far as she could tell. The only visible enemy was Stephen Pendleton, and he seemed to make a point of avoiding her these days. He certainly spent much less time with Mr Fraserman than he used to. She'd scratch his eyes out if he ever appeared again, but she wanted action now. "They can't just throw a university vice-chancellor out of a job, just because they feel like it. There's rules."

The Hon Ran shook his head. "Not Whitehall. No rules, barring the ones for themselves. But they've no guts either, so it's not so unequal a fight. They'll have to throw lots of sweeteners to shut me up, that's if I'm interested in taking them. Don't fret yourself, Karen, something will work out. What about you, my dear?"

"What about me?"

"You've stuck your neck out for us. Bound to be a comeback."

"I've been careful. I was warned off making enquiries and I've stayed warned off. Except Stephen Pendleton, and now I don't have to see him any more."

"Still and all. I owe you a favour or two, if you ever need them. Don't forget."

"I won't, and don't lose touch, whatever happens." She reached across the table and put her hand over his. He reciprocated with his other hand, and they looked into each other's eyes.

Oh God! Smoochy, smoochy, thought Karen, and she picked up her glass of wine and raised it high. "Here's to us!"

The other two disengaged and joined the toast, the Hon Ran relaxing in the female stand-down. They had spent the first half of the meeting circling one another like cats. It had been uncertain whether they'd make a meal of each other, or, by way of compromise, a meal of him, or (as had happened) declare peace.

LIII

SKIRMISHES

It only turned out to be the hit man on the gate. The one from the pub. He scowled at us as we walked in. "Funny guys. Funny guys. This who they send?" It sounded like mutual recognition.

We produced the security chits we'd been given and handed them to him. It seemed best to say nothing. He examined them at some length, with an expression of dislike. We waited. "You think you make jokes here, make noise, huh?" We both said no. "No is good. Not forgetting, no jokes, no noise. Just work. Understan', just work?" We said yes; wouldn't you have? His sense of dislike continued to surround him, like an aura, but he went into an office behind and re-emerged ten minutes later with passes. We were in. "Remember, no fuckin' jokes." We nodded and passed into a waiting area beyond the security gate. It wasn't a good start to our career as spies: we weren't exactly merging into the background. It wasn't clear whether the hit man had realised one of the people in our little pantomime had been his boss.

The rest of the day was quite boring. Security work isn't glamorous at the best, and we started by unpacking and packing vans: stationery, food for the staff canteen, toilet rolls: that sort of thing. We weren't allowed anywhere near the real security van that did arrive mid-afternoon. The brightest point in the day was at lunch in the canteen, when the vision of loveliness I'd seen briefly, just once, when we were keeping the outside under surveillance, appeared at the other side of the room. She seemed to be popular; no surprise there. I was still only conversing with Paul at that stage – they weren't a particularly friendly lot – so I didn't find out who she was.

It took three weeks, three days a week, packing and unpacking vans, running the gauntlet of the hit man's dislike and derision, stacking storerooms, keeping the unloading bay at the back tidy. I suppose somebody might have been tempted to plant a bomb there – I certainly was, just to liven things up – but I couldn't see what it had to do with security work; we were just general labourers. Then somebody called in sick. I'd managed to show a fraction more enthusiasm than Paul, so I was told to smarten up my uniform, put on my cap and come upstairs. I was on duty in Reception. On duty just meant standing about looking official, when anybody came in to or left the building, which wasn't often, so it was no less boring as a job than stacking storerooms. What was good, though, was that the vision of loveliness turned out to be the Receptionist. And I had, in effect, unlimited chat-up time.

She was called Valerie and lived in Greenwich with her parents. I learned all sorts of things about her, because once you'd got her started you couldn't get her stopped. After a while, I found I was glazing over and concentrated on her body, which was truly immaculate. Blond hair, waved, quite long, a delicate, quite broad face. Come to think of it, she had brown eyes, which would be quite unusual with the hair, I suppose. Her tits, well, they had a fascinating habit of hanging down as she leaned forward to answer the 'phone, grazing the desk gently. The rest of her was in perfect shape too, but I got to see less of her below the waist, because, of course, she was mostly sitting down. One view, though, when she bent to pick up a ball of paper she'd shied unsuccessfully at the bin, her skirt pulled tight over her bottom and a breast hanging down caused me a dramatic and embarrassing hard-on, which I had to diffuse by thinking hard about media design software.

"She told him where he could get off and he didn't like that, so he called her a slag and turned round and walked straight out, she shouted after him, who did he think he was using words like that, but he didn't listen, or say anything, just kept on walking, it wasn't very nice of him to say that, but then she shouldn't have spoiled everybody's night having a fit over who he danced with when she said she wasn't going to dance herself, what do you do at the weekends? … you're not listening, are you, Tad."

I snapped to attention. "Sorry, brings back memories. The pub. Do you go clubbing every weekend?"

She asked what memories, then, but I just waved my hand a bit from side to side and smiled, so she moved on. No she didn't, there were parties and sometimes they went up West, and that was her off again. I imagined her in party dress, but that was a bit too stimulating, and it was back to the media design software, so I got caught out again because I was looking gone out. I had to divert her hastily onto where she went to parties.

The conversation bounced along like this for most of the day, with occasional interruptions for visitors and periods of silence when she had to look at things on her holoscreen. Mostly within a radius of about three miles round Greenwich, incidentally. The weekends.

It was back to the vans and storerooms the next day, but I'd made a date with her by then. I couldn't concentrate hard enough on her chatter to convince her I was serious, though I got a very sweet goodnight kiss, but it did give me access to a lot more of the AFFREM building than I'd seen up to then. I was going on in a jokey way about only being allowed up from the cellars once a month to see the entrance area, what did they do in the rest of the building, turn gold into lead or something, and she said why don't you come and have a look, it's only offices, nothing to get excited about. So I pretended to need a guide, and that was our second date, after hours one evening, which gleaned me a second kiss and the hit man (who saw us leaving) a new repertoire of sour comments. I had no more success that time with her body, but I did get a good working knowledge of what was where in the building. She was right about that, it was just a big box of open-plan offices on four floors, chaotically muddled.

There was, over the next few weeks, some headway on the body front - on work premises too! - but I'm not going into detail, and I'll just say that how she looked gave no false promises. In the end, though, I just couldn't raise enough enthusiasm for the chatter, much as I loved its sound. But that's jumping ahead. First, I worked out where Stephen Pendleton's office was and, on one - it was not long before Christmas, and that floor of the building was empty - walked in and had a quick look round. Valerie was disapproving and jumpy about somebody finding us there, so next time I left her on the floor below, keeping lookout and, as they say, readjusting her dress. I said I needed the toilet, make sure no-one locks me in, but I homed straight in on his office and the filing cabinet in the corner. It was unlocked, but a quick riffle through the sparse contents turned up nothing of obvious interest. I had to go then, but I did notice a data stick on the desk and took a note of the manufacturer and model.

Next time I got up there, of course, it was gone, and the filing cabinet was locked. So were the desk drawers. The third visit, shortly after Christmas, it was back, and I did a quick substitution. Back home, I copied some interesting-looking files, put them in an obscure corner of the library when none of the librarians were about and well away from my research stuff, then copied them on to Karen, deleting the mail message as thoroughly as I could after sending.

I'd just taken a chance on Stephen Pendleton not coming in and noticing the strange blankness on his data stick, and that bit went to plan. I got up there again the following evening, minus Valerie this time; she was already complaining about so many of our trysts having to be in the office and I couldn't risk getting her too curious. Perhaps I should have. Anyway, I got into the office, but hadn't substituted data sticks or arranged things when I heard from behind me "You make jokes all over office? What you doing here?"

It's a cliché, but it really did feel like my blood froze. And that didn't help delivering the story I'd constructed in advance about hearing a noise and going to look. I'm a bad liar; Karen told me so, when she asked how I was, a few days after we split up. The hit man just said "Any noise, is you making. Jokes and noise. Problem, you tell me. You know?"

I nodded. "Sorry, I just didn't think. I'll remember next time."

"No next time. Too many jokes. And girlfriends – forbidden in office. You know?"

I tried to look puzzled. He smiled lasciviously; it was revolting. "You and Valerie." He laughed, which was worse: his breath stank.

"What about me and Valerie? You've got the wrong idea"

"I think different."

I carried on denying anything, if only for Valerie's sake, but he'd got me where he'd wanted me all along: in a position to be fired. And fired I was. There was no-one else there, or I swear he'd have assembled a parade, tearing off uniform badges, ceremonially burning my security pass, breaking the peak of my security cap in half across his knee and all that. As it was, I just handed them over, was told the balance of pay would come by post and that I was not to return, then I was ejected, not quite forcibly, onto the streets of Charlton, from where I took the tram and train back home.

It was a blow to the ego, but not the end of the world. I'd got something out of the spying and there'd been Valerie. Actually, it wasn't a bad excuse to bring that particular episode to a natural end; I'd definitely decided I didn't want to make anything serious or long-lasting of it. So I rang her the next day, said I'd had a bit of a row with the hit man (Stavros, I think he was called) and had left; it wasn't a bad thing really, because I was studying as well, and the job was starting to take too much time. So, got to move on, sorry, pleasant memories. She seemed quite upset, which surprised me; I'd expected some protests, but not this; made me feel like a right bastard if you want to know, so I found it quite upsetting too. But what was done was done, once I'd got it over with. The job was a relief to be done with, to be honest. It had been dead boring. The only good things had been Valerie and, of course, the pay. But I'd lived happily enough without those before and would do so again now.

The real unpleasantness kicked in three days later. I got home from AUP to find I'd been burgled. And not just burgled; they'd turned the flat over, kicked in partition walls, taken the doors apart. The holoscreen reported it had been used, and the avatar librarians said somebody had been in flashing a security pass. They didn't think they'd taken anything away, though. I checked on the quiet; the files were still where I'd put them. I'd chucked the data stick on the floor under a desk as we were going back to the security office, but obviously no-one had found it, and they'd made a few deductions from the blank substitute that Stephen Pendleton must have eventually looked at.

There were no more burglaries, so I think they must have either found the original, or decided that I'd not got hold of anything vital. But the landlord took exception to the damage – I had no insurance – and in lieu of making the place habitable again gave me immediate notice. For the past week, I've been sleeping on Paul's sofa. Luckily, he's still at work at ALBASEC, his speciality of gormless cluelessness having got him successfully through a grilling from the hit man. And he doesn't have much of a love life, so there's no necessity for overnight absences.

The day the final wage settlement from ALBASEC came through the post, I was called in by AUP Human Potentialities and told that regrettably there would be no place for me in the new structure. I was handed a letter which mentioned a miserable little lump sum of money I'd get ex gratia for my slightly less than two years service and told to pack my things up and get out. I've asked around since, but there's nothing I can do on the sort of money I've got and no appeal, because the new structure is a 'normalisation' process and apparently that counts as part of National Security. So that's it. A thoughtful New Year present from somewhere. The boot.

LIV

PLAYTIME

Quite insignificant looking, she thought; a small, metallic-black oblong, capped at one end. Lost in the lower reaches of her handbag for the last two weeks, it had slipped her memory. What had brought it back was Tad's becoming homeless and jobless because of what he'd copied onto it from Albasec. It had taken a five-minute search and turning her handbag upside down on the desk, but there it was. She thought she owed it to Tad to try and find out what all the fuss had been about. Mr Fraserman was out at another meeting with the loved one, Purveen, so she reckoned she had the right to half an hour of private business.

It was a yawn to start with. There were a few Holosheets with financial statements for Outvesta; she had a cursory look, but they didn't mean much; her ambitions had never taken in accountancy. There was a document called Approved Normalisation Procedures, which she had a look at, but it was full of the sort of thing managers say. The little she tried reading - about the preparations for normalisation before it began - seemed to have nothing to do with the conversations she'd observed between Mr Fraserman and Little Dick, let alone the advent of Leke. It was like trying to get what sex was about by reading a textbook.

Then she found the lists. Quite a few of those. There were the Rationalisations, Rightsizings and Upsizings. She went back to the Procedures document, but it wasn't much help, though it became clear that Rightsizing was just a fancy name for cutting pay. She had a look at that list; there were a lot of names on it, including, she noticed, Morrison and her friend Sue. Almost everybody else in AUP, judging by numbers, seemed to be on Rationalisations. They each had their present job listed, then another job next to that, so it must meant moving people about. Upsizings was quite a small list, including that creep Westwood. She hadn't found Mr Fraserman or herself yet.

She soon did, listed under 'In Play'. There were twenty or thirty other people 'In Play', mostly fairly senior, including Carl Trenchard. The other two lists were Modulerisations, which had just Carl Trenchard and Mr Fraserman, both with question marks alongside their names, and Eliminations, which was empty. What 'Modulerisations' or 'In Play' were supposed to mean was a mystery. Then she discovered another folder, called Players. This was bizarre; just a muddle of pictures and notes about the lives of the people shown, some of them well-known, like John F Kennedy, Joseph Stalin, or Marilyn Monroe, others vaguely familiar, most completely unfamiliar. Reading randomly a few of the unknowns, there seemed to be a lot who were businessmen, or businesswomen, but really it was just a hotchpotch. How it might relate to the In Play list was anyone's guess.

It was poking into a folder called Operations, most of it pretty boring, that turned up Playtime. It was another hotchpotch, this time of images and some video sequences, with or without sound. Some were of awards ceremonies, with smiling success stories holding trophies aloft. Others were of people sleeping on the streets. Then she found a video of a corpse. Not a peaceful corpse, either; the all-round, minute-long shot showed a scattering of bloodstains and what might have been burns about the face and neck; there was no sound commentary on that one.

The video sequence of a chained man being savagely beaten brought her searching to an abrupt halt. As it launched itself, she froze in disbelief, watching thirty seconds or so, before summoning up the will to turn it off. Her heart was beating so hard that she found it difficult to breathe, and she felt sick.

It took several minutes staring through the window at the bright but still wintry scene in the square outside before she took action. If this is what Little Dick got his rocks off on, then bad luck to him, but it was his lookout. She didn't, though, at all like the idea of connecting that (and whatever else 'Playtime' had to offer) with 'In Play', even if it was just a word. She decided to upload the lists, 'Playtime' and the normalisation stuff to MiMi, get it round as many people as she knew would be interested and tell them to pass it on. Someone might be able to stop it, whatever *it* was.

It took a while. As the upload reached the end, she saw the Hon Ran approaching from a corner of the square. He stopped to speak to somebody; it was time to wrap up. As an afterthought, she dumped the financial Holosheets down to Money Money Money. She didn't think they could possibly interest anyone, but it was quick, and putting something confidential out in public might just cause Little Dick some embarrassment.

The Hon Ran, as he walked in, was greeted sweetly by his PA, glancing up from her busy schedule of filing and administration.

LV

DATING (2)

Stepping into the virtual environment, she so nearly cannoned into John Librarian that her first impression was that he smelled of scorched dust. They spaced themselves a footfall further apart and exchanged apologies.

John raised his eyebrows a fraction. "Viola. What can we do for you?"

Was he being straight customer services, or did it have a dollop of insinuation in there? Viola treated it as straight. "Since you're offering."

It was a list of research queries, following up from her lecture, which was to be published as an extended article in one of the more prestigious of her professional journals. The activity would normally have given her great pleasure: it was open-ended and relatively undemanding, but an entirely virtuous way of spending an afternoon in pursuit of a coveted goal. The lion's share of the queries dispatched, he asked her what it was for and was both impressed and puzzled by her answer. Why was she so unhappy, unmistakably so? It took a little working round to, but he got there as they were tidying up the loose ends of the work. It was late by then, the day-shift assistants exchanging with the night workers.

"Just things. Nothing, really, I'm just a bit down at the moment."

"Really nothing?"

"No, nothing."

He knew about Carl's absence. "Perhaps you could help me celebrate."

"What's that?"

"I am to be encapped."

It took her a moment to realise the significance of this. "That's great. When?"

"Early next week. They say it will take a day or two to get used to life outside the library, though I'm getting training in that already, but by Wednesday or Thursday, I want to celebrate with an evening out. There would be nothing I'd like better than to spend it with you."

"What were you thinking of? I'd need to eat at some point, or were you thinking of a bit later?"

"Eating is not a problem. What would you do on an evening out? I have had no practice, you see."

Viola thought. She'd had much worse offers. Best to make sure the end to the proceedings was not too late. That way he could be let down gently on what she suspected was his ambition.

So they settled on the theatre and a meal, with Viola paying her half of the meal. She found she was looking forward to it.

"So how did you swing getting encapped? And what did it cost?" It had intrigued her for much of the past week how he had done it. Her theatre choice had been a musical, reckoning that a first night out in the real world was not a time for anything too cerebral. It had proved a good choice; the mood was now right for information gathering.

"A little over fifty thousand." His eyebrows flickered, as did hers.

"Quite expensive. How did you raise it?"

"I did not raise the money, myself, I haven't got that much anyway. The company paid."

"I thought you were a librarian."

"That is still true, but as of last month I am a member of the bourgeois tendency too."

What was he talking about? She stared at him.

"I had put in some money (a lot less than fifty thousand) to a consortium formed among some avatar friends. We have been looking for business opportunities and one came up towards the end of last year. A company that had overstretched itself and needed capital. They had tried a Rights issue, and it hadn't worked."

"What sort of business?"

"They do outsourcing: privatisation schemes."

"For the government?"

"Yes, among a lot of others."

"Doesn't that need a lot of money? Or do you have some very rich avatar friends?"

"Some richer than me, but none of us is filthy rich." He grinned. "A lot of avatars are trying to use their money. It is virtual, but then so is your money, or any of it that counts. You do not buy companies with hard cash, not usually. Mostly it's done on debt and getting the timing right. We avatars control the information anyway, so we are in the best position to use it."

She couldn't get her head round that, truth to tell and steered back to the original point. "So you're rich now and can afford encapping?"

"Not exactly rich. Not yet. And legally we must operate using a board of human beings. But we do control a heap of other people's money. The encapping was a decision that the directors needed proper mobility in the real world. That's where most of our customers are."

A waiter approached and they ordered. Viola had asked again what he'd do about eating, but it was fine: 'encapping is for everything; I can eat; I'm even programmed to enjoy it. It's just it goes straight to the waste bin, so we only do it socially'.

"What puzzles me is you've got this company – what's it called, incidentally?"

"Outvesta, but we are changing that. Too many dodgy decisions attached to the name."

"You've got this Outvesta company and it's in trouble with money. Where do you get the cash to pay for encapping the directors?"

"The money trouble is about servicing existing debts. It's on a huge scale and is the result of mis-management. We have already got rid of some of the more stupid commitments. Encapping is out of the loose change. There is always a small percentage of any budget that is within the margin of error. The way it's spent is a matter of priorities more than core business. When you are turning over the best part of twenty billion, even a tiny percentage means quite a lot of money."

"Twenty billion! Blimey!" Viola sat back.

"Outvesta is quite large."

"You can say that again. And now you're one of its directors?"

"That is right, yes."

"What's to stop the board of humans running your company just taking over and ignoring what the avatar owners decide. You said it's theirs to run, legally speaking."

"If they tried that, we would not fight on legalities. The humans on the board know very well that we exchange and shape the information that makes things happen. They have no effective control over that. We could bring the company down inside a week then buy it again with a different board."

She raised her glass of sparkling wine. "I don't pretend to understand how you've done it, or even what you've achieved, not exactly, but congratulations anyway."

They drank a toast. He looked her in the eyes for a few seconds, she staring defiantly back, then he said "so now you tell me about you. What is making you so unhappy? You are unhappy, aren't you?"

"What makes you think that?"

"Viola, it's obvious."

She found herself not in a mood to dissemble. "Well, Carl, he's my boss ..." and the rest, John thought, "... has taken this sudden sabbatical, no real reasons given, so the department's without a head just when we're coming up to a reorganisation that no-one'll tell the workers anything about."

John knew that she was being disingenuous. With two trips over to Vishiney in the last four months, she must know perfectly well what his 'sabbatical' was about. And she must know that her job wasn't under any serious threat. "There's more than that, isn't there? What's going on over the job and the department might make you nervous, but you are seriously unhappy. What is it?"

She didn't give way straight off, but a little sympathetic sparring did it.

"My friend Jane, they're trying to kill her. Bit by bit. It's horrible."

This was new. His job gave him access to just about everything that was going on and a librarian avatar's interest in following it, but this nudged no memory holding.

"Jane who? I don't know her, I think."

"No, you won't know her. Jane Fredricksson. She's a friend I made years ago, when I was doing work experience at a media company in the West End. She was one of the design strategists. We've kept in touch ever since. It's funny, we're not really one another's type: her main circle of friends is quite different from mine, but she's one of my closest friends, and I'm one of hers."

Piece by piece, he extracted the story from her. It appalled him. Bloody humans, they treated each other like chess pieces.

"Are you going to pay them?"

"We haven't got an alternative, but I don't know where the money will come from. Neil will chip in his own inheritance, which is about fifty thousand, and he's got the other relatives to agree to about another thirty. The Cowingdon could raise another thirty or forty between us if we had to, but that adds up to quite a bit short, and they're not budging, not even with Daoud on their back."

"That is difficult."

"It's impossible. It's why I think they're trying to kill her." The restaurant lighting left her face in semi-darkness, but the strain was visible.

He put his hand over hers, which was not withdrawn. A silence began and developed between them, accompanied only by eye movements, as each continued to observe the company around them. Viola shifting slightly in her chair to a more comfortable position. Neither looked at the other, except in passing. It was several minutes before he spoke. "Leave it to me; I will see if I can think of a way to help your friend."

"What sort of thing?"

"That I cannot say. Not yet. There must be some way round the problem, though. I will think about it."

It gave Viola little feeling of confidence, but it was comforting. The whole evening had been comforting, and she readily agreed when he suggested another. He extracted a goodnight kiss at her apartment door, but made no other move, to her relief: she felt exhausted. Next door's cat strolled over until almost within reach, demanding attention. They bent together, crouching down to reach out and run their fingertips along its fur. It permitted this, coolly, then came a little closer. Stroking alternately, all three surrendered themselves to the moment. Finally, her objectives achieved, the cat wriggled out of the laying on of hands and disappeared. John said "you realise that being a director of Outvesta puts me in some sense in charge of AUP? In charge of its normalisation, anyway."

"You mean Outvesta is doing our normalisation?"

"Nobody told you?"

"No. Along with all the other things they haven't told us."

"Well, yes, it is. As of six weeks ago. Just before their Rights Issue."

Viola raised her eyebrows. "Are you going to sack us all, then?"

"It depends what you mean by sack, I think," and she blushed, then laughed.

"So it's a reign of terror, then?"

He looked solemn. "It certainly terrifies me; it is a responsibility, and I have had very little time to get used to it. I would not be worried, though, about your job."

"Thanks. And thanks for listening to me about Jane. It helps."

"I hope I can give more tangible help once I have thought about it." She put her arms round him and kissed him again, unasked, then he left, taking his cue from the cat, raising his hand in farewell as Viola unlocked the apartment door and went in.

LVI

PAYBACK (1)

"Jack. I've been trying to get you for several days."

"Sorry, Stephen, it's been a busy time. What can I do for you?"

He should bloody well know that. He'd left enough messages with his airhead secretary. "Just needed to touch base with you about what's happening on the directorship and the arrangements on the consultancy fee."

"Sure. You got the papers?"

"I did. A couple of months ago. My lawyer checked them through and I signed and returned them two days later."

"That's good. Any problems?"

"No problems, Jack, just no response either. As a non-exec, I guess I have decisions and responsibilities regarding the Rights Issue, to take an instance."

"Hah! The Rights Issue. Forget that, Stephen, it's been canned."

"Canned! What do you mean, Jack?"

"I mean canned, Stephen. The investors wouldn't buy it, not even the Community Associations."

"Wasn't it intended to normalise the financial position?"

"That's all normalised. There've been developments."

Which he ought to know about. "I'd value clarification, Jack."

"Sure, but not now; I've got a meeting in minus five minutes. Can you ring me again this afternoon? About four, I'll be free."

He would lose face if he made a fuss. "That's a date." He rang off, fuming; they were giving him the run-around.

"Jack." He struggled not to sound pleading.

"Stephen. Good to talk to you. I was expecting a call from you. What goes?"

What went was three days of unavailability. Where in fuck had he been, and what in fuck was going on? "I missed you Tuesday afternoon. Something came up. Regarding our conversation earlier, you were to clarify the developments after the Rights Issue got canned."

"I was? Sure thing. Look, Stephen, it's complex. Better talk about this face to face. Can you make Monday, three o'clock?"

He haggled, for status purposes; they settled on Tuesday at six.

"Ah yes, Mr Pendleton. I have a message for you. Mr Kavkazian gives his apologies for not being able to meet you now. He's been called to a meeting with the Board at short notice. But he has put together the papers you were to discuss, and if you would like to read them now, in advance of a rearranged meeting, his office is at your disposal."

What papers? They had been talking about 'developments', not papers; you wiped your ass with those. He was getting the message, though, all right. For the sake of form, he rearranged the meeting, then settled into Jack's space-shuttle office chair in the adjoining office. On the expansive and expensive-looking desk in front of him was a neat pile of two bulky documents, a report and what looked like media releases. Trying to avoid knocking the seat controls – did they include an ejector facility? – he started with the media releases.

They were drafts, with a release time set for the next day: presumably what Jack's board meeting was about. On the first reading, his mind refused to engage with what it said; it seemed, oddly, more difficult to gauge something expressed in plain language; it might have been easier to start with the report. But a third reading forced it into his consciousness: Outvesta was being taken over. Jesus!

The report filled out the details. It had happened quickly and was being finalised with trembling haste; a sanitised financial statement was unable to conceal the reason why. A section on board arrangements talked about a commitment from and to existing board members under the new regime; there was a note from Jack stuck at the side of the page, to the effect that his appointment would be confirmed at the board meeting to which he had disappeared and that this would count as an 'existing arrangement'. Thank you Jack and no thanks. A clinical disengagement would have avoided any owning up to Herb Summerson, now overdue. The consultancy fee would have done just fine by itself the way things had gone. But he could see no way of stopping it at this stage.

He read on. One of the puzzles, resolved neither by the media releases nor by the report, was precisely who the people were who had done the taking over. The organisation name, AVT, meant nothing and was clearly just a name of convenience for what was identified as a consortium. No individual or company names appeared. He turned to the bulky documents, which turned out to be Heads of Agreement for the takeover and a draft Deed of Arrangement.

The Heads of Agreement gave the clue, in the Definitions section, three phrases. Firstly: "'Avatar" shall be taken within this document to mean a virtual reality construct whether encapsulated or not encapsulated and programmed to simulate the physical capabilities and bodily form, consciousness of self, application of intelligence and behavioural characteristics within an accepted cultural norm of a human being'. Secondly: 'Inasmuch as business capabilities, duties responsibilities and rewards shall be construed as appropriate and customary for a human being these also shall be taken within this document to apply without difference to an avatar'. Thirdly: 'The absence of a human being from either the executive or non-executive leadership of a company shall not, subject to the identification and agreement of human Guarantors, be admitted in the present context as an impediment to the recognition and acceptance of the fitness of that company to discharge its business duties and responsibilities, nor to its eligibility to receive and further develop customary and legally allowed business rewards'.

Holy shit! They had been taken over by a bunch of robots.

He must abort his non-exec appointment; he'd be mocked from here to Hawaii if he didn't. But the secretary had gone home, and there was nothing he could find about the location of the board meeting. In desperation, he tried videophoning Jack Kavkazian, but he was accepting messages only, and Stephen did not trust himself to leave anything reliably coherent and undamaging at the moment. The treacherous shit-eating motherfucker! No wonder he'd been out of touch or unable to talk for the past ten days.

Rage drove him in circles round the office and demolished a pot plant, before he gathered the various documents into his briefcase and stalked rapidly to the lift area before embarking on a fruitless, floor-by-floor search of the building, trying to find the meeting. The Odyssey was interrupted after a little less than half an hour by a security guard asking after his security credentials; he was shooed towards the exit when these were not forthcoming. It was only momentarily tempting to visit his frustrations on the person of the guard; it was a large person. Jet-propelled by a mixture of emotion and the sheer whirling momentum of his thoughts, as he tried vainly to find an acceptable way out of the situation, he walked away from

the Outvesta offices, blindly and at random. Somebody must suffer
for this.

433

LVII

FOREIGN AFFAIRS

It was when she saw the apartment door that she intuited trouble. Not being met at the airport had been no big deal; her visit was a last-minute arrangement, and she knew Vishiney well enough now to make her own way; Carl must be working. Perhaps he had a pupil with him now, though there was no sound of a piano, or of voices. But it was the door that threw her composure; you could tell just by looking that it was not securely closed. And that felt wrong. She walked over and pushed at it. The lock, not quite engaged, gave way. She walked in and shouted "hello", but there was no answer. She made her way into the living room, finding it empty, a chair on its side on the rug. The apartment was cold. She called again and pushed open the door to the bedroom, which was in semi-darkness, with the curtains drawn.

He was lying on his back, fully clothed, slantwise on the top of the bed, asleep, his face turned away towards the window. She went over quietly, not to wake him, just to see if he could make him more comfortable, throw a blanket over him or something. As she reached the side of the bed, he made a loud, rattling, snoring sound and turned over facing her.

At first, she was not quite sure it was him; his face was oddly unfamiliar. So she looked closer, bringing her face to within a foot or so of his. As she did so, she suddenly sneezed, and though she managed to turn aside, the noise woke him. He gave a sharp intake of breath, came to consciousness, subsided into steady breathing for several seconds, then stirred again, moving his head to look at her. Slowly, blinking determinedly, he forced his eyes to focus and after an interval spoke. "Viola."

It was Carl. "Yes. What's the matter?"

He said nothing, but with evident difficulty summoned up a smile. Then the smile vanished. "Viola. What time is it?"

She got up and drew back the curtains. A watery sun cast light but no warmth into the room. He turned to lie on his back, looking up at her. "What time is it? I was supposed to meet you."

She was shocked by his appearance. There was bruising all up the left-hand side of his face, starting from the jawbone and disappearing into the hairline. The eye on that side was half-closed, the eye socket puffy and discoloured. On the other side of his face and on his neck there were cuts and what looked like bloodstains, some of which had marked the bedclothes. He shivered and closed his eyes.

"Never mind about that." She wanted to hug him, but didn't know what she could touch without hurting him, so settled for a kiss on the less bruised side of his face. He opened his eyes again and looked at her. "What happened?"

He didn't answer straight away, just groaned, then said: "Sorry."

He needed to be more comfortable, not just lying out cold on the top of the bed. Then she'd try again. "Can you get up?"

Slowly, he rolled himself over to his left and tried to put weight on his left arm. With a short yelp of agony, he rolled on to his back again, the arm hanging to one side. His eyes filled with tears, and he broke out in a sweat, breathing convulsively. Viola sat by him on the bed and put a hand gently on his face, where it was less likely to hurt, wiping away the perspiration. Gradually, his breathing eased, and the sweating ceased. She covered him with a spare blanket she found in a corner of the room and put on the heater in the bedroom. At the least, his left arm was probably broken; she had to get him to a hospital.

"What do you do to get an ambulance here?"

"There's an emergency number, I don't know it. Mostly, you just get a taxi."

"Where to?"

"A cabbie will know."

She left the apartment and knocked on other doors, to see if anyone knew the emergency number, but there was no answer anywhere. It looked like it was going to be the taxi. She still had the card from the one that took her from the airport. First, though, she'd need to get him to his feet and walking. Trying to stand him up would risk a fall, but she didn't fancy leaving him entirely to the skills of some randomly chosen taxi driver. She returned to the bedroom.

"How are you feeling?"

"A bit better, thanks. Warmer."

"Let's try and get you up." Would his right arm take it? "If I touch this arm, tell me if it hurts." He nodded. She ran her hand carefully down and he didn't react. Then she tried tapping it gently at different places. It got an intake of breath at one spot, but nothing major. Then she tried holding upper and lower arms and moving it as a whole, very gently. He winced, but it seemed mobile.

"Can you try rolling over onto your right side?" she said. He did, moving slowly and cautiously. The arm was clearly sore, possibly bruised, but it could take his weight, and she managed to get him sitting up. After some dithering, she set about trying to coax him on to his feet and, if possible, into the living room. If that proved too difficult, she'd go all out for discovering the emergency number.

She turned the heater on in the living room and jammed the bedroom door open, before persuading him to hold the left arm rigid against his body, with his right and push himself up into her arms.

"If you feel you're going to faint, tell me, and I'll get you lying down as quickly as I can. Will you?"

He nodded, and they set off, slowly manoeuvring across and out of the bedroom. Still dazed, he needed help with balancing, and false moves could be painful. But, once started, he made it to the armchair in the living room largely without assistance. She tucked him in there with the blanket and rang for a taxi.

Dabbing at his face with a sponge, trying to remove the worst of the mess round his face, she returned to the story. "What happened?"

"A couple of police, I think they were, showed up at the door and took me by surprise, just started beating me up. I managed to get into the bedroom afterwards, but that's about all I can remember." He caught sight of the watch on her wrist and stared at it, trying to read it.

"It's just after four."

"In the afternoon?"

"It's daylight outside."

"Yes, of course. How long have you been here?"

"About an hour now."

"Christ!" He thought for a minute. "I must have been out more than twelve hours. I was getting ready for bed when they came."

"You shouldn't have opened the door to them."

"They sounded official. They'd have probably forced it if I hadn't."

The taxi turned up then, the driver proving more practiced and skilful than she had expected; it must be a regular part of his job. He suggested placing a chair by the lifts for Carl to rest on before attempting the descent and the walk out to the cab and the brief respite clearly helped. Blanket around his shoulders, Carl was badgered gently and slowly to the car, while Viola returned the chair to the apartment and collected a scarf and his coat to add to his outer layer of clothing, before locking up and following them down.

It was nearly midnight when they left the hospital. The arm was indeed broken, but it was a single clean break and had been set without trouble and plastered. The bruising was appalling; he had obviously been hit all over his body, but particularly on the left-hand side down to the waist. The hospital had given him some heavy-duty painkillers, and he was more in command of himself by this time, walked without assistance back into the apartment from the returning taxi. But it would be a day or two before he was fit and active again. Nobody was sure about concussion.

She put him to bed, lying on his back, a pillow under his plastered arm to prevent him rolling on to it in his sleep, before undressing herself and joining him there, on his "good" side. They drifted off to sleep together, her arm draped across his stomach, her hand positioned between bruises.

They woke early, not long after seven; she had forgotten to draw the curtains, and it was a bright, cold day outside. The events of the previous day hadn't included food, and they were both extremely hungry. Viola poked around the small kitchen and assembled a breakfast of sorts from the small end of bread that she found, the packet of crackers, the instant coffee powder that needed digging at and breaking up and the half-litre of orange juice that smelt more or less all right. Some milk went straight down the sink and some aged salami into the rubbish bin. It wasn't much of a meal, but they lingered over it until halfway into the morning.

"Have you any idea why you were attacked?"

"Nothing definite. I was threatened that time I tried to fly back to England – that they wouldn't be so kind next time. But I've done nothing provocative, I wouldn't have thought. Except maybe the Körthofer thing."

"Giving a workshop in Dresden?"

"Dresden, yes. Not that I've done anything about that yet."

"But Körthofer might have."

"I suppose he might." Carl nodded.

Viola knew this must be it. There'd been no robbery, unless they'd taken small change. And Carl had thought they might be police.

The immediate physical recovery was just a matter of the bruising subsiding and of getting used to a temporarily one-armed life. But the attack had shaken his confidence, making him uncharacteristically passive and withdrawn. Piano playing would come later still; there was, luckily no serious damage to his hands, but the left arm would be in plaster for six weeks or so. She would need to be around for a few days until he was coping fully by himself, so she rang AUP to announce a bad attack of 'flu.

In the evenings they talked: more than they'd done over the whole period of their relationship. She got to know a great deal about Carl's life and opinions and he, more selectively about hers. With some surprises. And there was AUP.

"Have you heard the company that's doing the normalisation got taken over? It only lasted a week or two from when we heard."

"One piranha eating another, I suppose."

"A bit stranger than that." She recounted what John had told her, with some editing of the circumstances.

"A public company run by avatars sounds like a first. I wouldn't have thought they had any legal standing."

"That's why the board of humans. But it seems to be theirs in any way that counts. I still can't see how they got their hands on it, though. Something about a Rights Issue that went wrong."

"A Rights Issue raises capital. Maybe they really needed the money for running expenses. If that went wrong, they could end up with a cash-flow problem."

Now that made more sense. She stored it up for interrogating John when she next saw him. "Now it's a new company, do you think you'll be allowed back?"

He raised his plastered arm and flicked his gaze between her and it.

"No, I suppose not. But why?"

"Why the arm, or why the not coming back?"

"Why keep you here in the first place?"

"Force you to take lots of holidays in Eastern Europe?" She didn't respond

"Well, seriously, I've had a lot of spare time to think about it and haven't come up with much. The authorities here aren't saying: I don't think they know anyway. David Wetherill certainly hasn't said, any time I've had the misfortune to meet him. The only thing I can think of is that I'm AUP Ancillary Music's nearest approximation to a celebrity and might have made things awkward for their normalisation if I'd been around. Started petitions, given interviews, that sort of thing. They just might have been right about that."

It had to suffice.

The daytime hours, with Carl one-handed and disinclined to get out much, threatened aimlessness. She hurled herself into a reform of his living conditions. Really, the place was ridiculously shabby and unwelcoming. There was no need for living out of suitcases, for leaving bathroom things cluttering up a corner of the living room, for a kitchen covered with odds and ends because there was nowhere to put them. One armchair. And even she could tell the piano wasn't up to much.

Cleaning the apartment, ordering some cheap but decent furniture and storage items, slapping paint, a co-opted Carl using his free hand, in cheerful colours on the living room and bedroom walls, her mind worried around the attack. Would they come again? What would happen if Carl did put in a request about Dresden? After a time, she realised it was nonsense trying to speculate; she simply had no idea what might happen. Neither, of course, would Carl, and the uncertainty was not going to help his state of mind. He was not in a state to take action at present; it was up to her, and she felt she must get it worked out before she went back.

On the Tuesday, she left him with a pot of paint, two walls, instructions as to both and a meal that just needed heating up. She equipped herself with an extra wad of cash from a bank machine and walked into the central police station. She had researched it and knew to ask for the Security Commissar if she wanted the man in charge. The Reception Clerk asked if she had an appointment, she handed her an opened envelope, and the banknote folded into the blank piece of paper inside it got her through to the Commissar's secretary, who was similarly persuaded, though with a much larger denomination note. It took just over an hour to be admitted to the presence.

The Security Commissar occupied a large and stylish office, with fake ancien régime furniture. He was a charmer. Sitting her down on one corner of a sofa, he perched himself loomingly on the other.

"This is your first time in Vishiney, Miss Trent?"

"No, I have often visited here."

"Then you like our city?" He smiled, ingratiatingly.

"I enjoy it very much."

"I am glad of that. What can I do for you?" He loomed a little closer.

Viola maintained her position and upright posture. "I have come to talk about Carl Trenchard."

Attentive, but neutral, he said nothing.

"You know of him, I think. He is the Englishman being held in Vishiney, not allowed to leave the country."

He still said nothing, but she had his attention.

"The real purpose of keeping him here is to stop him going back to England. Am I right in that?"

No response, but she continued.

"The only good reason for stopping him leaving here for other countries than England – I mean the UK – is that he might travel on from those countries to the UK. Is that right?"

A tiny raise of eyebrows might have been assent.

"But he would be arrested and sent back here if he landed in the UK anyway, wouldn't he? At the moment, every time you think he steps out of line, something happens. This can't go on. I want to discuss a deal."

The Commissar turned held up a hand for silence and, turning slightly to one side, said: "Mr Trenchard is known to us, yes, but his case concerns international security. I am afraid I am unable to discuss this matter further." Still holding up his hand in her direction, he waked across to the desk at the far end of the room, picked up a 'phone and said something rapidly into it. After a pause, he said what sounded like "spasiba", put the 'phone down and returned to the sofa.

"We can talk freely now. I will be honest with you. We have been a little surprised not to hear from Mr Trenchard before now. When you talk about a deal, what do you have in mind?"

"Something that gives freedom to move about, but with an undertaking not to visit the UK. Until the UK authorities change their mind, that is."

"Of course. But how would this … undertaking … be enforced?"

"By Carl not wishing to be arrested. That, I think will happen if he *does* travel to the UK. He is a respectable academic. The world of arrests and beatings …" She looked closely at him, but his face showed nothing "… is a strange one to him."

"I see. Nevertheless, we have given certain assurances to the UK authorities."

Viola seized the opening. "Perhaps some compensation would be needed - for the added administrative burden that the deal might cause."

"What compensation are you thinking of?"

"Two thousand." He thought for a moment, then looked at her sadly. "You misunderstand the scale of our commitments. It would have to be at least ten.

Viola had not been under Daoud's tutelage for nothing. Another thirty minutes or so of cordial, but intensive bargaining brought him down, for immediate cash payment, to just half as much again on her opening bid. Payment in hard euros rather than the local currency she had opened with was the decider, and they shook hands on that. Carl was to keep the width of one country away from the UK, which in practical terms eliminated Scandinavia, Benelux, Iberia and France west of Strasbourg. But he was free again for everywhere else. Any attempt to access the UK and he was back to the position as it had been. She parted with almost all the cash she had on her person – Carl would make almost nothing out of his first Dresden workshop – but it felt like a good enough deal to her. Her instinct was that the Commissar would honour it; Carl was not of any direct concern to them.

She left the Commissar on friendly terms and was smiled at by the secretary and the receptionist on her way out. It had, in all, taken just over two hours. Would that Denmark Hill nick, she thought, could ever show such pragmatism or efficiency. She returned in time to help Carl with both the painting and the meal, enlightening him as to the demolition of his workshop earnings over the one and the lifting of his country-arrest over the other.

In the remaining three days of her stay, in between continued assaults on the apartment, she coaxed Carl round half a dozen music shops of varying decrepitude and found a second-hand Schimmel upright piano in decent condition, which was delivered just before she went; he could pay her back out of earnings, as and when.

Carl's passivity started to dissipate as the days went on, buffeted by the sheer energy of Viola's reforms. The pivotal change was the treaty with the Commissar. He actually felt physically lighter once the threat of further attacks had receded and there was no longer the need to face asking permission for a visit to Dresden. It did not entirely free him from anxiety, but gut feel, driven by Viola's sense of certainty, was that the agreement would work in practice. Traitorous inner thoughts, as he worked on painting and other one-handed chores, dwelt on the more relaxed, bachelor regime to come, but their days together were, for Carl, something special. When it came to it, he found the parting at the airport more than usually difficult.

445

LVIII

SUMMIT CONFERENCE

They were all there, sitting attentively around his desk. Karen in pole position, in the centre, on the executive chair. That's my girl, he thought, disciplining himself not to allow a smile or any other change of expression onto his face.

Arrayed around her were Sue from Corporate Planning, Leke and Morrison. He didn't suppose Leke would follow a word, but Karen could fill him in afterwards. While he was filling her, he thought, continuing to be careful not to change his expression.

What's he keep smirking about? Karen thought.

"Thank you for making the time to come here. I've spoken to all of you individually at different times this week, but I wanted to speak to you as a team. Above all, I wanted to leave you entirely clear about what is being offered before this afternoon's general announcement. All sorts of questions are likely to be flying around following that, and it is only right that you, my core team, know the answers to those pertinent to yourselves."

Yeah, yeah, thought Karen. Get on with it.

"As you all already know, I'll be leaving AUP; I resigned formally this morning. The precise timing of my departure isn't certain at the moment, but it is unlikely to be later than the end of March, and may well be the end of February. You will also know that I am taking up the post of Head of Administration at the ..." he paused and consulted the paper in his hand, enunciating slowly and in an ineluctably English accent " ... Aykol National Superior day Bow Arts Virtuals."

He really is going to need some tuition, thought Karen. She mentally lined up Eva.

"In Paris", he added, which made things a bit clearer. "As part of the arrangement, I shall be taking a small inner cabinet of assistants. Each of you has been asked to be part of this team and has shown interest in taking the opportunity up. In fact, I am pleased to tell you that no-one has so far turned it down, and I would like to thank you again for showing faith in an unusual, but exciting venture. A tremendous boost to your CVs I need hardly say and I think it's going to be fun."

"Your letters are with Karen. Karen, could you ...?" He gestured. Karen produced three envelopes from her bag and handed them round. "Clearly, it will be up to you to decide. AUP is unlikely to deprive you of a job, though relatively few details below the most senior levels are yet clear, but undoubtedly the next few months will be a time of some considerable uncertainty, and no jobs, or job grades are guaranteed. I can say that I sincerely hope that you will all be joining our expedition across the Channel, our little raft of English common sense that will float on an ocean of, well, merde probably. Let's drink to that." He grabbed a bottle of sparkling wine and opened it with practised expertise, while Karen reached into a filing cabinet and produced glasses. No letters had yet been opened, but they all drank and the bottle and a second and third bottle disappeared with speed and ease. Halfway through the second bottle, the Hon Ran raised his hand for silence. "There is one more thing to say, which will probably be news to all of you. There will be one more member of the team, working in the area of personnel relations. She may be known to some of you, as she worked at AUP for a time, some years ago. Sadie Conant. She has not been able to be here today, but I know that you will find her a very able colleague and will give her a warm welcome when she joins us in Paris. Now, a refill, perhaps."

Sadie! So he'd been shagging her all along. The dirty old bastard! Karen felt troubled about this revealed defect to her radar. No problems about the appointment; she liked Sadie, such as she had seen of her, and a source of information from the bedroom would be a real addition to her network. That one was certainly going to be about Personnel Relations.

The office had become an oasis of light and warmth in the unspeakably dismal day that surrounded them outside the building. Heavy intermittent rain from louring clouds, with gusts of wind and near-freezing temperatures suggested the Almighty's displeasure with his creatures. Looking from the lighted room into the murk of the exterior world, Karen became aware of a watcher, paused in the middle of the square and looking up with a scowl at the celebration, effectively on a stage set, as nobody had thought to draw the blinds. It was Little Dick, and he had his Pitchfork expression on, doubtless disapproving of the jollity or the alcohol or both. Well fuck him! They could afford not to have to worry about his dislikes and attitudes any longer.

The Playtime stuff hadn't gone anywhere; MiMi barred it as unsuitable, so she was reduced to sending it out to people she knew, one at a time, and that just wasn't quick enough. But Money Money Money had really liked what she sent them. It was one of their most popular posts for a couple of weeks and, in some way she didn't understand, had knackered the company Little Dick had given his 'normalisation' to. Didn't save their jobs at AUP, mind, but who cared with Paris to go to, and it left a warm feeling that they'd got them where it hurt, even if it was only by chance. She hoisted her wine glass in Little Dick's direction, in a simulacrum of a raised finger and turned away to talk to Sue.

Morrison saw him too and growled, mentally. His department had indeed been atomised, but not without concessions. Certainly, accommodation would be better all round. Ceramics would remain in China, but with staff, for the first time, paid an out-of-zone allowance. It could have been much worse: he had the Paris job to go to, and a sense of satisfaction at having fought them hard this time. He raised his glass slightly, in a toast to Pendleton's damnation, ironic rather than bitter.

The Hon Ran didn't see him, but did catch the stiffening in Morrison's expression. The Labrador-become-Rottweiler phenomenon was welcome, but still perplexing. It could be useful in dealing with the Frogs, though. The new job looked straightforward. They needed some of the professors sacking and were too gutless to do it themselves. He'd sort that out in the first month. Quite how things would go after that, dealing with a bunch of foreign artistic weirdoes, speaking a language he'd never taken much beyond school lessons, remained to be seen. And he didn't doubt they'd resent a foreigner, an Anglo-Saxon, invading one of their holy of holies, but if there was one thing an army training gave you, it was confidence in dealing with foreigners. He turned to start a dialogue with Leke, in pidgin Albanian, about future security arrangements.

LIX

WE'RE IN THE MONEY?

Viola did not have to wait long. A mere five days after the night out with John Librarian, she returned from work to find a holo-message lighting up the study: 'HAVE AN IDEA TO HELP YOUR FRIEND. PLEASE CONTACT. TALK ABOUT IT OVER DINNER?' She changed, after some dithering, into something casual, loose but colour-coordinated, expressing adequate rather than optimum smartness. She picked up a research paper and, thus armed and expressed, stepped through the Library gateway.

John was out, so she left her own holo-message and went to pursue the background to the paper. Half an hour sufficed for that, so she left again, but the Holoscreen flickered into life only ten minutes after her return, as she was assembling a meal from the random collection of leftovers in the ridge. 'WHAT ABOUT NOW', it said. She answered, 'Okay' and they found themselves twenty minutes later in the local Thai restaurant with an assortment of blisteringly hot dishes on order; she wondered how far his software would cope.

He was smartly turned out, definitely one notch ahead of her. Damn! She decided on direct assault. "What's this idea, then?"

"The one I left you a message about?"

What else? "Yes. I'm intrigued."

"Intrigued is good," he said, adjusting his tie. He was even wearing a tie!

"Maybe. So what is it?"

"You humans are so impatient," he said, smiling. She did not reciprocate. "But yes, I have had an idea. Quite a good idea, I think. It depends a lot on your ladies club, though … what was their name?"

"The Cowingdon?"

"Yes, that. How ready would they be to put themselves forward as performance artists?"

She frowned. Was he taking the piss? "What sort of performance artists?"

"Restaurant artists. They would repeat a standard evening-out, once or twice, and it would be recorded."

"You mean having a meal then trashing the restaurant? That's what got Jane into this problem in the first place. We don't want to risk any more."

He held up his hands for calm. "Wait. There is nothing risky. It would be in a recording studio. The only police would be hired extras."

She couldn't see where it was leading, but took it on its own terms. "It might be possible. Sylv would always be on for that sort of thing, and I suppose I could persuade some of the others at least. But I don't see how any of this would help Jane."

"It could help her a great deal if the performance got a substantial grant from Outvesta's Arts Leverage Fund."

She started to see some light. "You think that's possible?"

"Very possible. I am the director who makes the decisions on the fund. It would only cover part of the ransom, perhaps sixty or seventy thousand, and some of the money would have to go on the recording. But it would help, and I will look out for any other funds that might be added."

Viola resisted furiously the sense of liberation that started to overtake her. Too many possible solutions had previously evaporated or been blocked for her to allow herself to believe straight away that this was it. But intuitively she knew that suddenly they were there, that they could now look forward to Jane's release in a limited time. On an impulse, she leaned over the table, put her hand on John's shoulder and kissed him. Then she realised she wanted to cry and fled the restaurant, with a "sorry, I'll be back," walking up and down outside for five minutes to regain face.

She returned. The food arrived and was disposed about the table, the waitress inscrutably dispassionate, with just the hint of a glare at John. The conversation settled, piecemeal onto practicalities.

It was just after settling the bill that he brought up the other matter. "Your friend, Daoud Amin. You got to know him through this case of your friend, Jane?"

"I did; he represented the Memories of Kandahar waiters who got scooped up into jail at the same time. We met him at the Security Condominium when we were both there for meetings."

"Has he ever said anything about either waiter and what they might have been charged with?"

She thought. "He did once say something about Farooz choosing his company badly but being no criminal. Mohammed seems to have been completely innocent. Why do you ask?"

"Since you told me the story of this, I have been researching it, and there is almost nothing to find; the police and OSC have covered their tracks very thoroughly, even for somebody with my levels of access to information. I did find a snippet about Farooz, though: something he did, nearly three years ago now. I am not able to say whether it is relevant to what has happened here, and it is confidential information, so I cannot tell you what it is, even. I would suggest questioning Daoud if you can, to see if there is more involved here than he is saying."

"You can't say any more than that?"

"No, I'm sorry, I cannot. Daoud might be able to."

She nodded, taken aback. Daoud had become a sort of lifeline, the only person she knew with both the knowledge of the case and the negotiation skills to give any realistic sense of hope. One shift of the ground under an entrenched situation was a cause of joy; two shifts was unsettling.

LX

PAYBACK (2)

The paper was covered with words, he could see them, he could read them. One at a time. But they meant nothing. The hand holding the paper was shaking. It was important to make sense of what was on the paper. But he couldn't. Why was it important? Why was the hand shaking? His hand.

Try again. He put the paper down on the desk. The text steadied. He read the first sentence. The second sentence. The third sentence. The fourth sentence. He could skim-read the whole page as normal. But how did the first sentence relate to the second? The second to the third? The third to the fourth? What did it say on the page? Nothing. He could connect nothing, understand nothing. He picked the paper up again. It shook. He read again. And again. And again. Still nothing.

Try again. Why must he know? Why must he know what it said? He sat down, aware that he was trembling. The writing came into focus, but not its meaning. He leaned forward and supported his chin in his hands, attempting to calm himself, but without result. He looked again at the writing. Still no meaning. He stood up again and walked once around the desk. Why was it important to understand? Why was he here like this?

A face, talking. In his mind. Almost there, but it vanished as he tried to concentrate. He picked up a second piece of paper. It shook uncontrollably in his hand. He read the writing on it. The first sentence. The second sentence. The third sentence. But no connection emerged, no meaning. Just the face again, saying something. Disappearing again, the words dimmed below the level of sense. A taste of bitterness. What was happening? He sat again and fell for some minutes into a stupor.

"Are you feeling all right Mr Crabtree?" Another face. He flailed his right arm feebly and grunted, instinctively denying. The face went away. A briefcase near his feet. It was his, he remembered. The papers, the writing. Why were they important? Were they important? A niggling sense they were not; not now. But why? The stupor returned, and he even dozed briefly, before waking as he started to roll off the chair, steadying himself and catching sight again of the briefcase. He was flooded with a sense of dread. It came to him that he must go home. Why? No reason came to him. But he must go, must get away.

Mother. Remembering her was like a punch to the head. What to tell her? He looked again at the papers. Writing, words, blank spaces, nothing. He stood again, wandering aimlessly around the small office, avoiding obstacles of chairs piled with stacks of files, a trailing power-lead, a box of stationery. He reached down to the briefcase. His body surprised him with its unwilled motive power. On automatic pilot, he picked up the papers on the desk, stuffed them at random into the briefcase and fastened it. He walked out of the office holding it. The coat on the back of the door, unseen, remained in place.

He walked, detached, almost unhearing, seeing only the next few moments' way ahead, out of the building and onto the street. It was cold. He shivered, but could not tell where the trembling left off and the shivering began. Home. He left his body to navigate. Mother. What to tell her? His mind slithered and slipped around this; the face returning, talking. Saying what? Again a sense of dread. More sliding. He walked across the square, then, on reflex, walked in the Nunhead direction. People flowed around him, in turbulent knots where the pavement narrowed, their voices, their footsteps, the sounds from the shops, the sounds of a tram, blurred into a background sound-track. Were they real?

Let go. Had they let go? Should he let go? Home. Go home. Mother. What was he to say to her? Ideas fled from him. He stood, unmoving for several seconds, then turned and slowly retraced some steps, before turning again, aiming itself towards the station. The briefcase was pulling him down. The papers? What did they mean? He staggered slightly, saw a bench and sat on it, trying again to calm himself, regain his thoughts. Leaning forward, still holding the briefcase, he felt himself pulled down into stupor, letting go, but a small gust of wind racked him with a new onset of shivering, and impelled him on.

The face again. Whose? Saying what? His thoughts misfired still. A sign on a shop-front: 'Compensation'. No, none. Why did he think that? What was he to say to mother? Nothing came to him. Home. He got up and walked on.

By the railway bridge, the face came to mind again and he got it. Stephen Pendleton. He stopped. Should he go back? But there was no sense to be made. No sense of what was said. He must go home. Mother. Could she explain? He stood, unable to move forward or back.

Stephen Pendleton. His mind worried at the name, at the face, chipping at a hard nut of memory. The wind gusted again, and the cold drove him into shelter. The station.
Ambient noise, echoing, now diffuse now intense; he felt detached and as if drowning. At the stairs, a change of note, shouts, a brief lull in the sound, brought it suddenly back and he put the pieces together as he walked up to the platform and along where he always waited, for the rear carriages.

Stephen Pendleton, his manager. The last half-year. Turned on him. Like a snake. Letting go. Letting him go. Thrown out. Twenty-two years. Bitterness and dread invaded him. Normalisation. He knew that well. What it meant. Too well. No reference, no appeal, no compensation. Only good will. Sudden hostility, ferocious hostility. Where from? Unable to answer, resist. Hopeless.

The train approaching. Home. Mother. Mother might understand, explain. But what must he say? The papers he had taken from the desk? His mind recoiled and set him shaking. He was cold; the wind was strong, raised up here. Home. The train pouring in past the end of the platform, he leaned forward to greet a familiar. A friend. Time for home. Dread immersed him. Falling. Reaching for home. Mother. Forgive.

LXI

TAKING CONTROL

That felt better. A good elimination was always enjoyable, even just as pretence. It made him feel more in control again. He would throw him something in a day or two, but the little asshole could squirm till then. Destroying him had been almost too easy; he was made for silent obstruction, not for teeth-baring aggression. Pity to see him go, really; he had had his uses, particularly the vomit bucket they called a financial system round here. But there was a score to be settled over accommodation, and there was nothing for him in the normalised organisation; he had to have the skids put under him sooner or later. Electing to put them sooner had generated a mood of masterful euphoria.

Things were moving. There were the other eliminations, always the fun bit of the process, to look forward to; there'd be no soft landing for any of those. Carl Trenchard was the irritant; too well known to crucify properly. But he'd do what he could; pay the son of a bitch back for that expression. When they first met. Talking about Phoniotics. The distanced gaze, the sense that he'd heard something slightly humorous. He hadn't missed it; the Brits did it all the time; he was used to looking for it. Well screw you, he thought, you'll be in the Russian Sector for as long as I can keep you there.

Time to get some sense out of Jack Kavkazian. He called him up on the videophone and this time got straight through. Things were looking up. "Jack. I missed you on Tuesday."

"Ah that. Sorry, Stephen, events got pretty hectic. What can I do for you?"

"We need closure on the consultancy fee, Jack. And we need dialogue respecting the non-executive directorship. Parameters have changed."

"The directorship is all settled, Stephen. Tuesday's meeting. You were voted in."

Shit! That needed unravelling. But first, the money. "Thank you, Jack, that is good news. Can you offer the same on the consultancy fee?"

"No worries about the consultancy fee, Stephen, it's been put aside in a fund. One hundred and seventy, if I remember right."

"Two hundred and fifty."

"Whatever. It's earmarked. The thing is, we have a transition situation at the moment, changes in ownership, changes in the board. All non-essential expenditure is frozen while budgets are re-evaluated. It's just a question of time, while the position gets regularised. You know how it is."

"Sure, I understand the position. The key issue, though, is Outvesta's identifying the consultancy fee as non-essential expenditure. This is a payment in fulfilment of a contract, originally scheduled for payment not much off two months ago."

"A contract, sure. A verbal contract. That's the difficulty. A short-term difficulty, it goes without saying, but a difficulty all the same. I would prioritise the payment today, but that decision is out of my hands, and the person with the hands didn't make the verbal contract. Don't misinterpret what I'm saying Stephen; it's as good as done, the money's allocated, sitting by itself under a 'Consultancy Contingencies' budget. It'll just need a little patience."

Trouble was there was nothing he could threaten him with except being cut out of future deals, and it sounded only borderline whether Jack would have much to do with any future deals that Outvesta made. "All right. For now. But there are serious issues of contractual obligations and business ethics involved here. Keep the pressure up on the man with the hands, won't you."

"Will do. Anything else?"

"You say the directorship has been confirmed?"

"Yeah, voted in, nem con."

"I have not received any notification."

"In a day or two, Stephen. There's a letter in the post. Take this as confirmation, if you want."

"Thank you, Jack; I'll wait for it in writing."

They rang off. He was being stalled, no question. Devoid of ideas for effective action, he fretted, walking backwards and forwards in little bursts of energy, interspersed by rumination. He remembered the saying that revenge was a dish best served cold and started contemplating what he would do in due course to Jack Kavkazian. This occupied him happily enough as he left the office and crossed the square, to seek out transport to the AFFREM offices. Darkness had descended to the milk-chocolate level and lights were coming on. One, in what he recognised as Fraserman's office, showed a small group holding glasses and drinking. Well, that sort of thing would stop soon enough when Fraserman had gone. It would not be long now. Two of the company, not quite in synchrony, appeared to raise their glasses in his direction. He ignored them, of course, but a feeling of the camaraderie that he might have enjoyed in other lines of work troubled the journey. He willed it to go away, but without success.

The 'phone was ringing as he regained his AFFREM office. Alan Westwood, and he sounded upset. "Stephen, I think you ought to know immediately."

"Yes, what is it?"

"We're not one hundred per cent sure yet, the police are still investigating and there'll need to be a formal identification. They rang me, because they got his briefcase afterwards and found the university number."

"I don't understand. What you are trying to say?"

"It's Crabtree. He seems to have walked from the university earlier this afternoon to the station and either thrown himself, or fallen under a train. No-one seems quite sure, but apparently several people noticed him looking agitated and acting oddly before it happened."

Pendleton froze, standing before the desk, unable for nearly a minute either to move or to speak. This could be serious. Taking an elimination literally was okay for somebody earmarked, if that's what it took. Seeing off one of your own was something else; it could see off his career too. If anybody found out about the meeting before Crabtree left … this could require major fuck-up management, depending on what they found in the briefcase.

Westwood was droning on, he'd taken nothing of it in. " … terrible shock for the university, terrible shock for me. He wasn't the most popular character, but something like this … poor bugger!"

He had to shut him up and allow himself time to think. "Alan, you need to give yourself space … time to think. This is a sad event, but there is nothing we can now do for Crabtree himself, so let us focus on practicalities. What did the police say they found in the briefcase?"

It didn't sound like much, apart from a work address and 'phone number, but of course they hadn't said much, just given the news. The first imperative was to get to Crabtree's office and sanitise what might still be lying on his desk. No saying the police would bother to look themselves, but somebody would, once it was known. He called for a cab.

LXII

MOVING ON (1)

With Karen it's been a bit like 'Decline and Fall': she may have kicked me out, but she's never let me down. Three weeks of sharing Paul's flat, and I thought I'd had enough. Then ALBASEC laid him off too, and suddenly he was around a lot more of the time. But it was the girlfriend that really did it. Yes, Paul got a girlfriend. Alison's younger sister, Carly. She turned up in the flat with him one day, all bright smile, short skirt, long perfect legs, nice tits. Another vision of loveliness, friendly and pleasant with it. She was achingly fanciable, which made, as I lay sleepless on the lumpy sofa bed in the main room, the occasional random sounds from Paul's bedroom beyond a joke.

I appealed to Karen for help. Accommodation and a job. It was her plans that had got me into this, after all. The outcome was amazing. Just four more nights of ordeal by sofa bed and I had my own room in another flat. In Brockley. With Eva. Basically, Alison had just moved out to live with Ben Cordell and left a room free. Karen dispatched me to meet Eva in situ and negotiate terms.

I should mention that Karen definitely owed me at the time. The data stick had given up some interesting details about the way AFFREM worked. Best of all (though this wasn't obvious until later) was the confidential statement on Outvesta's finances. Karen got it onto the media, and it really got everybody's interest. Details like valuation of assets that included 'Organic Ideas Bank'. A sub-clause to some very small print showed that to be the ideas for improvement and development assumed to be present in the brains of their members of staff, and it was a very large number. Just goes to show they do value us after all. In their way. I'm told it put the mockers on what's called a Rights Issue. I'm not absolutely sure what that is, but it didn't sound like a good thing to happen. Not for Outvesta.

Eva greeted me with one of her rare smiles when I arrived, though it was wary. Then I got a detailed tour of the flat: the kitchen, the kitchen cupboard lower shelf (hers), the kitchen cupboard upper shelf (mine), the smaller bedroom overlooking the road (formerly Eva's, now mine), the bathroom, the bathroom cabinet lower shelf (Eva's), the bathroom cabinet upper shelf (mine), the toilet seat (down), the living room, the living room bookcase upper two shelves (Eva's), the living room bookcase lower two shelves (mine), the media centre (Eva's and Alison's), the conditions for use of the media centre, the small garden, the garden furniture (Eva's and Alison's), the conditions of use of the garden furniture, the utility room by the backdoor.

"Has Karen told you what's been arranged on the rent?"

"Only that I'm all right up to the end of the month."

She nodded. "Alison paid till then. You'll have to try claiming on SHIRT after that."

"I'll apply tomorrow. I might have a job by then, of course." I should have been able to get something out of SHIRT (Social and Housing Interim Regulation (Temporary)), as I'd been out of any sort of job for four weeks by that time and hadn't had a penny compensation from anywhere. But I hoped Karen would work her magic on employment as well.

"You may not be the only one looking for one of those. What are you going for?"

"Media design."

"That's what you were doing?"

"Yeah."

"Do you like it?"

"It's not bad. Interesting enough, and I'm good at it. Some of the projects are a slog sometimes, that's all."

She nodded, looking thoughtful. "I wish I could say the same about what I do. It can be really boring. Not all of the time, but quite a lot. Sometimes it starts to look pointless too."

"You're one of Alan Westwood's lot, aren't you?"

She rolled her eyes slightly. "Yes."

"Ancillary Music's all right, I'd have thought."

"It is, but not the way Alan Westwood does it. He's never been a practitioner, so it's all theory. It's not very inspired theory, either. He spends a lot of his time correcting your English in reports and papers."

"Couldn't you find another department to work in?"

"I could try, I suppose. But everyone's just looking after the jobs they've got at the moment. You know, with this normalisation thing going on."

I did. All too well. She went back to being businesslike. "I was told the deal was you'd do the cooking and the cleaning for the time being. Until you get an income."

"That's right. I do a mean baked beans on toast." She grimaced. "Only joking. I can cook."

"When are you moving in?"

I thought of the sofa bed. "Now, if I could. Will tomorrow be all right?"

"Tomorrow will be fine. "You'll have to sign a renting agreement, and then I can give you a key."

"I could sign it now if you want." She went into her bedroom to look for it. I had a quick read of it – they're very standard, so I just made sure there were no funny extras – then signed and got the key. I could move all my stuff over the following day, in two or three journeys if I had to. "I don't know if my cooking duties start now, but it's a bit late to get anything together (I'd called in on her after work). Do you fancy finding something at the pub? We could toast a beautiful flatmateship."

She laughed. "Say that again in a month." She dithered a bit. There was some work to finish, but it didn't sound very important. Ten minutes or so later she gave in, went to garb herself in coat, scarf and gloves, and we set out. As we strode rapidly along (it was bloody cold out), I jokingly said, "well, Eva, you're the experienced flat sharer. Any tips?"

She said, "you can start by getting my name right. It's not Eever. It's not Ayver either, it's Evva." And she threw me a sideways glance.

I glanced back. "Okay, 'Ever' it is."

"No. Too breathy and English. And it's not 'err' at the end. Evva. A good Polish boy like you should know that."

"My grandfather was the last of our family lived in Poland. Give us a chance." I tried again, and this time got modified approval. It's odd, but the new (correct) pronunciation suited her; perhaps it's its faintly combative sound. I've used it without prompting ever since.

I moved in, as planned, the following day, leaving Paul and Carly an unencumbered love-nest and some wine and chocolates as thanks. The same day I applied to SHIRT. Four months later, their adjudication gave me a lump sum of one hundred and seventy six pounds (for no discernible reason), but refused anything towards the rent. Karen engineered an introduction, though, and I got a job from it. It started only two weeks into the next month, so I paid out of my own pocket from the start.

The job - which I'm really enjoying - is in Croydon. That's an awful looking place, lined from one end to the other with high-rise buildings a century old and looking as if no-one's done anything to them since they were built. It makes it cheap, of course, so it's popular with small media companies just starting up, among others. But you don't want to be alone on the streets late at night. Not like in Peckham.

LXIII

PICKING OVER THE BONES

"Daoud."

"Yes, Viola?"

"As my grandmother used to say, I've a bone to pick with you."

"Ah." He slowed his pace and turned slightly towards her. "Is this a large, beat-about-the-head bone, or a small bone sharpened to a point?"

"Neither, I hope. But it is a bone, and I can't carry on gnawing at it without asking you what it means. Something somebody said implied there was more to Farooz's detention than just the police sweeping up a bystander with their idea of the wrong skin colour. Is that true? I mean, has he had some involvement in actual terrorism."

"In actual terrorism, absolutely no."

"But in something?"

"But in something, yes. You remember that I told you, when we first talked together, that Farooz was a young man not always wise in his choice of friends?"

"Yes."

"That is in the past. He married nearly a year ago now – his wife was much distressed by his detention – and has broken off communication with the friends I talk of. His friends are such as Mohammed nowadays. And there is little enough in the past to note."

"But he has a past?"

Daoud sighed and said "a visit to family in Afghanistan five years ago was to more than just family. He told me everything, when it became necessary to learn everything. He spent time with a group that talked about freedom in Afghanistan, which is still not free in any useful sense that you would recognise. That is all: they talked. He kept contact with the group when he returned to London, but has now broken off contact."

"Knowing this earlier might have helped, though I should have asked what exactly you meant about Farooz and his unwise friends."

"Helped in what way?"

"Can't you see?" She stopped walking and turned to him. "It means the police have got some shred of justification for the position they've taken on Jane's case. We may know it's rubbish, but it gives them an excuse."

He faced her square on, gesturing with his arms. "If I am at fault for concealing anything, Viola, then truly I apologise. But think. Does it seem likely to you that your friend would have been held as she has been if the authorities did not believe they could leech on her for large sums of money? Farooz, or no Farooz, the restaurant incident was an opportunity for some nice bail money and performance pay for the police, then somebody else came to believe they could make much more. Money has driven this, and it did so just the same for Farooz and Mohammed."

"Possibly." She looked at the ground, then over his shoulder at the late afternoon light on the river, half-convinced.

"Consider this also, Viola. What Farooz is guilty of, if that is the word, is talk. The group he so unwisely got to know are also 'guilty' to my certain knowledge of no more than talk. Talk of freedom. Freedom in my community's native country is not an academic question, but terrorism is an academic question if there is no intent to act. There has been little political questioning here in this country for a long time now. Perhaps everything is perfect, or perhaps it is all just sufficiently comfortable as it is. But there used to be a great deal of political questioning. Many joined the Communist Party, to take an example. Only a handful of these took any form of action towards the revolution they thought they preached. For most it was just talk, and at some point they left it behind. Some were kept under observation, but once they had left the movement the stain was not assumed indelible. Why is it now indelible for what is called terrorism, which in recent decades is mostly just more talk? This country despised America for the McCarthy era and its hysteria over Communism. Why has it imported that era for something new? Why?"

His gestures had become impassioned, and he was, she saw, perspiring slightly, in spite of the cold. "I don't know, Daoud. I'm going to have to think about it. But I take your point about Farooz anyway." She thought she would discuss it with Joe; she wasn't expecting to meet Carl for another month or so and had learned to distrust the confidentiality of the videophone.

"Thank you, Viola. It is always a pleasure talking to you."

She laughed. "Tell that to the Inspector."

"I think the Inspector also takes pleasure in talking to you. One could wish it were more productive in freeing your friend, Jane."

"Vile. Over here." Sylv was ensconced at a large corner table in the coffee bar, with Clare and John Librarian. "We were just getting to know your boyfriend." John looked amused as Viola struggled to recast the relationship more accurately. They ordered coffee and a sample of the cakes that confirmed this particular café as their regular meeting place. They ordered also for Neil, who came in shortly after.

Viola spoke. "John has news to give, though he's been mysterious about it up to now. Does anyone else have anything to say first?" Nobody did. "John."

"I have good news, but it comes with a catch. Viola has talked to some of your group about the catch. Which do you want to hear about first?"

"Give us the good news," said Sylv. "We'll let you know if we want to hear about the catch."

"Yes, we need any good news," said Clare. Viola and Neil both nodded.

"We can raise a little more than one hundred and ninety thousand, which should be equivalent to more or less all the money for Jane. The catch, and you do need to know this, is that you'll be getting it as a Performance Art ensemble. That means that about fifteen thousand will have to be spent on a recording. That will go into our archives, in case anyone should ask what the grant was about."

"Is this this thing about being filmed beating up a restaurant?" asked Sylv.

"Yes. The Cowingdon group in action." Sylv and Clare looked blank.

"It's a name Joe suggested, " said Viola.

"Sounds an okay deal to me," said Sylv.

Clare looked worried. "I've not done much of the actual smashing up of restaurants, and I've never acted. Will we be told what to do?"

"It'll all be choreographed, Clare. You'll just follow instructions."

"Hey, we're not doing ballet or something?" said Sylv.

"No, just what comes naturally, neatened up for a recording." Though, Viola reflected, synchronised hurling of lamb fusillade from one side of a set to the other wouldn't be as different from contemporary dance as you might expect.

"Throw in a free meal and I'm on," said Sylv.

"The meal's part of it. You'll be filmed eating, though."

There wasn't much doubt about the deal. They'd need to find about twenty-five thousand between them to cover the balance of the bail money and some compensation for the restaurant, but this was straightforward. They had been contemplating much worse. The remaining uncertainty was over the Inspector's ability to square OSC.

Half an hour later he appeared, picking his way through the tables like a tank edging through a suburban housing estate.

"How do!" Viola and Clare responded verbally, Daoud and Neil nodded, Sylv stared back, widening her eyes to large black pools, before looking down at the table and settling into a waiting slump, her legs crossed. The Inspector took his reception in good humour. "Thought on't lass?" he said to Viola, who looked puzzled, uncertain whether a question had been addressed to her. "A bit more time, right you are. How are we doing on the money, then?"

Neil sighed and looked depressed. Sylv snorted, though gently. Viola roused herself to respond, but was cut off by Daoud. "We must first ask how you and your friends are doing on the money. There is little point our doing anything until that is known."

The Inspector cast a glance in his direction before refocusing on Viola. "Fair does. OSC want one hundred and ninety two. If that's what you meant by my friends."

"And the police and anyone else?"

"My lot will settle for that. Don't know who you mean by anyone else."

"The Superintendent?"

"Like I said, the police will settle." His coffee appeared. He picked up the cup and took a gulp.

"The tame judge you found and the MP."

He exploded with laughter, spraying coffee over shirt and trousers. "Shit!" He dabbed with a grubby handkerchief, to little effect. "Pardon me, ladies." Sylv raised her head and looked at him briefly and disdainfully. Clare and Viola chose not to have noticed anything. "You mean Warrendell? Haven't you heard? He'll be settling debts for the time being, not trying to collect them."

"What about Tom Warrendell?" said Viola. "We haven't heard anything." Clare had, but she kept silent.

"It was in all the media yesterday. Caught transferring funds from a company he'd made bankrupt to his fancy woman's bank account. Incompetent or what? You need to keep up. So did he" He sniggered. A brief smile flitted over Sylv's face, and she uncrossed her legs, though she continued to look down at the table.

"So there will be no payout needed to the MP?"

"No. Nothing but payback there. Stupid bugger!" He looked reflective.

"And the judge?"

"Looked to by OSC. Anyhow, I've no idea who it was. Probably someone new; they're a sight more cooperative and they come cheap."

"One hundred and ninety two, then. Would that cover everything for Jane Fredricksson's release? There will be no extras or surcharges or arrangement fees growing out of the dung heap later on? We give your people one hundred and ninety two thousand and you give us Jane, no strings attached, is that it?"

The Inspector spoke to Viola. "He knows how to promise your money, doesn't he? How do you feel about it?"

"Daoud speaks for us all. What's your answer to his question?"

"One hundred and ninety two is everything. It will get your friend unconditional bail in the usual way."

Daoud said, "then we need a discussion among ourselves before giving you an answer. Can you wait? Somewhere else?"

"I'll be at yon hotel." He inclined his head outwards, looking over the river, before turning and winking at Viola, who looked at him blankly.

As he was getting up and buttoning his coat, Clare said, "aren't you afraid we might have videoed this conversation, to put it on the media?"

"Videoed what? A discussion about bail terms. Happens all the time. But don't try getting funny with me, lass. Any of that media crap. I wasn't born yesterday." He stared at her for a moment, then, treating them to an affable nod, raised his hand in farewell and navigated, surprisingly neatly, to the door, walking away towards Tower Bridge. Sylv blew a raspberry, but not too loudly.

"Resist the urge to provoke them, please, Clare, Sylvia. They are too powerful." Daoud was concerned to keep the team in reasonable order, but did not feel that the Inspector had taken offence. "Have we got a deal now, do you think?"

"It's gone up another two thousand," Sylv said.

"True, but the hundred and ninety was the Inspector's estimate." (Clare).

"I doubt that he would have been allowed to meet us before without a precise figure, but the truth is that they have the whip hand here. If they feel they can extort another two thousand, they will" (Daoud).

"I think we can manage this now and should take it. Before they stick it up another twenty" (Viola). "John, Neil, you've been very quiet. What do you think?"

"I would agree with Viola. But you are the ones whose personal finances will be hit." (John)

"We need to get it done now we can. Try for something better, and it could end up a lot worse." (Neil)

"Yeah" (Sylv).

"Yes" (Clare).

"That is agreed by everybody then" (Daoud).

And so Jane's captivity came to an end, ten months after it had started. There were formalities in raising the money to make the payment, but four days after the last Action Committee (as it had come to think of itself), they all convened at Denmark Hill to watch Viola sign the bail papers and greet Jane as she was led out of the remand area to which she had been transported the previous evening.

It was a bright day of early spring, cold in the shadows but with a warm sun in a cloudless sky. A cheerful day, and the group, in spite of the financial sacrifices, was in a cheerful mood.

Jane came from a different world. Pallid, wearing an ill-matched assortment of the clothes they had taken to her in prison at various times, her hair kempt and apparently clean, but cut without obvious style, carrying her possessions in a cheap cotton bag, she seemed hardly to register the group's presence, greeting just Viola with a protracted, rather limp hug and Sylv with a desultory wave of the hand. She did not speak. They had hired a taxi to get Jane back to Viola's apartment, where she would stay for the time being. Viola and Clare accompanied her, the others dispersing, subdued.

Back in the flat, of which she showed no immediate recognition (though it was true that she had spent little time there in the past), she was shown the spare bedroom, put her bag down by the bed, gave Viola another quick hug, looked in Clare's direction, acknowledging her, then lay down on the bed, staring at the ceiling and breathing deeply, in and out.

Clare said, "Do you need anything, Jane." Jane looked at her as she said her name, but said nothing, looking back at the ceiling, then nodding her head after a lapse of half a minute or so. Their presence was clearly redundant and, after an interval of uncertainty, they left the room. Clare and Viola chatted for a while in the sitting room, checking on Jane a couple of times – she continued simply to lie awake, staring at the ceiling – before Clare left her to it.

The group celebration so happily talked about before the release had not necessarily been expected to happen on the day of the release, but it retreated into the future and eventually fizzled out, as the days turning into weeks brought no appreciable change in Jane's condition. She was perfectly amenable to being told to get out of or return to bed, to wash, to dress, to eat; she was not a difficult guest in that sense. But a vital spring seemed to have broken; to Viola it seemed that none of those things would have happened without her being told to do them. And between directed events, there was nothing; she simply sat or lay, unspeaking, in passive acceptance of time's passage. Occasionally she would utter a word or two, a yes, or no, or thanks, but it was purely responsive. At some point in the second week, she started referring to Viola as Vi, though with an air of uncertainty. Questions about how she was feeling would get no response, other, perhaps, than a shake of the head, or audible breathing for some minutes afterwards, and Viola, sensing that it might be causing her friend distress, ceased asking at an early stage. What she did during the day, when Viola was at work was a mystery, but there was little evidence of activity, so Viola presumed that she remained inert except where driven by need. Sylv's and Clare's observation when sitting in for her in the first few days tended to confirm this.

It was towards the end of the third week that John Librarian suggested an evening out to celebrate what was at any rate an end to Jane's captivity, and she gladly accepted. It was just the two of them; she had no qualms now about Jane's safety in being left alone, but there was no question of including her; she reacted with suspicion and signs of withdrawal even to the presence of people she could be expected to know, such as Sylv and Clare. Viola was the only exception to that; exposure to a public place might be disastrous.

Viola was complicit; she invited him in for a drink at the end of the evening. They ended up in bed together. There were no software faults this time; indeed, no faults of any sort, and it was to a feeling of relaxation and contentment that she woke on the following morning. She became gradually aware that she had woken to a sound, but could not place it. Then it happened again, a rustle of wind and a door banging gently, the front door. Her first reaction was alarm, and she shook John, who stirred, opened his eyes, closed them again, flung an arm around her and drew closer, the beginnings of an erection pushing against the side of her right buttock. "No, there's been enough of that for now. The door. The front door. It's open. There's somebody there."

He didn't exactly leap to action, but, spurred by the urgency in her voice, heaved himself, still partly asleep, out of bed, stood up, penis still at half mast and grabbed a dressing gown from the back of the bedroom door. One of Viola's, it covered only just enough for decency, but thus attired he went out of the room in search of the intruder. Viola swung herself out of bed, grabbed another dressing gown, more successful in its concealment and followed. He called,

"Viola" and she found him outside the front door, standing in front of Jane, who was just outside the door, on the balcony corridor, sitting in sunlight on the ground and stroking the next-door cat, who was purring loudly. Going outside and fraternising with the cat were two advances over three weeks of social catatonia; however, she was stark naked. Mindful of the neighbours, she and John grouped themselves, squatting, around her as best they could, contributing odd strokes to the cat worship and working on chivvying her gradually back inside. But she was quite content with the situation, and Viola was considering a joint effort to hoist her indoors more or less forcibly, when Jane became aware of John. Specifically, from her vantage point on the ground, the goods, only approximately covered by the dressing gown, were on full view, still short of flaccid neutrality. She peered at this, then looked him briefly in the eye, peering again, then blinking and moving her hands to cover herself. Viola then persuaded her, without difficulty, to go back indoors; the cat had in any case got bored and strolled away sleekly, with feline dignity. John and she helped Jane to her room, where Viola encouraged her to dress, and Jane's daily routine of sedentary vacancy resumed. But John became accepted as a presence without cause for alarm.

Back in Viola's bedroom, John was in a mind to resume where they had left off, but she kissed him lightly and pushed him away. "Another time." She started to dress, and he followed suit. She gave voice to something that had been puzzling her. "Why do you chase humans like me, John? Aren't you supposed to chase avatar females"

Struggling with a sock, he said, without hesitation. "I am a sort of mutant, you see," before pulling down a corner of his mouth with a finger and squinting his eyes, gazing up at her.

"Stop it." She passed her hands over his face, and he caught her arms, pulling her over onto him. "That too." She stood up and looked down at him, eyebrows just perceptibly raised. "So what sort of a mutant am I going out with, then? What happened to the programming?"

"I don't know exactly, but something did. Happen, I mean. I have chased female avatars, and they sometimes chase me, but I just do not find them as interesting as humans. You human girls are all different, much more intriguing. Avatars really are all the same, well, all one of about half a dozen types, and I just do not find any of the half-dozen very seductive. I ought to, but I don't: it must be a coding error."

"Maybe there are female coding errors too."

"Possibly, but I have never met any. Avatars in our present form have only been around for thirty or forty years. Even with a dozen or so software upgrades each year, that has given us little time for mutations to develop, so perhaps it is just me. One thing that I do know is that I care very much for you. If it meant anything in the case of an avatar, I would say that I love you."

Viola, staring into the dressing table mirror, adjusted a necklace with great care.

"You know about Carl Trenchard and me, don't you?"

"I do."

"Though it's only once every two months or so, I'll keep seeing him. For the time being. Does that bother you?"

"If you will see me as well, I'm happy. It is just a matter of programming."

Viola wasn't sure that was what she'd wanted to hear, really, but then, what was that anyway? It would have to do for now.

John, the socks laboriously in place, pulled on his trousers. They went to the kitchen to get breakfast together. Viola looked in on Jane, but she was dozing in her armchair.

Towards the end of the morning, John said he'd better be getting back. "When will I see you again?"

"This evening?"

That was the answer that he had wanted to hear. Smiling, he kissed her. "Six o'clock? Here?"

"I'll see you then."

At the door of the flat he turned to look at her. "By the way, I should have told you before. You will hear officially in a day or two: somebody from the Appointments Committee, but I thought I would give you a bit of warning. You know how things are for Carl Trenchard, I think?"

"You mean that he won't be coming back. Yes, I do."

"I am sorry about that, as I suppose you are, but it is not something we can prevent. His exile, I mean. It is out of our hands; the Government is involved in some way. What it does mean, though, is that a professorship is vacant, and I know that it will be offered to you."

"Won't Ben Cordell have a claim?"

"If the post were exactly the same as Carl's, yes he would, though I am unsure whether he would get it. He is too much associated with Carl's regime. But the nature of the job is changing. It will be a chair in Virtual Paginatorics, and your lecture in Bucharest last summer impressed a lot of people. You will have to apply formally, but it will be your job if you want it. Think about it, but please do not imagine that holding back would make any difference to Carl. His exile may or may not be permanent, I do not know myself, but there will be no return to AUP."

Pleasure at the news mixed with unease over how Ben might take it and a sense of guilt in relation to Carl. It felt as though she had been unfaithful to him and would now snaffle his job, but that was absurd. She felt tremendous affection for Carl, but the sexual relationship had always been a little more of a quid pro quo for the music than a romantic liaison and now occurred not more frequently than once every couple of months, when she was able to get across to Vishiney. There was no template for how an avatar might react to the prospect of being a shared sexual partner; she would have to work round to that somehow, but John felt like the important relationship just now. As to the job, well, as John said, it was all too clear that whoever was to do Carl's job at AUP in the future, it would not be Carl; that was something that none of them seemed able to challenge.

He kissed her, opened the door, said "six o'clock, then" over his shoulder and strode away along the balcony corridor.

She thought about the job at length over the weekend; John found her preoccupied and so, subconsciously, did Jane. But when Monday came and with it the call from the Appointments Committee, she put in her application. As the new professor-in-waiting, she decided to attend Crabtree's funeral on the Thursday.

LXIV

RITES OF PASSAGE

"Though I did not know Jedediah well myself, I have, in talking to his relatives and to his colleagues, been left with impressions of a life of service to others, of an integrity in his personal and working lives and of an even-handedness in his dealings with others that sat well with his professional competence … "

Meaning that everyone got the same shit, the Hon Ran thought. Except him, of course. Crabtree had been a useful fixer. Until he threw in his lot with Pendleton, at any rate. The parson wasn't making too bad a job of eulogising someone he clearly didn't know; they must get a lot of practice in that sort of thing, parsons. He'd be on himself in five minutes. The notes were to hand; important thing was to avoid saying anything about the actual death. Accidental death was what the coroner had said, but people didn't just fall in front of trains, not unless it was a heart attack or something, and there had been no sign of that. But no reason that anyone could work out for a suicide. Odd! Very odd!

" … much loved by his family. Our thoughts should be with his mother … " He nodded in the direction of a small, aged woman, dressed largely in black, who sat on the bench at the front. A younger woman sitting next to her, presumably a relative, put her hand over hers, but she made no response and showed no expression. " … in conclusion, let us sit in silent prayer for a moment, in memory of this man, taken from us in so untimely a manner."

All dutifully bent their heads in silence.

Alison, sitting next to Ben, thought with indignation of the way in which he had been pushed aside for promotion. Still, he was looking around and should get something soon. And look on the bright side;

he'd have been spending a lot more time away from her if he'd got the professorship. Things were going nicely. She'd almost got his flat civilised now; it looked quite like a home. Just the study, though there might be more difficulty there. Just a feeling; it would have to be taken by stealth.

Eva, sitting with the two of them, wondered again why she was there. It had been to keep Alison company, but wonder-boy seemed to provide quite enough of that. Anyway, it shouldn't be too long; English crematorium services were always fairly brief, unlike some of the Catholic equivalents.

The Hon Ran cast an eye over his notes.

Karen, sitting next to him with Leke, felt unaccountably sad. It was not as if she'd liked the little creep when he was alive. He hadn't even really been on their side the last six months. But there was something definitely not right about the way he'd died. Driving others to suicide from boredom or frustration maybe, but he'd been too up his own arse to think of it for himself. Something must have happened. She was quite sure it had been suicide.

Leke thought of his brother's funeral, all those years ago in Albania and felt sad too.

Crabtree's mother's thoughts wandered on vacancy, only peripherally aware that her niece had taken her hand again.

"And now, the Honourable Ranulph Fraserman, vice-chancellor of the Arts University of Peckham, to which Jedediah Crabtree gave the benefit of his professional skills, would like to say a few words of remembrance."

He got up and walked over to the lectern. The turnout, all things considered, was surprisingly good; the crem. chapel was half full. Probably curiosity as much as anything. Surprising number of relatives, but then he'd only been fifty-four; possibly the first of his generation to go.   Glad they were sending him off decently. Arranging his notes and clearing his throat, he set off on a well-polished routine.

Viola, sitting by herself on the other side of the chapel from Ben – she had arrived as the service started – reflected on what she had known of Crabtree. It was not much, and not favourable. She had had few dealings with him herself, but he had driven Carl to apoplectic incoherence on more than one occasion, and John had talked of the avatars' ever-present fear that one of his seemingly arbitrary budget attacks might condemn some or all of them to archive storage or even deletion. Carl would have felt it essential to attend the funeral, though, as head of department, and, as the heir apparent, she had come in his place. The VC seemed to be doing a professional job of hagiography. Not that he was to be VC for long now; this must be among the last of his duties.

They stood up and sang a hymn. There were some prayers. Then the minister announced Mr David Wetherill of the Ancient Fellowship of Franchised Reamers, to give an appreciation. Everyone woke up: who was he?

"It is my privilege to celebrate the achievements of Jedediah Crabtree, Resource Officer to the Faculty of Ancillary Music in AUP for many years and a principal mover in the normalisation process that is currently bringing the university into line with the most advanced interpretations of the business paradigm in the academic context. It may be less well known that Jedediah pursued, in such little time as he could spare from his duties at the university, the discipline of Ancillary Musicologist, defining the material environment and information access requirements for a Musicologist to perform at optimum effectiveness. Though the actual pursuit of musicology, particularly in the S-class context, is largely discouraged in your country and, indeed, in mine, that does not obviate the need for a clear and consistent methodology, crystallising and containing the perceptive links from a normalised media-arts-centred environment … "

They had all glazed over. Must make a point of thanking David afterwards; a pro at this sort of address, no question. It could all have been very different if he hadn't acted quickly. By the time anyone had thought of looking at Crabtree's office, it had all been nicely sanitised. The papers they found in the briefcase seemed to be a random selection of letters and reports that he'd picked up. Nothing to cause waves. Now it was all going to go out in a eulogy that no-one was listening to. That was the way. He allowed himself a brief satisfied smile.

Adjusting the position of her bum on the very hard bench with the torturing back-rest, Karen, half-turned, caught the smile and wondered what Little Dick was smirking at.

David Wetherill finished and there was a silence of several seconds, until the minister, revived and announced the final hymn.

" … earth to earth, ashes to ashes, dust to dust: in sure and certain hope of the resurrection to eternal life …" Crabtree's mother looked neither convinced nor unconvinced; her face an unvarying mask. The Committal followed, the coffin descending to a position just below floor level. The relatives stood up and shuffled towards the exit, past the coffin. His mother went first, standing in front of the coffin in silence for what must have been a minute or two, though it felt much more protracted to the onlookers. Then, suddenly, she broke down, sobbing, knelt down and reached forward to touch the coffin, still just within reach, with both hands, wailing "my boy, my boy" over and over again, as if she would wrench him back into the world.

Nobody quite knew what to do. Most were embarrassed. Eva was appalled at herself for having thought it just a routine ceremony up till now. The niece and one of the ushers took the mother by each arm and gradually persuaded her to let go of the coffin and be raised up and half-carried out of the chapel. The remainder of the congregation filed out quickly, it being close on time for the next service. Three other relatives did the honours shaking hands; there was no question of involving Crabtree's mother, still sobbing and being comforted by the niece and by the minister, the usher standing by in case of need.

'Blessed are those who mourn, for they will be comforted': he didn't get that right did he, thought Stephen Pendleton, standing to one side. He had been chatting with David Wetherill, who was now turned away, talking to Alan Westwood. An involuntary smile flitted over his face at the thought. These people never learned how to behave.

Karen caught that one too and then she knew. No detail, no proof, nothing. But she knew, for certain. Crabtree had been Playtime. Even Crabtree hadn't deserved that, still less his mother, poor woman. Impelled by fury but calm to outward appearance, she walked the thirty feet or so separating them, through a gap in the crowd, stood in front of him for a moment in which he registered a mild astonishment at her presence, then walloped him across the face right-handed, with the full force that she could achieve. Still outwardly calm and looking away from him, she walked back to where she had been.

The sound of the slap resonated from the walls and porch of the building. Conversation ceased for several seconds as people looked at what had happened. David Wetherill turned, dumbfounded, before moving hastily away. Stephen Pendleton, as one of the centres of attention, had the presence of mind to say nothing, attempt no remonstrances and keep as still a facial expression as he could. But nobody attempted sympathy, or sought an explanation. Universally, they turned away, leaving him isolated at the edge of the crowd. Reaching up to rub some of the smart out of his face, he found that Karen's signet ring had cut his cheek, drawing a small amount of blood. Attending to this with his handkerchief occupied a useful two or three minutes; it wouldn't do to leave in an undignified scuttle. But he departed soon after, unremarked.

Crabtree's mother had been shocked into silence. The minister said some words that he hoped would be comforting, and she responded gratefully, before allowing herself to be led away. The company dispersed.

LXV

MOVING ON (2)

The front door opened and shut and there was just silence. I went to have a look after a couple of minutes and found her in the hall, taking her jacket off, or to be exact, with her jacket half off, but no sign of further action. She was looking down at the floor. It is quiet living with Eva – for one thing she spends every other weekend up in Cambridge – but not usually as quiet as this. I settled on breezy.

"How was the funeral, then?"

After a few seconds, she replied. "It was awful." Then she started to cry, gently at first, so you'd hardly notice, but then she put her hands over her face and got going properly. I didn't know what to do, really. I couldn't just leave her like that, and there wasn't anything obvious I could say for the moment. Rather gingerly – it's a serious no-touch policy with flatmates – I went over and put an arm round her shoulder. Policy or not, she responded immediately by turning towards me, and I put my other arm round her and held her for several minutes while the tears gradually subsided. She wiped her eyes roughly with a handkerchief and blew her nose in the genteel way girls have when they know they're under observation. Then she put her arms round me and held me for a short while, before disengaging. "I'm being silly, don't take any notice of me."

An admission of imperfection from Eva: that was a first, but I just said, "do you want a cup of tea" and she said yes. She stood around in the kitchen, not saying anything, while I made two cups of builder's, then we went and sat down in the living room.

"What happened?"

She told me the story. "It was just so awful, his mother having to go through all that, then not being able to. And knowing what happened. Do you think it was an accident?"

Crabtree's death had been widely discussed. "Not sure. It didn't look it, though."

"No. I think his mother thought so too. Imagine having to go through that. Then after that there was the thing with Karen. It was just a bit too much. I'd only gone along because of Alison, and she disappeared with Ben straightaway afterwards." She frowned a little as she said that; she doesn't seem very favourable towards Ben. "Why do you think Karen did that?"

It was a mystery, but I didn't see Karen as an aggrieved girlfriend. I know she detests Stephen Pendleton; besides, Leke would have turned him into dog meat long since if there'd been any of that. Eva hadn't thought so either. We speculated for some time, then I suggested the pub and she grabbed at the diversion. It was Friday evening, so the pub was crowded, but we managed to find a corner sufficiently quiet to hear each other. Shouting sometimes, but hearing, which is better than it sometimes is. It got late, and she rang to put her visit to Bernard's off till the morning. As she calmed down, she told me the good news from the reorganisation, the 'normalisation', as it had affected her. She had been moved away from Alan Westwood's dismal fiefdom and into Ben Cordell's area. Still doing the same work, which seemed a bit mysterious, but with a boss who at least did some serious research, even if she didn't seem to think that much of him personally. She was over her upset by the end of the evening: even managed to laugh a bit.

LXVI

IN THE CAN

It had been a long, hard-worked day for the Cowingdon and assorted extras, but it was now down to the editors and, above all, to the cleaners. Lamb Fusillade and a variety of exotic chicken and vegetable concoctions covered not just the restaurant set, but also the studio wall up to eight feet from the ground, not forgetting the results of a few exceptionally delivered throws that had gone, in just one case, up to fourteen feet. Only the lighting had entirely escaped; the studio crew certainly had not. The day had been accounted a success. The producer, hired in for the occasion, had been excited by the concept and the vigour of its execution and clearly had ambitions for the recording.

Daoud, with Tala surveyed the wreckage. "It is as well they have not been waging a real war."

"If we women waged a real war, there would be no studio for you to survey."

"Without question, light of my life. Would you seek to destroy the walls with the lamb, the chicken or the vegetable ammunition?"

"That is quite enough of that Daoud. I was being serious."

"I would never presume otherwise. And would the ammunition be spiced or plain?"

Viola saw her plant a swift sideways kick on his shin. Unmoved in expression, he said, "we were discussing women at war. It is an impressive scene."

"You can say that again. I'd avoided the more recent restaurant break-ups. I hadn't realised how enthusiastic everyone had become. Even Clare." Particularly memorable had been Sylv in full cry, a piled plate in each hand.

"The waiters were, I noticed, assisting here and there, when the cameras appeared to be looking elsewhere."

"I think that a certain amount of that went on with the real thing. Jane's ventures used to keep some of the less ambitious places alive, as far as I could tell, so there was good reason to make sure the more disastrous bits of décor got well daubed."

"Talking of Jane, how is she getting along? She was not here today."

"No, it wouldn't have been safe for her. The best I can say is that she's making slow progress. She's in good enough health, but not really with it."

A shadow passed over Tala 's face, and she clicked her tongue. Daoud said, "I'm sorry. If there is anything we can do …"

"There will be, but not just yet. She's okay with me and with John. And the cat. But twitchy with anyone else, even Sylv or Clare."

John joined them. "I had never realised eating out in Camberwell could be so exciting."

"I don't think it will be again, not in this way. Or only as art."

John could feel a speculation coming on about the virtulisation of experience through performance art as a complement to the virtualisation of bodies through avatars like himself, X-Gloves etc, but the company was spared this through the advent of Sylv, fired up and wearing an outfit that left nothing north of the nipple or south of the crotch to the imagination. She smiled broadly at Daoud and ogled

John, who winked at her. "Good one, Vile. When are we doing it again?"

"When we get the next grant. Not in public." That probably meant never, whatever the producer thought.

"Pity. You're the man with the money, aren't you?" she said to John, giving him a coy smile and adding "how about it then?"

"Depends on what you're thinking of," he said, raising his eyebrows, "but you only have to ask."

Viola was about to divert the conversational direction, when Karen appeared. Viola had asked her along as a useful extra in the video, after a summons to the VC's office to discuss the professorship application had matched curiosity with opportunity and led her to ask what had been going on at Crabtree's funeral. Karen had treated her to a brief but adequate viewing of Playtime.

"Thanks for helping us out".

"Enjoyed it. I hope Paris turns out as lively."

"When are you going?" asked Clare, who had joined the group with her."

"End of this week."

"You looking forward to it?" from Sylv.

"Yeah. It looks like fun." That was if the old bastard didn't start a new World War. He'd gone over to start work six days ahead of her, and was always a danger zone, especially left to himself. A good thing the Parisians were mostly still on holiday.

The company drifted away, in search of a pub. John and Viola were left together. "I think that went well."

"Very well. It may even have a life beyond our arts fund archives."

Viola had her doubts. However …

"If you have projects that need funding, it will always be worth trying our Arts Fund."

"You must have run through your budget just on this."

He shook his head. "When we were doing due diligence on the accounts, we found quite a few pots of spare money for this and that contingency. There were a few millions just for Eliminations Management. If they had had any idea about how to run a business nowadays, they would have used a small fraction of it to hire a good avatar information distributor and saved themselves a lot of trouble. Anyway, one of the many of these budgets was Consultancy Contingencies. No-one knew what that was for and it hadn't been committed, so I shoehorned it into this. One hundred and sixty thousand in all. The Arts Fund only had to put up a modest sum. Its management has passed on to one of my colleagues now, but I could give you an introduction."

She gave thanks inwardly for the money conduit no longer being so blatantly direct.

LXVII

PAYBACK (3)

' … the name change to Avatvesta clarifies our unique position in the market and is expected to deliver synergistic benefits from product identification in the virtual community. As you will already be aware, we have undertaken a general review of company policies and, in tandem with this, have taken the decision to restructure and to review the functions and competencies of our non-executive directorships. As a result, we regret to inform you that no place has been found appropriate to your skills in the new structure and we must therefore terminate your contract with immediate effect. May I, on behalf of the Chairman, express Outvesta's warmest appreciation of the contribution you have made over a very difficult transitional period in the Company's history and wish you all the best in pursuing alternative opportunities elsewhere …'

Where was his consultancy fee? He put a call through to Jack Kavkazian. The usual secretary answered and pondered his request briefly. "I am sorry, we are unable to help you. Mr Kavkazian is no longer working for the company. Shall I put you through to his successor, Mr … ?" It wasn't a name he recognised.

"Have you got a number that I can contact Jack on?"

"I'm sorry, Mr Pendleton, we are unable to provide that information. Would you like to be put through?" He rang off. There was no way he was taking a newcomer through the details of the consultancy fee. The many nuances held endless possibilities of misunderstanding.

Later in the day, punishment scenarios for Jack Kavkazian having paled as an entertainment, he realised it was time to cover his bases and rang Herb Summerson.

"Herb. Stephen Pendleton here."

"Hi there, Stephen. Nice to talk to you. What can I do for you?"

"Well, Herb, we've not spoken for a while, and I need to update you. I'm pretty nearly finished here., just a couple of junior appointments to push through and the usual paperwork. Thought I'd get in touch about the next assignment." Keeping up this jocular tone was a strain, but effort, he thought, well spent with Herb.

"Well there, that's still cooking, as they say. If I were you, I'd take a little time out. You've been a year, just short, at AUP. Time for a spell on the beach."

"Thanks, Herb, I appreciate the thought. But I've never felt fitter, I'd like to keep the momentum going, take on the next project management assignment while I'm still in gear. I can schedule a few days into that, if you're sure I must."

"Glad to hear you're raring to go, Stephen. And there's no shortage of project management jobs waiting just now. But how they'll go is all in the melting pot. Board decision. So like I said, take a bit of time off. You've earned it. We'll be in touch."

This batted back on forth for a little while longer. He pushed a little for the Southwell University project, which he knew was coming up next, then terminated the conversation as a note of impatience made itself felt in Herb's voice. He reckoned he had put a claim, but hadn't liked Herb's attitude. He'd appeal higher up, maybe even the Global Master.

The hell he'd get Southwell, thought Herb Summerson, as he rang off. There were accounts to settle over AUP first, like what he thought he'd been doing with that damn-fool non-executive directorship that he hadn't declared. The AUP project was a heap of shit. 'Not enough blood' had been the Global Master's comment. Except for the bean counter, what was he called? That could have been very nasty. Trouble with characters like Stephen Pendleton, they missed the point. Eliminations weren't just fun, they were power, making a point. The money and the fun came later. You didn't waste your time on sideshows that weren't even your enemy, especially if it stymied the main acts. And the robots muscling in … okay, that had come out of left field. Avatar organisations were not unknown, but never a public company before. If they got a habit for it, they could foul up AFFREM's plans big time. It had lost them their command centre at AUP; that would have to be at Southwell. Presently, they were seriously short of ways to coerce avatars outside their programming control into doing what they wanted.

Too many things left to chance, and the luck had run against them.

All of which might be appraised and eventually forgiven, but for one other thing. If you screwed up on a project, you had to be careful about where you did it. If there was one area where screw-ups were never forgiven or forgotten it was funerals. AFFREM was a God-fearing organisation, praise the Lord! Respect for the dead was high on its priorities. Weakness of the flesh was one thing. Let he who is without sin cast the first stone and all that. Desecrating the solemnity and dignity of a funeral by having a row with the evidence of that weakness was quite another.

He'd argue Pendleton's case while they kept him stewing, and if he was wise he'd keep quiet and out of the way; things could get wild if the Global Master got a bead on you. Southwell would get someone who could reliably turn in the expected outcomes, somebody like David Wetherill. He laughed to himself at the thought of David in charge. Poor old Southwell! It could be tough being the means that justified the end. Pendleton, frankly, would be lucky to be kept on at any level in project work: might have to settle for processing invoices.

LXVIII

PUSHING THE BOUNDARIES

The music landed with a splat. Resignedly, the room porter shuffled across, bent down and picked it up. Pete took it from him with a nod and restored it to the piano's music stand.

"Right, let's have another go at that. This time, though, remember something. No matter how smooth your choreography, how correctly minimal your movements, how well characterised and passionate your rendering, it counts for nothing at all with an audience if you end up with the music on the floor. Unless it's Hegyi." The students laughed dutifully, but nervously. Hegyi specialised in paginatoric routines that deliberately went wrong. His most famous piece, which still awaited its first authentic performance, ended in the ritual suicide of everyone taking part, including the instrumentalists.

"You need to develop a sense at any moment through the performance of how far you can go without causing disaster. That is a sense that I keep with me as I perform, as Paul here keeps with him as he performs. You will find yourselves able gradually to push those boundaries out as your technique develops. But remember, in your first year it is highly unlikely that any of you will be able to push those anywhere near what we can achieve. All else apart, we've been at this game for thirty years. So don't try too hard. Try to make sure you develop that sense of danger and learn how to stay just within it. From the top again."

Pete and Henry swung into action. The students lolloped inexpertly around, taking greater care with their moves, but after another ten minutes the music was on the floor again, the lugubrious porter advancing on it with snail-like determination. It was always burlesque, Carl reflected, with first-year students in the American zone. They were not supposed to have anything to do with S-Class music while

495

they were under-age, so they mostly got no experience trying it out. By the second year, the more lumpen had usually transferred to something less demanding, but it took four or five years of study and two or three years as someone's Sorcerer's Apprentice, fetching, carrying and helping in small ways, before many of them could be trusted in a professional context.

The master class lurched to its conclusion, Carl demonstrating moves as necessary. With a word of thanks to Pete and Henry and a promise to meet them later at a restaurant, he collected the music: a much-valued United Rossello edition, well-bound, good- quality, heavy paper, tough as old boots, perfect for first-years. They'd been his printers of choice for the MacLeish.

"Well, Paul, they're not shaping too badly."

"They are not, I think, too good, either."

"It's early days."

"Early, that is it. They come here, they know the music not. You, Carl, I, we know the music fifteen years before we come to university."

It was why the best students were coming from the Russian and Chinese sectors. "There is talent still there to work on, though."

"I hope, yes."

They went out together. Strasbourg, cheerful in spring light, the current western boundary of his world. Viola had met him there by arrangement when he arrived the previous day. They had found a room at the Conservatoire for music-making. And he had been careful to book a good-sized double room at the hotel. She had been no disappointment, but had seemed preoccupied and had disappeared back to London immediately after breakfast. The truth was, he saw more of Janet, if not in the biblical sense, nowadays. It was going to be difficult keeping up a long-distance relationship with no end date in view for too much longer.

He and Paul had a reception to go on to, a melange of the diplomatic, the academic and the cultural. They fortified themselves first with coffee and cake. The conference centre foyer was showing its age, but the room was smart enough, the walls hung with what looked like magnified, plasticated animal remains. Two glasses of wine down after just twenty minutes, it occurred to Carl that such rooms were designed to give a sense of existential unease, of transience. Hence the need for alcohol and like sedatives. Paul had wandered away, conversing with a distinguished (and fairly drunk) Eastern European composer. Carl turned to his immediate neighbour, an attractive young woman of Eurasian appearance and held out his hand.

"Hello. I'm Carl."

"Purveen. What do you do?"

Purveen. He knew the name from somewhere. "I'm a Paginist, if that means anything." Pianist might hit the wrong note; this was Western Europe.

"Part of Ancillary Music?"

"That's right. We do the page-turning bit. What about you?"

"I'm with OCSE."

"I'm afraid you're ahead of me on that."

"Organisation Coopératif pour Securité Economique," she said with a creditable French accent.

"It sounds impressive, but I've led a sheltered life."

She laughed. "It means only a little more to me. I've been out here less than a month. Basically, it's a European organisation and it does economic development."

"I see. So you are an economist."

"Not really, though I did a bit of that at university. I'm English government service."

"Well, charmed to meet you. My only contacts with the government service were through the reports we used to get. Reading them, I'm afraid, was like trying to eat old leather."

She grimaced. "Don't. The avatars downstairs used to write those. I always had to get them up to interpret if I was in any sort of hurry. What department did you deal with?"

"We always called it ASBA. I'm only half clear what that stood for."

"That was my department. You were in education, then?"

"Yes, earning an honest coin as a professor."

Light dawned. "You're not Carl Trenchard, are you?"

"The one. How do you know that?"

Purveen was divided between curiosity and a sense of shame. Curiosity triumphed. "What are you doing now? I was so sorry about what was done to you."

"You know I'm effectively in exile, then?"

"Yes, though I shouldn't be talking to you about it. Actually, I'm probably supposed to go away and do some ritual purification for being in the same room." She giggled and took a swig of wine.

Carl signalled to a passing waiter, and the glasses were topped up. "Well, life's not too bad at all, though it was dicey at the beginning. I'm here because of a visiting lectureship that gets me workshops at various places around Europe. Just so long as I don't get too near England. Strasbourg's about as far west as I'm allowed."

"And if you get on a plane and just go?"

"I don't. I find myself in front of some security official before the flight takes off, and that's the end of that. I'm told similar things would happen with trains and cars. I've not tried horseback; it's a long way."

She thought back to what Giles had said when she went to discuss the possibility of the transfer to OCSE: "you could go far here, you know. Don't throw it away over some misplaced sentimentality. Carl Trenchard is on ice and will be staying there for quite some time to come. There's nothing you or I could do to change that, even if we wanted." It was precisely that powerlessness to affect even the most outrageous of decisions that had finally decided her on taking the transfer. She chose not to retail the bit about the ice. It would only be discouraging, and Carl seemed to have got things sorted. "I'm sorry. I had nothing to do with it."

"I haven't assumed you did, my dear. Mostly it was down to a character from an organisation called AFFREM, who afflicted us for a while."

"Stephen Pendleton?"

"That's the one. Pitchfork, as I called him. Curious character."

"Pitchfork." She laughed. She liked it. "You're very forgiving, only calling him curious. It was more than just Stephen Pendleton, though. ASBA was involved and I think maybe others higher up still. I've no idea why."

"I'm not really forgiving, just lazy about expending energy hating a pathology. He seemed to be suffering from some kind of power virus. As to the others, I've always found government service motives as obscure as their reports. I seem to be one of ASBA's collective hysterias. I suppose it must have been something to do with security. Rational sense seems to fly out of the window when security flies in, and you really can't get bitter and twisted about a witch hunt pursued by people you don't know. Besides, they do look after me in a penny-pinching way, and I've started to make a new life."

"Actually, I think Stephen Pendleton is making a new life too. I saw him the other day, in the centre of Paris. He was shuffling along with a bad limp and didn't look too good."

Well, well! "Sounds like he got across one too many people."

"Possibly." She looked, unfocused, thinking, to one side, not seeming much concerned.

It clicked. He'd got it. "I thought your name was familiar. Weren't you Ranulph Fraserman's contact at ASBA?"

She looked up at him. "Yes, for a while. He's in Paris now."

"I heard."

"Perhaps we could keep in touch."

"A very good idea." Carl dug out an infocard, newly minted. "I'll be in Strasbourg two or three times a year, so it should be possible."

"Oh, well, the thing is, my base is in Paris; I'm here just to see some people from the Parliament."

"Ah. Do you get trips out east of here?"

"I hope so. We're supposed to cover the whole of Europe."

"If we let each other know when we travel, maybe we'll coincide eventually."

Parting company, they found that the reception had thinned out to the hard-core survivors. Carl went in search of Körthofer.

LXIX

ET ITERUM

The Faculty Resources Committee was in session in the Symposium Room. A minute's silence had been observed for Crabtree, Viola had been formally welcomed as the new member, the minutes of the previous meeting (twelve months earlier) adopted and the non-agenda action points, now largely dissipated into irrelevance, solemnly discussed and closed.

Viola struggled to remain alert and attentive. Ben's girlfriend was in the middle of a Holopoint presentation of an Internal Audit report: 'Summary on Health and Safety Procedures Applicable to Ancillary Music Teaching Practice'. Carried over, unadopted, from the previous meeting, it had not improved with age. Concluding, it provoked little discussion; there was general agreement that the Committee needed time to think about the recommendations. Alison was thanked, and the report carried forward to the next meeting.

Carl, had he been there, would have noticed little change in personnel or environment. Pitchfork was not there, but then he had been but as a comet to the Committee's solar system: a short-lived visiting blaze of energy with a core of ice, distributing alarm, disturbance and, some said, viruses and alien life-forms, with impartial generosity. A comet might have lasting impact on the Faculty itself, even on the University, but only a meteorite could have hoped to discompose the Committee. Alan Westwood was there, but now promoted (on one interpretation) to Ancillary Music Resources Co-ordinator. Since no-one, least of all Alan himself, could really explain what the job was for, it had been interpreted, in Committee terms, as minute-taker. He had just scribbled 'c/f' across a paper copy of Alison's slides. The layout of table and chairs remained unchanged, as did the positioning of the plate of biscuits in the centre. Apparently unchanged in composition, they could have been a dusted-off resurrection from the last meeting. Only the clock above the entrance, still stuck on winter time, suggested any capacity for variation.

Rupert Llewellyn, now Head of Ancillary Music Crafts, slipped into the room with a muttered apology and took his seat.

Item six drifted into reach: the faculty budgets. Graham Fender, still chairman, the conceptual slipperiness of the position having defeated the security-driven certainties of the normalisation process, called upon the Resources Officer.

Taking over from Crabtree was an heroic labour: the Byzantine sinuosities of his systems of control demanded a flexible intellect and an instinct for creating obstructions to which the pallid young man, Kevin, now standing was entirely unequal. Which is not to say that he did not try. Brandishing the device of a year with more weeks in it than normally enjoyed by mankind, he waded into battle.

"Committed expenditure from the previous year's budget that has not yet been invoiced will be considered as part of Week 53 expenditure if of a revenue nature, or as Week 54 if capital. Committed expenditure from the last financial year not invoiced by the last Friday in May will, where possible, be cancelled and the reclaimed balance held in suspense, for reallocation to the current year. Committed expenditure that cannot be cancelled will be carried forward to Weeks 55 or 56, according as to whether the expenditure is of a revenue or capital nature. Are you all clear about that?"

A series of baffled grunts sounded from around the table. Viola kept quiet; she was going to have to put in some homework on this gobbledegook. John should be able to help.

It was the desired response. He went on. "Your budget bids will need to be submitted in writing on the standard form for the purpose. At this stage, however, it is not possible to accurately assess the correct balance between budgetary demands and budgetary provision for the forthcoming fiscal year until the corresponding balance has been struck for the fiscal year just passed."

"Meaning we still haven't got budgets for the year that's just ended." It was Mike Esther, newly confident as a Senior Lecturer.

"That's right, they were deferred last time we met, and nothing more happened." Rupert spoke up.

Shit! They'd understood that one. He attempted to scramble to the high ground of professional inscrutability. "Viring budget monies, whether retrospective or projective must conform to PISFA standards."

"What do PISFA standards say about spending money first and setting budgets afterwards?"

He had lost the game. Graham Fender spoke up. "I propose that budgets for the fiscal year just finished be declared equal to actual expenditure up to the last day of the financial year. Anything committed but not yet spent must go into this year." Everyone, the Resources Officer excepted, agreed, and the resolution was swiftly seconded and passed. Graham reached for, unwrapped and devoured the chocolate orange cream.

Kevin, too demoralised even to join the others in seizing a biscuit, sat in near despair. Closing the accounts at the end of Week 52 would make him a laughing stock in the profession. A limited salvation started to take shape as he successfully resisted an immediate agreement on budgets for the next year. He had another month's lease in which to refine his professional skills. The cost overruns from this year would be a good starting point to deny the budget demands now being put forward by the Heads of Department.

Viola allowed herself to relax a little once her pitch was done. The meeting had moved onto the crisis in toilet roll provision in the Manucussionists block. Her relaxation was premature. Rupert's

Achilles Heel was a tendency to undue exasperation over small stupidities, and AUP's ongoing refusal to supply toilet rolls (though there was no shortage of toilet roll holders) to the Manucussionists who were now his staff was driving him to heights of oratory, in an accent that grew more Welsh as the speech became more impassioned.

" … Manucussionists, the very name tells you, are skilled, highly skilled I should say, in, and I quote, 'assisting percussion operatives in optimisation of their performance through a timely provision of the correct percussion accessory for the moment, whether it be the correct variety of drum stick, the correct quality of tambourine, or the correct length, load-bearing capacity and frictional hold of the string from which a triangle is suspended. This involves considerable logistical ability and manual dexterity.' Manual dexterity, that tells you. Hands. Hands that are needed for professional purposes, not as the raw material for bottom wiping. I can say with confidence, the utmost confidence, that this is the only university in this fair kingdom, that seems to see bottom-wiping as an integral part of music practice. Of the practice of helping others to hit things. To hit things, look you, not wipe them. If our name was Coprophilia Studies I could understand, but … "

"Yes, yes," Graham interjected hastily, "what do you need to remedy this."

"A small budget and the university to supply toilet rolls."

"Kevin?"

Kevin seized his moment. "Sorry, no can do."

"Why not?"

"Security."

"Security? What in hell's name has that to do with toilet rolls? Terrorism is about shit happening, not about wiping it up."

"Guidelines from PISFA. Toilet rolls are capable of being used in conjunction with certain types of drum sticks to form an offensive weapon."

Rupert protested a little further, before subsiding. There was no challenging an appeal to security. Kevin felt good. Appealing to security invoked the Public Institute for Financial Security and Accounting's very name. The neophyte had scored for the first time. He was left him with a warm feeling that he had played a small but honourable part in upholding a tradition. The rest of the company, with one exception, enjoyed the argument, but without taking sides. They had heard it all two years ago from Alan Westwood. No doubt the Manucussionists would continue to buy their toilet paper from KostKrunch round the corner and charge it to the Miscellaneous Stationery budget.

For Viola, the security mantra inevitably brought her to Jane, now back in a secure psychiatric unit. One paid for out of family funds, but still a hospital. Not thought likely to stay there long, just enough to stabilise and maybe prevent more episodes. Security and money, she thought, the illness and the aftermath. It wasn't the only illness that had gripped them this last year, if you counted the normalisation. Consuming what must have been a great deal of money, it had simply taken them round in a circle. Everyone had been tumbled around and a few, notably Carl and Crabtree, spun out haphazard in the course of the revolution. Her sighting of Playtime told her they had, overall, been lucky. A storm cloud had wandered over to cover them and been sent on its way with nothing more than a pinch of small lightning strikes. A lot was owed to John and his friends, though few would ever realise it. Whatever agenda had been played out over the last year, it was hard to see security as anything more than the convenient excuse. Money, she thought, made a much more plausible binding thread. Jane, her morphed friend, had been, she supposed, Any Other Business.

And that was, finally, where they had arrived. Maundering, aloud or in silence, about a friend destroyed would do nothing for her professional reputation. Viola snapped to, the better to look attentive and say nothing. Mike Esther asked when the stocks of waxed paper used to hold and separate violin strings immediately before use would be replenished. Rupert suggested applying for toilet paper, the shiny kind. Kevin smiled and kept his counsel. Graham moved on to fixing the next meeting. A date was consigned to diaries, the new entry stretching its tentacles, reshaping and shrinking the future within its reach. Viola sensed the presence of further dates, further meetings, not yet defined, but stretching indefinitely forward. Did the Committee in some sense make them exist as an expression of sheer Juggernaut momentum? She'd ask Joe what he thought; it was the type of philosophical speculation he'd love.